Praise for

EVE SILVER

"Oh, how I have missed books like this!"
—*New York Times* bestselling author Linda Lael Miller

"Silver thrusts the classic gothic romance into the next century
with the ideal merging of chilling and dark mystery elements
and heated sexual tension."
—*RT Book Reviews*

"Hot romance and truly cool paranormal world building
make Silver a welcome addition to the genre."
—*New York Times* bestselling author Kelley Armstrong

"[Silver] is going to be a force to reckon with
in the future and [I] look forward to reading her books
as she heads up the bestseller chart."
—*Paranormalromancewriters.com*

"Silver's climb to the top is proving to be a rapid one!"
—*RT Book Reviews*

"Eve Silver makes magic!"
—*USA TODAY* bestselling author Cheyenne McCray

"This author is on a hot streak, providing a new gothic voice
that infuses the traditions of the genre with updated twists
and sizzling sensuality."
—*RT Book Reviews*

Don't miss the rest of the chillingly sexy
Otherkin series from

EVE SILVER

and HQN Books!

Sins of the Soul
Available September 2010

Sins of the Flesh
Available October 2010

EVE SILVER

SINS OF THE HEART

HQN™

Recycling programs
for this product may
not exist in your area.

ISBN-13: 978-0-373-77482-1

SINS OF THE HEART

www.HQNBooks.com

Printed in U.S.A.

Acknowledgments

Thank you to my editor, Tara Parsons, whose enthusiasm for this project is boundless, and who gave me the gift of allowing me to see my work through her eyes. To my agent, Karen Solem, who offered me the bounty of her wisdom and experience, answered my endless questions and gave me a much-appreciated push in the right direction.

To everyone at Harlequin Books who had a hand in helping this bouncing baby book along the way.

To Nancy Frost, for more than a decade of hanging in there with me. To Michelle Rowen, for lunches and hugs and pep talks and last-minute reads. To Ann Christopher, Caroline Linden, Kristi Cook/Astor, Laura Drewry, Lori Devoti and Sally MacKenzie because they make the good times better and the hard times easier, and because, together, we come up with the best new words.

Thank you to my family. To Dylan, my light; Sheridan, my joy; and Henning, my forever love. They fill my heart and replenish my well.

And a special thank-you to my readers who open the door and let my stories in.

Dedicated to the memory of Margaret Schorbach,
who cracked jokes right to the end
and found joy in every day

SINS OF THE
HEART

Watch. Listen. Evaluate. Revise. My father taught me these things. As a kid, I thought "revise" was most important. My father's wrath was physical in nature, and it descended if my thoughts didn't percolate quickly enough. If he was in a mellow mood, I might be allowed to have an opinion of my own. But if his mood perched on the edge of a blade, then I was allowed no opinion but his. I still watch, listen, evaluate, revise, but now I use those tools to form my own ideas rather than emulate his. Took me a while. Dear old Dad can be the very devil to deal with.

—Dagan Krayl

CHAPTER ONE

Save me from that god who steals souls,
Who laps up corruption, who lives on what is
putrid,
Who is in charge of darkness, who lives in gloom,
Of whom those who are among the languid ones
are afraid.
Who is he? He is Seth.
He is Sutekh.

—The Egyptian Book of the Dead, Chapter 17

Chicago, Illinois, eleven years ago

IN THE FAR CORNER OF A ROOM in the basement of an abandoned factory, a woman huddled on a filthy mattress. Her wrists and ankles were bound by yellow nylon rope. Her head was bowed, dark, glossy ringlets falling forward to obscure her face. The harsh glare of the naked overhead bulb accented the curved line of her back.

Terror had a way of making mortals scream.

Dagan Krayl wondered why this one wasn't.

He shifted to get a better view through the half-inch crack in the door. Small, bare room. Concrete floor. Particleboard walls. No windows.

There were stains on the mattress. Old stains, reddish-brown, dark and stiff. Someone's blood.

Not hers.

Not yet.

But whoever had left her here would be back. So she had reason enough to be terrified. Reason enough to scream. Human females cried. And, at times, human males. But not this female.

Both her silence and her odd movements piqued Dagan's curiosity.

Her head bobbed like a buoy in choppy water. Up. Down. He could hear the distinct rasp of each breath, more scrape than sob, accompanied by a muted grinding.

What the hell was she doing? From this position, he couldn't tell.

She paused, shifted a bit to one side and rolled her shoulder up against her cheek to push back the long, corkscrew strands of her hair. Then she dipped her head and went back to her task. The grinding resumed, and he realized that she was gnawing at the rope with her teeth, making a play for freedom.

A flicker of interest ignited. It appeared that despite the desperation of her circumstances her spirit was tattered but not crushed.

A fighting spirit.

Something to be admired.

He blinked, startled by the thought. She was none of his concern. He was here to harvest and kill.

But not her.

The prey he sought had a tarnished soul, one smeared with the worst sort of slime, the accumulated malfeasance and malady of a lifetime. Nothing less

would satisfy dear old Dad. Sutekh, the Lord of Chaos. He dined only on malevolence and vice. Evil was the delicacy he craved.

As a soul reaper, Dagan was tasked with providing it. He was not just any soul reaper, but Sutekh's eldest son. The old man had a small army of soul reapers to harvest for him, but he had only four sons, and he had exacting expectations of his progeny.

He glanced over his shoulder down the narrow, dark corridor. He'd already checked the massive empty space upstairs. Only the underground bowels of the abandoned factory remained unexplored. His prey was here somewhere, and he ought to continue the hunt, not stand here watching the woman.

But something kept him from leaving her and prowling off in search of a darksoul. He knew what it felt like to struggle and strive, to ache for freedom. Be careful what you wish for—wasn't that a common mortal adage? Freedom wasn't always delicious.

Reaching into the back pocket of his faded, torn jeans, he took out a lollipop. The clear plastic wrapper crinkled as he pulled it off. He popped the sucker in his mouth and waited—flavor exploded. Coconut...pineapple. Piña colada. Not his favorite. He'd remember that next time.

He folded the cellophane in half, then quarters and shoved it in his pocket, because littering went against his grain, even in this condemned shithole of an abandoned factory in Chicago's far South Side. The clear paper crinkled and crunched in the quiet.

The woman's head jerked up. She must have heard the sound.

She turned her face toward him, blinked a couple of

times and then froze. He didn't know if she cold see him, but she definitely heard him. That was a surprise.

A long scratch marked her neck and a fresh bruise darkened her right cheek, swollen and red against the smooth toffee cream of her skin. She'd been roughed up a bit, but she still had her clothes on. Didn't look like she'd been raped. Yet.

Dagan figured she had to count that as a good thing.

She wasn't gagged. Her captor hadn't bothered, either because there was no one around to hear her or because the guy liked to listen to her scream. Only she wasn't. Screaming.

He found that interesting.

Stepping deeper into the room, Dagan lifted his finger to his lips—*stay quiet*—and reached back to pull the door closed behind him. He wasn't sure why he wanted her quiet. Letting her scream would only bring her captor running, which would save Dagan the trouble of hunting him down. But he wanted a moment with her. One moment.

Why? One moment to do what? He came up with fuck-all for an answer.

Her eyes widened, then narrowed. Beautiful eyes, green and bronze, the shape almond tipped. The color was startling against her dark skin and even darker lashes.

For an instant, he saw only her eyes, tiger fierce. The room disappeared, and he saw only those eyes. They reached inside him, found something he hadn't known he'd lost, hadn't known he had in the first place.

The instant passed, leaving his pulse beating a little harder, his breath coming a little faster. He recognized that the source wasn't mere sexual attraction. It was…something else.

His gaze dipped to her mouth—full lips, lush and plump—and dipped lower to follow the thick silver chain that snaked beneath the neckline of her dirt-smeared tank top to disappear between the generous swell of her breasts. The room was like a meat locker, and the distinct outline of her nipples left no doubt that she was cold. He was in no hurry to look away; he couldn't help but appreciate the view.

I could warm her, ease her fear.

The uncharacteristic thought held distinct appeal.

Her breasts rose and fell with each rapid breath. He dragged his gaze away, let it rake her at a more leisurely pace, and he felt a distinct unease as he noticed things he'd missed the first time around. Things like incredibly smooth, taut skin. Not a wrinkle. Not a line. Not a single flaw.

Hell. He had no business staring at her breasts, her nipples. He saw now that she wasn't a woman at all. Barely more than a kid. Nineteen, maybe twenty.

"How old are you?"

"Nineteen." She frowned. "And a half."

And a half. That sealed the deal. Too young. She was far too young for him. And mortal, to boot. He generally didn't bother with mortals. They were too… human. There were more than enough female genies and demigods in the Underworld to choose from if he needed to scratch an itch.

But he'd pulled his gaze away too late. She'd seen exactly where his attention had strayed.

"Old enough to put up a fight." Her voice was low and fierce. "You won't get any without a fight, white boy."

His gaze flicked to the yellow ropes that bound her.

"I'm not in the habit of tying my lovers up." A slow smile curved his lips. "Unless they ask."

"I'm not asking."

She stared at him, her posture and expression putting him in mind of a cornered cat. Ready to fight. Claws. Teeth. Whatever it took.

Guts and grit. And beauty. He found the combination appealing. Nineteen. And a half.

"Fuck." He was here to harvest a darksoul, not think about getting laid, and he was rapidly coming to the conclusion that the faster he got done and got going, the better. He set his teeth against the lollipop, sheared off a shard of candy and ground it between his molars.

"*Fuck,*" she echoed. "Yeah, that about sums it up, vanilla bean."

He didn't surprise easily, but that did the trick. She'd been beaten, bound and left to stew in her own terror, but she had the brass balls left to call him vanilla bean. And white boy.

He'd been called worse. With reason.

"You in this with him?" Despite the show of bravado, the question held a telltale tremble.

He took the lollipop from his mouth, studied her for a second, then popped the candy back in and used his tongue to push it off to one side. She held perfectly still, only her eyes moving as she tracked his actions.

"By *him,* I assume you mean your captor." At her sharp nod, he finished, "No, I'm not in it with him."

Hope flickered to life in her eyes. "You here to free me?"

"Free you?" He almost laughed. "No." If she were looking for a savior, she was in for disappointment. No

one was coming. No one but him. Which was unfortunate for her.

At his answer, her cheeks paled, but her chin kicked up a little higher. "You gonna kill me, then?" Her eyes narrowed. "'Cause if y'are, get in line. I think the asshole who tied me up will call dibs."

Not tonight, he wouldn't. Dagan had no intention of letting the bastard touch her.

The second the thought formed, he ground it to dust beneath his boot. He wasn't here to protect this oddly alluring girl. He was here to kill and take what he needed—a darksoul to feed Sutekh's power.

But not from her. Her soul was bright as a xenon arc lamp. Sutekh would cough it up like a hairball.

"This isn't your night to die."

"Real talk?" She tipped her head and thrust one shoulder back in a cocky pose. Almost made him believe it. More bravado. And still no tears.

Interesting.

"Real talk?" he echoed, floundering. Then he realized she was asking if he was telling the truth. "I'm not here for you. I came for a darksoul."

She frowned at the term but didn't ask for an explanation. She had other things on her mind. "Good for you. Maybe you could help me with this little inconvenience first?" Her voice dripped sarcasm. Jerking her bound hands up, she separated them by the quarter inch the rope allowed and winced as it rubbed her already chaffed skin. "You got a knife?"

As he stared at the red, inflamed marks that braceletted her wrists, something odd and unfamiliar raised its head and uncoiled deep inside him. He'd seen thousands of wounds, caused most of them himself. But the

sight of her beautiful brown skin, abraded and bloody, was…unsettling. He felt a second's disorientation. He had no reason to care about her pain.

"A knife?" she prompted. And he heard *asshole* implied in her tone. Or maybe *dickhead*.

"No knife." He didn't need one. In three strides he closed the space between them. He took the rolled paper lollipop stick from between his lips, tucked it away in his pocket then hunkered down and caught the rope in his fist.

Her pupils dilated and she gasped. Every muscle in her sleek frame tensed. But she didn't jerk away. Only watched him with those incredible eyes.

A sound carried from the hallway. Footsteps.

"Cut me loose!" she hissed.

"After." He was already rising and backing away.

"After what?" Her breath came in short, sharp pants, her gaze flicking to the closed door, her fear clearly escalating. Bemused, he wondered why she was all swagger and sass talking to him, but she was terrified of the human in the hallway. She had her priorities ass-backwards.

Lifting a finger to his lips once more, Dagan cautioned her to silence as he eased back into the narrow space between the door frame and the wall. If she were smart, she'd be quiet. If she gave him away, it would only make his job…messier.

Jaw clenched, fingers curled into her palms, she followed his movements and offered a short nod as, with a creak, the door opened halfway. A blonde in tight jeans and stilettos sashayed into the room, shouldering the door fully open. Close behind her was a tall man, dressed all in black, greasy brown hair hanging lank to his shoulders. He had one hand clasped tight around

the blonde's wrist, the other holding a long hunting knife down by his thigh.

The girl on the mattress lurched up and rasped, "Marcie! You're alive. Oh, thank God."

Marcie froze, and the guy holding her tightened his grip.

Looked like the bastard meant to rape and murder not one girl but *two*.

Ambitious.

Disgust curdled in Dagan's gut. He was as far from good as anyone could be, but he did have a code. He always settled his debts. His word was his law. He refused to lie. And he sure as sugar never fucked girls barely out of high school then slit their throats.

Marcie tossed her hair back from her face and cocked one hip to the side. She had a hard look about her, like she knew the score and liked it that way. Turning her head, she slanted a glance toward the mattress and the girl.

That was all.

Just a glance.

No expression at all.

Not horror. Not fear. Not empathy.

Understanding arrowed deep, a sharp, bright barb, and Dagan narrowed his eyes, seeing things with new clarity.

Marcie wasn't bound. She didn't lean away from the grasp of her tormentor; instead, she relaxed into his grip. The way she held herself, shoulders back, head high, was anything but fearful. And her lips were curved in the faintest smile.

Well, fuck me raw.

The bastard didn't have two girls captive. He had one girl he was all set to rape and murder.

And one girl who was all set to help him.

The Underworld, the Territory of Sutekh

GAHIJI STOOD ON THE SANDSTONE GALLERY and looked down at the line of souls awaiting entry, petitioning for a moment, but a moment, of Sutekh's time. They knew him by that name, and others: Seth, Set, Seteh, Lord of Chaos, Lord of Evil, Lord of the Desert, Mighty One of Twofold Strength. Some even called him by the Greek name Typhon, a god known for cruelty and blind rage. Those who thought that knew him not at all. Sutekh never devolved into blind rage; he was far more dangerous than that: coldly analytical, methodical in his actions, his fury more blade than bludgeon. He was a businessman who could see every angle, map out all possible future ramifications of every decision.

The line of souls stretched so far that Gahiji had no hope of seeing the end. Each time one at the front was allowed entry, dozens more joined the line at the far end. They came to beg favors of the Lord of Chaos. Some were minor deities themselves, far below Sutekh in rank and power, here to wheedle and finagle a deal. Some were the souls of those who had failed to find the Field of Reeds, the paradise of life after death. Perhaps they had done dark deeds in life. Perhaps they had failed the tests of their chosen deity. Some could not pass the twenty-one gates of Osiris. Others lacked the payment for Charon and so would not be ferried across the river Styx. The Underworld was divied up into tidy territories, each god and demigod holding sway in their own kingdom. Souls had to play by the rules to get in.

But sometimes, they didn't even know the rules. So they came to Sutekh, the most powerful lord of the Underworld, to plead for an exemption or a back door into the afterworld of choice.

Each one had a story, each one wanted Sutekh's boon. Most would be turned away.

At times, Gahiji wondered if that in itself was a boon, to be sent to wander the nothingness of the lakes of fire rather than be allowed into Sutekh's dark presence. Not that he himself had cause to complain. He had never regretted the moment he had abased himself before his master, never regretted this afterlife, and the power it had brought him.

He turned his head as a servant approached, carrying a parchment scroll inscribed with names. Bowing low, she delivered the list and departed, never turning her back on Gahiji. A show of respect. The interaction was enough to draw the attention of those below.

Heads tipped back; faces turned to him. They looked up and saw him standing above them. A few opened their mouths as though to call out, then appeared to take his measure, and one by one, their mouths snapped shut.

He knew what they saw. A man of medium height, heavyset, his face a mask of anger and menace not by intent but by a fluke of design, by the arrangement of thin, pale lips and small dark eyes, a hawklike nose and wide forehead, all set in a massive skull adorned by a carefully shorn ring of steel-gray hair. He had not been a handsome man in life. His afterlife as a soul reaper had not improved that.

Turning away from the endless line of petitioners, he returned to Sutekh's greeting chamber. It was a vast space with pale sandstone walls and floor. The ceiling

was high. The columns that ran the length of the room bore brilliant paintings: the river, the delta, rich soil and fields and classic Egyptian depictions of slaves at their labor. The back of the chamber opened to a secluded garden with palm trees and lotus blossoms and a tranquil pool that played home to exotic fish from the river Nile.

The room itself was mostly empty, save for a small seating arrangement at the far end. The chairs were made of fine wood from Lebanon, inlaid with silver and ivory and tightly stretched leather. Above that seating area, raised on a dais, was a single chair, elaborately carved and decorated with gold—in truth, a throne—occupied by Gahiji's master.

Today, Sutekh had chosen to be beautiful, to wear the guise of humanity, to take on the fair coloring of three of his four sons. It was a lie. He looked nothing like the golden-skinned, golden-haired man who sat, regal and relaxed, upon his golden throne. Sutekh changed his appearance like others changed clothes. No one knew his true form, not even Gahiji, who had been with him for almost two thousand human years.

Though Kemetic depictions were of a man with a forked tail and doglike head, squared ears and a snout like an aardvark, long and downturned, Gahiji had never seen his master take that form. He thought Sutekh's true appearance must be something darker, something more frightening.

"Anyone of interest?" Sutekh asked, helping himself to a morsel of honeyed sweets that sat on a table by his right hand.

"The usual emissaries from other territories looking for your support." Neighboring gods and demigods,

each jockeying for position in the Underworld, each trying to cement an alliance with the most powerful of them all, were always sending underlings bearing gifts. Gahiji glanced at the list in his hand and read off several names.

Listening intently, Sutekh appeared to weigh each one. "No," he interjected, and again, "No." Then, "Yes, he has Hades' ear. He may have a proposition I am interested in. Put him last."

And so he arranged the visits, until Gahiji murmured, "Abasi Abubakar, High Reverend of the mortal cult Setnakht, worshippers of Sutekh. He forfeited his life as a means to speak with you."

Sutekh turned his head and glanced to his right. There, in a dim corner, back against the far wall, face to the room, sat Lokan, Sutekh's youngest son.

He was Sutekh's emissary, his ambassador to the other territories. Often, it was Lokan standing in an endless line, waiting for his chance to present his father's words to another deity. But not today. Today, he sat in his father's shadow, watching, listening. Learning.

Though they dared not ask outright, Gahiji knew there were those in the Underworld who wondered at Sutekh's political hierarchy, wondered why it was the youngest son and not the oldest who sat at Sutekh's hand. The truth was simplicity itself. The Lord of Chaos preferred to train the son who was eager to be trained, who chose this role and reveled in it. Lokan was a born politician, his father's son in so many ways.

At a slight nod from Sutekh, Lokan leaned forward so his forearms rested on his thighs, and asked, "How did Abasi Abubakar accomplish this?"

"He chose six innocents and killed them, face-to-face, slowly, with a ceremonial dagger. With each death, he absorbed the evil of his actions, allowing his darksoul to feed. Then he chanted and prayed and begged for a soul reaper to come to him."

"Innovative." Lokan leaned back in his chair, posture upright once more. "But soul reapers do not answer human summons."

"No, they do not. And humans do not forfeit their lives for a mere conversation. Not even one with me." There was no scorn in Sutekh's tone. He was thinking, mulling over the information. It was his way. Listen. Evaluate. Understand. See the reasons and ramifications. Sutekh never acted in haste. At length, he asked, "And when no soul reaper came to the High Reverend?"

"He continued to beseech and pray, eating nothing, drinking nothing, sequestering himself in a room with the dead, until he, too, died."

Sutekh was quiet for a moment. The smell of lotus blossoms carried in from the garden. The sound of the water trickling down a cascade of rocks into the pool was soft and relaxing, the environment deceptively calm. "I will see him after Hades' minion. I am interested to know what this human was willing to sacrifice his life for and how that sacrifice may be of benefit to me."

And so it began, the endless procession. The chosen souls were granted their time. Sutekh was unfailingly polite, listening to each plea. The end was invariably the same. He explained kindly, softly, that no, sadly, he could not return them to life. That was not within his power. Then he offered a boon, a gift, to each one.

Would they like a loved one left behind to come into some money? Would they like a child to have a chance for an education? Perhaps aging parents to be comforted in their time of mourning?

When the supplicants grasped his hand and thanked him, he shook his head and said, "This I am very glad to do for you. I do it with an open heart. The heart of a friend. Friends do for each other, care for each other. I do this for you and you become part of me." He watched them carefully, his golden beauty and soft voice and air of steely command lulling them. Gahiji had seen it so many times before. "I will keep you here, with me, my friend. Right here. Not in a distant place, but close to me, as close as can be. Do you want that?"

Eagerly, they nodded and voiced their agreement.

He waited only for that, their clear and unwavering agreement.

Then he had Gahiji write the terms in the large book that stood open on a pedestal in the very center of the great, airy room. Sutekh was very particular that every detail be recorded. He had no wish to rob them in the end. He liked to be fair. It was important to him to be fair.

So Gahiji wrote in neat, legible script in the book that was bound in human skin treated with tannin and turned to leather. The pages were parchment made of more of the same. But that was a secret, known only to Sutekh and Gahiji. A little shared joke between them.

Each in turn, the supplicants slumped in relief as the record was written. They had not achieved the specific goal they came for—a return to the life they had left

behind—but they had achieved *something*. They always seemed to find that uplifting. Perhaps it made them think the afterlife in the Underworld would not be so very bad.

When Sutekh held out his hand, they came close to take it. They were always so pathetically grateful.

Until he opened his jaws, let them unhinge like the jaws of a snake, and swallowed the supplicant's soul whole, doing exactly what he said he would do, keeping that soul as close to him as could be. Of course, they never suspected he meant to truly make them part of him, feed off their energy, their power.

Sutekh liked the dark ones the best. The ones laced with the greed and malice and hate that they had brought with them from life. They were the tastiest meals, the most nourishing.

It was left to Gahiji to arrange for contact with the mortal left behind in the world of man, to ensure that all Sutekh had promised was carried out. Sutekh believed in fulfilling his bargain to the soul he had ingested, terminated, robbed of any hope for rebirth or future life.

Not only a life snuffed, but an immortality taken. There was no afterlife for that soul, no heaven or hell or Field of Reeds. No Valhalla or any other version of a next world. Nothing. There was only Sutekh's voracious hunger.

In exchange, Sutekh gave their loved one exactly what he had agreed to, and in doing so, doomed that loved one to the exact same fate.

After all, a contract was a contract, and at the end of their lives, they would come to Sutekh when he called.

In the corner of the room, Lokan sat and watched and learned. But it did not escape Gahiji's notice that at the moment of the soul's ingestion, the son's expression betrayed distaste, perhaps even disgust, suggesting that the human half of him had some remnants of tender emotion, perhaps empathy, for these pathetic souls.

Gahiji never dared to point that out to his master. He liked his role as a soul reaper and Sutekh's trusted second far too much to open his mouth unwisely in criticism of his master's son, and find himself the meal rather than the meal provider.

But he planned to continue to keep an eye on Lokan. Just in case.

He felt a certain…rage…at all Sutekh's sons. They had no idea the gift that had been given them, the honor, the power, the beauty of what they were. He, Gahiji, had been made a soul reaper, his human body strengthened and transformed, but it could never compare to the gift they had been given. They were Sutekh's *sons,* fruit of his loins. The gifted. The chosen. However powerful Gahiji was, they were more so. A part of him hated them for that.

At length, Gahiji led Abasi Abubakar into the chamber. Sutekh's manner was different now. He was reserved, quiet, making no effort to put the supplicant at ease.

"Master," the High Reverend whispered, and threw himself to the ground, his fingers reaching for the tips of Sutekh's toes, close, but not touching. That would be beyond brave.

The High Reverend was weeping, his shoulders shaking, and when Sutekh bid him "Rise," he managed

only to lift his face from the floor, his expression one of fanatic's joy.

Sutekh cut a glance at Gahiji, who moved forward to close his meaty hand around the supplicant's upper arm and help him to his knees.

"Speak," Sutekh urged, his voice gentle.

Abasi glanced at Gahiji, and his brow drew tight in a frown. Then his head jerked up as he spied Lokan, who sat in the corner, still as death.

The High Reverend wet his lips, his expression distraught. "May I speak with you alone?"

Gahiji almost laughed in surprise. He could not recall such a request, not in all the long years he had been Sutekh's most loyal servant.

His expression one of commiseration and regret, Sutekh murmured, "You are in the presence of my son and my trusted servant. They are as the thumb and forefinger of my right hand. Speak freely. Know they will never betray what they hear." He paused. "Would you have me insult their honor by sending them from me?" Words kindly spoken, laced with the promise of terrifying retribution should insult be made.

The High Reverend paled, swallowed, and began to speak, and as he revealed the layers of his knowledge, Gahiji was hard-pressed not to betray his surprise. They had a plan, these mortals of the cult of Setnakht. One that might well succeed.

"Now, if it pleases you, Master," said Abasi, his tone growing more confident with the telling, "let me share with you my knowledge of the Daughters of Aset."

Again, Gahiji masked his surprise. The Daughters of Aset were Sutekh's ancient enemies, as were Aset herself, and her husband, Osiris.

"It pleases me," Sutekh replied with a negligent wave of his hand, and he leaned back on his throne as Abasi began to speak.

CHAPTER TWO

Chicago, Illinois

"HEAR THAT, JERRY?" Marcie tipped her head to the side. "She's happy I'm alive. Isn't that sweet?"

Roxy Tam jerked back, the words hitting her like a powerful blow, sending emotions tumbling one against the next. Fear, horror, dawning understanding.

Marcie had been the lure, her partner the trap.

And Roxy'd fallen for it like some fool kid from the suburbs.

They meant to kill her. *Marcie* meant to kill her.

The breath whooshed out of her, leaving her deflated, shaken, physically ill.

She opened her mouth, but no words came out. She ought to do something, say something. But she never got the chance.

Because he killed her.

The blond guy stepped from behind the door and thrust his hand through Marcie's chest. Like it was nothing. Like he'd done it a million times before. There was a sharp snap as ribs shattered and the short, high note of Marcie's scream, cut off at the crescendo. For an endless, chilling second, Marcie hung there like a coat on a hook, her toes barely

grazing the floor, her body jerking, her blood dripping down her torso.

Roxy shrank back and her teeth sank into her lower lip, hard enough to draw blood, hard enough to hold back the cry that bubbled and swelled in her throat. *Don't make a sound. Not a sound. He'll look your way if you do. He'll do that to you.*

Marcie's partner—what had she called him?...Jerry—dove for the blond guy with a snarl. The guy didn't even glance up. Just shot his free hand out and back so his fingers clamped the bastard's throat and held him there above the ground, feet twitching, body squirming like a worm.

The knife fell from Jerry's hand, clattered to the floor and spun away. Roxy stared at it, panting. But she'd have to go past the killing field to get it.

Don't think. Just move. She undulated like an inchworm, aiming for the knife.

Another sharp crack of bone. Another rib splintering. Her attention jerked back to the horror before her.

With the fingers of his right hand still clamped around Jerry's throat, the blond guy dug his left hand deeper into Marcie's chest. She hung there, arms limp, head lolling like a broken doll.

There was a monstrous squishy, sucking sound. Roxy froze, every muscle taut, horror icing her veins as something hot sprayed her cheek.

The raindrop patter of blood.

Oh, God, the blood.

Marcie slumped to the ground as he pulled his hand free.

He turned to Jerry then, and asked softly, "How many before this one?"

Jerry clawed at the fingers that choked him. He struggled, feet twitching as he stretched his toes to try and reach the floor.

"How many, Jerry?" The blond guy jerked his head toward Roxy. "How many girls did you rape and murder before this one?" His tone never changed. Low. Polite. Like he was asking how many pairs of shoes Jerry owned.

"Seven. Lucky seven," Jerry croaked. "And Marcie did three more while I watched." He made a gagging sound, took a raspy breath. "You do the math."

"Perfect." The blond guy nodded and smiled and killed him. Held him dangling above the ground, tore open his chest, and ripped his heart out, just like he'd done to Marcie.

Clamping her jaw tight, Roxy refused to scream, because she had a feeling that once she started, she'd never stop. Shock, revulsion, dread—they held her pinned, her body crouched and contorted by her bonds, her breath locked in her throat. She'd staved off her terror the whole time they'd left her here, bound and alone. Held it in check when the blond guy had shown up, as she tried to decide exactly what his role was, his surfer-boy hair and the lollipop stick between his lips somehow making him seem less threatening.

Talk about irony.

He was the scariest fucking thing she could ever have imagined.

There were two bodies on the floor, lying in a pool of gore. A goddamned lake of it. They were dead. And their murderer slowly turned his face toward her.

Her heart thundered in her chest.

His gaze flashed to hers. Gray eyes. Like fog at dusk. Colder than Lake Michigan in January.

The coldest eyes she'd ever seen.

There was nothing there. Nothing behind those eyes. Not a flicker of emotion.

Her skin prickled and the fine hairs on her forearms stood upright. The silence stretched until she thought it would break her.

"You killed them." Nice. She was mistress of the obvious.

"It's what I do. Kill the evildoer. Harvest the dark-souls." He didn't sound contrite. He didn't sound *any-thing*. To him, the words were simply a statement of fact.

The evildoer? "What are you?" she whispered before she could stop herself. "An angel of death?"

That earned her the barest whisper of a smile. "Death, yes." The smile edged tighter. "Angel, no."

He lifted his hands. They glistened beneath the naked overhead bulb, wet and dark. He held the two hearts, one in each fist. Like he was a butcher holding fresh-cut meat. *Oh, God.* If she lived through this, she was never going to eat steak again. She swore it. On her life, she swore it.

She saw then that he had a battered leather pouch slung across one shoulder, and he opened it to drop the hearts inside. Then he squatted beside Marcie's body and reached into the hole he'd torn in her chest. He frowned, reached deeper and rooted around a bit.

When he pulled his hand free, he was clutching... *smoke.* Smoke the color of an oil slick, the texture of it simultaneously amorphous and greasy. It writhed and twined up around his forearm, then down again, only to slither away from his skin and ooze up, up, until it hovered just above his shoulder like a bloated black balloon tethered by a gossamer string so bright it hurt to look at it.

Roxy cringed back against the wall and wished she could dissolve into the concrete blocks like water into sand. She was shaking so hard her shoulder bumped the wall again and again.

He glanced at her, his expression ruthlessly neutral. Terrifyingly so.

She'd called him vanilla bean. She'd called a fucking monster vanilla bean.

"Stop," he said.

Only in that second did she realize that every time she exhaled, she made a high-pitched whining sound.

"Stop. Now." A hard edge crept into his tone.

And she did. She snapped her mouth shut so quickly that her teeth clacked together vigorously enough to hurt.

"Thank you." Soft. Polite.

She whispered, "You're welcome," and as the words left her lips, she recognized how ludicrous they were. A laugh tore free, against her will, against any sort of good judgment. Too loud, too wild, it rang with the sharp peal of hysteria.

Keep it together, sister. Don't you lose it now.

Ignoring her outburst, he turned back to the bodies, moved to Jerry's corpse and shoved his hand into the lacerated chest. Again, oily smoke coiled up his forearm and coalesced into a second black balloon that slithered up to join the one he'd pulled from Marcie.

Roxy's every instinct screamed for her to escape, to run while he was occupied elsewhere. But instinct and the reality of her bound limbs didn't mesh. Her gaze skittered once more to the knife that'd landed in the corner, and she wriggled and twisted, suddenly wholly focused on the gleaming blade. Her efforts only served to snag his unwanted attention.

He looked at her with those glacier eyes.

"You're shaking."

Give the man a prize.

He rose and strode toward her, the grotesque balloons writhing behind him like fat, slimy slugs.

She shook harder. And it pissed her off that her body wasn't doing anything her mind was telling it. She wasn't a coward. Growing up in Rogers Park, she'd seen all kinds of shit. Shit that had seemed so big, so bad. Shit she'd been adept at avoiding. But all that suddenly seemed small in comparison to what she'd just witnessed.

Fear gnawed at her as he approached and stood over her, studying her. Like she'd studied the frog in tenth-grade biology, all pinned out and cut open. It had been interesting in a dead, gross, reeking kind of way. A part of her had felt disgust, but the bigger part had wanted to get her hands dirty and figure out how the thing worked.

Right now, she was feeling a mighty kinship to that frog.

Behind him, the two smoky, black balloons bobbed and dipped on their glittering tethers. One dropped and bounced against her forearm, icy cold. With a gasp, she yanked her hand away.

"You see them." A statement, not a question. But he was surprised. Even though there wasn't a flicker of emotion in his features, and his eyes stayed flat and cold, she knew he was surprised.

Lie? Tell the truth? She'd say anything if he just let her live, but something told her the truth would serve her better.

"Yeah." Her answer was more breath than formed word.

"Do you know what they are?"

"No." *Maybe.* They were something dark. Something evil. And they'd come from inside the two people, two killers, who had in turn been killed. What had he said earlier? That he was here for a darksoul. Was that what those slimy balloons were? Darksouls?

Did she have one inside her, obsidian and oily?

After what she had and hadn't done, the choices she'd made—choices that had indirectly led her here— she thought she might. What she'd done…did it make her a monster now?

She felt like one, for sure. *Rhianna.* Her foster sister. It hurt even to think her name. So she locked it away in a dark corner of her mind and she pressed her parched lips tight. It didn't help. She was shaking so hard that her teeth clacked together like a jackhammer.

The events of the past two days were catching up to her, big-time.

"She wasn't your friend. You know that, yes?"

Horror congealed in her gut. He *knew.* About Rhianna. How?

Then he glanced at the bodies, and she realized he was talking about Marcie, telling her that Marcie hadn't been her friend.

"Yeah." She did know it, *now,* though she hadn't when she'd followed Marcie here like a lamb to the slaughter.

"What's your name?"

She tried to focus on the question. She was cold. So cold.

"W-w-what's yours?" she shot back, but her chattering drained the force of her demand.

"Dagan Krayl." He tipped his head to the side, waiting.

Perversely, she said nothing.

He shrugged, hunkered down and caught her bound

wrists. She recoiled from his bloody hands. With an impatient sound, he rubbed them on his jeans, leaving long, dark smears on the denim that stretched taut over his muscled thighs.

"Hold still." He tore the rope.

Tore it. No knife. Just his hands. Inch-thick nylon rope, and he tore through it as if it was nothing.

Above them, the slimy darksouls danced and bobbed. Bile crawled up her throat, stinging the back of her tongue. She fought it, digging her nails deep into her palms, straining for control.

He was careful not to let the glowing tethers he held in his right hand touch her skin, but he wasn't so careful about the remnants of blood on his fingers; his touch left a trail, marking her as it marked him.

A monster. A killer.

Marcie's blood. Marcie's darksoul.

Now Marcie was dead. Dead. Dead. Dead.

And if Dagan Krayl hadn't shown up when he did, it would be Roxy who was dead.

Was she supposed to feel guilty that she was alive?

She didn't. She was glad it wasn't her. Fiercely glad. Light-headed with gratitude. Or maybe that was fatigue and fear.

As he worked at unwinding her bonds, she noticed a long, deep scratch on his wrist. Marcie or Jerry—one of them had fought hard enough to score him. His blood mixed with theirs.

He bled. She thought that was important, but she had no idea why. The shudders that racked her were making her fuzzy. That, and more than twenty-four hours without food or water or sleep.

Again he rubbed his palm against his denim-clad

thigh. Then he fished through his pocket and pulled something out. She glanced at his offering and felt the world tip and tilt. A lollipop. He was offering her a yellow lollipop.

"Sugar," he said. "You need it."

Vaguely, she realized he was right. But she thought there was something wrong with this plan.

"No...c-c-can—" Not taking candy from a stranger.

He didn't seem inclined to chat. He carefully removed the wrapper, folded it in half, then in half again, tucked the paper in his pocket and ordered, "Open your mouth."

And she did. Maybe that was stupid. Or maybe it was the smartest thing she'd ever done, she thought a moment later as the first hint of sugar rush amped through her. He rocked back on his heels and shrugged out of his battered leather jacket, then leaned in to drape it over her. It was warm. Deliciously, tear-wrenchingly warm. And she wanted to howl with gratitude.

Right after she got her hands on the knife in the corner. Just in case.

He watched her in silence, and by the time the candy was half gone, she was shaking a little less, thinking a little clearer.

The whole thing was insane. She was sitting in a room that had been turned into a slaughterhouse, sucking on a lollipop.

"Think I jumped down the rabbit hole. Head first."

Again, the whisper of a smile. "You think?"

Her heart slammed against her ribs. She couldn't look away from his face. A part of her didn't want to.

If she looked away, she wouldn't see him come for her. She wouldn't have a hope in hell of escape.

She *didn't* have a hope in hell. She'd seen how fast he moved. Inhumanly fast, his hands a blur. But some corner of her mind was convinced that if she just kept him in her sights, she'd stay alive.

Stupid, really.

Reaching out, he caught her right hand and dragged it forward, her puny resistance no deterrent. His touch was firm, his skin warm. She was hyperaware of their contact, skin to skin. Turning her palm up, then down, he examined her torn wrist. Then he did the same with her left hand.

And there she was, shaking like a leaf the whole time, even though he hadn't made a single threatening move toward her. But he'd told her he wasn't here to free her, then he'd gone ahead and done exactly that. He'd wrapped her in his jacket and he'd fed her candy. She wasn't a fan of contradictions. Besides—her gaze slid to the broken bodies on the floor, then away—she couldn't say she was crazy about his methods.

Slowly, he raised his head, sun-bright hair sliding along his cheek. "You'll heal."

Was he trying to reassure her? She fought the urge to laugh maniacally. To scream. Instead, she stared at him and nodded. Or tried to, anyway. She was still trembling, which made her movements less than smooth.

But she would heal. She was okay. She was alive. Thanks to him. Thanks to a man who'd just torn two people apart with his bare hands and pulled out—what? Their souls?

"I'll tear you up some if you try to do that to me."

He'd definitely been right about the sugar. It had given her a boost. Her words were clearer now, her tongue and lips actually obeying her will.

"You can retract your claws. If I meant to hurt you, it'd be a done deal."

No shit. "Why're you helping me?" she whispered.

He blinked. Hit her with that endless stare. Shrugged. "I have no fucking idea."

His answer was oddly comforting. "Good to know."

He smiled for real now. White teeth. Tanned skin. A dimple in his left cheek. The light from the naked bulb overhead painted him gold and bronze.

Her breath froze, then she inhaled sharply. Until that moment, she hadn't really *seen* him. But as she studied him now, she realized that he didn't look anything like he ought to. He was some sort of fiend, but he looked like a man. A beautifully sculpted, smiling man. Older than her. Maybe thirty. Shoulder-length blond hair, thick and wavy, tied back at his nape, a few strands falling free to frame his face. Chiseled features. Slashing cheekbones. A hard, square jaw dusted by dark gold stubble.

Handsome, in an all-edges, no-curves kind of way.

His good looks made everything worse.

He was a handsome monster that ripped out hearts without a flicker of emotion.

A monster who'd saved her life. Who'd set her free and examined her wounds with solemn-faced concern. Wrapped her in his decadently warm jacket. And fed her a lemon-flavored sucker.

Barely daring to breathe, she held still as he bent his head and tore through the rope at her ankles. The second they were free, she scuttled awkwardly along the

wall, trying to get away. Her prickling, numb limbs refused to properly obey her command. She didn't get far. A wide metal duct jutting out of the wall stopped her dead.

He followed her.

"Relax. We've already established that I'm not going to kill you tonight."

That was reassuring. Not going to kill her *tonight*. "Do tell. Tomorrow night, then? Next week?" She couldn't stop herself from looking over at the corpses. Tonight, he'd come to kill them. Marcie and her partner. Why them and not her?

"You only kill...murderers?" That was the only possible explanation.

His expression was cold, detached. "Not exclusively."

"Children? Small, furry animals?" Her voice cracked.

For a second she thought she'd gone too far. The expression she'd noticed earlier was back, not flitting now, but holding its place.

His gaze dropped to her mouth. Her heart slammed against her ribs.

He was going to kiss her.

And she was truly, truly bat-shit crazy, because a part of her wanted him to.

Then he smiled—just with his lips, not with his eyes—and said, "That mouth ever get you in trouble?"

More often than she'd ever admit.

Forever got crammed into about three seconds. Then he looked away, jaw clenched, eyes focusing on the far wall. She didn't dare move. Didn't dare breathe.

She didn't know where to look. Not at him. He only

amped her confusion into redline. And she sure didn't want to look at the bodies again. That was a sure path to losing whatever pretense of self-control she'd mustered.

Confusion and hope and, yeah, gratitude mixed together in a bubbling stew. Because she owed him for saving her life.

Question was: What would he demand in return?

"No one does something for nothing," she muttered.

Above them, the darksouls dipped and swayed, blocking the light of the bulb for an instant, leaving her in shadow.

Was that what he wanted from her? A darksoul? No. Because if he did, why bother to be nice?

Suddenly, everything slammed her at once. Everything she'd seen and heard. Impossible things. She shook her head, shock setting in.

"Are you—" She couldn't believe what she was thinking here. What she was considering. But she knew what she'd seen, and what she'd seen wasn't anything a normal man could do. She swallowed and forced the question out. In for a penny, in for a pound. "Are you human?"

He studied her, focused, intent. "No."

Don't ask the question if you don't want to know the answer. She swallowed. "What are you?"

He laughed, a sinful, dark sound. "Something else."

CHAPTER THREE

You have your blood, O Aset
You have your power, O Aset
You have your magic, O Aset

—The Egyptian Book of the Dead, Chapter 156

Present day
Amarillo, Texas

NOT MUCH TO SEE IN THE SLASH of moonlight that cut through the crack in the dusty curtains. Purple-and-brown paisley carpet. Brown-and-purple papered walls. A low suspended ceiling.

Roxy Tam paused in the doorway of room 9 at the Tee Pee Inn and looked back to check the empty parking lot. If anyone saw her, they'd take her for a hooker. She'd dressed the part with that in mind. Too much bronzer on her toffee-cream skin, eyes outlined with black liner and garish green shadow, sleek, dark ringlets left free about her shoulders. Her skirt so short it barely covered her ass.

Not her usual look, but she was nothing if not adaptable.

At the far end of the lot a neon yellow sign declared there were vacancies, and below that, spelled out in black: $10.00 ALL NIGHT.

A bargain.

Her gaze pierced the shadows. Nothing stirred. Not even the breeze.

Stepping into the room, she reached back and eased the door shut behind her. The air smelled of stale tobacco, lavender air freshener and...a faint whiff of piss. The door to the toilet was wide-open, and if she had to guess, she'd say that Frank Marin hadn't flushed.

For an instant, the smells triggered an arctic blast of crappy memories. How many run-down motel rooms had been her home for the first five years of her life?

There was a dresser by the window, a single night table with a shadeless lamp, and a double bed shoved up against the wall. A snoring lump lay beneath the thin, threadbare sheet, but there was no sign of the kid.

Damn it to fucking hell.

Crossing to the bed, Roxy closed her fingers around Marin's throat, pressing hard enough to cut off his air. *Rise 'n' shine, sunshine.* He came awake with a lurch and a choked caw, his hands flying up to claw at her wrist. She felt it then, a low-level psychic buzz. So Marin had a touch of the supernatural in his blood. She wondered if he even knew it.

"Where's the kid, you bag of shit?" she asked, all polite and nice.

He croaked and clawed at her some more, but she held him with ease, stronger than any mortal. A side benefit of what she'd become that long-ago night when the soul reaper had saved her sorry ass.

"The kid?" Loosening her hold enough that he could speak, she waited.

"Closet," he rasped, his eyes showing white as he darted a glance in that direction.

Roxy clicked on the lamp, 60 watts of yellowish light illuminating Frank Marin's features. He looked like a weasel. Thinning black hair. Sharp, pointed nose. Close-set eyes. The left one had three teardrops tattooed underneath.

"You ever do time in Australia, Frank?" She already knew the answer. She made a point of researching her quarry before she hunted.

"Seven years."

Revulsion surged. For most people, the number of teardrops represented the number of people they'd murdered. For some it represented loved ones lost. But in Australian prisons, inmates forcibly tattooed convicted child molesters. "You get those tattoos in Australia?"

Frank Marin kept his mouth shut.

Which was answer enough. She snagged a set of cuffs from her belt, looped the chain around the headboard and clamped his wrists. Safety first. She'd be no use to the kid in the closet if Marin plugged her in the back. Not that a bullet was likely to kill her. But it would be inconvenient and unpleasant.

Leaning her weight on the hand at Marin's throat, her fingers biting deep, she reached under the spare pillow with her free hand and pulled out his gun. He struggled, which was little more than a nuisance. A bit more pressure and he stilled. Guess he liked breathing.

She let go of Marin and stepped back as he snarled and cursed, but the cuffs held.

"Shut. Up." She smiled and leveled the gun lower.

His jaw snapped shut with teeth-rattling force. Guess he preferred to keep his equipment intact.

"So, what do we have here?" She glanced at the gun. "Hmm…semiautomatic."

She preferred knives herself—she was all about the personal touch—but in her business it paid to know the weapons favored by the enemy. So she knew the drill: Push the magazine release. Remove. Pull the slide back and lock it. Visual confirmation that the chamber was empty. She tossed the magazine across the floor in one direction and the empty gun in the other. Then she jerked open the night-table drawer. It was empty. Jackass didn't even have a backup.

Marin started up swearing again.

Reaching for the sheath on her belt, Roxy slid her knife free and turned it so the blade caught the light.

And that caught his attention. He stopped midcurse.

"Easy," he rasped. "Hey, now…easy, there. You don't want to hurt me—"

"Easy, there? Is that like 'Whoa, girl'? I'm not a horse." She brought the tip of the knife to rest against his Adam's apple. "As to my not wanting to hurt you…yeah—" she pushed hard enough that his skin gave way with a faint pop, like pricking a grape "—actually, yeah. I really do want to hurt you."

"I have information—"

She dug the tip a little deeper, effectively cutting off his attempt to bargain.

"You stay nice and quiet, Marin. For the moment, if you stay quiet, you stay alive. You speak when I tell you to, and not before. If I want to hear what you have to say, I'll let you know." She watched a rivulet of blood snake along his pale skin, the urge to reach out and catch it on her finger—or better yet, on her tongue—was nearly overwhelming. It had been too long since she'd fed. Finally, she raised her gaze to his. "Nod, just so I know you understand."

He nodded—a spare movement, because anything more might just slit his throat.

The only sounds in the room were the harsh rasps of Marin's breathing and the soft shush of metal on cloth as Roxy wiped the tip of her blade clean on the pillowcase.

Deftly, she slit away a long, wide strip, sliced it in two and sheathed the knife. The she grabbed Marin's hair, yanked his head back, wadded one piece of the pillowcase into a ball and shoved it his mouth, using the second piece to hold it in place.

"Sit. Stay."

If he followed her instructions any better, he'd have grown a tail.

Crossing to the closet, Roxy yanked open the door to find a little girl curled in the corner, huddled beneath a snot-green blanket that Marin must have pulled from the bed. Probably the only decent thing he'd done in the past decade. Although maybe he just hadn't wanted to risk damaging the goods.

The kid's eyes were closed, her chest fluttering as she breathed through the gag Marin had tied around her mouth. At least she *was* breathing, a bonus as far as Roxy was concerned. No way she wanted to head back with a cold little body instead of a warm one.

Been there. Done that.

Which was one of the many reasons she generally avoided jobs that involved kids. But this job wasn't actually about the kid. It was about getting information. And it was about following orders.

Her directive was simple. One of Sutekh's soul reapers had been butchered. Her job was to gather information to ensure that the dead soul reaper stayed dead.

Not an easy task, since she had no clue what the dead reaper had to do with the live kid. Calliope Kane, her direct superior in the Asetian Guard, had made it clear that information was need-to-know only. No surprise there. The Daughters of Aset were rarely forthcoming with anything but the most spare and sparse details. After nearly a decade, Roxy was still little more than a foot soldier in the ranks, which meant they figured she needed to know very little.

Usually, that sat just fine on her shoulders. But lately, she'd had the feeling that something was going down. Something outside the ordinary. And not knowing a damned thing was starting to wear thin.

Plus there was something about this job that made her uneasy. There hadn't been anything in Calliope's manner to say otherwise, but Roxy's gut was telling her that the kid was more important than her mentor had let on, that she wasn't just incidental. Which made Roxy wonder why it had been so all-important to hide that fact.

With the closet door blocking Marin's sight line, Roxy squatted down and pulled an inhaler from her pocket. She undid the gag, then the girl's hands.

"Dana, wake up."

The child's head lolled, and she didn't open her eyes. Roxy looped one arm around her thin shoulders and hauled her upright, giving her just enough of a shake to rouse her.

"Come on, kid. Don't make me regret this." *Don't make me face your mom and tell her you died.*

Dana opened her eyes. They were denim-blue, bleary and unfocused. Roxy held up the inhaler. The girl stared at her, but that was it. Every line of her

body, every shallow, wheezing breath spoke of fear and tension. Which left Roxy at a loss. She had almost no experience with kids. She'd barely had a chance to be one herself, so there was no help there.

Or maybe there was.

What's your name?

Roxy Tam.

Where do you live, Roxy? She remembered his voice, low and calm and kind. They'd sat in a small room with two chairs and a table, the overhead light too bright. His skin had been brown, his eyes almost black, his uniform blue. He'd given her a soda and some chocolate wafer cookies. Despite his kindness, she hated chocolate to this day.

You're safe now, Roxy. No one's going to hurt you.

Bingo.

"Dana, you're safe now. No one's going to hurt you." She dragged the words from the mire of her memories, then doctored them a bit to fit the circumstances. "I'm going to take you back to your mom."

No one had promised to take Roxy back to her mom, because there had been no mom to take her back to. No big deal. She'd survived.

Seconds ticked past, and Roxy was back to searching for more words when Dana reached for the inhaler. Her fingers brushed Roxy's, ice cold. The girl knew the routine, gave the inhaler a quick shake and breathed deep. Then she shrank back into the corner as the dollop of trust she'd mustered vaporized like mist under the noonday sun.

Roxy leaned back to clear the closet door and glanced at Marin. He sat exactly as she'd left him, quiet during the entire exchange, not even moaning

into the gag. Guess he believed that she'd follow through on her threat. Give the weasel a gold star.

Her movements slow and nonthreatening, Roxy turned back to the kid, reached into her pocket and withdrew a small, floppy stuffed toy. A cat, threadbare and well loved. "Your mom sent this. To keep you company till you get home. She said its name is Flopsy."

"Not *it*," Dana whispered. She reached, retreated, then finally took the cat, snatching it close to embrace against her chest. *"Her."*

"Okay. Her," Roxy agreed softly. "You stay here a minute, Dana. I'm gonna close the door again for just a minute—"

"No!"

"It'll be okay. You have Flopsy."

Dana didn't look convinced.

The bed creaked as Marin shifted, and Dana's eyes rolled with fright.

Keeping her movements slow and easy, Roxy reached into the small, black backpack she had slung over her shoulder and drew out an iPod attached to a set of noise-canceling headphones. She was nothing if not prepared. She'd had Dana's mom load up the kid's favorite songs anticipating exactly this occasion. There were things she needed to say to Mr. Marin…things she definitely didn't want Dana to hear.

The kid was watching her, eyes dipping to the bright pink iPod with the white cat stickers on the back, then back to Roxy's face.

"Your mom sent this." Roxy reached out and carefully settled the headphones on Dana's ears.

Dana's eyes widened as Roxy set the volume on low

and hit Play. Roxy lifted off one earphone. Behind her, she could hear the harsh rasp of Marin's breathing and the creak of the bed as he stirred. She figured he was probably almost out of patience.

"Your mom said you love 'The Locomotion.'" The kid hesitated then nodded solemnly. Roxy thumbed through her choices until she found the song she wanted. When she hit Play, Dana exhaled. Her shoulders came down. "I want you to, uh, sing to Flopsy," Roxy said, "so she won't be scared. Sing along with the music, Dana, nice and loud. I just need to—" she glanced over her shoulder at Marin. From this angle, all she could see were his feet "—I need to tie up a couple of loose ends, and then we're going to find your mom. Okay?"

The kid watched Roxy, still wary, her faded-denim eyes way too big, her expression solemn. She nodded but didn't say another word.

Shit.

For a second, Roxy hesitated, but she saw no other way. Leaving the kid in the closet was better than having her witness what was to come. And locking her alone in the car in this neighborhood while she came back inside to do what needed to be done just wasn't an option.

"Sing, Dana. If you sing to Flopsy, she won't be afraid."

She settled the earphone back against Dana's ear, offered what she hoped was a reassuring smile— exactly how was one supposed to smile at a six-year-old?—and played with the volume a bit more until she was satisfied that it was loud enough to block ambient noise.

Straightening, she studied the closet door. She figured the kid was so freaked that she'd stay put until Roxy came back for her, so instead of shutting the door all the way, she angled it so it completely blocked any view of the bed, but she left it open a few inches to let the light in. Finally, she stepped away. There was a second of silence, and then a tiny voice carried through the plywood: "...do the locomotion with me..."

Roxy turned back to the bed and found Marin watching her with wary eyes. She closed the space between them, held him by his hair and ripped out the gag.

"Ouch!" He rubbed the back of his head. "You tore off my bloody scalp!"

"Cry me a river." She tossed aside the gag and withdrew her knife once more, flipping it into the air then catching it on the downswing. Marin's head tipped and bobbed. Up, then down.

"So, what now? You gonna kill me?" He tried for cocky but ended up with something between a squeak and a whine.

"I fucking want to kill you," Roxy said, low and furious. She leaned close, her eyes locked on his. "You nabbed a kid. A little kid. And you were going to sell her." She took a slow breath, mastering her emotions. Marin didn't so much as blink. Guess she'd made an impression. "So now, I'm ready to let you talk. You give me useful information, you get to live." She paused. "Maybe."

Marin nodded frantically, his attention fixed on the knife. "Anything. Yeah. Just ask."

Like she needed his permission. Roxy yanked up her left sleeve, baring her forearm, and turned it until

her mark was clearly visible. Etched in her skin was an ankh with wings and horns, a finely rendered piece of art, a match to the pendant that hung around her neck. It wasn't a tattoo. The design was scored in her flesh, and it had taken a long time to put it there. She'd let it heal, then scored it again and again until it was perfect. The dark mark. It claimed her as a Daughter of Aset, an ancient line of immortals who walked among humans, watching, guiding, guarding. Fighting for mankind when they must. Fighting for their own survival the rest of the time. The mark's placement on her forearm told those who would recognize its importance that she was of the lineage of the Keeper, a guardian among her kind.

But Frank Marin wouldn't know anything about that.

"You've seen this mark before, yes? Upside down on a man's chest. Not scored like mine. Tattooed, in black ink." She knew that much, but nothing more. And she needed answers because time was running out. The Underworld buzz was that there were those who wanted to see the dead reaper reanimated. Talk about opening a can of worms; that would be more like snakes on a plane.

In the Underworld everyone wanted his piece of the pie. Osiris. Hades. Pluto. Sutekh—the überlord of chaos and malevolence. A slew of lesser gods, demigods and genies that populated all major and minor religions. The place was divied up all neat and tidy, the same way Topworld crime syndicates marked territory in human cities.

But alliances were fragile, the balance determined by territorial and volatile creatures. Tip the scale just a little and a 6,000-year-old ceasefire could be over.

Last week, someone had decided to try to tip the scale.

That someone had butchered a soul reaper.

Seemed like every Topworld grunt had the word out trying to find out who and how, and Roxy was certain that the Underworld was buzzing even more. Of course, the only way to know that for sure was to visit, and you only got to visit if you were dead.

Bottom line was that mortals didn't get a free pass to go below, and high-power gods and demigods couldn't come up. Only a handful of beings could travel between Topworld and the Underworld.

She wasn't one of them.

But soul reapers were. They could go back and forth at will. Which was exactly why this whole assignment didn't sit quite right.

"If the reaper's dead, then his soul's gone to the Underworld," Roxy had pointed out to Calliope last night, wondering why the obvious didn't seem so obvious to her mentor in the Asetian Guard. "Why doesn't Sutekh just ask him who the killers are?"

"The soul reaper was murdered, but his soul never went to the Underworld. We've checked every territory. Questioned every god and demigod. The reaper isn't there. And he isn't Topworld. He doesn't appear to be anywhere."

That news had been anything but reassuring. "How is that possible?"

Calliope had shaken her head and spread her hands, palms up. "If I knew that, I would have all the answers. But that's your task. To find answers. We suspect that if one of Sutekh's minions or allies finds the remains first, they'll complete a reanimation ceremony. Draw

the reaper's soul back from wherever it has gone. I trust you understand exactly how dire that could be?"

She understood that the Daughters of Aset had to find the reaper's remains before anyone else did. Because common lore claimed that reapers weren't supposed to die. In fact, once they made their choice and swore fealty to Sutekh, he forced their souls back into their bodies and modified them using dark magic and the souls of the innocent. So if Sutekh's minions found the reaper's remains first, it would stand to reason that they could work that same dark magic to bring him back. Reanimate him. And he'd sing like the fat lady, fingering the ones who'd killed him.

The possibility didn't give her the warm and fuzzies because she couldn't shake the feeling that the Daughters of Aset just might be the ones who'd done the deed, in which case they'd take a direct hit when Sutekh opened the figurative floodgates. But regardless of the culprit, in the end, all would suffer, because once he identified the perpetrator, they'd all be sucked in as Sutekh unleashed his vengeance: a war to end all wars.

Roxy meant to make certain that never happened. The dead reaper would stay dead, his soul trapped in whatever limbo it had gone to. Unreachable. Untouchable.

And that was the way it was gonna be. All she needed to do to make certain of that was figure out the clues.

The piece of shit she'd cuffed to the bed had information that might help her solve the puzzle. She needed to find out what Frank Marin had seen the night the soul reaper was killed.

"Tell me about the tattoo and the guy, Frank," she said, whisper soft.

Staring at her forearm, Marin swallowed and shook his head. "Nope. Never seen it."

She moved with lethal speed, one hand slapping down to seal his lips, muffling his cry so as not to scare the kid, the other bringing the knife down to slice skin and muscle clear to his rib. Bone gleamed white in the lamplight.

Marin's back arched, his entire frame humming with pain and fear.

Leaning in until her lips rested against his ear, she promised, "Next cut is *between* the ribs, maybe clear to your heart. Now, talk. What I need to know is where you saw him, and when."

Marin nodded wildly and she eased back, letting him speak.

"Yeah. Okay, yeah," he said, suddenly all cooperative. Guess he didn't like her carving skills. He grimaced, pain lacing his features. "I seen that mark. Big guy. Blond. He was in chains and that—" he jutted his chin toward her mark "—was on his chest."

Big guy. Blond. A chill skittered up her spine. Not Dagan Krayl. She didn't want it to be him.

Are you here to free me? She'd been so damned naive.

No.

You gonna kill me, then?

This isn't your night to die.

He hadn't just let her live. He'd saved her life. He'd given her hope. He'd inadvertently given her direction when he warned her off the Daughters of Aset—a warning she'd chosen to ignore. And he'd given her

enough money to build a life. So she didn't want the big, blond, *dead* reaper to be him.

"You saw the actual tattoo in the flesh, Marin? Saw it on the guy's chest?"

"Yeah. I did. Yeah."

She leaned in nice and close, staring into his eyes. "Saw him get skinned alive, or just watched the video?"

Someone had used fucking YouTube to circulate a video of a gloved hand wielding the blade that skinned the reaper's chest. YouTube had pulled the clip pretty quick. But rumor had it that a week later, the skin had been sent to Sutekh as a gift, stretched and pinned in place like a macabre picture complete with shiny, black plastic frame. Supposedly, the Wal-Mart sticker was still intact.

Whoever had done that had balls of carbon steel. Or a death wish.

"The video?" Marin swallowed again, and for a second Roxy thought he was going to ask what she was talking about. Then he gave a short, huffing exhalation and said, "Nah. Saw the actual tattoo when they brought the guy in. But, uh, not what followed…" He paused. "You, uh, you seen it?"

"Not in the flesh." She offered a dark smile.

So he hadn't been there for the actual killing. A shame. It meant his information was less valuable than she'd hoped.

"Frank, you're not giving me shit. Tell me something I can use." She smiled and turned the knife so the blade caught the light. "Or don't. I need to practice my carving skills. Thanksgiving's just around the corner."

His eyes rolled until only the whites showed.

Keeping her expression blank, Roxy murmured, "I'm betting there were other witnesses, Frank. Wanna tell me about them?"

He blinked, then shrugged. "No one. Didn't see no one."

"You're lying."

Pressing his lips together, he glared at her. "You think I'm stupid?"

"I'm guessing that's a rhetorical question." He just stared at her, terror and rage glittering in his gaze. She almost laughed. "Are any of those witnesses still alive? Is that it? Everyone who watched the skinning is dead? And you're not inclined to join them in hell?"

Live witnesses were a liability, which explained Marin's reticence.

A live witness would be invaluable to Sutekh. A dead one would be invaluable to his opponent. So the soul reaper's executioner would be inclined to kill the witness and take the soul to a territory off-limits to the Lord of Chaos.

Either way, it was war.

Once the battle started, it wouldn't stop in the Underworld. It'd spill Topworld, into the mortal realm.

The thought chilled her like an Arctic wind.

CHAPTER FOUR

As for any god or any goddess who shall oppose themselves to me
They shall be handed over to those…who live on hearts

—The Egyptian Book of the Dead, Chapter 124

St. Louis, Missouri

DAGAN KRAYL PROPPED ONE shoulder against a burned-out streetlamp and surveyed the dilapidated house before him. The angle of the moon sent his shadow slicing like a dark arrow deep into the overgrown yard, past the maze of old truck tires to the skeletons of two rusting, graffiti-covered cars. The place was little more than a shack, with boarded-up windows and a wide plank nailed across the door.

No one home.

But *someone* watched him, hidden… Where?

Turning his head to the left, he scanned the small, single-story house across the street. There. The pale oval of a face framed by a cracked and grime-flaked front window. From behind a tattered curtain an old woman watched him, white hair hanging in stringy threads past her shoulders, her back hunched and

twisted. His gaze met hers, and he looked beyond her face, beyond age spots and wrinkles and dull eyes. To her soul.

She jerked back, trembling. With some justification, he supposed. Part of the reason he had come here was to kill.

But she wasn't on the job board. Not tonight. She was already near the end of her time; no need for him to hasten her course. Her greatest sin lay at the bottom of a gin bottle, and so her soul was not for him to harvest.

Too shiny.

Dear old Dad would choke on it. Sutekh preferred to dine on those that were obsidian and opaque, stinking of rot and malice. Darksouls.

The wind picked up, dancing an empty cardboard box down the deserted street. Dagan reached into his pocket and pulled out a lollipop, removed the wrapper and folded it once, twice and tucked it away in his pocket. Then he popped the candy in his mouth. Cherry. Nice. He and his brothers each had their own poison. His was lollipops. Alastor liked English toffee. They could just as easily have downed spoonfuls of sugar. The goal was a quick hit of glucose. Their half human, half god metabolism demanded inordinate amounts.

He pushed off the lamppost and vaulted the teetering spikes of wood that passed for a picket fence. He crossed the yard, took the steps two at a time, then followed the sloping porch, his boot heels beating an easy rhythm. Cobwebs draped the overhang, and a pile of old, dry leaves was pushed into the corner, barely visible in the shadows.

Around back, he paused beside a window, examining the board laid flat across. It wasn't nailed down. There were hinges at the top and the board was on springs, designed to automatically slam back in place if lifted.

Fascinating.

Someone had gone to a good deal of trouble to rig that board. An escape hatch. A secret entry. Perhaps a little of both.

He knew who that someone was. Dagan had spent the better part of the last two days watching him. Joe Marin. A killer. A man most mortals would brand a monster.

Sutekh would call him a snack.

Curling his fingers around the edge, Dagan pulled up on the plank and climbed through the window frame, avoiding the jagged remnants of broken glass that protruded into the opening like a serpent's teeth. The board sprang back into place behind him with a clack of wood on wood, sharp in the quiet night.

Inside, he paused, doing a quick scan of his surroundings. Pale fingers of light bled from the neighboring house, reaching through narrow cracks in the boards to touch the piles of trash—bottles, cans, empty pizza boxes—and an ancient, ragged recliner shoved in the corner.

Rustling and scratching told him he wasn't the only live creature in the place, a suspicion that was proved true when a rat scurried across the floor.

His cell phone vibrated. He pulled the lollipop out, stared at it for a second and ignored the summons. The old man could wait.

Or not.

Dagan's lips quirked in a bitter smile as intrusive tendrils of dark power poked at the edges of his thoughts. They had the subtlety of a hurricane, but no more substance than fog. He brushed them aside with ease. The time had long since passed that his father could force his way into Dagan's mind. He could only gain entry now if Dagan let him. That wasn't going to happen anytime soon.

Seconds later, the squeak of metal hinges told him that the spring-loaded board behind him had been pulled open. A thud sounded as the new arrival climbed through the window, then the board banged shut. Dagan sighed, put the candy back in his mouth and crunched it until it was gone. But he didn't turn.

"Didn't ask for anyone to watch my back, Alastor," he drawled.

He should have answered his father's call. Maybe then the old man wouldn't have sent his brother to play guard dog. But Dad already had one dead son, and he wasn't interested in losing another.

After all, good help was so hard to find.

"Not here to watch your back, Dae." A lie. After Lokan's death, the old man had decreed that each of his three remaining sons team up with each other or with another soul reaper. They were supposed to watch each other's backs, because Sutekh hadn't wanted to risk losing another son to the bastards who'd killed his youngest.

But who were the bastards? Wasn't that the question of the hour? Every hour.

"Not here to watch my back?" Dagan glanced at him and snorted. "That's a class-five storm of crap. I'll just wait till it passes."

"I'm not interested in a row, though you seem to be spoiling for one." A faint hint of an English accent clipped Alastor's words, evidence that he'd grown up in a far different place than Dagan. Each of the brothers had. It was all part of Sutekh's philosophy on child-rearing. Keep them apart. Don't let them bond. Engender a rabid sense of competition and distrust. The old man hadn't been too happy when it turned out that despite distance and deprivation—or perhaps because of it—the brothers ended up with an unbreakable connection.

They couldn't climb inside each other's thoughts, not the way Sutekh could in the early years, but they could sense when one of them needed the others. Sort of a psychic 911.

Each of them had felt Lokan's death. In vivid, Technicolor detail.

So, in a way, Dagan was glad that his brother was here—not because his back needed watching, but because it meant he could keep an eye on Alastor, be certain he was safe.

He stepped deeper into the room, glancing about. A used condom was draped over the back of the recliner, and what looked like a pool of vomit had dried to a crusty splotch on the floor.

"Lovely decor," Alastor muttered, his fine sense of aesthetic obviously insulted.

"Yeah." Dagan shoved the paper lollipop stick into his pocket. "Mortals leave such a disgusting mess."

Alastor made an odd choked sound. "Bit of the pot calling the kettle black?"

Unfamiliar with the reference to pots and kettles, Dagan shrugged. Unlike Alastor, he hadn't spent his formative years in the world of mortals. He didn't

understand all their idioms, and he wasn't interested enough to ask. He settled on a generic reply. "We're not here to admire the furniture."

"Why *are* we here?"

Dagan glanced over his shoulder at his brother. In the dim light, Alastor's thick blond hair—a match to his own—gleamed pale and bright. Alastor's was trimmed and styled to perfection, while Dagan's hair was long, past his shoulders, tied back at his nape with a thin scrap of leather. Their features were almost identical, unless someone took care to look closely. Then the differences became apparent. Dagan's face was narrower, his jaw more squared, his eyes gray while Alastor's were blue. But those were subtle differences. There was no doubt they were brothers. Two of four.

No. Now two of only three.

Lokan was dead. Murdered. Now *there* was a word. *Murdered.* It hardly seemed to fit the circumstance. *Butchered* was more accurate.

Rage surged, an acid tide. He felt as if he'd been doused with liquid nitrogen, cold and hot, the pain so intense it stole his breath. The first time he'd felt that, he'd been staring down at the blood-soaked ground where his brother had been skinned and hacked to bits.

Initially, he hadn't recognized the sensation as emotion. He'd only known that it had consumed him. *Hurt* him.

Eventually, he'd come to understand that it was grief and loss and pain.

Whoever had done the deed, he'd find them. And for the first time in his long existence, he would take their souls not purely because it was his task, but for sheer enjoyment.

He'd make it last. And he'd make it hurt.

"Don't know why you're here, but *I'm* here to do a job, Alastor." Dagan locked away the seething rage. It wouldn't help him find Lokan's killers, but coolheaded logic might.

"What job would that be, mate?" Alastor's tone was mild, but there was an undercurrent of tension.

"I may have picked up a lead," Dagan admitted. He didn't need to clarify that it was a lead on Lokan's killers. "Obscure, but worth a look. Police report on a homeless guy who swore he'd barely escaped a run-down shack with his life."

"I suspect you mean *this* run-down shack." Alastor paused and seemed to take his silence for an affirmative. "Anything else in that report? Did the local constabulary check it out?"

"Local *constabulary?*" Dagan snorted. "The *cops* did a drive-by and a cursory check. Place belongs to a guy by the name of Joe Marin. He and his brother, Frank, inherited it three years ago when their mother died. She's the one who got Joe's name inscribed in the old man's book of records. She asked for the mortgage to be paid off on this place.

"The brother, Frank, is overseas, last anyone knows. Cops chatted with Joe. Decided he was squeaky clean. So they closed the file."

Turning, he studied the graffiti on the opposite wall. *Life Sux.*

True, but he could argue that death sucked more.

He stepped closer, examined the letters, let his fingertips almost touch the words. Not the usual sort of paint...

"Waste of perfectly good blood," Alastor murmured from behind him.

"You think?" They exchanged a glance. Humans. They did such odd things. "Let's see what other marvels this place holds."

Dagan walked along the narrow hallway to the back of the house, peripherally aware of his brother a step behind him. He paused at the end, studying the door.

"What makes you think there's something here to find?" Alastor asked.

"Apart from a *new* deadbolt—" Dagan tapped his index finger against the cool metal "—on the outside of an *old* basement door?"

"Looks like the bloke was planning to keep something in rather than keep it out." Alastor shrugged. "But you weren't aware of that before you got here. So what brought you here in the first place?"

"Two things." Dagan slid the bolt. "First, the old man offered up Joe Marin's name. Time for payback."

"And second?"

"The police report said the homeless guy couldn't describe his captor, but he offered vivid details of a silver pendant in the shape of an ankh. With wings. And horns."

Alastor gave a low whistle. "The dark mark."

A mark the Daughters of Aset generally took care to keep from prying mortal eyes.

"Same as the mark burned in the ground where Lokan was killed."

"One more reason to hate the Daughters of Aset."

Dagan glanced at his brother, a little startled by his vehemence. "I'm not ready to jump to conclusions at this point. Could be someone playing on an old enmity. Could be they weren't involved at all."

"Could be," Alastor agreed, but Dagan wasn't con-

vinced he meant it. So for now, he kept his mouth shut about the pendant he'd seen before.

He remembered it. Remembered *her*. Smooth skin the color of coffee, double cream. Brown-black ringlets tumbling over her shoulders and hanging halfway down her back. Almond-tipped eyes, a unique shade of bronze and green, bright with fire and fury.

He remembered her guts and grit. Her smart mouth.

In the years since, long periods had passed where he didn't allow himself to think of her at all.

Interspersed with short periods where he did.

This moment was one of them.

You stay away from the Otherkin. Anyone with the mark of Aset. He'd paused in the doorway and spoken without looking back.

Aset?

He'd glanced at her over his shoulder then, wanting to see her expression, to judge it for guile. She was sitting between the corpses, wrapped in his jacket, clutching it closed. *That symbol on your necklace. It's an ankh, yeah, but it has wings and horns. That makes it…special. You see anyone with that mark cut in their skin, an ankh with wings and horns, you run. As fast and as far as you can. You trust me on that.*

Why should I run? A breathless whisper.

Because if they catch you, they'll keep you. And that'd make you my enemy. You want me for an enemy, little girl?

He'd warned her off the Daughters of Aset. He'd figured she'd be smart enough to listen.

What were the odds she was in any way connected to any of this? To Lokan's murder?

Next to impossible.

But nearly three hundred years of existence had taught him not to trust coincidence, and the dark mark was turning up in too many places to ignore.

"You tell Da'?" Alastor asked.

Dagan's head jerked up. His tension eased only when he realized Alastor was asking not about the girl but about the possible link between Lokan's murder and Aset. Also known as Isis. Wife of Osiris. Eternal enemy of Sutekh.

"And start an apocalyptic war? Sutekh and Aset aren't exactly lunch buddies." And if he proved a link between Aset and Lokan's death, things would get damned ugly. Not just between the two of them, but between all the gods and demigods who would invariably choose sides—or start a new side—until the whole damned Underworld was twisted up tighter than a Gordian knot, the situation more explosive than C-4.

Turning back to the basement door, Dagan opened it and flicked the light switch. Nothing. So he went down into the dark. Actually, he liked it better dark. Bright sunlight hurt his eyes; even hazy days could be a pain. But night was his time. He could see as well in pitch-black as under a hundred-watt bulb. One of the perks of being the old man's spawn.

The air was musty and stained with rot. The smell was distinctive—aged meat and old blood—poorly camouflaged by the heavier stink of bleach, a smell that grew stronger as Dagan turned to his left. Following his nose, he moved to stand before a padlocked wooden door.

There were carvings in the wood. In the centre of the door itself was a deeply grooved eye of Horus, the symbol of protection and royal power. A symbol linked to Horus's mother, Aset. Isis.

Another fucking coincidence? Right.

On the door frame were crude hieroglyphics, barely readable. Dagan did a quick translation, reading aloud.

"For all men who shall enter this place...impure... there will be judgment...an end shall be made for him...I shall cast the fear of myself into him...his head cut off, his soul putrefied...for this is the first of twenty-one gates to the domain of Osiris."

Since all of those gates were in the Underworld in the territory of Osiris, Dagan knew for a fact that this door was not one of them.

"What's he playing at?" Alastor stood at his shoulder.

"Let's find out." Dagan closed his fist around the lock and yanked hard. One side of his mouth curved up as the metal gave way. The door opened soundlessly, the hinges well oiled. The old-penny stink of blood was so thick he could almost reach out and touch it. "Smells like we hit the mother lode."

He stepped into the windowless room and turned a slow circle. The concrete floor sloped away from the bare brick walls in a subtle grade to a drain in the center. In the corner was a plastic tub sink and beside it a fridge plugged into a portable generator that chugged with a steady hum.

"High-end generator," Alastor observed.

"Let's see what's so special..." Cold air rushed free as Dagan opened the refrigerator door and, with it, a whole can of worms. Plastic wrap couldn't obscure the contents: a half dozen neatly arranged human heads in various stages of decomposition and an open box of baking soda.

"Wonder if he changes it every three months." Dagan held up the box.

His brother arched a brow.

Dagan replaced the baking soda, let the door swing shut and then checked the freezer; it held its own unique surprises—a neatly stacked array of plastic-wrapped severed hands.

A body cut into bits, some parts stored here and the rest left…where? These humans had been butchered, just like Lokan. But that's where the similarity ended. Finding and reassembling all the body bits of a dead human wouldn't change the outcome. They'd still be dead.

Finding Lokan's parts, though, was a whole different story. Because Lokan hadn't been human. He was a soul reaper, the youngest son of Sutekh, and he could be brought back. He could live and breathe again if Dagan and his brothers could find him in time, before he ate the food of the dead and severed his connection to the world of the living.

Problem was, Dagan had no clue where Lokan's parts were, and without them, his brother's life force, his Ka, was confined to an unknown limbo. He didn't walk the mortal realm and he wasn't in the Underworld. He was somewhere else. Somewhere none of them could travel, his spirit locked away from them by an unseen barrier. They couldn't sense him. Their psychic link failed them.

So far, every effort Dagan and his two remaining brothers had made to find Lokan's body had been met with failure. Fucking failure.

And thinking about it brought out unfamiliar, un-welcome emotions, not the least of which was guilt. Dagan was the oldest. The strongest. He should have been there. Should have protected him.

Turning away from the freezer and its neatly aligned, plastic-wrapped packages, he studied the metal shelves on the opposite wall. Empty eye sockets stared back at him from skulls devoid of flesh, arranged in perfect symmetry.

"This smacks of ritual," Alastor murmured.

"Doesn't it, though? Thing is, I never knew Osiris or Aset to call for human sacrifice. So is this guy just doing his own thing?" He glanced at his brother. "Or did he move from sacrificing mortals to sacrificing a soul reaper?"

"Not pissing likely." Alastor shook his head. "A mortal wouldn't have stood a chance against Lokan."

The truth of that hung between them.

A supernatural had to be involved, and all fingers were currently pointing at Aset's Daughters. But was that the truth or a convenient fiction meant to throw them off the true scent? He'd long ago learned not to trust the obvious.

Dagan hunkered down. On the bottom shelf was a plug-in hot plate along with a metal pot big enough to hold a severed head and boil it like a chicken. No stretch to figure out how the killer had gotten the flesh off the skulls.

Straightening, he poked at a clear plastic box filled with little ivory bones. They were cube shaped and small, which made him guess wrist bones. This guy was nothing if not organized. Everything had its place.

A black, rectangular box on the top shelf yielded a detailed pictographic record of the killer's escapades, neatly organized with crisp cardboard dividers. Dagan flipped through the photos, froze, flipped back.

He slid the picture from the box and studied it. It

was old, with a wide, white stripe at the bottom. One of those self-developing photos that had been popular a few decades back. It showed a woman's neck and torso, but not her face. Her necklace was visible in the open neck of her shirt. A silver pendant. An ankh.

Just like the one the homeless guy had described.

Just like the one Dagan remembered seeing around the girl's neck a decade ago. He studied the picture. Same girl? Probably not. Lots of women wore jewelry, and an Egyptian motif wasn't an unusual choice. But the wings and horns *were*.

He remembered the way he'd leaned in close, the feel of the heavy silver chain in his hand as he gathered the pendant from between her breasts and lifted it for a closer look.

You know what this symbol means?

It's an ankh. The ancient Egyptian symbol of life.

Where did you get it?

Why d'you wanna know? She'd snapped, her anger blatant armor against her fear. Then she'd finally admitted, *From my mother.*

Where did she get it?

Haven't seen her since I was five. But if she shows up out of the blue, I'll be sure to ask.

Damn. The picture in his hand took on a whole crapload of new possibilities. He closed and replaced the box but kept the photo.

"All these victims were mortal." Alastor picked up a skull, lobbed it in the air, then caught it as it fell. "I sense no remnants of supernatural energy here."

Dagan had to agree. He picked up no supernatural vibe at all, despite the markings on the door. Did they actually mean anything? Were they connected to the

Underworld, or all for show? Dagan was inclined to believe the latter, but there were factions—supporters of Aset and Osiris among them—that would like nothing better than to sow the seeds of turmoil and reap the rewards of a new balance in the Underworld, one where Sutekh wasn't at the pinnacle of power. Which meant Dagan couldn't discount any possibilities, however unlikely.

"Can't be a one-off. If this killer, this *mortal,* took Lokan," Alastor continued, "wouldn't he have had to practice on something weaker than a soul reaper first? Shouldn't there be something other than human bones and body parts in the mix? Maybe a lesser Underlord or a succubus?" Again, he tossed the skull and caught it.

"Put it back," Dagan ordered, his tone mild.

Alastor gave a snort of incredulity. "It's a lump of dead mineralized cells."

"Now it is." Dagan stared him down. "But it used to be a living being."

That drew a startled laugh. "Blimey, you think of the strangest things. You take souls, steal hearts. Literally. What do you care about a human skull?"

"I care about respect." His answer sucked, but it was all he had.

"Respect," Alastor echoed, glancing at the skull.

"It might have been someone's brother."

The silence stretched until Alastor gave a deceptively lazy shrug and set the skull back on the shelf. Their eyes met and held, both grief and the unspoken promise of retribution hanging thickly between them.

"Maybe he killed a supernatural elsewhere," Dagan said, shifting the conversation back to Alastor's

original question. He passed his brother the photo-graph. Alastor studied it, then shrugged and shook his head.

"Look again."

Alastor did, taking his time. "The pendant," he said at length, handing the photo back. "You think he killed one of Aset's Daughters?"

"I think he killed *someone* and took a photograph. Can't say if it was one of Aset's Daughters." Or if it was a smart-mouthed girl with toffee-cream skin and sleek, dark ringlets that fell over her shoulders. The possibility made him feel like he was going to burst out of his skin.

"What do you know about Aset's Daughters?" Alastor's question hurtled him into the past. He'd asked her almost the same thing as he'd held her necklace in his hand, studying the hieroglyphics on the back, leaning so close he could hear her heartbeat.

You ever hear of the Otherkin or the Daughters of Aset?

No.

You ever hear of Sutekh?

No. But if we're playing twenty questions, I have a few.

He'd been on her before she could exhale, pressing his palm across her mouth, cutting off her questions. He hadn't wanted to tell her a damned thing. He'd wanted her to walk out of that blood-soaked room and build some sort of life.

Shh. She'd watched him with those tiger eyes. *You have a chance for a life, little girl. Don't waste it.*

"Dagan?"

"Yeah, just thinking…" He scrubbed his hand along his jaw. "I don't know much about them. You?"

"Only that they're supposed to be guardians of humankind when called upon, and seekers of self-realization."

"Supposed to be," Dagan agreed.

"But you don't think so."

"What I know is that Aset and the old man have never precisely gotten along."

"A polite way of putting it. They bloody well hate each other's guts."

Couldn't argue with that.

"That girl in the picture…you think she was a Daughter of Aset? You think the bloke might have practiced on her before killing Lokan?"

"Maybe."

Alastor frowned. "You're answering *maybe* to which question?"

"Dunno. Neither. Both."

"Cryptic gets old fast, Dae."

"Can't give you answers I don't have. The pendant in the picture could be coincidence—" he didn't bother to hide his cynicism "—could have nothing to do with the Daughters of Aset. Could be just pretty jewelry. Hard to—"

The squeak of the stair made him stop midsentence and turn toward the open door. "Showtime," he murmured as he flicked off the light.

CHAPTER FIVE

Amarillo, Texas

"YOU KNOW, MARIN, YOU AREN'T being particularly helpful." Roxy flipped the knife again, higher this time. "Let's try a different question. Where'd you see the guy with the tattoo? Give me a city. Preferably an intersection. Better still, an exact address."

He stared at the knife, apparently contemplating his options.

"I *will* kill you," Roxy promised, her tone cheerful.

"Toronto. He was there with these priests." The words tumbled one into the next. "Part of some freaky cult."

Toronto. She was being strangled by coincidences. And she was pissed that whoever was responsible for this debacle had decided to crap in her backyard.

"A cult?" Like he didn't know what they were called. He was giving her just enough to pacify without nailing himself to the cross. "The Setnakhts?" she prompted sweetly. Offshoot worshippers of Sutekh. Which made no sense. Why would Sutekh's fanboys nab one of his reapers? Kill him?

Who would be crazy enough to poke the devil with his own tail?

"Yeah. Yeah. Setnakhts. That was it. They have this temple there."

"And you were involved because…"

"I was hired to…uh…to—" his gaze darted to the closet "—supply a certain…entertainment."

That answer made Roxy want to let him live. Minus his dick and balls. Because she didn't need to look in the closet again to know exactly what sort of entertainment he meant.

But something didn't add up. She'd lay bets that he was improvising, giving up answers that had nothing to do with more valuable truths.

"You were hired to provide entertainment. So you nabbed a kid in Oklahoma City and dragged her to Amarillo. Long way from Toronto, isn't it?"

Marin darted another glance at the closet and his breathing sped up.

"The Setnakhts wanted *any* entertainment," Roxy prodded, "or this kid in particular?"

"Any kid," he hastened to assure. "Any kid."

Which made her certain that he lied. He'd chosen this particular kid for a reason. If she could figure out what that was, she'd have another fragment of the puzzle.

"Don't lie to me, Marin." She brought the knife down and nicked him on the cheek. "Three cuts, three strikes."

He yelped and wrenched at the cuffs. "It wasn't just the kid. I was hired to supply information," he squawked. "They wanted to know about someone." He froze, then shot her a sly glance. "Maybe there's someone you want to know about? I'm good at that. Knowing things. I have power. Great power."

Roxy snorted. She could read exactly what he was: a low-level psychic, his power little more than an annoying fizzle. Whatever he knew was at best 10 percent truth and 90 percent smoke and mirrors. He was a typical Topworld grunt, a mortal or near mortal the Underworlders used to do their dirty work.

She was definitely a step or two above him as far as paranormal enhancements went. She was physically stronger. Her wounds healed at an accelerated rate. Her senses were sharper, and she had a sixth sense that let her recognize when there was a supernatural in the vicinity—all useful tools in her line of work.

She could hear the kid shifting in the closet, growing restless.

"So those priests who hired you to supply the entertainment," she said flatly, suddenly tired of the game. She needed to be done with this, needed to get the kid back to a set of loving arms. Not that she'd ever be the same. Take a peek into the dark world and you never forget it. Roxy knew that better than most. "They were looking for information about something else. *Someone* else. Who?"

"I can't. I can't." Marin shook his head wildly back and forth, terror bleeding from every pore. Now they were getting somewhere. Roxy slid the tip of the knife back into the cut she'd made in his chest.

"No," he cried. "Can't do it." But he didn't sound so sure.

Roxy smiled. "Then you're a dead man."

Marin wrenched and yanked at the cuffs, all the while trying to hold his chest still. "You said you wouldn't kill me. You said!"

"Like *you* never tell a lie?" Roxy laughed. "Who're they looking for, Marin?"

He was breathing faster, his chest rising and falling in a frantic rhythm. "Some woman."

"Her name?"

"They'll kill me."

"*I'll* kill you." She scored his skin an inch above the first cut, just deep enough to draw blood. The scent teased her, copper sweet. He gave a choked sob. "They're far away," she continued. "You can hide from them, but not from me. Her name."

He swallowed. "Kelley Tam."

No. Effing. Way.

"Kelley Tam," Roxy repeated, careful not to betray even a flicker of emotion. "You certain?"

"Yeah. Yeah."

"You know why they're looking for her?"

"No."

"You know where she is?"

He shook his head. "Nah. Couldn't find much. Her dad was from Jamaica. Mom from Chicago. She was born there. Grew up there. Then disappeared, leaving two kids behind. She pulled off one hell of a vanishing act. I couldn't find even a breadcrumb to mark the trail. I swear it. I swear it on my mother's grave."

Yeah. Like she put stock in that.

The thing was, Marin hadn't revealed a damned thing that she didn't already know. Which made her suspicious.

There were probably a lot of women named Kelley Tam in this world, but Roxy would lay a bet in blood that Marin was talking about one in particular. The same one Roxy had been looking for most of her life.

Kelley Tam had walked out on her five-year-old daughter twenty-five years ago and never looked back.

Left her huddled in a dim hallway, wearing pink pajamas and cornrows. In all the years since, with considerable resources at her disposal, Roxy hadn't been able to find a trace.

She doubted Marin and the Setnakhts would have better luck. The question was, why were they even trying?

Something didn't ring true. He'd given up that name way too easily, almost without a fight.

Marin's cheap watch ticked off the seconds. Was he telling the truth? Had the Setnakhts really sent him after Kelley Tam, or had his weak psychic senses kicked in and offered him the jackpot, snagging the name from Roxy's thoughts?

"What do they want with her?"

"Don't know. I swear it on my dick. I don't know."

Interesting. He'd upgraded from swearing on his mother's grave.

"Give me another name. This one having to do with the blond guy's death. That's not so much to offer in exchange for your life."

Protecting her thoughts from whatever psy talent Marin had, making certain he couldn't reach in and grab a stray idea, Roxy pictured an endless void—an energy shield—in her mind.

Marin stared up at her, sweating, shaking, his teeth clacking together.

"Tell me," she ordered, whisper soft.

"Krayl. I heard the name Krayl."

Her heart slammed against her ribs. Whatever she'd expected Marin to say, it wasn't that. Ten years ago, Dagan Krayl had left her in a room where the walls wept blood and death after he'd done something to

her, something evil, insidious and quiet. Something that made her both more and less than human.

She remembered the look in his eyes as he'd reached for her, focused, intent. He'd wanted the pendant dangling between her breasts. She'd thought he wanted her breasts.

With a snarl, she'd lunged, her nails clawing at his face, her teeth sinking into his forearm, hard enough to break skin. His blood had filled her mouth, copper sharp on her tongue.

Damn, she could almost taste it even now.

She'd held on like a starving hyena on a piece of meat.

Then he'd hit her, a hard thump of his open palm against her chest, forcing the air from her lungs and sending her sprawling.

She'd lain where she'd fallen in the puddle of his coat on the stinking mattress, glaring up at him, breathless, her fingers clawed in ready defense.

"I told you—" she'd struggled for breath "—that I'd tear you up if you tried anything on me. I told you."

Blood had seeped from the crescent marks left by her teeth and snaked down his forearm in thick rivulets.

"You're a fucking hair-trigger disaster zone. I was reaching for your pendant, not your tits."

Her first thought was that she hated that word, and something told her that he knew it, that he'd chosen it on purpose.

Her second thought was that she'd bitten him. Bitten an otherworldly monster that ripped people apart for kicks.

Only he hadn't ripped her apart. Instead, he'd left her sitting in a pool of blood, surrounded by death, left

her to figure out on her own exactly what he'd done to her.

She hadn't even realized it for months, and when she had, she'd been too horrified to accept it until it was almost too late. He'd saved her and damned her and left her mind and emotions tangled up worse than Christmas lights stored in the attic.

Was he the soul reaper who'd been killed?

She ought to be relieved, even happy, if he was. Soul reapers were Sutekh's minions, and that made them no friends of the Daughters of Aset.

So why did she feel a flicker of regret?

Maybe because in a bizarre, convoluted way, he'd been almost...kind to her.

"I want you to build a life that keeps you away from places like this," he'd said. "Mortals like that—" he'd jerked his head toward the bloody corpses "—A good human life, whatever that entails." He'd stared at her, his gray eyes bright and intent. "A safe life. I want you to have a safe life."

Safe. She'd never been safe. She'd always just stayed one step ahead, dancing as fast as she could, trying to stay on the log before it rolled and took her under.

Tension crawled through her and she realized the tip of her knife was centimeters from Marin's eye. She eased back a bit and snarled, "Was Krayl the villain or the victim?"

"All I heard was a name. I don't know what his role was, I swear." The words were garbled, mangled by Marin's sobs. She believed him.

"We're done," Roxy said, choking off the unwelcome emotions that swelled and surged. Too many co-

incidences. Too many bits of her past being dumped into the mix. *Krayl.* Dagan Krayl? Was he dead? Skinned and hacked to bits?

The possibility rubbed at her like grit in a wound.

Because part of her figured that if anyone got to kill him, it ought to be her. And the other part remembered his eyes, colder than frost, the way his mouth quirked at the corner in the whisper of a smile and the feel of his soft, warm jacket wrapped around her like an embrace.

But she also remembered the sickness that had slowly consumed her in the months that followed. A sickness he'd left her to face alone. Confused. Completely unprepared.

She ground the memory to dust.

"No, please, we're not done," Marin blubbered. "Don't kill me. Please don't kill me." He jerked so hard the cuffs cut deep into his wrist, leaving raw abrasions. "I have more. I can tell you about the soul reaper."

Roxy tapped the tip of the knife against his cheek. "Go on," she urged.

"The dead reaper—"

She waited, and when he just squirmed and shook, she made a sound of frustration and nicked his other cheek so he had twin oozing cuts.

He squawked and blurted, "Not just any reaper. Sutekh's son. The dead reaper was one of Sutekh's four sons."

Roxy felt as if she'd been slammed in the head with a brick. Who the hell had enough power—or the brass balls—to take down not just a soul reaper but Sutekh's son?

"That's good, right? That's good information. You didn't know that, did you?" Marin babbled. "You'll let me loose now." He jiggled the cuffs. "Let me loose."

Keeping her expression ruthlessly neutral, Roxy slid the phone on the nightstand closer to the bed and lifted the receiver to make certain there was a dial tone. The dead reaper was Sutekh's son. Sutekh's fucking son. She needed time to wrap her head around that.

"Here's the way this is going to play out, Marin. I'm going to slit your throat—"

"What the fuck? What the fuck?" He dug his heels into the mattress, flopping around like a landed fish, jerking his bound wrists with enough violence to tear away skin.

"Shut up. Don't interrupt." Roxy rammed the heel of her palm against his forehead, sending his head back to bang loudly on the headboard.

Reaching for Marin's hands, she undid the cuff on one wrist. He flailed and tugged, but she was stronger than him, thanks to that long-ago mouthful of soul reaper blood.

"You fucking stole a kid," she continued. "And it isn't the first time you've done it, you worthless piece of shit. But I'm a woman of my word. I said I wouldn't kill you, and I won't."

He stared at her, wild eyed and panting, a faint flicker of hope flitting across his features. She squashed it like a rotten grape.

"I'm going to slit your throat. Not deep enough to hit the artery, which would see you bleed out in seconds. Just deep enough to nick the vein. That'll buy you minutes. You shove your finger in the hole, press hard,

and you live. Problem is, with one hand chained to the bed, you're going to have to pull your finger out to dial for help." She laughed. "Decisions, decisions."

He held up his free hand, slapping at her, trying to ward her off. She caught his hair in her fist, jerked his head to the side and slashed her blade across his throat.

Blood welled, dark and red.

Luscious.

Marin's mouth opened and closed, but the only sound that came out was a mewling whimper. The smell of urine grew stronger and Roxy glanced down. He was sitting in a puddle.

Grabbing his hand, she hauled it to his throat and pressed his fingers against the cut. The bleeding slowed. With a grin, she let go, raised her fingers to her lips and held them there, closing her eyes, letting the scent of his blood tease her. Then she opened her eyes and slowly licked her fingers clean.

He watched her with abject horror.

Energy surged, and she leashed the urge to bend over and suck him dry. Time had taught her to master her need. She took only what she must, a few drops.

Enough to slake her hunger.

Enough that if she ever chose to track him, she'd be able to single him out as surely as if she'd planted a GPS under his skin. One taste of his blood and it was like having his blueprint on file.

But, damn, it tasted so good.

He'd done this to her. Dagan Krayl. Saved her. Doomed her. Made her what she was.

He hadn't warned her, hadn't prepared her, hadn't said a word.

And now he might be dead.

She'd dig him up just to kill him again. Or just to be certain he was dead. Or just to see him in the flesh one last time.

She shook her head. Look up *ambivalent* in the dictionary and there'd be a picture of Roxy Tam.

Eyes bulging, Marin darted his gaze wildly between her and the phone on the night table.

"Tough choice," she commiserated. "Keep your finger in the hole or reach for the phone? I wouldn't waste energy trying to scream for help. The motel's empty. I checked. And the kid at the front desk is probably fast asleep." She paused. "One last question, Frank. And remember, I've tasted your blood. I know your heart. I'll know if you lie." This in itself was a lie, but he had no way to know that. "Did you *touch* that kid?"

His gaze shot to hers, his fingers pressing tightly against his slashed throat. He knew exactly what she was asking. "I didn't touch her!" he rasped. "I didn't! She wasn't for me. She was for them. The Setnakhts."

She patted his cheek. "I believe you." Mostly because her research had revealed that Marin's Australian victims had all been little boys.

Marin was blubbering now. Begging. Terror, shock, confusion—the panoply of emotion that flitted across his features was priceless.

Of course, he could always use his mouth to take the receiver off the hook. Use his nose to punch 911. She didn't offer those helpful tips, but she did offer a backhanded wave. "Too bad I can't stick around to see how this plays out. Good luck, Marin."

She crossed to the closet and pulled off her denim jacket. Then she did a cursory check to make sure it

wasn't splattered with Marin's blood. Good to go. Not a drop.

Opening the door just enough to reach the kid without offering her a view of the carnage on the bed, Roxy summoned what she hoped was a reassuring smile. Dana was still singing, so low it was more breath than melody. She stopped and looked up, her fingers tightening around Flopsy.

"We're outta here." Roxy pulled away the musty blanket, wrapped Dana in the jacket and lifted her from the floor. She was stiff and awkward, clearly traumatized. Pressing the kid's head against her chest, Roxy shielded her view as they left the room. She hoped the headphones blocked the sound of Marin's babbling pleas.

Reaching behind her, she jerked the front door shut. Marin howled.

With Dana clinging to her like a monkey, Roxy hauled out a prepaid, disposable cell phone and dialed 911. Not out of the goodness of her heart. That organ was as shriveled and black as coal. She did it because she wanted Marin alive and scared enough to shit himself. The first thing he'd do was run back to whoever was pulling the strings. And Roxy could find him if she wanted.

Balancing the kid on her hip, she gave the motel's address and Marin's room number as she headed to the rented convertible Corvette parked at the far end of the lot. Ignoring the instruction to stay on the line, she ended the call.

"Your mom's waiting for you in Oklahoma City," she said, after turning off the iPod and buckling Dana up nice and safe. She'd disabled the airbag earlier and

picked up this cloth contraption that wrapped around the seat belt to modify it for the kid's small size. Because she took her work seriously. Do it right or don't do it at all. "She'll be hugging you in about four hours."

Roxy didn't expect a reply, but Dana surprised her.

"How long is four hours?"

Damn. Smart kid.

Roxy opened her mouth. Closed it. Glanced at the clock in the dash. She pointed at the number on the left. "Do you know what this is?"

"A one," Dana whispered.

"Do you know what a five looks like?"

The kid stared at her, then slowly held up one hand, fingers extended.

"Yeah, that's, um, good. But do you know what the *number* five looks like?"

Dana leaned forward and pressed the tip of her finger to the number on the far right. A five. It was 1:35 a.m.

"Okay, then. When the one turns into a five, your mom will be there to give you a hug."

"Okay, then," Dana parroted, and she closed her eyes and promptly fell asleep.

Roxy stared at her for a minute, nonplussed. Then she tossed the phone into a sorry-looking clump of bushes, gave a quick scan of the perimeter and rounded the hood. The breeze ruffled her hair. She froze, skin prickling, wariness scratching at her. Slowly, she turned.

Behind her, not ten feet away, was Dagan Krayl. He looked exactly as she recalled. Same long, honey-blond hair. Same piercing gray eyes. He looked straight at her and then turned toward the motel, as though he, too, thought they were being watched.

With a sigh, she ignored him. He wasn't real. She knew that for a fact because this wasn't the first time she'd had this sort of waking dream. First time it'd happened, she'd thought it really was him. Maybe even the second or third time. Eventually, she'd figured out she was just a bit touched in the head, dreaming about him with her eyes wide-open.

The illusion or delusion or dream or whatever the hell he was tended to pop by periodically, appearing like her own fucking fairy godmother or early-warning system when she was anxious or on alert.

And sometimes he came to her when her eyes were closed in the darkest heart of the night...

She blew out a breath and looked past him, studying the shadows. All she saw were street and walls and clumps of ragged grass. And when her gaze shifted back to where he'd been, he was gone. No surprise. He tended to do that, too. Disappear at will.

With the driver's door open, she rested her forearm on the roof of the car and drummed her fingers in a staccato burst. Again, she scanned the lot, turning all the way around to study the empty field across the road.

Nothing there that she could see.

Which didn't actually mean that there was nothing there.

She climbed in, shifted into gear and drove to the exit. Again, she felt an odd crackling sensation, like her skin was charged and sensitized.

Shooting a look in the rearview mirror, she thought she saw something move across the deserted parking lot, something fast. She slowed, stopped, slung her arm over Dana's seat back and looked back. Seconds ticked past.

Nothing. There was nothing back there except a worthless low-level psychic that she probably ought to have killed.

She wanted to believe that, but her gut told her she was wrong. That there *was* something there. Something powerful enough to camouflage its signature.

Paranoia? Maybe. She'd long ago adopted it as her middle name.

Either way, it was time to go.

She got the car moving and turned toward the highway. With her index finger, she loaded the CD. "(Get Your Kicks On) Route 66" came on. A glance at Dana showed she was out for the count. Turning up the volume a bit, Roxy let the old Depeche Mode cover rock her and Dana along Route 66.

Well, not exactly Route 66. Eastbound on the I-40.

Four hours, give or take, and she'd be running solo again. Heading for Toronto. Heading for home. What were the odds that it was also home to the Setnakhts?

Focusing her thoughts, she picked apart the information Marin had supplied. Not that he'd given her much she could use. Just a possible link to the Setnakhts, and a name: *Krayl.*

Premonition skittered up her spine.

Dagan Krayl had left her in a room he'd turned into a slaughterhouse.

Left her alive, with a stack of bills and a dire warning not to make herself his enemy, not to ally with the Daughters of Aset. And damn if she hadn't gone and done exactly that. Wasn't she the queen of good choices?

But he'd left her to become the creature he'd made her. Without an instruction manual.

So she owed him. Yeah, she *owed* him.

And if he wasn't the reaper who'd been butchered and skinned, she meant to honor her debt.

CHAPTER SIX

I have come against that enemy of mine,
And he is given over to me
He is finished and silent...

—Egyptian Book of the Dead, Chapter 65

St. Louis, Missouri

ALASTOR REACHED FOR THE BOX of photos then stepped to the corner, blending with the shadows. Dagan shot him a questioning look, but his brother just shrugged, silently slipped the top off the box and started flipping through the collection.

There was no time to wonder what he was about. Dagan watched the doorway, waiting for his prey to step into view. Medium-size guy. Sharp features. Neatly dressed. Mouse-brown hair slicked down to one side. The kind of guy you'd pass on the street and not even notice.

He was boring beige on the outside, monster on the inside. Perfect for Dagan's purposes.

They watched each other in silence for an instant, a flicker of annoyance registering on the killer's face.

"Hello, Joe."

"You know my name. You have me at a disadvantage."

Dagan grinned. "You have no idea."

The guy looked relaxed, calm. Dagan wasn't buying the act. He'd penetrated the inner sanctum, desecrated the killer's lair. No way was he as cool and detached as he seemed.

"Time to change the baking soda?" Dagan goaded.

"Did you disturb anything? Move anything?" Small, dark eyes flicked to the fridge. There was an edge to Joe's tone now. A bit of tension around his mouth. He didn't like the idea of someone else touching his treasures.

"Oh, yeah." Dagan smiled. "Unwrapped every shiny package. Wanna see?"

"I'll see it when I open the door to put your parts away." The guy's lips peeled back in a snarl, revealing small white teeth, like a child's. "Generally, I prefer a female and a knife, but needs must—" Lifting his arm, he leveled a 9mm Glock at Dagan's head. "So, what are you? PI? Cop?" He pursed his lips. "Fed?"

Dagan kept his eyes on Joe, but he was peripherally aware of Alastor shifting from the shadows as the gun came up.

"None of the above." He held out the photograph. "Humor me before you carve me up for dinner. Tell me about the pendant. The one in the picture."

Joe glanced at the photo but didn't step closer. "Ah," he said, lips twisting in a sneer. "And you want to know…why?"

"Curiosity."

"Curiosity killed the cat." His eyes glittered. "I took the necklace from her. It was her treasure. Then it became one of mine. She was young. Early twenties.

Pretty. Mixed heritage. Black. Chinese. A little of each, I'd say. Maybe something else thrown into the mix." He inhaled deeply, and his pupils dilated as he drew on the memories. "I remember her skin. The smell of it. The feel. Dark and smooth." He licked his lips. "She was brave. She didn't want to scream. I put quite an effort into that—making her scream."

The killer's victim sounded a lot like the girl Dagan remembered. An unfamiliar tension coiled in his gut. What were the chances that he'd left her alive only to have her get nabbed by this prick? What the fuck were the chances of that?

And why the fuck did he care?

Because he'd told her to build a life. A nice, boring, safe life. He'd wanted that for her, though he couldn't understand why.

"Year?" he rasped.

"Year?"

"The day you killed her. What year was it?" At least that'd point him in the right direction. Tell him if the girl in the picture could possibly be the same one he tried so hard not to think about. Tried so hard not to find.

"I'll never tell." Joe waggled his brows. "I'll never tell."

He held the gun rock-steady. There was nothing about this situation that fazed him. Not yet. He thought he was in control, the undisputed winner.

He was about to find out that his prize was a dud.

"She was your friend?" Joe whispered. "Was it your friend I sliced till she screamed?" He waited a heartbeat and, seeing he would get no reply, continued. "But that was a long time ago. A very long time. She was one of my first. I kept her beneath the floorboards in my closet.

Took her out and held her in my arms at night. She was lovely. I kept her for a very long while before I carved her."

He wanted a reaction and Dagan wasn't about to oblige. Instead, he asked, "The marks on the door... they have a particular meaning, or were you just expressing your artistic side?"

"That's quite the change of topic." The killer tipped his head, his eyes rolling up and to the right, his expression thoughtful, assessing. Then he said, "They're ancient Mayan markings. My kills are sacrifices to the Mayan god of the Underworld."

"Yeah? Who would that be?"

He blinked, paused. "Uh...Toth."

Dagan laughed. He couldn't help it. "Actually, the symbols are Egyptian. And the Mayan god of the Underworld is Ah Puch. Nice guy. A bit bloodthirsty."

Joe's lips thinned and his breathing grew deeper, faster. Anger. He didn't like being corrected.

And Dagan was tired of the game. He had whatever answers he was going to get, which amounted to pretty much a heap of nothing. Sutekh would do better. Souls invariably opened up to him. One way or another.

"We're done," he said, and stepped forward to reach past the weapon, so quick his movements were little more than a blur. Not quick enough.

A shot rang out. Dagan moved to avoid the bullet but at the same time braced to take a hit.

Alastor was already in motion, coming at Joe from the opposite side. He leaped, twisted in midair, making his chest a broad target for the shot meant for Dagan. His body jerked as the bullet tore through flesh and

bone, then he came down hard, his shoulder taking the brunt of the fall.

"What the fuck?" Dagan snarled, spinning to kick the Glock out of Joe's hand. It went flying across the room and slammed against the wall, then skittered across the floor, finally coming to stop beside the fridge. Dagan positioned himself between Joe and the gun. He could feel his features twist in an expression of feral rage.

Joe backed up a step, his hands coming up as though they could ward off the coming assault.

Pressing the side of his fist against his bleeding chest, Alastor pushed to a sitting position, his lips peeled back. "I think the bugger cracked my sternum."

"For fuck's sake." Dagan snatched Joe's collar as the bastard tried to back away. Joe struggled and squeaked, clawing at Dagan's wrist. Yeah, like that'd do him good.

Dagan glared at Alastor. "Was there a point to the heroics?"

"I wasn't thinking in terms of heroics. I didn't plan for the wanker to actually hit me—" Alastor pressed his fist tighter against his chest "—just planned to make sure he didn't hit you."

"Not like a bullet would kill me," Dagan pointed out, giving Joe a hard shake and he tried to break the hold on his collar.

"Or me." Alastor sent him a half-hearted grin, the effect ruined by the blood dripping down his pristine white shirt. "But, bloody hell, it hurts like a bitch."

Dagan couldn't argue that. Not when he'd taken a bullet or a knife more than once for his brothers. And each time, it hurt. Hurt like a fucking bitch.

Soul reapers were immortal, not impervious.

"You planning to gut the sodding bastard, or shall I?" Alastor asked, bracing one hand on his thigh as he pushed to his feet.

"He's mine," Dagan said as he turned and hauled Joe close.

Joe's eyes widened as the thin light from the open door hit Dagan's face. "You—"

Dagan struck. His fingers tore through skin and muscle, ribs cracking as his bare hand sank deep. It was like deboning raw chicken without a knife.

Eyes wide, Joe stared at him. Something flared. Some sort of recognition.

"You," he said again. Then he made a gurgling gasp that might have been a laugh. "Thought there was only…one way…for a man to…guarantee…immortality.… Guess I was…wrong.…" His eyes glazed and he died with a last gasp, his body loosing a torrent of waste as the muscles of his sphincter relaxed.

Dagan's head jerked up and he met Alastor's startled gaze. "He recognized me."

"You ever seen him before?"

Tightening his grip on the heart, Dagan glanced at the dead man's face. His head lolled to one side, eyes open, seeing nothing. "No."

"You certain?"

"Yeah."

"Then he didn't recognize you." Alastor shrugged and dropped his gaze back to the box of photos. "Perhaps he recognized death."

"Maybe." Maybe not. There had been something definitive in Joe Marin's gaze, something personal. Like they'd met before. Which hadn't happened. Dagan

revealed himself to very few humans, and 99.99 percent of the time they ended up dead. The other .01 percent were Topworld informers who had no clue what he was, or the rare woman who ended up naked in his bed.

And, of course, the girl. The one mouthy, memorable girl, with her bronze-green eyes shooting sparks and her guts and grit laid out there for him to see.

With a twist and yank, he wrenched the heart free. As he withdrew his hand from the chest cavity, the body dropped to the floor like a sack of garbage. A chain slid free of Joe Marin's open collar, followed by a faint clink as metal hit concrete.

The pendant from the photo.

Dagan stared at the necklace.

Was she dead? He didn't want her to be dead.

Without intent, he closed his fist tightly around the heart he'd ripped free. Blood spurted from the stubs of the torn blood vessels, emptying the ventricles. It sprayed the walls and floor and the array of skulls on the shelves, splattering dark crimson against Dagan's white T-shirt and the skin of his neck and cheek.

"It's not like you to be so sloppy," Alastor chided.

"You think?"

For an instant, Dagan's emotions had been so powerful that he'd forgotten his brother was there. Forgotten everything but the kill. This one had been personal. Fuck. It was *never* personal.

But the possible link to the girl made it so.

Which made no sense. He hadn't seen her in eleven years. Dreamed about her, yeah. Vivid, Technicolor dreams that made him feel as if he could reach out and touch her, talk to her, thread his fingers through her

silky, dark ringlets. Which also made no sense, because reapers didn't dream.

With conscious effort, he eased his grip on Joe Marin's heart, tucked it away in the leather bag slung across his shoulder and wiped the back of his free hand across his mouth. He was breathing heavily, his heart racing. Adrenaline high.

Glancing up, he caught Alastor rubbing the bullet wound in his chest.

"Did the bullet go through?" He rose, grabbed Alastor's shoulder and turned him, checking his back. "Ah, it did."

"Blimey, that's a bit of good news." Sarcasm dripped from his words.

"I wouldn't go so far as to call it good," Dagan offered, relieved that the damage wasn't as bad as it could have been. "But having the bullet go clean through is better than having me shove my fingers in the hole and dig around for it." They exchanged a glance. Wouldn't be the first time one of them had had to apply some down-and-dirty first aid. "You'll live."

The second the words were out, his thoughts barreled down a road he didn't want to travel, and from the look on Alastor's face, his were walking the same path. Despite the bullet that had ripped through his chest, cracking his sternum and probably taking a chunk of lung with it, Alastor *would* live.

That was exactly the problem.

They were soul reapers, with the added bonus of being Sutekh's biological sons. Nothing could kill them. Not even a bullet through the chest.

But something *had* killed Lokan.

Could that same something kill any one of them?

Only…they wouldn't see it coming, because they didn't have a clue what it was.

Squatting by Joe's body, Dagan reached inside the gaping chest and waited. The darksoul came to him, so cold it burned. It writhed and twined up around his forearm like a wet, slimy worm, then down again, only to dissipate into a greasy haze and ooze up, up, until it hovered just above his shoulder.

Absently, he yanked it free of its mortal tether and collared it with a band of fire. Then he rifled through Joe's pockets. A handful of change. A stick of gum. A wallet. He went through that. Credit cards. ID. A couple of twenties. An emergency contact card with a name scrawled in red pen. *Frank Marin.* So maybe the brother wasn't overseas. Dagan tucked that card in his pocket. It was worth checking out.

The last card caught Dagan's attention. Expensive cream-colored paper. Burgundy ink so dark it looked black. No name. No logo. Just an address. In Toronto. And folded up behind the card, a receipt for parking in a lot on College Street. Also in Toronto.

"That's the day before Lokan was killed," Alastor said, reading the stub over his shoulder.

Dagan nodded, and he passed the wallet and its contents to his brother.

"You need to see this, too." Alastor held out a short stack of photographs. Dagan flipped through them. They showed human torsos, denuded of skin.

Just like Lokan.

Silently, he handed them back to Alastor and turned his attention to the body before him.

What the fuck was going on here? Was this pathetic human Lokan's murderer? How was that even pos-

sible? How had a mere human skinned a soul reaper and cut him to pieces?

He hadn't.

That was the only possible answer.

"There's something here that we're missing." There had to be.

He reached for the pendant hanging around Joe's neck and pulled on the chain so he could get a better look at the design. An ankh with wings and horns.

He flipped it over. Familiar hieroglyphs. Just like the ones he'd seen before on the girl's pendant.

He inhaled sharply, not liking what he saw.

"Definitely looks like the symbol of the Daughters of Aset," Alastor murmured, grimacing and pressing the flat of his hand to his chest as he hunkered down to get a better look.

"Only they don't wear it on a necklace. They cut it into their flesh in a ritual of self-discovery and control."

Alastor sent him a measured look. "Thought you didn't know much about them."

"That isn't much given the amount of time I've spent trying to research them. They're divided into three essential lineages. Keeper, Guide and Adaptive."

"And?"

Dagan huffed a short laugh. "That's all I know. They're elitist and secretive. It's almost as if they don't actually exist."

He stared at the pendant. His bloody fingers had left prints on the metal. For some inexplicable reason, that bothered him. He set the necklace down and rubbed his palms along his thighs, leaving dark smears on the faded denim. He froze.

Déjà vu.

Shit.

He remembered wiping his hands before he'd touched the girl. Her face coalesced in his mind, the look of ferocious determination in her bronze-green eyes.

She was just one more human in a sea of humans, but he'd let her live. He'd slit her bonds to set her free. He'd wrapped her in his jacket. He'd left her money. Why her?

He hadn't been tempted to do the same for anyone before or since.

The pendant and the photo he'd found meant there might be a link between her and the stack of body parts in this stinking room. Was there? Was there some link between her and the guy he'd just killed? Between her and Lokan's death?

The likelihood was minimal, but he didn't like co-incidences. Didn't trust them. Yet here he was, drowning in them.

"How the fuck does she fit into this?" he muttered.

"She? You referring to Aset?"

"No." Dagan closed his fist on the pendant and dragged it over the dead guy's head. Then he rose, shrugged. Alastor stared at him, eyes narrowed, interest growing, until Dagan figured he'd better offer something. Not the whole story, but something. "I think I might have seen this pendant before."

"Where?"

Dagan wasn't ready to share. He preferred to hunt down this particular lead on his own. "I'll follow it up."

He was tilting at windmills, trying to make connections where, in all likelihood, none existed. Because he had no other leads. Not one thing to work from.

Someone had killed Sutekh's youngest son, and no one seemed to know a thing. He'd put out feelers

throughout the Underworld as soon as they learned of Lokan's murder, but either no one knew anything or no one was talking.

The second option was the more likely of the two. Fear was a powerful motivator, and an equally powerful suppressant.

Idly, he turned the pendant over, read the hieroglyphs on the flat base.

> O my heart which I received from my mother,
> My heart which I received from my mother,
> My heart of my different ages,
> Do not stand up against me as a witness.

It was the same verse he'd read on another pendant a decade past. Or maybe the same pendant. He didn't want to entertain that possibility.

"The reference to mother…" Alastor murmured.

"Yeah. The goddess of motherhood and fertility… Aset." *Isis.* Another fucking coincidence. With a sharp yank, Dagan handed the writhing darksoul off to Alastor, along with the bloody bag containing the heart. "Mind taking the old man his dinner for me?"

"My bloody pleasure. I live to serve." The words dripped sarcasm, underlain with bitter truth. They all lived to serve. It was why they'd been spawned. None of the most powerful gods of the Underworld could travel Topworld at will. Including Sutekh. The greater their power, the less mobile they were. It was a safeguard set in place six thousand years past to ensure they didn't encroach on each others' territories or the human realm. So Sutekh needed emissaries, worker bees, to be his eyes and ears Topworld. He called them "associates."

Most were converted souls, carefully handpicked from the endless stream that came before him, offered the opportunity to become one of the Underworld's elite: a soul reaper.

But four had been bred to the role.

What better way to ensure an associate's loyalty than to breed one himself? In fact, he'd been so successful the first time, that he'd bred three more. Four sons on three human women.

And yeah, they were loyal. To each other. And to Sutekh, though that was a tangled mess because they all both loathed and loved him.

Still, it was family first. Even if they were dysfunctional as all hell.

"And I need you to check out the contents of the wallet," Dagan said, handing that over, as well. "Follow up on the emergency contact, Frank Marin. The brother. And check out exactly what sort of business is located at the address on that card."

Alastor laughed. "Right away, your bleeding lordship."

Dagan shot him a look and affected a mock British accent. "I ain't the one who's bleeding, mate."

With a pained grimace, Alastor shook his head. "Don't. Even. Try. So what exactly will you be doing while I bimble off to obey your every command?"

What would he be doing? His fingers clamped tightly on the pendant.

Turning away, he mastered his emotions, fighting the sudden surge of black rage that boiled up and threatened to steal his voice, his thoughts, his sanity. Before Lokan's death, he had never known the like, but since, his frustration at his failure to find his brother's

remains, to find his killer—hell, to have stopped the killing from happening in the first place—meant he'd not been able to lock it down completely. Part of his rage was directed at himself. And part of his rage was directed at his father. For being what he was. For making Lokan a target. For not using his vast power to protect his son.

He wasn't being fair. He knew that. Sutekh couldn't be everywhere at once, couldn't know everything. But when the red tide of his fury swamped him, rationality didn't seem to matter.

"Tell me where you're off to, Dae." Alastor's tone took on a harder edge.

An ugly laugh escaped him as he opened his fist and glanced at the necklace but saw the girl's face in his mind's eye. Instinct was telling him she was involved. Somehow, she was involved.

"I'm going hunting," he rasped. "For the one that lived."

Toronto, Canada

PYOTR KUSNETZOV, HIGH REVEREND of the Setnakhts, glanced at the diners up and down the long, low wooden table where they gathered for a ceremonial meal in the Temple of Setnakht. "A blood sacrifice is necessary to move forward."

All conversation died. All eyes fixed on him. As he let the silence grow, feeding on itself, neighbors shifted where they sat cross-legged on layered carpets, glancing warily to the left, the right. He let them stew, knowing exactly what thoughts percolated in their minds.

He'd heard the whispers. There were rumors that

there had already been blood sacrifices in recent months. Three of their members had left the group, quietly, without notice or farewell. After years, and in one case decades, of membership in the Cult of Setnakht, they were simply...gone.

The congregation had been told that the missing members had rethought their allegiance. That they had withdrawn from the group and moved to another city. An unheard-of desertion.

No one believed those assurances. But no one dared to disbelieve them, either. Not openly.

Pyotr knew the truth.

The missing had wavered in their faith. They had failed when tested. They had betrayed the precepts of the Setnakhts.

Were that all they had done, Pyotr would have set them free. He would have pitied them for their choices and sent them off to make their own way in the world.

What sealed their fates was their alliance with each other, their agreement to share knowledge among themselves and to use it to create an offshoot sect, a group that wanted to steal all that the Setnakhts had worked so hard to build. Their actions were tantamount to treason.

That, he could never allow.

A lifetime of planning and dedication had brought him to the brink of success. He had come to the fold as a mere child, angry, aggressive, a poster boy for the rebellious teenage years. His mentor, Abasi Abubakar, had trained him, nurtured him and in the end entrusted him with the vision he had created.

The earliest foundations, the sacrifice of one of Aset's Daughters, had been before Pyotr's time. But in the past eleven years, since he had donned the mantle

of power, Pyotr had lived up to the sacred trust he had sworn to carry on the great leader's work.

High Reverend Abubakar was more to Pyotr than father or mother or lover or friend. He had been a visionary, totally dedicated to his cause, to the eradication of famine and war and hatred. He saw the way to end such pain: by calling forth from the Underworld the most powerful deity, to rule with a wise and fair hand. Who better to leash chaos than the Lord of Chaos? He had sacrificed his very life to plead his case before Sutekh. His dedication was a thing of glory, and in the intervening years, Pyotr's admiration for his mentor had grown to near fervent worship.

Pyotr could not allow three foolish men and their lack of faith to shatter plans more than twenty-five years in the making. He had and *would* continue Abasi's work, and in so doing, ensure his own place in Sutekh's hierarchy.

For Sutekh *would* come. And he would rule. Disbelievers would be punished, and his faithful would be rewarded.

The trials of the three betrayers had been quick—a private accusation followed by denial, then explanation, then whimpered pleas and finally the thrust of Pytor's knife. They had been his friends, his *family,* for decades, so he owed them that: swift and personal justice.

He smiled now at the assembled diners, letting the warmth of his personality fall upon them like sunlight. His smile brought the first hints of relief. Taut shoulders relaxed. Jaws unclenched, but there was still a level of wariness humming in the air.

"The sacrifice will be a sheep," Pyotr said. The tension in the room ratcheted down another level. Their

relief was palpable. "The animal will be slaughtered humanely under government guidelines. I have made arrangements with a slaughterhouse. The meat distributed to the poor."

An instant of silence as all present assimilated his edict, then smiles returned. The first whispers of conversation grew to a dull roar and, along with the clink of cutlery on plates, filled the room once more.

Pyotr ate and chatted and held court from his place at the head of the table, and then with casual insignificance to any who might observe, his gaze slid to his left, far down the table to Marie Matheson, who sat quiet and docile, picking daintily at the food on the plate before her.

He smiled, his blood quickening. She was utterly, absolutely perfect. Innocent. Lovely. And in her blood, the faintest trace of Aset's lineage. He had hoped for a stronger link, a full Daughter of Aset. He had even found such a rare jewel, a girl by the name of Naphré. But he had been unable to lure her to the fold no matter what enticement he offered. So Marie Matheson—with her far weaker blood—it would have to be.

As though she sensed his regard, Marie lifted her head and sent him a sidelong look through her lashes. There was no guile in her action. The shyness was genuine. She was new to the group—a six-month acolyte—uncertain as yet of her place. She was new to the city, with only an aunt in Ottawa, nearly five hours away. The Setnakhts had become her family. Or so he let her believe. For now.

Soon enough, she would learn that along with the public sacrifice of the sheep, Pyotr would make a per-

sonal and private sacrifice. A sweet, naive little lamb, newly brought to the fold.

A lamb ripe for the slaughter.

CHAPTER SEVEN

Blood of Aset, words of power of Aset, glory of Aset,
It is a protection for this great one,
A protection against wickedness.

—The Papyrus of Ani, Chapter 156

Toronto, Canada

BONE TIRED AND ACHING FOR BED, Roxy headed along Richmond Street. Earlier in the evening, she'd made a dozen phone calls, putting out subtle feelers about the dead reaper and the kid, Dana.

But no one had heard anything. No one knew anything. It was like talking to the three wise monkeys. Except none of the Topworld grunts she talked to were what she'd call wise.

The lack of information bugged her. Something didn't add up. Her gut was telling her she was missing the obvious, but her brain couldn't seem to connect the dots.

Fed up with the phone, she'd tried the direct approach. Armed with a story about being referred by a guy she'd met on the plane, Frank...Something— Darn, she couldn't remember his last name; maybe

they could help her with that?—she'd walked through the chrome-and-glass front doors of the eighteenth-century factory that had been converted into the Temple of Setnakht.

She'd spent the next three fucking hours getting the grand tour. The sanctuary. The banquet hall. Even the gleaming kitchen. They'd hustled her past the private offices at the back of the building when she slowed to catch a glimpse, but they were particularly proud of the green roof garden and thrilled to linger there. They'd been friendly and forthright, offering reams of information, none of which suited her purposes or answered her actual questions. And, of course, they'd hit her up for a donation.

Fun didn't begin to describe it.

Unfortunately, any effort to turn the conversation back to Frank, the nice guy she'd met on the plane who'd sent her their way, had been met with a blank stare.

But the visit hadn't been a total waste. She'd seen pictures of several High Reverends hanging on the walls, with glossy name plaques underneath. She'd pass on names and descriptions to Calliope and do her own search, as well.

The night was crisp, but there was no wind, and the stars were out now. As out as they could be in the middle of downtown.

Within a few blocks of the temple, she had the eerie sensation that she was being followed, watched. She stopped to stare at a display of geriatric bathroom aids and thought she spotted a guy's reflection in the window. Tall. Blond. She kept walking. Two blocks later, he was still there, reflected in the window of a pawn

shop. She took her time studying the image. It was a bit blurred at the edges, and she could see the traffic through the guy's translucent chest. With a sigh, she turned. The wind caught his hair and whipped it around his face.

Only there was no wind. The night was dead calm.

She couldn't see his features, but she didn't doubt his identity. She'd had these waking dreams in the years since she'd last seen Dagan Krayl. She'd thought they were just conjurings of the part of her psyche that had never moved past that night in the old factory.

But now, she wondered if this were something else.

The Daughters of Aset believed that the soul was made up of five parts: *Ren, Ba, Ka, Sheut,* and *Ib.* The body was the *ha*—the sum of bodily parts. The dead reaper had been butchered and skinned, his parts scattered.

If that reaper were Dagan, then the thing following her could be any of the parts of his soul.

Did soul reapers have souls? How the fuck was she supposed to know?

"You warning me off?" she asked. "Or telling me I'm heading in the right direction?"

He didn't answer. She hadn't expected him to.

With a shake of her head, she headed for Tesso's Bar and Grill and didn't stop to look in any more windows along the way. If he were still there, she didn't want to know it. At least, that's what she told herself.

At Tesso's there was no line, but there was a burly guy guarding the door. She wasn't a regular, but her face was familiar enough that he let her through after he palmed the bill she offered.

Calliope was going to hate her expense report this

month, because it took another five bills to get her into the back room, a setting so cliché it ought to have been in a B movie.

Sitting around a table, playing poker and drinking cheap Scotch were a handful of Topworld grunts who ran prostitutes for Asmodeus, the Underworld demon of lust. One of them glanced her way as she came through the door. He grunted. "No women."

The three girls in the corner stared at her through flat, blank eyes.

The grunt didn't consider them women. They were property. Different thing entirely.

"Don't get your dander up. I brought gifts." Before he could answer, Roxy held out the box and opened the lid. Cuban cigars. She figured they wouldn't resist.

"I said no—"

"It's okay," one of the other grunts interrupted. He called himself Big Ralph even though he was lean and hard, and he'd leeringly told her more than once that he'd show her the reason for the nickname anytime she asked.

She never asked.

"I seen her here before," he continued, motioning her over. "She likes to watch us play. Wants to learn the game."

He nodded at her and she forced her lips to shape a smile. Asshole. She'd bought her way into his game three times before and dropped thousands each time, letting him win. Because he liked to chat between hands. He was usually a fount of information.

All friendly and shit, she sauntered over. Even lit his cigar for him.

Then she stood around, gritting her teeth while the

rest of them lit up and puffed fat rings of smoke, reminding herself that gutting all four of them and hauling the three girls out of here wasn't playing nice. It wouldn't get her the information she needed, and it wouldn't save those girls. They were already marked by Asmodeus. The only way to save them was to get him to set them free.

Once you made a deal with a demon, there was almost no way to go back.

"Xaphan still wants that girl. Everybody knows it."

Roxy's ears perked up and she slid deeper into the shadow, hoping they'd forget she was there. Could it be this easy? Her pulse picked up its pace.

"Yeah, but she doesn't want nothing to do with him." More smoke. More laughter.

"Heard she's under Butcher's protection."

Roxy frowned at the name. She'd heard it a time or two. And the bubble of anticipation she'd floated was already sinking before Big Ralph said, "I don't think he'd like it if his Naphré ended up as Xaphan's concubine."

They weren't talking about Dana.

The night was a bust.

ROXY SOUNDLESSLY PULLED THE FRONT door shut behind her and breathed in the familiar scent of lemon cleaner. Three years ago, she'd bought the dilapidated church just north of the city and lovingly restored it. She'd hired a local artist to replace cracked fragments of the stained-glass windows. She'd taken out the pews with her own hands and laid new strips of hardwood. Plumbing and wiring were beyond her knowledge, so she'd been forced to hire contractors for those jobs. But in the end, her stamp was on every stair and every beam.

Home, sweet home.

And after nearly forty-eight hours awake and on the move, she was damned glad to be here.

Closing her eyes, she let her senses reach for any hint of an unfamiliar supernatural energy signature. A humorless smile tugged at her lips. Of course; nothing was ever easy.

She rested her hand on the smooth, cool marble of the console table and dropped her keys into the rose-colored glass bowl. She'd nabbed the mail from her box on the way home, and she quickly rifled through the pile. Bills. Bills. An envelope from the National Urban League…probably a receipt for her donation. Another envelope from the University of Chicago Medical Center. She hoped they'd earmarked the money for the burn unit. She always included a note asking them to when she sent the check.

Reaching up, she flicked off the entry-hall light, then tossed the pile down beside the glass bowl and rolled her shoulders forward, then back.

She was tempted to crawl into bed, pull the covers over her head and sleep for a week. But duty came first.

Peeling off her jacket, she left it where it dropped, tipped back her head for a jaw-cracking yawn, then kinked her neck to one side and then the other. Muscles and tendons pulled and twinged. She needed a re-charge.

It was either sleep…or blood.

Instinct screamed for blood; long years of forcing her nature under rigid control made her choose sleep. She headed for her bedroom and paused in the door-way, checking every nook and cranny. She kept her posture easy and relaxed as a shadow uncoiled from the

overstuffed chair in the corner and then glided along the wall toward her.

Soundless.

Graceful.

Deadly.

Roxy didn't give herself away, not by word or action, she just kept moving through the bedroom as though she didn't know she was being stalked.

Too soon…wait…wait…

On a sharp inhalation, she squatted, taking her weight on her bent right leg, kicking out hard with her left in a sweeping arc. The momentum nearly toppled her when the impact she expected never happened. Her foot kept going, never connecting with her attacker. Because her attacker was no longer there.

Heart pounding, she tucked, rolled and came up three feet away. She was on her feet and spinning, not thinking, just doing, letting her enhanced senses lead her actions. A sharp hit with the heel of her right hand. Turn, sway. A closed fist aimed for where her attacker ought to be.

This time, she was rewarded by a satisfying grunt. And then she went down as her opponent's leg swept her own feet from under her.

Her ass hit the carpet. Her breath left her in a whoosh.

The tip of a very long blade pressed against the skin of her throat.

"Almost had me this time." The voice was cool and even, like a mountain spring running over smooth rocks.

"Almost only counts in horseshoes and hand grenades," Roxy groused as she took the proffered hand

and let herself be dragged back to her feet. "You know, locks were invented to keep intruders out."

"I'm sure they're usually quite effective," the intruder replied. She disengaged from the shadows as Roxy turned on the bedside lamp.

If Roxy was colored in shades of coffee and bronze, Calliope Kane was painted in hues of a snowy winter's night. Her skin was pale, her hair almost black, hanging in a straight, thick curtain halfway down her back. Accented by straight-cut bangs and dark lashes, her eyes glowed cat-green, the color too vivid to be natural. But it was. Roxy knew because she'd asked, years ago. And while Calliope might evade or conveniently omit information, she never outright lied.

"Hey," Roxy greeted her mentor.

"Good evening." Calliope glanced at her watch. "Or rather, good morning. You look tired," she finished without malice.

"Thanks. I am," Roxy replied with a wry smile. "I need sleep." She needed blood, but sleep would do. "Is this a formal interview?" In which case, she'd remain at attention to give her report.

"Informal."

"Thank Aset." Roxy blew out a sharp breath and sank down on the side of the bed. "Kid's back with her mom. The mom's a ditz." But a loving one. She'd been sobbing and laughing, hugging Dana. Hugging Roxy.

Yeah, Roxy could have done without *that*. She'd stood like a post, accepting the woman's touch though she'd have preferred to jerk away and set a good ten feet between them.

From the shelter of her mother's embrace, the kid had looked at Roxy as if she'd hung the moon. Which

had made Roxy feel a bit guilty for the small betrayal she'd perpetrated while the kid was dozing in the car. But what the hell. In her sleep, the kid had scratched a scab, and little beads of blood had welled in a neat line. The kid hadn't even stirred as Roxy wiped the blood away with her baby finger. That miniscule taste was insurance; her preternatural version of GPS would kick in if Dana ever disappeared again.

"Did you terminate Mr. Marin?" Calliope asked as she returned to the comfy chair and folded herself with effortless grace into its embrace.

"That wasn't my assignment, was it?"

One dark brow lifted a fraction of an inch. "No, but I have no doubt that it was your inclination."

Roxy snorted. "Well, I followed orders. I did slit his throat, but I didn't kill him. I figured he might be of more use alive. That way, I can have another chat with him if the need arises."

"Providing you can find him."

"Not a problem." Roxy didn't offer any information about tracking him via his blood. She never spoke about her *peculiarity,* or the added benefits. Having subtle supernatural talents was one thing—all the Daughters of Aset had their own unique gifts—but being a parasite who survived by taking blood from human hosts was quite another. So what was she supposed to say? *By the way, before I met you, I got turned into a bloodsucking leech that can track those I've fed on. Except for the asshole who made me. Him, I can't track even though I got a generous helping of his blood.*

Oh, yeah. That'd be an interesting conversation.

"Did Mr. Marin reveal anything of value before you cut his throat?"

"Pretty much a fuckload of nothing." Roxy pinched the bridge of her nose. Her eyes felt as if they'd been sandblasted. "He gave me a name. Krayl. But whether he's the dead reaper or the one doing the killing, I got no clue."

"Krayl…" Calliope mused. "I'm not familiar with the name. A demon?"

"Soul reaper."

Calliope gave her a sharp look, and Roxy realized it seemed odd for her to know that with certainty. Reapers didn't exactly go around advertising their names. She kept mum on how she knew Krayl was a reaper and dropped a different bomb instead. "And Marin said the dead guy wasn't just a reaper. He was Sutekh's fucking son."

Calliope was silent for several seconds. Her eyes didn't widen. Her body didn't tense. Not even fractionally. Which told Roxy that Marin's big reveal was no surprise to Calliope. She might not have known the name Krayl, but she'd known the dead guy was Sutekh's son.

"You might have mentioned that to me beforehand," Roxy muttered.

"It wasn't relevant."

Guess they had different definitions of the word.

"Why would a soul reaper kill one of his own?" Calliope mused.

"Is that relevant?" Roxy didn't bother to mask her sarcasm.

"Feeling prickly this evening, Roxy?"

"Very. Which makes this evening different from every other evening…how?"

Calliope laughed, a smooth, controlled sound, soft

and warm. No belly laughs for Calliope. "What other tidbits did Mr. Marin share?"

"He said the Setnakhts are involved." She gave Calliope a concise description of her evening's escapades, including the names and descriptions of the High Reverends whose portraits she'd seen hanging on the walls of the temple. "They could be the brains. Or the brawn. Again, good old Frank gave me just enough to tease but not enough to solve the riddle."

"He gave you a name and a link to Sutekh's worshippers. I'd say that's a bit more than a 'fuckload—'" Calliope's nose wrinkled in distaste for the terminology "—of nothing. It's more than we had before."

"Yeah, but it isn't enough. I still can't connect the dots."

"Give it time, Roxy. You're always so impatient."

Roxy met Calliope's gaze. "I might not have time. There was someone else there, outside the Tee Pee Inn. Someone powerful enough to camouflage their energy signature."

Calliope's cat-green eyes reflected the light, taking on an eerie glow. "If it was camouflaged, then how did you know there was someone there?"

"My gut told me. I didn't see anything, didn't really feel anything, other than a serious case of the creeps when I was leaving the motel with the kid. There was something watching me. Or her. Or us." Roxy laced her fingers behind her head and flopped back, the mattress bouncing a bit under her weight. It felt so good to lie down. She stared at the ceiling, weighing her words, then said, "I think it might have been a reaper."

"A soul reaper?" For once, Calliope's tone veered from cool and even, the question laced with disbelief.

Roxy turned her head.

Calliope just stared at her, and Roxy figured it was time to scale back the sass. She knew her mentor's limits, and she'd already pushed them, hard.

"You were that close to a soul reaper and he let you live?"

Now, wasn't that a fine question? She couldn't see a way to suddenly admit that this wasn't the first, but the second time a soul reaper had done exactly that. How was she supposed to explain the fact that one of their enemies had not just set her free the last time they'd met but had saved her life and given her a stake to get started...along with a mouthful of his blood? And how was she supposed to justify having failed to mention it for so many years? Not a place she wanted to go at the moment.

Instead, she shrugged. "*Something* was there. Soul reaper's the most likely answer. And the worst-case scenario, isn't it?"

Calliope was silent for a moment. "Yes, I'd say it is."

Closing her eyes, Roxy pressed against her gritty lids with her thumb and forefinger. "They want to bring the dead back to life." She dropped her hand and glanced at Calliope. "That *is* what they want, right? And we want to make certain the dead stay dead. So I'd say that if a reaper has me in his sights, our odds of success just dropped to the bottom of the toilet. I'd also venture to guess that we're onto something. Otherwise, why would they bother with me?"

"It wasn't a soul reaper." Calliope's tone was uncharacteristically emphatic.

"And you know this because…?"

"Because you sensed the being that was watching you, and if it had been a reaper, you would never have known he was there. Not unless he wanted you to. They can practically move between molecules, disturbing nothing. Not air. Not sound. Not light. They are there, but not there."

Calliope wasn't telling her anything she didn't already know. And, as always, she wondered why Dagan Krayl had let her see him all those years ago. Why he'd saved her. Helped her. Why he'd let her live. She couldn't ask Calliope those questions. It would only raise suspicion about her own loyalty to the Daughters of Aset.

They'd wonder if she were a spy.

Damn. Faced with the same set of facts, she'd wonder that herself.

She sighed and then bolted upright as she was struck by a new and not-so-lovely thought. "You need to move the kid." She'd been stupid. She saw that with sudden, blinding clarity. "I'd like to say that I'm certain I wasn't followed, but, see, that's the thing. Play along with me for a sec." She slammed the side of her fist against her thigh. "If it *was* a reaper, he could have followed me to the kid's house, and all my precautions aren't worth a damn, 'cause I'd never have known he was behind me."

She should have considered that before. She'd watched her tail, been certain there was nothing there, but this conversation with Calliope left her feeling less secure in her certainty. If she *had* been followed, it was likely that she was the target. But what if she wasn't? What if it was the kid they wanted? After all, Dana had already been a target once.

"I'll send an apprentice to relocate them."

"Will the kid's mom agree to this?" Roxy asked.

"She came to us when the child was snatched. I suspect she'll agree to whatever will keep Dana from being taken once more."

"She came to us?" Roxy echoed. That struck her as odd. How did a mortal woman know about the Otherkin?

But Calliope was already making the call to Oklahoma City, using the phone by the bed, a secure landline. A brief exchange set the wheels in motion.

One worry taken care of. Another flared. As Calliope replaced the receiver, Roxy pointed out, "If it was a soul reaper, he could have followed me here without me ever having a clue."

"Yes." Calliope fell silent and crossed her arms over her chest. Like she was waiting for something. Some sort of big reveal. Say…something about a blond reaper?

Roxy pressed her lips together and looked away, figuring her guilty conscience had her imagining things. A part of her wanted to tell all. The other part was busy shoving that impulse, along with the memories, under a moth-eaten rug in the farthest corner of her thoughts. She'd never told anyone about that night. She wasn't about to change that now. It was all about self-preservation.

The Asetian Guard viewed Sutekh and soul reapers as their enemies because of an ancient feud. Hell, she could understand the hate-on. Sutekh had slaughtered Aset's husband and dismembered his body. Then he'd gone after her son, Horus. So Roxy didn't imagine revealing that she'd known a reaper all up close and personal—that he had, in fact, converted her to a blood-drinking fiend—would go over all that well.

After a long moment, Calliope said, "Good night, Roxy. Sleep tight." She sounded as cool and calm as ever, and Roxy told herself that if she heard a whisper of disappointment, of hurt, it was all in her very tired imagination.

When she opened her eyes, Calliope was gone.

Yeah. Good-fucking-night. She was supposed to sleep, knowing a soul reaper might be sniffing around outside her door? If he were, her best bet was to stay put. Let him come. Then take him down. Or die trying. Running wouldn't do her a damned bit of good. If he wanted her, he'd find her.

A comforting thought.

You want me for an enemy, little girl?

Not so much. But her choices had made him one all the same.

She'd chosen to become a member of the Asetian Guard, and she'd never regretted it. It had kept her sane. Kept her safe. Given her a purpose and a place. Given her a chance to be part of something bigger than herself, to be part of a sisterhood and atone in a sort of bizarre, twisted way for other choices she'd made, ones she regretted to the core of her soul.

For a second, she could smell the acrid scent of the hospital, hear the machines and the labored rasp of Rhianna's every breath.

Her fists curled into the pillow, just as they'd done that day in the hospital.

She could see Rhianna's face, her dark skin faded to a terrible yellowish-gray, her brown eyes pleading, sliding from Roxy's face to the pillow clutched in her hands. *Don't...please...*

Memories. Ugly, stinking memories.

Fuck, she wasn't going there.

Waste of time and energy to wonder what the outcome would have been if she'd taken the other fork in the road.

She sighed, headed for the bathroom and got ready for bed. When she was done, she flipped off the lights and made her way in the dark. Familiar territory. She didn't need a light.

She flopped on her side, tugged on the blankets and shoved the pillow under her head.

Hunger coiled in her belly. Not the kind that could be satisfied with a candy bar or a carton of ice cream—though either one was moderately appealing. She wanted blood. More than a tiny taste. A whole vat of it, red and dark. She wanted to take a fucking bath in it.

With a snarl, she rolled onto her back and willed herself to sleep.

Do when you can. Sleep when there is nothing you can do.

Ten years of training to live by that motto let her close her eyes and drift off almost immediately. And she dreamed. The same damned dream she'd had again and again over the years.

At first, there was only sensation. Warmth against her cheek and her breasts. The feel and scent of skin. Male skin.

She stroked her tongue along the curve of hip bone, tasted salt and man. Hunger surged. She wanted to lick him, taste him, sink her teeth into his flesh. Savor him. Mark him.

Opening her eyes, she saw that she was kneeling, naked. Only then did she register the sensation of

carpet against her shins and knees. Her arms were wrapped around a man's muscled thighs, her wrists bound by yellow nylon rope—his ropes binding her, her arms binding him. Her cheek brushed his hip; his skin was smooth and hot. The fine hairs on his legs teased her nipples with each breath she took. And it felt good. So good. She wanted more.

She tipped her head back and looked up at his face. Hard. Handsome. Crystal-gray eyes glittering in the dimness, catching moonlight as it streamed through an open window.

Beautiful eyes. So familiar. No translucent being, this. Not Ka or Ba flown free of the corporeal form, but man. Hot, hard, man.

She wet her lips and turned her head a little. Wanting. Yearning. A tight coil of desire spiraled deep and tied her in knots. The head of his cock stroked her lips. Her tongue darted out. She couldn't help it. He was thick and hard, and as she turned her head and took him in her mouth, he let out a slow hiss of pleasure.

His hand cradled the back of her head, holding her in place, and he pumped slowly into her mouth—not too deep…just enough to make her moan and arch to take more. She inhaled through her nose, taking in the luscious scent of his skin. She remembered that smell—fresh, faintly citrus. He smelled of himself. He smelled so damned good she wanted to swallow him whole.

So she did. She took him as deep as she could, and still she couldn't take the whole of him. Her bound wrists made it impossible to clutch the muscled globes of his buttocks. And she wanted that. Wanted to dig her fingers into his solid flesh. Frustrated by her bindings,

she wriggled closer, pressed herself full against his thighs and took him deeper still.

He groaned. Arched. A smooth, pumping grind. Filling her mouth as she tongued him and sucked him. She used her teeth, biting just hard enough to make him inhale sharply. Then sucking hard enough to make him swell, impossibly thick.

Bound, kneeling before him, *she* was the one with the power here.

Then her bonds were gone, dissipating into thin air, her hands free to roam. She grabbed his ass, digging her fingers into hard muscle, her lips and tongue and teeth working his cock. Making him hers.

"Fuck." The sound of his voice, hard and low, made her shiver.

A whimper of distress tore free as he pulled from her mouth, his hands fisted in her hair. He looked down at her, and his lips curved in a dark, wicked smile. She felt the promise of that smile like a molten river coursing through her limbs, her breasts and low in her belly.

He tumbled her onto her back, one hand hooked behind her knee, lifting her leg until she was open, aching, the other hand outstretched to hold his weight, his palm flat beside her shoulder.

She felt the heat of him then, pushing at her opening, the broad head of his cock sliding in with a shallow thrust. Stretching her. A tiny discomfort overwhelmed by liquid need. It wasn't enough. God, she wanted him, hot and full and deep inside her.

Arching her hips, she tried to take what she wanted: all of that steely, wonderful length. But he held himself apart. Aloof. Giving her only a bit. A taste. A tease.

She cried out in frustration, straining toward him. With a low, dark laugh, he let her take more, take it all, in a smooth, slick glide. So good. Thrust and grind. Keen pleasure, making her muscles tense, her whole body throb, her every thought centered on the place they joined.

Yes. Like that. And…ahh…like that. "Please. Dagan. Please."

A smile curved his hard, luscious mouth, a stark baring of straight white teeth, telling her he liked that. Liked to hear her plead. He liked the illusion of his dominion, but it wasn't his, it was hers.

Rearing up, she tore his skin with her teeth, biting deep into the swell of lean muscle that layered his chest. He grunted but didn't pull away. Blood filled her mouth, hot, red, luscious blood. She knew the taste of him. Ambrosia.

She drank from him as he pumped harder, faster, his cock taking her higher, his blood feeding her need.

Tearing her mouth from his flesh, she arched back, moaning as she ground her hips against him, the friction hitting her in all the right places. His thrusts were deep, rhythmic, working her to the razor's edge. She took her pleasure from him.

And he took her heart.

He thrust his cock deep inside her and his hand into her chest.

As she tore over the edge of her orgasm, he tore her heart out and held it cradled in his palm.

There was no pain. Only pleasure. Profound pleasure that made her buck and scream.

Their bodies rubbed together, slick with sweat, slick with blood. Her blood. His blood.

He held her heart.

She wanted his. Wanted his heart.

"Dagan…" His name was her beacon, her light in the darkness, and then he was gone and she was alone.

Alone.

"Dagan!"

With a cry, Roxy jerked awake and vaulted to a sitting position, chest heaving, eyes wide.

Tears pricked her eyes, of loss and disappointment. Just a dream.

Always the same damned, fucking dream.

Scrubbing one hand over her face, she reached blindly and turned on the bedside lamp. The pillows were strewn across the room. The blankets and sheets were twisted and lay half off the bed, puddling on the floor. Her gaze skittered from corner to corner, her ears straining to hear any sound.

Nothing there. There never was.

She was alone. Always alone.

But the thing that got her, that made her chest twist up tight, was the knowledge that in her darkest heart, she didn't want to be.

CHAPTER EIGHT

I know you, and I know your name,
And I know the names of the two and forty gods
Who live in the Hall of the Two Truths,
Who imprison the sinners, and feed upon their
blood.

—The Egyptian Book of the Dead,
The Judgment of the Dead

The Underworld, the Territory of Osiris

MALTHUS KRAYL WALKED the endless trek to the Hall of Two Truths. How long had he been here? Could be an hour. Could be a week. Hard to tell. Time played out differently in the realm of Osiris.

His footsteps echoed hollowly on the stone floor.

Mammoth columns rose on either side of him, so high their tops were swallowed by shadow. Beyond them was a void of utter blackness. Each column was etched with ancient symbols—hieroglyphics that predated the language unlocked by the Rosetta Stone—and each was guarded by a sentry. Their hands, their bodies, even their faces were obscured by the long robes that draped their forms, the purple cloth so dark

it looked almost black in the eerie greenish light that guided his way.

"You will be judged," one cowled creature whispered as he passed.

Yeah. He figured.

Red eyes glowed from beneath the hood, the face in shadow except for the snout. A dog or a jackal. Mal was betting on jackal because, hey, Anubis had a twisted sense of humor.

A second sentry spoke, "Leave this place. Only Lokan Krayl may pass."

"Lokan Krayl is dead." The words were like ash on his tongue. "I am here in his place."

Wherever *here* was. An illusion, most likely, conjured by Osiris's power for the benefit of the souls of the dead and soon-to-be-judged.

This part of the Underworld was Osiris's domain, a place where Sutekh did not venture. None of the gods and demigods ventured into the territory of another. Talk about an Underworld faux pas.

Except Lokan. He'd had what amounted to a free pass, crossing borders with ease because he'd been an emissary. An ambassador.

A pawn.

Now it was Mal's turn to do the job, because Lokan was dead. The fact hadn't quite settled. He still expected to feel a bruising punch to his shoulder and turn to find his brother standing behind him.

But if Lokan were alive, Mal wouldn't be here at all.

Rules were rules.

Osiris suffered the company of only one of Sutekh's spawn at a time. And he was no gracious host. He didn't welcome the presence of a soul reaper on his

turf, only grudgingly tolerated it because someone had to keep the peace between Osiris, Hades, Satan, Xaphan and a slew of lesser demons and demigods. Rulers of the Underworld could be so territorial at times. So someone needed to be a politician: part power broker, part impartial negotiator. Part god-whisperer.

That had been Lokan. He could charm the scales off a snake or the shell off a scarab beetle. Not to mention the skirt off one of Xaphan's concubines. But Lokan was dead. Butchered. His body parts scattered like leaves in the wind. Which made Mal the youngest by default.

So, like his brother before him, Mal came here as his father's representative.

He'd drawn the short straw by way of birth order, and because he'd expressed a modicum of interest in the family business a time or two. That'd been enough to seal his fate.

Mal paused, an uneasy feeling stirring in his gut. A sound behind him made him turn. Disbelief surged. His brothers knew better. They wouldn't—

They would. The black void before him undulated and pulsed until it disgorged a form of haze and smoke that slowly coalesced into…Dagan.

Shit.

It was tough enough to convince Osiris to let one son of Sutekh breach his domain. With reason. Sutekh had once carved Osiris into little pieces and fed his dick to a fish. His wife, Aset, hadn't been too happy about that. She'd pined for him and searched for him and eventually reanimated him for a single night of bliss before he was forced into the Underworld, denied the

Topworld because…well, because he was dead. Or so the story went. Couldn't blame old Osiris for holding a grudge. Or Aset, as far as Mal was concerned, but it wasn't as if he'd make that observation out loud.

"What are you doing here?" Mal asked, not even trying to temper the frustration that leaked into his words. "You looking to fire up trouble?"

"Not so much." Dagan folded his arms across his chest, legs planted shoulder-width apart. "I'm staying. You're going."

Mal laughed. They didn't get to choose their place in Sutekh's hierarchy, or their roles. The job of liaison was his whether he wanted it or not. And that was definitely a *not*. But passing it off to Dagan really wasn't an option, no matter how appealing the thought.

"Thanks for the offer, Dae." He made a shooing motion. "But you can run along now, like a good lad."

"Running along's a fine plan, Mal." Dagan mimicked Mal in both tone and action. "*You* be a good lad. I'll face Osiris."

"You will be judged," whispered the sentry to their left.

"Dandy," Dagan muttered.

Mal clenched his jaw, then he used the only argument that might sway big brother, with *might* being the key concept. "When Sutekh gives an order, he expects it to be obeyed."

Not that Mal had even the slightest desire to take on the task of intermediary. He was no good little soldier. In fact, he had a bit of a problem with authority. But he had his reasons for wanting to obey this particular command: If he stepped up to the plate and took the job parleying with Osiris and the others, then his

brothers would be spared. An important consideration, but he had another reason, one he wasn't about to blurt in front of an endless procession of Osiris's sentries.

He wanted to face Osiris, question him, find out what he knew. Because he didn't buy the platitudes Osiris had sent to each of them when Lokan died, the messages identical, written on papyrus with shiny gold leaf. *So sorry for your loss. I understand your pain. I, too, was murdered and dismembered. By my own brother.*

Those statements were as multitiered as a cruise ship.

What the hell was Osiris implying? That *he* had butchered Lokan? Payment in kind for what Set had done to him. Set. Sutekh, Lord of the Desert. Lord of Chaos. God of Storms. God of Darkness. Seth. Seteh. So many forgotten names. In the end, they were one. Sutekh.

The Krayl boys called him daddy dearest. Sort of. Actually, Dagan called him "the old man." Alastor called him Dad. And Mal just used his name. It was the best he could do, given that he loathed his father. And loved him.

Would Osiris dare to tip the balance by killing Lokan? And why now? What could he hope to gain? It had been millennia since Sutekh betrayed him. Why seek vengeance by killing his son now?

Mal had been over the possibilities again and again. Maybe Osiris's message of condolence had had a different intent. Maybe he meant to suggest that one of Lokan's own brothers had killed him.

If that's what he meant, it was easy enough to discount. Given the right provocation, any one of them might have pummeled Lokan senseless. And Lokan would have given it right back to them. But murder? They might fight and squabble and glare, but in the end, they watched out for each other. Neither Dagan nor

Alastor would have killed Lokan. It wasn't the way they rolled. And Mal knew for a fact that *he* hadn't done the deed.

Which left Osiris's message as exactly what it appeared to be: an expression of condolence.

Mal wasn't buying it. But trying to figure out the motivations of an Egyptian god who'd been around for millennia, who was versed in every possible twist and treacherous move, was an endeavor doomed to failure.

"Mal—"

"You trespass sacred grounds," the sentry hissed.

"Get lost, Dae." Mal stepped forward, shouldering his brother aside, but Dagan grabbed his forearm, fingers closing like a vise, his gray eyes glittering in the odd greenish light. There was concern there, and affection. Damn. It was the affection that hit Mal where he lived.

"There are things you don't know, and I don't have time to tell you everything." Dagan leaned in close and spoke so low that Mal had to strain to catch the words. "But I'll give you the abbreviated version. I've spent two days following up a lead that led me to a shitload of questions. Apparently, there was a witness. Frank Marin. Alastor's all over that, but it looks like the Daughters of Aset got to him first and he's gone to ground."

"Like a worm." Mal crossed his arms, imitating Dagan's implacable posture.

"Exactly like." Slinging an arm across Mal's shoulders, Dagan glanced at the silent sentry and shifted even closer. "Xaphan's concubines know something. They've been stirring up shit. Asking questions. Stepping over territorial lines. I need you to go talk to them. You'll do better with them than I will."

That was an inarguable fact. Dagan wasn't exactly

known for his easygoing way with the ladies. Drop him in a pit for a match with a hellhound. Leave him in a room with a pile of ancient scrolls. Send him out to navigate the gates of Osiris and the lakes of fire. Not a problem. Dagan'd do fine with any of the above. Choice D: sweet-talk a female. Not so much.

As though he sensed that he'd made headway, Dagan pressed. "Mal, you're the better choice to meet with Xaphan's fire genies, and I'm the better choice to face Osiris. Even if he was the one who took out Lokan, no way he'll take out the old man's firstborn. But anyone—*everyone*—else is fair game. Including you or Alastor. I'm the only one who's safe here. You know it. I know it." His mouth hardened. "The old man knows it."

Nothing but the truth. Sutekh knew the risks. But he'd still sent Mal to do the job.

Mal stared at Dagan, and when he spoke, he knew his voice was raw with all the pent-up emotion he'd harbored since his brother's death. "*How* did they take out Lokan? How could anyone, anything, kill a soul reaper?"

It was nearly impossible. The only way to terminate a soul reaper was with his permission and by his will. Occasionally, one got tired of eternal life, jaded, sick with the endless cycle of harvesting darksouls, and chose to walk into a lake of fire. That was the key word. *Chose.* But Lokan hadn't been any soul reaper. He'd had the added benefit of being Sutekh's son. Half god. And he'd been full of life, full of laughter. It was not a choice he would have made. So how the fucking hell had he ended up dead?

"Alastor'll brief you about Marin and the kid," Dagan said. "Go. Every second we waste arguing brings us closer to really pissing off Osiris. And given

that I'm here to ask for his help, I figure angry isn't a mood I want to put him in."

"I don't like it." But even as the statement left his mouth, he knew Dae would take it for the acquiescence it was. Osiris would know that two soul reapers had walked into his territory, but if only one remained to face him, the damage could be minimized.

Mal throttled the urge to argue further. Instead, he grasped his brother's forearm, hauled him close and thumped his fist against Dae's chest.

"Just don't get yourself hacked to bits."

One side of Dagan's mouth quirked up. "Wouldn't say it's at the top of my to-do list."

Toronto, Canada

PYOTR TURNED TO CONVERSE with the man on his left, meaningless words. He ate and drank and enjoyed the meal, the second of the celebratory dinners since he had chosen Marie as his perfect sacrifice. He smiled and laughed at appropriate moments. He was very good at soothing his congregation, even when he called only a fraction of his charm and wiles into play.

As the honeyed cakes and mint tea were brought out to end the repast, he caught the eye of High Reverend Djeserit Bast, who sat at the head of the table next to his own. He dipped his head toward her. It was enough. She excused herself and rose and, moments later, Pyotr followed.

"Are you aware that we had a visitor? One of Aset's Daughters?" Djeserit asked without tact or foreplay as Pyotr joined her in her private office.

Djeserit was a tall, imposing woman with piercing

black eyes and a strong nose. As long as he had known her, she had chosen the path of the traditional Egyptian priest, plucking or waxing or doing whatever it was she did so there was not a single hair on her head. No eyebrows, no eyelashes. She was completely hairless. Pyotr assumed that she extended the practice to the rest of her body. Not that he had devoted a great deal of time to pondering the issue; it was simply a logical conclusion. But theirs was not the sort of relationship that would allow him to investigate firsthand.

Nor would he wish to. She was too strong. Too bold. Yes, she was highly intelligent, and he liked that in a consort. Stimulating conversation was as important as a willing mouth or pussy or ass. But he preferred his partners beautiful, and somewhat reserved. There was something about breaching a woman's defenses, coaxing and wooing her responses, subtly breaking through her every defense until she not only agreed to, but begged for, anything he desired. That appealed to him on the most visceral level.

He could not imagine Djeserit being coaxed or wooed, could not imagine her begging.

"I am aware. She was treated to the grand tour." He allowed himself a brief smile. "And she made a donation." There was a distinct irony in that, one of Aset's Daughters giving money to Sutekh's worshippers. "She's a foot soldier, nothing more. They didn't even bother to send an opponent of worth."

"You are certain that she learned nothing?"

"She learned that we have a roof garden." He shrugged. "Roxy Tam is of no consequence."

"But bears watching, nonetheless," Djeserit insisted.

Pyotr inclined his head. "If you wish. Send one of

your men." She wouldn't. It was a waste of manpower. They both knew it. Roxy Tam had asked her questions and left without answers. As would be the outcome if she returned.

"Who have you chosen?" Djeserit asked, changing the subject in her typical abrupt manner.

"I suggest our newest member," he replied. It was not a suggestion. It was an absolute. But let Djeserit pretend her opinion mattered. It cost him nothing to pretend.

She moved to stand by her desk, a massive affair of chrome and glass that dominated the far wall. The room was luxurious, fitted with rich carpets and over-stuffed brown leather couches. Windowless. Only one entry, a door guarded by two sentries, Djeserit's personal picks, loyal to her unto death. The room and hallway beyond were scoured for bugs morning and evening. There was absolutely no possibility that their privacy would be breached.

Though they were equal in the Cult of Setnakht, High Reverends both, Djeserit had chosen to have this meeting on her turf without clarifying his assent. A petty insult. One Pyotr was not interested in repaying. If he got his nose out of joint for every small snub or affront, he would be a poor leader, indeed. And he meant to be a great leader, a supreme leader, an immortal leader.

He could afford to be magnanimous.

Djeserit walked around the desk then and sat in her custom-designed ergonomic chair, a luxury paid for by the congregation at the astonishing cost of nearly ten thousand dollars.

Her actions were yet another effort to place herself in a position of power, sitting while she left him stand-

ing, separated by her desk. But her expression remained completely neutral, betraying nothing of her thoughts.

"I am surprised by your choice." She didn't sound surprised. But then, she never did.

"Why is that?" Uninvited, Pyotr crossed to the sidebar and poured himself a cup of the rich, strong Turkish coffee Djeserit preferred. Personally, he favored café hufuch, a foamy, creamy beverage made with unfiltered coffee. But small things were not worth his temper.

"She is innocent." Bold, bordering on rude, Djeserit's tone never changed as she made her observations. It was her way. Instead of questioning his choice, she would simply point out the obvious and rely on him to see his own wayward path. "I fail to see her value as bait for a soul reaper. She has no darksoul."

Pyotr shot her a glance, sipped his coffee, suppressed a shudder at the bitter taste and smiled. Without waiting for an invitation, he settled on one of the low couches and leaned back. "Precisely."

Djeserit was missing the obvious. No matter how much they might wish it otherwise, they had no power to summon a soul reaper. The minions of their master, Sutekh, did not answer mortal command. They could kill the most heinous villains and end up with nothing to show for their efforts other than a river of blood. No, they must be cunning. Wise. They must choose their victim with care. Not someone to lure a reaper, but rather a sacrifice to lure another sacrifice, to lure yet another who might ultimately attract the attention of the one they wanted. Layers upon layers.

Killing an innocent was more productive than killing one whose deeds had already blackened their soul.

"She will traverse the twenty-one gates of Osiris, her

heart will be weighed, she will be found righteous and Anubis will allow her to proceed to the Field of Reeds." Again, Djeserit asked no question. She merely pointed out that which she found obvious, believing her superior intellect would sway him to her point of view. But he heard what she did not ask. *What is to be gained by her death?*

Pyotr sipped again at the bitter brew. He set the small white cup on its matched saucer, taking his time, letting her wait. "How do you know she will go to the realm of Osiris? She may go to another afterlife entirely."

A fleeting expression touched Djeserit's implacable features, surprise, perhaps dismay. "Your words are blasphemy."

"Not at all," he demurred. "I only point out that the Underworld has many gods, many lords. Endless territories. And I do not even touch on other possibilities for the afterlife. Her soul may go to any one of thousands of places. But the unassailable truth is that it matters not where the lamb's soul settles, only that it does not remain in her current incarnation."

She missed his point, but she was careful not to betray her confusion. He let the silence grow and stretch, in no rush to explain. Let her wonder. Djeserit saw only the obvious. Despite her intellect, she was too literal to grasp the nuances of his plan. She stared at him, unblinking. Finally, when his coffee was done, the dregs dark at the bottom of the cup, he leaned forward to place it carefully on the edge of the glass and chrome monstrosity of a coffee table, then raised his gaze to hers.

"The taking of the innocent life is merely a means to the end. It is the blackening of another's darksoul, one already dipped in fetid rot, that is the goal, Djeserit.

The killer kills the innocent, and then another and another, until we have layered a soul so thick with tar and rot that a soul reaper cannot help but notice. One will come to ensure the monster's darksoul is carried to Sutekh. It will be a morsel too delicious to ignore." He said nothing of the prophecy, or the blood. That was the most delicious morsel of all. The soul reaper's blood, to be mixed with that of a Daughter of Aset. And the god would live again.

A slow smile lit Djeserit's face. If ever a woman ought not smile, it was Djeserit Bast. Lines creased her cheeks and the pouches beneath her eyes puffed and crinkled. Not attractive in the least.

"Kill the killer." She leaned forward on the opposite couch, engaged now, excited. "Really, you surpass yourself Pyotr. The plan is quite lovely. Did you have someone in mind?"

The Underworld, the Territory of Osiris

"Dae…"

"Too late to argue."

"It was too late before I even started." Mal's frustration was evident as he scraped his fingers through his straight, dark hair, dragging it back from his forehead. He was the only one of the brothers who had dark hair. Since Sutekh didn't have a mortal corporeal form, his sons took the genetic blueprint of their appearance from their mothers. Dagan and Alastor's mother had been fair, as had Lokan's. Only Mal's mother had had dark hair and olive skin, and Mal had her coloring.

His thick platinum hoops—two in each ear—glinted

in the eerie greenish lights. There was a platinum ring in the shape of a stylized skull on his baby finger. Red silk shirt. Dark jeans. Black boots.

Dagan shook his head. Mal was a pirate. Always had been. Always would be. A couple of hundred years one way or the other didn't change that.

The thought was oddly reassuring.

Sometimes, those with extreme longevity who traversed both Topworld and the Underworld became withdrawn, despondent, clinging to the old ways, unable to change as the world changed. Eventually, they chose to remain in the Underworld, isolated, alone. Some went mad. Others went into the lakes of fire. It was one of the few ways most Underworlders could make certain the end was the end.

But Mal would never be one of them. He embraced everything the Topworld had to offer. Foods. Fashions. Gadgets. Ideas. His pattern of speech changed as the world birthed each new generation. He was a chameleon, always blending.

To a degree, all of them were. They had to be. But Mal was the master, and he reveled in making those changes. So long as he saw a way to profit from it, Mal was all over it, whatever *it* might be.

Mal opened his mouth. Closed it.

"What?" Dagan asked.

"Bro, Osiris is bound to try and screw you."

"Thanks for the insight. You have some brilliant suggestion on how to avoid it?"

"Nah." He flashed a grin. "Just be alert when he tells you to drop your pants."

With a laugh, he turned and sauntered away. After a dozen steps, he lifted a hand and tossed a casual wave

without looking back. Then, in a parting gesture, he extended his middle finger, a low chuckle drifting behind him as he was swallowed by distance and darkness.

For some reason, the nearly universal symbol made Dagan think of the girl. It was something she'd do, flip him the bird.

She'd been on his mind incessantly since he'd left the serial killer's lair. Made sense, since he'd spent the past few days trying to find out something about her, and about the pendant. Name. Address. E-mail addy. Anything.

He'd come up empty.

But that didn't stop her from invading his thoughts. Nothing new. Over the years, she'd had a habit of doing that—when he let her, which wasn't often. But not an hour ago, he'd let her. He'd been in the shower, hot water beating on his back, his hand fisted around his cock. And she'd been right there with him, dark hair slicked back from her face, water beading on her coffee, double-cream skin. And her mouth…damn… the things she'd done with her mouth.

Vivid waking dreams.

Soul reapers didn't dream. But he dreamed of her. What the fuck was he supposed to make of that?

Dagan cleared his thoughts and walked deeper into Osiris's lair. Moments later, he paused at the foot of a wide stone staircase. At the top stood a creature with the body of a man and the head of a jackal. There was a flail tucked in the crook of his arm, and he held a golden ankh, the symbol of life. But unlike the pendant Dagan had hauled off the serial killer, the jackal's ankh had neither wings nor horns.

"Anubis," Dagan greeted him, inclining his head in a spare nod.

"Dagan Krayl." The voice reverberated in his thoughts. "You are not welcome here."

Why was he not surprised?

"I have not come as Sutekh's son." He smiled dryly. "Think of me as a negotiator, one without allegiance to any party. One who seeks only to maintain the balance."

The jackal stared at him, weighing his words. Dagan stared back, the silence stretching like an infinite piece of string.

"You are always first and foremost Sutekh's son," Anubis said at last.

Dagan had to admit there was a hefty degree of truth in that observation. He'd spent a chunk of his life trying to be his father's perfect son. In the early years, he'd learned to fear nothing except his father's disappointment. At times, Sutekh's wrath had been physical in nature. At times, psychological. He had used every means and underhanded trick to teach Dagan that *his* was the only opinion that mattered. Loyalty to him was tantamount.

He'd instilled the belief that failing to rise to his potential, failing to attain the heights he knew Dagan could reach, was the greatest of all sins.

Of course, the height Dagan aspired to had to be one Sutekh condoned.

In the beginning Dagan had been in his father's thrall, and so he had had his father's approval. Then, slowly, like a seed unfurling, he'd begun to form his own opinions. He'd stopped blindly following his father's will. Sutekh had not been pleased. Those had

been dark years, and the resulting freedom had not been sweet. It had been a yoke to bear in its own right.

The loss of his father's favorable opinion had been devastating, for that approval had defined all he was.

So, layer by layer, Dagan built his own new identity and chose to include Sutekh's lessons in loyalty and fealty. Only he switched 'em up. Sutekh meant that fealty to extend only to him. Dagan stretched the umbrella over his brothers.

But Anubis wasn't far off. In many ways, Dagan *was* first and foremost his father's son. But in more important ways, he wasn't.

"I have information to share," Dagan offered.

"That may be true, son of Sutekh. But you would not come here for that. You have come because there is information you *seek*."

Again, a truth he couldn't deny. It had been four days since he'd harvested Joe Marin's darksoul. He hadn't managed to find out a damned thing about the girl since then. But he'd heard a shitload about the cult that called itself the Setnakhts. And he'd found out that he wasn't the only one interested in that fact. Turned out, Xaphan and his concubines were very interested in Frank Marin. The same guy the Setnakht's were asking questions about. The same guy the Daughters of Aset had gone sniffing after. Who just happened to be Joe Marin's brother.

He had coincidences coming out his ass.

Problem was, he'd hit a dead end. His information had stopped at that, teasers without substance, nothing solid to move forward with. He couldn't go directly to Xaphan. Sutekh had a history with the keeper of the lakes of fire, and it wasn't exactly friendly.

He sure as sugar couldn't approach Aset. She'd as soon shred one of Sutekh's sons as talk to him.

Which left only Osiris, her brother, who also just happened to be her husband. Dagan knew there was a squick factor there for mortals, but he figured, hey, to each his own. Not his business who slept with whom.

He had a more immediate concern: to find a way into Osiris's inner sanctum, Dagan needed to pass Anubis, who was currently looking at him as though he were dog shit and Anubis were a shoe.

"Agreed. I do seek information. But I'm willing to share equally." This was one occasion where the truth would serve him better than a lie. "The flow of knowledge will benefit us both. There's a group that calls itself the Setnakhts. And they may be a threat to us all." He trod carefully, choosing each word, because Anubis was waiting to pounce on anything he might construe as an insult.

"The Setnakhts are Sutekh's minions."

Yeah…how to parry that?

"They worship Sutekh," Dagan agreed. "By *their* choice. He did not recruit them or invite their worship."

"He does not discourage it."

Sutekh? Discourage adoration? Not fucking likely. "He allows them their free will. It is their mortal right," Dagan hedged.

"You cloud the topic, soul reaper, arguing both sides. Do you defend them or condemn them?"

"Their motives are unknown. Quite possibly impure."

"You condemn them."

"No." He sucked at this. Give him a darksoul to reap and he was good to go. But this doublespeak

wasn't for him. "They are mortals who dabble in things they do not understand, and those dabblings are creating…imbalances."

"We have felt that." Anubis's obsidian eyes glittered in the eerie light. "What do you want of Osiris?"

"I seek information and wish for an ally in my quest."

"An ally, son of Sutekh?"

Dagan heard what wasn't said: son of Osiris's enemy.

But he'd said his piece, and he didn't think it would help much to point out that in the Underworld, friends were enemies, allies were traitors, and no one was trustworthy. No one.

The silence was quickly becoming uncomfortable. Then Anubis extended his hand, palm up, and curled his fingers inward. "Come, Dagan Krayl. You will be judged."

"So I've been told," he muttered and loped up the sandstone stairs, taking them two at a time. Reaching the top, he paused, waiting for Anubis to offer instruction.

"We will begin. Speak the declarations of purity."

Dagan's head jerked up. He stared into the eyes of the jackal, black and fathomless, and he said nothing. The forty-two declarations of purity were absolute. To lie at this point would mean his destruction, and even his position as the old man's firstborn wouldn't save him.

Because Osiris was one of the few beings with enough power to bring him down. Was that what had happened to Lokan? Had he pissed off Osiris at one of their meetings? Pissed him off enough to sign his own death warrant?

No way to know for certain. Not yet. But Dagan meant to ensure that the tally didn't jump to *two* dead reapers, because he wasn't in the mood to offer himself up as anyone's sacrificial lamb.

Besides, another dead reaper would definitively set them all on a path to war.

But whoever had killed Lokan had exactly that in mind. You didn't take down a prince and expect that the king wouldn't retaliate.

"The declarations, son of Sutekh," Anubis prodded.

I have driven away wickedness. I have not done iniquity to mankind. I have not caused misery. I have not caused affliction. Yeah, like he could swear to any of those without lying.

Then an honest declaration slid through his thoughts and the words came easily to his lips. "I have not done harm unto animals. And, uh, I have not stolen milk from the mouths of children. And, yeah, I have not put out a fire when it should burn." That about summed it up.

"So you value honesty." The jackal laughed, the sound anything but warm. "Let us proceed directly to judgment, then." He paused, as though waiting for a reply, and when Dagan offered none, he continued. "Unlike your brother, you are one of few words."

No. He had many words. He just weighed them before he set them free. He'd spent the first part of his life pretty much alone. That sort of upbringing didn't lend one toward verbosity.

Anubis made an encompassing gesture, indicating the length of Dagan's body. "I will need your Ib."

His heart. The seat of his emotion and thought, will and intention.

The jackal smiled, a stark baring of pointed teeth that gleamed white in the dim light. "The Ib must be weighed against the feather of Maat—truth—before you may proceed any further."

Of course it must.

"Only if you are deemed worthy will you be permitted into the presence of Osiris." Anubis extended the hand that held the ankh and Dagan saw then that it was a dagger, the golden hilt formed into the symbol for life.

Nice. Lokan had never mentioned this part. Of course, secrecy was key to any negotiations that took place here. That's what had made Lokan such a great negotiator. He'd known how to read the mood of every god and demigod, every demon and genie, and he'd known how to keep his mouth shut.

Keeping his eyes on the jackal, Dagan pulled the hem of his T-shirt free of his jeans and dragged it off over his head, thinking as he did so that Mal had been right. He was so screwed, because no way would his dark heart measure up.

Anubis froze. His expression remained ruthlessly neutral, but Dagan felt the charge in the air, the tension.

"Son of Sutekh," he whispered. "You dare to don the mark of Osiris?"

The pendant. Dagan had put it around his neck and hadn't taken it off since he'd pulled it from the serial killer's corpse.

"Not Osiris's mark. You see the wings and horns," he replied carefully as he turned fully toward Anubis, giving him a chance to examine the necklace. "I am the son of Sutekh but choose to carry Aset's sign." The sign of the Daughters of Aset, anyway.

"The sons of Sutekh are enemies of Aset."

You think?

"I wear it as proof of my aspiration toward neutrality." Oh, yeah. That sounded good. "And as a gesture of respect for the sister and wife of Osiris." And that sounded political. Sort of.

"Approach." Anubis's voice echoed through the vast space, and he sounded pissed.

Dagan drew closer to the massive gleaming scales that appeared out of nowhere to loom before him. On one side was a single white feather, the feather of Maat. Truth. The other side was empty.

"Proceed."

Accepting the dagger, Dagan took a breath, held it, then plunged the blade between the fourth and fifth ribs on his left side, deep enough to slit through the skin and layers of muscle, but not deep enough to hit organs. Blood dripped down his chest and belly, sliding under the waistband of his jeans.

He let the dagger clatter to the ground. Curling the fingers of his right hand under the fourth rib, and the fingers of his left hand over the fifth, he cracked them wide.

Blood welled, red and hot, the pain hotter still. The human part of him flinched and inwardly cried out in agony. The part of him that was the son of Sutekh didn't even blink.

"Your heart," Anubis demanded. Was there a certain amount of glee in his tone?

Asshole.

Closing his fist around his pulsing heart, Dagan yanked it from his thorax and tossed it on the empty side of the scale. Blood puddled on the scale's golden plate and dripped over the edges to splatter the ground like red paint.

Nausea boiled in his gut, and his legs felt like celery stalks left in the back of the fridge for a month. But he showed none of that. He only held his place and kept his eyes on the scale.

For an instant, the side with his heart sank low, weighted by sin and transgression. Then it slowly rose until the side with the feather dipped and held even. Just barely.

Well, fuck me raw.

He'd been judged, and he was more than a little surprised by the results.

His gaze flicked to Anubis. If the jackal were equally surprised, he didn't show it.

"We done here?"

Anubis inclined his head in a shallow gesture of assent and intoned, "You may enter. Osiris will speak with you."

Dagan's lips curled in dark humor.

Lucky him.

Reaching out, he closed his hand around his still-twitching heart and thrust it back inside his chest. Pain rocked him as the great vessels sealed to the gaping holes, and bone and muscle healed. He stared straight ahead, betraying nothing.

Pain was weakness.

Weakness was failure.

And Dagan had learned at the old man's knee not to accept failure.

CHAPTER NINE

Toronto, Canada

SOMEONE WAS HUNTING HER.

Perched on the rail of the bell tower that rose from the north end of the deconsecrated church, Roxy turned her face to the wind—stronger and colder up here so far from the ground—and opened her senses. Yes, someone was out there, and that made hard-edged rage ignite in her gut.

This was her *home*. After a lifetime of doing without, she'd made herself a home.

Now, someone dared to slink onto her turf, uninvited. Stalking her.

She breathed deep, her head coming up, her skin crackling with awareness as she studied the night shadows. Whoever was out there was good. She couldn't hear him. Couldn't see him.

But she knew he was there.

Her own fault. She'd been careful not to tip her hand, dancing around the name *Krayl* as she made her inquiries. Obviously, she hadn't been careful enough.

All she'd gotten back on her queries was the vacuum of a black hole. No one had told her anything, but it looked like someone had ratted her out, sent word

along the chain that she was poking around in soul reaper business. Sutekh's business.

Bad idea to poke at the Überlord of Chaos and Evil. He tended to poke back.

So she was pretty damned certain that her unwelcome visitor was a soul reaper.

Not the way she would have preferred to play this, but she'd learned that sometimes you just eat what's served.

She slid off the rail and clambered down the metal ladder set in the inside wall of the tower, silent, focused. At the base, she paused, closing her eyes and letting the charge in her blood seek what was out there.

No one. Her senses reached, and found only cool air, the faint, distant rustle of branches in the wind and the scent of the lemon cleaner she'd used to wash the floor. There wasn't a single thing that gave him away.

Easing open the scarred wooden door, polished to a glossy patina, she stepped out of the tower into what had once been the chancel but was now her living room.

To her left, the faintest shush of sound. She made a half turn—

As fast as she was, he was faster.

Her heart didn't even have the chance to finish a beat before he was on her. His body slammed against hers, spinning her, caging her.

Pulse ramping into redline, she brought one palm up to slap the wall as she cushioned the impact. Her neck twisted to the side and her cheek mashed against cool plaster.

She jabbed back hard with her free elbow. Anticipating the move, he arched beyond her reach. Then he

crushed her with his full weight, making her the filling in a reaper/wall sandwich.

Her breath whooshed out. The heat of her captor's body pressed full against her back, his stubbled jaw resting against her temple. She could feel the smooth hum of his power, purring like the engine of a finely tuned Bugati. No doubt about it; she was outgunned.

Mind racing, she evaluated her options and came up with damned few.

Damn. Double damn.

Squashed as she was, a shallow inhalation was all she could manage. It was enough to tickle her senses with the scent of his skin, citrus and spice. Luscious. Clean. Faintly familiar. A hazy memory.

A memory that had coalesced into solid muscle and male heat, pressed up against her closer than paint on plaster. She knew it was him a millisecond before he spoke.

"Hello, Roxy," he murmured, his voice smoke and crème brûlée, smooth and rich with just a hint of crackle. She'd heard that voice a million times in her dreams. She hadn't told him her name that long-ago night. But he knew it now, and the sound of his voice pounded through her.

A part of her had waited for him for eleven years, warring with the part that had prayed he'd never come.

Memories stirred. For an instant, she wasn't here in her stone church far north of the city. She was more than a decade in the past, back in a deserted factory, in a room that percolated mildew and sweat and white-hot terror.

Are you here to free me?

No.

To kill me?

No. He'd been there to do his job: harvest the dark-souls, denying them any hope of rebirth or redemption.

Bastard.

She wriggled a little, testing his hold. His weight was like a cement block on her back. But cement could crumble; she just needed to find the right angle and hit it hard. Her preternatural strength and enhanced senses would be little help in this battle.

She wasn't up against a mortal, but a soul reaper. However powerful she was, he was more so.

"It's...good to see you," he murmured against her ear.

"You can't see anything but the back of my head."

He laughed. She could feel the movement of his chest against her back.

"Get off," she rasped.

A pause. He shifted, the front of his thighs melding to the backs of hers, the ridges and bumps of his pelvis hard against her buttocks. He was lean and honed, his body a weapon.

"Get off?" He sounded amused, and she realized the alternate ways her comment could be taken. Then his tone hardened. "I think not."

"Can't blame a girl for trying." Her quip was a poor mask for the panic that threatened to overtake her as she groped for a plan. She hated the cloying fear, hated herself for feeling it. The Asetian Guard had trained her better than this.

Angry is better than afraid. Cunning is better than angry. Calliope Kane's voice echoed in her thoughts. Her mentor had shared damned few bits of advice over the years, so when she'd offered even the most obscure tidbits, Roxy'd perked up and listened.

She could do angry. But under the circumstances—

wall in front, soul reaping bastard behind, hands trapped, feet in the wrong position to land a solid kick—cunning wasn't even in the cards.

Shifting her shoulders, she tried to adjust her position so she could free her hand. Her pulse raced as the reaper moved with her, an inch this way, an inch back, his weight pinning her, his breath feathering her cheek.

She forced herself to be still then, to think and plot and…nothing came to her. So she stopped thinking and let instinct lead.

"Stop squirming. I'm here to—"

With a snarl, she sank her teeth into his forearm. Hard enough to hurt like hell. Not hard enough to make him bleed. She'd tried that once and hadn't liked the results.

Hissing out a breath, he shook his arm to get it free of her teeth and jerked back just a bit. Millimeters.

It was enough.

A hard twist of her hips. The scrape of the wall against her skin as she tore one hand free.

A surge of adrenaline shot her to the stratosphere.

She rammed her elbow sharply into his side. This time she was fast enough that her blow glanced his ribs even though he arched to avoid it. Satisfaction surged. Not that she believed she'd actually hurt him. But his movement gave her opportunity.

Curling at the waist, she used her shoulder as a bolster and ripped her other hand free. Less than a second, and he slammed her hard into the wall once more, crushing the breath out of her.

Too late, sucka. She almost felt sorry for him as she

whipped her right arm straight back so her palm flashed down and her fingers clawed between his legs.

Survival in favor of modesty—not that she cared much for that, anyway.

She grabbed his balls and held on tight. "Back off, asshole."

"I just want information." A rough whisper. He sounded...amused. Again. Did he think she wouldn't do a little nut cracking? She squeezed the goods and smiled when he tensed.

"Information?" she echoed, her tone flat, her grip growing ever tighter. "Try 411." She gave a neat little twist of the wrist to make a point.

He stopped breathing. His weight left her, and he carefully eased back as far as her grip let him.

Guess he got the point.

Her free hand snaked down to her belt and she flicked open the sheath that held her knife. But didn't pull it. Not yet. She would wait for the moment.

She wasn't a nineteen-year-old kid anymore. She wasn't anything she'd been back then. She was a Daughter of Aset. A member of the Asetian Guard. Anyone's match.

Even his.

"Truce." His mouth was close to her ear when he spoke, his tone low and smooth, offering no evidence of the pain he must be feeling given the overexuberance of her hold on his balls. "I just want information. Tell me about Frank Marin."

Right. A Daughter of Aset offering info to a son of Sutekh. That'd be a *not*.

When she didn't respond, he made a sound that might have been a laugh. Then he closed his hand around her

wrist, pressing hard on the tendons at the front. She fought it, her wrist going numb, her fingers uncoiling of their own volition until she had no choice but to let go.

He quickly shifted to the side, getting his personal gear beyond her reach. Feeling mighty pleased with himself, no doubt.

Plan B, then.

With no more warning than a sharp exhale, she freed her blade and plunged it into his thigh. To the hilt. Blood spurted over her fingers, accompanied by a smoother-than-warm-caramel swell of satisfaction when he gave a pained grunt.

But she wasn't about to risk her life by getting cocky. It was a lucky strike. She knew it. He was still faster and stronger, but she'd had the element of surprise. And that was gone now.

She spun and sprinted flat out for the back door. She was running from him, and from herself. What the fuck was wrong with her that something inside her was *glad* to see him? Glad he wasn't dead. Or butchered. Or skinned. She vaulted the couch, one foot on the seat, the other slamming the back until the whole thing tipped over exactly as she wanted, carrying her forward while creating an obstacle in his path.

Her blood pounded in her ears.

Almost there. She reached out with her numbed hand, scrabbling for the doorknob.

Almost.

There.

He grabbed a hank of her hair, yanked her up short and hauled her back against the solid wall of his body. He wasn't even breathing hard.

Because he wasn't human. She had to remember

that. For all the red blood that had poured from his thigh, he wasn't human.

But then again, neither was she. Not exactly. Not anymore.

He yanked on her hair again, harder. Her scalp prickled and throbbed. Figuring he expected a struggle, she let herself go limp, hoping to throw him off balance. But he seemed to expect that, as well, holding her weight easily.

"For fuck's sake," he snarled. "Just stay still and listen."

Something pressed against the back of her thigh near her buttock. Hard. Smooth. The handle of her knife. How had he moved so fast with a blade in his thigh?

Balling her fist, she slammed it against the hilt, shifting the angle and burying the blade deeper in his flesh. She could swear she heard it scrape bone.

But still he held her, his fist twisting tighter in her hair.

"Information," he snarled, looping his arm around her waist as she tried to tear free. He lifted her clear off her feet and plastered her against him like shrink-wrap on meat, her ass pressed to his pubic bone. Then he stepped to the side, hauling her along as he went. "I want fucking information, not a brawl."

He let go of her hair then, but not her waist, holding her so her toes barely grazed the ground. Panting, she hung there, trying to guess his next move. A click sounded a millisecond before light flooded the space. She blinked, focused. He'd turned on the overhead chandelier, the one she'd had shipped from Italy.

Instinct screamed for her to claw and fight as he

dropped her to her feet and jerked her around to face him.

And for an endless, frozen second, they just stared at each other. She read the glint of steel and snow in his gaze.

She'd seen those eyes a thousand times in her dreams. Mercury gray. Both bright and opaque at once. Rimmed by dark brown lashes. Cold as a high mountain lake or an endless icy abyss.

For the briefest instant, his gaze warmed as it slid along her features, nose, chin, down to her toes and up again. That warmth reached inside her and unloaded a king-size carton of confusion.

She slapped it back, holding out for her chance. She needed to get away from him, but there was no sense wasting energy. She would lose in a match of brute strength.

Cunning is better than angry.

So she offered no resistance as he switched his grip from her waist to her wrists. Squelching the urge to squirm and writhe against his hold, she forced herself to be still, to watch for her chance. He'd secured her hands. He had no idea what she could do with her knees.

But the way his eyes narrowed warned her that he didn't trust her acquiescence.

"Figured you for the type who'd prefer the dark," she muttered, tipping her head toward the chandelier.

"You figured right. Dark works for me. But unlike you—" he shot her an unreadable look "—I'm trying to be accommodating. I figured you for the type who prefers the light."

"Slamming me against a wall and yanking out my

hair is being accommodating?" She'd hate to see him being disobliging. "You're killing me with kindness."

He shifted his weight and winced. "You stabbed me."

No shit, Sherlock. She shrugged. "You grabbed me."

One side of his mouth moved in the barest hint of a smile. "I wasn't questioning the appropriateness of the action, but rather the fact that you succeeded."

There was that.

Her own lips twitched before she squelched even the hint of humor. She shouldn't give a flying flip that reaper boy seemed to have a bit of respect for her knife work, despite the fact that it'd been him she was carving.

"It's a gift."

His smile widened until she saw a flash of white teeth. Heart pounding, she stared, taken aback. He looked exactly as she recalled. Exactly the way he looked in her dreams.

Mmm-hmm, he was *fine*.

Beautiful in the way of a weapon, honed and sleek and deadly.

And she had a liking for weapons. *Damn.*

"Run, and I'll catch you." He loosened his grip enough that she could pull free, and she took her time rubbing first one wrist and then the other. "Make me chase you, and I'll be—" his voice dropped to a menacing rasp "—unhappy."

I'll bet.

Reaching down, he pulled her knife out of his thigh. A little fountain of blood surged. He made a sound of irritation, ripped the hem off his T-shirt and then ripped that in half again. One part he folded with meticulous

care and pressed hard on the wound. After a few seconds, he used the second piece to tie off the first. But his watchful gaze never left her.

She thought about bolting—

"Do not even think it."

"I'm not." Not anymore.

He wiped her knife on his jeans. Leaking from beneath his makeshift bandage was a three-inch margin that was dark and wet with blood. The scent of it—

She froze, mastering her nature. Instinct screamed for her to lean down, rip his jeans and open her mouth against his skin, latch on to him like a suckerfish and drink and drink and drink like the parasite she was. The power of her need was startling. Disturbing. Rarely did it hit her so hard.

Was it because his blood was supernatural? Or because it was his fault that she felt such cravings at all? Eleven years ago, he had awakened the seeds of the creature she had become. He had ended her old life and given her a new one, set her on the winding path that had brought her to this moment.

And then he'd walked away.

Had he ever given that a second thought? Given *her* a second thought?

No. He'd left her to make her way all on her own. To stumble and fall and almost give up. To hate him and curse him.

To fear him.

To dream of him and yearn for him, twisting the fact that he'd saved her life into some sort of attraction. That was the worst part. The nights she woke thrashing and covered in sweat—not because she was terrified but because she'd been dreaming about him.

Filling her. Taking her.

On those nights, she hated herself more than she could ever hate him.

And now, here he was, as beautiful and deadly as she recalled.

He was her maker. And he was the enemy of her kind. *Her* enemy.

He flipped the knife, offering it to her, hilt first.

A hard bark of laughter escaped her. "What are you, a sucker for punishment?"

"Use that on me again and I'll snap it in half." His tone was flat, even. "Then I'll snap your fingers."

Her gaze flashed to his. Yeah, he would. "Promises, promises." But he didn't promise to kill her. Which meant he wanted her alive.

Because he wanted something from her.

What?

"You remember me?" he asked.

Dumb-ass question. "Yeah, I remember you, vanilla bean. Reaper boy." *I remember everything.* The screams. The bodies. The blood. The terror.

The overwhelming swell of gratitude because he'd left her alive. Because, in a twisted way, he'd even been kind.

She remembered the sound of his voice. The scent of his skin. The way his knuckles had felt as they grazed her cheek.

Everything.

In the year after that terrible night, she'd bounced through three therapists. Stockholm syndrome. Trauma bonding. Capture bonding. They'd offered all sorts of pat answers. Problem was, Dagan Krayl hadn't kidnapped her or captured her. He'd saved her ass.

Was that trauma? Not hardly.

Besides, she couldn't tell any of them what had really gone down. Couldn't tell them about the hearts and the blood and the darksouls. They'd have locked her away and put her on lithium.

So she'd told them only half a story, which meant they'd been able to offer only shallow understanding and half-baked diagnoses. And she'd continued to dream of blood and hearts and greasy, slithering dark-souls tethered by bands of fire.

Oh, and she'd continued to dream of *him*.

"Reaper boy," he echoed, and she cursed herself for that mistake. Should have kept her mouth shut. "You know what I am."

She gave a one-shouldered shrug. No point lying. She'd already given away the game. "Soul reaper."

"You know what I do."

Duh? She spread her hands, palms up. "Reap souls?"

His gaze dipped to her lips, and she felt the heat of that look all the way to her toes. "I see you still have a mouth that gets you into trouble."

"Guess I do." There were all kinds of trouble her mouth could get into. With him.

Crap.

He stared at her, saying nothing. The reflection of the dozen tiny bulbs of the chandelier danced in his eyes as he studied her. She shivered.

He was still holding the knife out toward her, and she reached for it, happy for the distraction.

"Can't kill you anyway, can I?" she asked, taking it from him. Their fingers brushed, skin to skin. She felt the contact like a lightning bolt zinging along her limb.

"No. Whatever carnage you inflict will heal. But if you stab me, I do feel pain—"

"Glad to hear it."

"—and given the choice, I'd rather not," he finished.

"Like I care what you'd rather?"

"You made that abundantly clear when you ignored the advice I gave you." He sounded aggrieved, like she'd somehow wounded him.

Lightning fast, he reached out and caught her wrist, shoved her sleeve up and bared her forearm. Her mark stared up at both of them. "I told you to run like hell, and instead you ran straight to the Daughters of Aset."

"Not *straight* to them." His fingers were hot against her skin, his touch electric. She pulled her hand from his grasp, knowing that she did so only because he let her. "It took a little over a year for me to find them."

"You didn't."

"Excuse me?"

"You didn't find them. You could have searched your entire life and never found them. *They* found you. Never doubt it."

She fisted her hand at her side. It wasn't that he told her anything she hadn't suspected all along, but for some reason hearing him say it pissed her off.

"What did you tell them about me?"

"Not a damned, fucking thing." She'd never revealed what he'd done to her, what he'd made her. And the truth was, no one ever asked. Need-to-know only. That was the motto of the Daughters of Aset and their elite guard. They didn't ask about her. She didn't ask about them. Whatever knowledge they offered, she sucked up like a sponge, but she learned early on not to look for more.

The secretive, elitist, bizarre world of the Daughters of Aset and the Asetian Guard had become her own, making her feel as if she wasn't the only totally screwed-up creature in this world or the next.

"Why didn't you tell them about me?"

"Didn't think you were important enough to mention."

"No?" He reached out and trailed his thumb over her lower lip. She jerked her face to the side, fighting the urge to sink her teeth into his flesh, hard enough to draw blood—hot, luscious blood—and the equally inappropriate urge to suck his thumb into her mouth.

His voice dropped to a rough whisper. "Then why did you keep my jacket?"

CHAPTER TEN

*I have come for what my heart desires
Into the Lake of Fire which is quenched for me*

—Egyptian Book of the Dead, Chapter 22

"HOW DID YOU KNOW ABOUT—" Roxy choked off the question.

"I like what you've done with the place. Nice kitchen. Rosewood cabinets with black granite counters. You have expensive taste. And the bedroom…" Dagan's voice trailed away.

Fury suffused her. He'd been here, in her home, poking around, touching her things. He'd been in her bedroom, found his jacket tucked away in the back of her closet.

"Tell me what you want, why you came here. Or better yet, leave," she snarled.

He raised a brow. "Any particular reason for your hostility?"

Apart from the fact that he'd violated her home? That he could move like smoke, could kill his victims before they even knew he was there? And the *way* he killed, the finality of what he took—the darksoul—denying his prey any hope of being born anew. The Daughters of Aset believed that the soul was eternal,

born again and again into earthly vessels. The cycle preserved.

Apart from the fact that seeing him in the flesh made her remember eleven years' worth of dark, secret dreams.

"No *particular* reason." She tapped her index finger against her chin. "Maybe I don't like your aftershave."

Any warmth she'd imagined in his gaze evaporated, leaving his eyes the color of asphalt and ice. "I don't suffer fools, Roxy. I've done you no harm—"

"Not yet."

"Not yet," he agreed, the implied threat heavy in the air. Then he cocked a brow and waited for her to answer his original question.

"You break the cycle," she said at last. "You harvest darksouls. You act as both judge and executioner, denying your victims the Hall of Two Truths, the chance to be fairly judged. You feed them to Sutekh, a meal of pure power. And then they are gone for eternity. Have I got that right?" She stared him down, daring in the face of her seemingly hopeless circumstances, weighted by the knowledge that he could do that to her. Rip out her darksoul and end her existence. Not just this life, but any future life she might have laid claim to.

The scent of his blood called to her, and she couldn't stop herself from looking at his injured thigh. If she took his blood again, fed on *his* power, would it make her stronger, make her his match?

The thought—the potential ramifications—left her dizzy. Look what she had become with one *mouthful* of his blood. Imagine what she would be if she drained him dry.

A shiver chased up her spine. She could feel him watching her, feel the heat that radiated from his body. And she could smell the old penny lure of his blood. To her, it smelled like ambrosia. Her lips parted.

No. Not going there. Not now. Not ever.

He was a soul reaper. She had to be crazy to be thinking about sucking anything out of him. Not energy. Not blood. Or anything else. Nada. Zip.

"I don't act as judge." He gave an odd, indecipherable smile, layered with self-awareness and derision. "Only executioner."

"Good to know."

His smile turned mocking. "Pretty speech, but I want the truth, Roxy. Why the hostility?"

She kicked her chin up a notch. "You know why. I'm one of them now. A Daughter of Aset. Otherkin. It was you who told me that if I found them, they'd keep me, and that would make me your enemy. Well, I found them, and they kept me. You're batting two for two. You claiming the enemy thing was a lie?"

"No."

The breath left her in a rush, and only then did she realize that a part of her had wanted him to give an entirely different answer, even though she knew there was no other answer to give.

Dipping her head, she feigned interest in her task as she sheathed the knife and fastened the snap, careful to betray none of her unease. She didn't like giving up the advantage that having blade in hand afforded her, but she didn't doubt he would break her fingers, just as he'd promised.

Besides, that avenue was closed now. He knew what to expect. She'd laid out her cards too early.

Time would offer another opportunity, a different opportunity. And like any smart survivor, she just needed to recognize the driftwood and grab it fast when it floated her way.

The soul reaper stepped forward. Too close. If she breathed deeply, her breasts would brush his chest, obliterating the safe zone between them.

She felt like she *knew* him. After so many nights spent in his dream embrace, she felt like her body recognized him. And her soul.

The direction of her thoughts sent every alarm bell she had clanging.

"If you're so concerned about the right of a soul to be judged, tell me what you know," he murmured.

"That's a pretty sweeping request." She gave the position of her knife a final adjustment, though it didn't need it, took a step back and lifted her head. "I know lots of things. A great recipe for apple cobbler. How to ride a Segway. I'm still mastering Twitter, but I'll gladly tell you the basics."

If his stone-faced silence was any indication, he wasn't amused.

"What did Frank Marin tell you?" He used his size to crowd her. She held her ground.

"Sack of shit told me a fuckload of nothing, except the name Krayl." She stared him down. "But that's not much help to you, is it, Dagan Krayl?"

"Was Marin working for the Setnakhts?"

"If you already know the answers, why are you asking the questions?"

He crowded her a little more, until there wasn't even air between them.

Unwilling to edge backward and offer him game

point, she tried to keep the match even by flattening her palms against his chest and shoving him back with as much force as she could muster.

Which wasn't enough. He didn't budge. He didn't even exhale.

"I warn you—I fight fair, Roxy Tam." He lifted his hand and flattened his palm against her chest, just above the swell of her breast, his fingers curving over her collarbone.

She froze. "What's that supposed to mean?"

"You shove me, I shove back. You hit me, I hit back." He brought his lips a breath away from hers and whispered, "Shall I return blow for blow?"

The question was, why hadn't he done exactly that already? She had a feeling she might not like the answer.

"I'd prefer you didn't." Because despite her enhanced speed and strength, she doubted she'd be left standing. Or conscious.

It'd be her brains, not her brawn, that beat him.

Catching his wrist, she jerked his hand from her chest and stepped back, knowing that she did so only because he let her. "How did you find me?"

"I cut my heart out and offered it up on a platter." One side of his mouth curved. Not a nice smile.

"Sorry?" His answer made about as much sense as him being here at all.

"So am I. It hurt like a bitch."

Clearly he wasn't going to explain, which was fine by her. She couldn't care less about his cryptic bullshit.

"So, about that information. What exactly was it you wanted to know?" she asked, wondering if perhaps his questions would in themselves provide her with some answers.

One straight brow arched in question. "Why the sudden urge to cooperate?"

"Figure I owe you."

"For what?"

"You didn't kill me last time we met—" that earned her a snort of laughter "—and I hate being in anyone's debt."

"Well, let's set parameters, then," he said. "An answer or two won't clear your tab, but it'll make a dent."

"What—" She closed her mouth; she didn't want to know what *would* clear her tab.

Reaching up, he dragged a pendant free of his T-shirt and turned it to the light. The silver gleamed against his skin. She saw an oval on a stem and a crossbar. Wings. Horns.

She shook her head, stunned. The feelings that slammed through her coalesced into a single shining recollection: A woman leaning close, her face so similar to Roxy's own, tears glistening in her dark brown eyes and leaving silvery tracks on her cheeks. The smell of her hair, like herbs and flowers. The brush of her lips on Roxy's forehead.

The pendant resting on Dagan Krayl's broad palm, cradled by his long, elegant fingers was a match to the one hanging around Roxy's neck beneath her shirt and a match to the symbol that was etched in her flesh, put there by her own hand.

"You recognize it." Not a question.

"Nope."

"You have one exactly like it."

"Nope."

"It's the mark of the Daughters of Aset." She opened her mouth for another denial, but his cold glare stopped

her. "It's carved in your forearm and it was burned into the ground where my brother was butchered." He paused to let that revelation sink in. "Know anything about that?"

"Nothing." And this time, she wasn't lying or hedging. What he'd just told her was news to her. Definitely not good news. She'd known a bastardized, inverted version of Aset's mark had been tattooed in the dead reaper's skin. But she hadn't known about it being burned into the ground.

Guess she'd been right. Letting him ask his questions had definitely given her some answers.

Was Calliope aware of any of this? Maybe. Maybe not.

And, of course, Roxy couldn't discount the possibility that the Asetian Guard had actually killed and skinned the reaper in the first place, though she couldn't see a purpose to such action. If they had done it, though, it would have been nice if they'd mentioned that small fact.

Fuck.

She set her jaw and kept her mouth shut.

Stalemate. He stared at her. She stared at him.

At length, he asked, "Whose pendant is this?"

"I dunno." But she did. And the knowledge brought an ache to her chest.

What was he doing with her mother's pendant? Where had he found it? How had he found it?

No sense asking. If he had answers, he wouldn't be here firing questions.

She forced herself to shrug, her brows rising in mocking query. "Since it's hanging around your neck, I'd guess it's...yours?"

Something flickered in his gaze, something hot enough to singe.

"Evidence suggests the owner is dead." His voice was low, the words harsh. They hit her like bullets, tearing through her defenses.

Dead.

Her mother was dead.

Evidence suggests—suggests, not conclusively *proves.* She latched on to that, preferring—*needing*—to think that maybe he was wrong.

He was studying her responses, watching her, judging her, leaving her feeling bare and vulnerable. Not a place she liked to be. She fired off her last defense. "Fuck off."

"That mouth again," he murmured.

Before she could come up with even a lame reply, he closed his fingers around her upper arm and dragged her up against him. She wasn't sure if he wanted to kiss her or kill her, or maybe do both, but she was left with absolutely no doubt that she roused some sort of passion in his cold reaper's heart.

His lips compressed in a hard line and his eyes narrowed.

But not in threat.

Something else.

Her heart jerked to a stop, then slammed into redline, beating so hard she swore she could feel it hammering against her ribs.

"I came here—" He broke off and looked away, his jaw tight. She waited, her breath coming too fast, suffused by a strange anxiety as she waited for what he might say next. Finally, he returned his gaze to her face. "I came because I needed to know the pendant wasn't yours."

Not hers. Her mother's.

His words, his tone, reached inside her and twisted her like a screw. Because the way he said it told her in no uncertain terms that the owner of that necklace *was* dead. No maybes about it.

Which meant her mother was dead.

The pain was sharp as the scab ripped off the old wound.

Then his choice of wording seeped through her grief. *I came because I needed to know the pendant wasn't yours.*

Slowly, she shook her head from side to side. "It's not mine."

She wet her lips and locked the door on her grief. She'd take it out later. Right now, she couldn't think about it.

His exhalation was long and slow. Measured. Like he was forcing himself to be calm when he wasn't.

"Why did you need to know that it wasn't mine?" she whispered. Had he carried her memory as she had carried his? That was impossible. Crazy.

"Because you were supposed to build a life." He was practically snarling. "A safe life." *You were supposed to live, not die,* he didn't say, but she heard it anyway.

She scuffed the toe of her boot against the floor and retreated behind her customary wall. "And here I thought you came looking for information."

"That's information." He was still holding her arm, not tight enough to bruise but definitely tight enough to keep her in place. With his free hand, he caught hold of a dark ringlet where it lay across her shoulder, frowning slightly as he tested the spring in the curl.

"You wanna lose a finger?" She disengaged her hair with meticulous, unhurried care and brushed his hand

aside. He let her. His strength—both physical and supernatural—was such that he could do pretty much anything he pleased. And what he pleased was to touch her, stroke her hair, study her features...all of which made her distinctly uneasy.

"Roxy." He said her name like he was tasting it, savoring the flavor. Tensing, she waited for some revelation, some declaration. Of what? She had no idea. But he when he spoke again, he didn't say anything she thought to expect. "Why did you kill Frank Marin?"

The question came out of nowhere. She blinked. Anger flared. The bastard. The lowlife, shithead bastard. "What? You figured you wouldn't get answers just plain asking, so you tried to—" She stopped, at a loss for words. Really, he hadn't done anything more, or less, than say her name. Was it his fault that it had sent a shiver of awareness sluicing through her?

Then the content of his question registered. Frank Marin was *dead*. She'd left him alive. A bit battered, but alive. "Don't know anyone by the name of Marin," she said sullenly.

"Of course not."

The silence stretched. She used the opportunity to press her supernatural borders, to reach for Frank Marin's genetic signature, to use her bizarre blood-tracking abilities. She came up empty. There was only a void where once there had been the current of life.

So it wasn't a lie. Someone *had* killed Marin. And the only thing she knew for certain was that it hadn't been her.

He tipped his head to the side and abruptly changed tack. "Who killed my brother?"

"Can't say. I never met your brother." That much she

could swear was true. She had a feeling that if she'd met another Krayl, she'd remember.

"Can't say, or won't say?"

"What are you, five? I don't know who killed your brother." The Setnakhts? The Asetian Guard? Any one of the gods and demigods fighting for supremacy in the Underworld?

His gaze came up and snagged hers. "Not particularly forthcoming, are you?"

"Can't give you answers I don't have."

"Here's the thing, Roxy." He stroked his fingers along her cheek, over the line of her jaw to her throat, then he flattened his palm against her skin. She could feel her own pulse, too hard, too loud. "I think that's a lie. I think you have plenty of answers you aren't inclined to share."

The smile he flashed her was positively chilling. He let his thumb stretch until his hand encircled the front of her neck, not pressing or hurting, just resting there. A promise. One she didn't like. She jerked away, glaring daggers. Too bad she wasn't in a position to sink a few into his black, shriveled heart.

"I can be patient," he said softly, dropping his hand to his side. Funny, she didn't feel relieved. "But until I have my answers, we're going to be joined at the hip. I hope you're in the mood for company."

"You know," she mused, "you're like a shower. For a minute, the water's all pleasant and nice, until someone flushes. Then its burning hot, and you feel like a lobster in a pot."

He blinked. Then laughed. "I suppose I should feel lucky that you compared me to the shower and not the toilet."

"Semantics." She shrugged.

The way he looked at her made her feel as if he was searching for something. Whatever it was, he found it, because a gleam of satisfaction lit his mercury-bright eyes. "We're going to get to know each other, Roxy Tam."

Not if she had any say about it.

He tucked the pendant away inside his shirt; she felt a pang to see it go. It was hers by rights. But now wasn't the time to insist on that.

"You've changed," he said after a long moment, brows drawing together in a quizzical frown.

You have no idea.

Last time he'd seen her, she'd been a naive kid. She hadn't known a thing about the Setnakhts or the Daughters of Aset, about Sutekh and soul reapers and the vast Underworld. She still didn't know everything; she'd barely scratched the surface. But she knew enough to recognize the danger of his far-superior power.

If she was a summer storm, he was a level-5 hurricane.

"You speak differently."

"I grew up. Lost the slang. Oh, and I went to college."

"Ah. You put the money I left you to good use."

"Never make assumptions. I did put it to good use, but not the way you think. I invested it." She was gratified to see a hint of surprise. "I already had a college scholarship before you ever came along."

"Did you?" He tipped his head to the side, studying her. "Your words that night led me to believe you felt a degree of hopelessness about your future."

She froze, horrified that he remembered that, but

definitely not willing to share the true source of her tirade, the guilt she'd felt—and still felt—about Rhianna. "You believed wrong."

For a long moment, he said nothing, only stared at her like he could see clear through to her soul. Not a nice feeling, to have a soul reaper examining her soul. Was he thinking it'd make a nice, light snack?

Whatever he saw made him decide to give her some space. He eased back a couple of inches and raked his fingers through the thick strands of his hair. His efforts only served to muss it up even more. The tie at his nape came away altogether and the shimmering length fell free, loose waves cut blunt to his shoulders, one strand curving along the hollow of his cheekbone.

For an instant she saw him not as a soul reaper but as a male. Handsome. Alluring. He was rough and a little unkempt with his long hair and lean features, scuffed boots and faded jeans. Wild. Frightening. Certainly not pretty-boy polished.

Dangerous on so many levels.

How many nights had she woken up in a cold sweat, torn from a nightmare where he'd come for her, ripped her chest open, taken her heart?

And how many nights had she woken from a dream where he'd come for her and saved her life? Touched her hair. Her cheek. Gentle, so gentle. Not a dream. A memory.

"Why didn't you kill me that night?" The question was out and she couldn't call it back.

He shrugged, watching her with his cold, beautiful eyes, the gray of his irises tinged in this light with purple and blue. "It wasn't your night to die."

A step and he was so close that she could smell his

skin, faintly citrus. Definitely male. She wanted to lean even closer, breathe deeper.

She didn't.

But he did. He was there against her, his face lowering until the side of his nose grazed her cheek. He breathed in. Only that. A slow inhalation. It made her pulse jump and her blood heat.

Confusion slapped her.

What the hell was she thinking? He was a creature who ripped souls from mortals and carried them to the Underworld to feed Sutekh's voracious appetite. The fact that they were darksouls yanked from human monsters didn't change the facts. Maybe he didn't limit himself to those. How was she to know?

What she *did* know was that Sutekh was Aset's nemesis, her enemy, and so he was Roxy's enemy. The foe of the entire Asetian Guard.

Which made Dagan Krayl her enemy, because he was not only Sutekh's minion but his son.

And she knew it was his job to kill.

Once he got the information he sought, he just might decide to kill *her.* Because the information he sought was ultimately about his brother's killer, and Roxy had the uneasy suspicion that maybe, just maybe, the Asetian Guard had somehow been involved.

Worse—she shuddered—what if *she'd* somehow been involved? What if one of her multitude of tasks has somehow linked to the reaper's death? It wasn't outside the realm of possibility.

Her palms were damp, and she resisted the urge to rub them on her thighs. Everything going through her head was reason enough to ignore his broad shoulders and damned inexplicable appeal.

Only she didn't step away.

Her heart twisted and froze as he shifted so his lips rested against the angle of her jaw where it met her throat. If she turned her face just a little, her lips would brush his. Horror congealed in her gut. She was close enough to trail her tongue along his lips, his jaw. The artery pulsing at his throat. How many nights had she dreamed of this?

As many as she'd dreamed of killing him.

He gave a short, huffing exhalation and drew back, the cool air of the church filling the space between them. She was breathing too fast, her heart pounding, and she could sense the thrum of his blood.

Her mouth grew dry and she ached to pull her blade, to slit his vein, to seal her mouth to that luscious fountain as his blood spurted. The song of his solidly beating pulse combined with the lure of the power he harbored; it was potent and tempting, like hundred-year-old brandy sliding down her throat.

A taste. Just one taste.

Crossing her arms over her abdomen, she tried to master the wild cadence of her heart.

Slitting a soul reaper's throat and drinking from him was *so* not a plan.

Suddenly, something changed. Shifted. His attention left her and settled on the door at the far end of the church.

The air stirred, the molecules vibrating at an altered rate. She could feel it. Someone coming.

His eyes narrowed, his expression changing, hardening, telling her that he felt it, too. She slammed the lid on the swirling eddy of emotion that clawed at her. Looked like for the moment she had bigger problems

than the bizarre repulsion-attraction she felt for Dagan Krayl.

Within seconds she heard faint crackling sounds that confirmed the soul reaper wasn't her only late-night visitor. His gaze clipped from the door to the row of windows on the far wall.

"You expecting someone?"

"No. You?"

The look he sent her was enough to confirm that whatever was out there might not be after her, but him.

"Stay behind me."

As if. Trusting someone else to protect her wasn't up there on her to-do list. Drawing her knife from its sheath once more, she held it in an easy grip.

He raised a brow. "Guess I don't need to ask if you're any good with that."

With a jerk of her chin toward his blood-soaked jeans, she gave a soft snort. "Good enough."

Reaching down, she slid a second blade from her boot.

Again, that incredible smile curved his lips, wider now, showing straight, white teeth. Of course. They couldn't be crooked and yellow. Or missing. That would be asking for too much.

"Then at least stay *beside* me."

"No promises."

The smile disappeared. "Remember, if you run, I *will* find you."

"Promises, promises." But that was just it. He made it sounds like a promise rather than a threat, as if he thought she'd *want* him to find her.

His gaze dropped to her lips, her breasts, her knives. Back to her breasts. The heat in that look singed every-where it touched.

"What? Danger cranks your handle?"

"Cranks my—" He laughed, low and dark. "Yeah. Maybe it does. Or maybe *you* do."

Before she could think or move or clip him in the jaw, he curled his fingers around the back of her neck and dipped his head. Then his mouth was on hers, smooth, firm lips opening on her own, his tongue in her mouth. Sweet heat.

A tight coil of hard-edged lust twisted low in her gut.

She had a knife in each hand, or she'd have grabbed his ass.

Wrong place. Wrong time.

Didn't matter.

His fingers were rough and calloused on the back of her neck, his mouth hot on hers. He didn't touch her anywhere else. Not hips or thighs—and damn, she wanted to press up against him until there wasn't a molecule of air between them. He kissed her like he knew her, knew every secret part of her. Exactly like he'd done in her dreams.

Her skin felt like it was on fire. And her underwear grew damp. From a kiss. One hungry, luscious kiss.

He withdrew. She chased him, running the tip of her tongue along the corner of his mouth, the squared edges of his teeth. She pushed deep, wanting more of the taste of him. She'd never tasted anything so damned, fucking good.

The air around them crackled with supernatural power. Not his or hers. Something else.

Jerking away, she stared at him, chest heaving, senses humming. Pupils dilated and dark, he watched her, waiting for something. What?

Deliberately, she wiped the back of her hand across her mouth, her fingers still curled around the hilt of her knife.

He dipped his chin toward her hand and grinned.

"You're gorgeous when you're stabbing things, Roxy Tam."

CHAPTER ELEVEN

O you who bring the ferryboat of Re,
Strengthen your rope in the north wind.
Ferry upstream to the Island of Fire
Beside the realm of the dead,
Collect this magic from wherever it may be

—The Egyptian Book of the Dead, Chapter 24

LOKAN KRAYL TRIED TO LIFT his head. Once. Twice. He lay there, panting, his muscles refusing to obey the commands of his brain. Embarrassment was his first reaction. Anger his second. He didn't recall ever being this weak. This feeble.

Or his emotions being this far outside his control.

The ground at his back was cold and hard, the sky above him heavy with clouds. Not white or gray. Reddish-brown—earthworm-red—the edges stained a darker hue.

Again, he tried to lift his head, this attempt a success only because he wouldn't settle for anything less. Teeth gritted, he stared down at himself, waiting for his eyes to focus.

There was no blood on his hands.

Good. That was good.

Wasn't it?

The skin of his chest and belly was smooth. Undam-

aged. Intact. No tattoo. No blood. Somehow, that didn't make him as happy as it ought to. Problem was, he couldn't recall why.

His head dropped back, cracking against the ground. Another bit of information. Whatever he was lying on was as hard as concrete. He rolled to the side, paused to catch his breath and then pushed up on all fours, head spinning, thoughts reeling. Well, there you go; it *was* concrete.

He took stock. Ten fingers. Ten toes. And all major parts in between. He didn't hurt. Not exactly. But he wouldn't go so far as to say he felt good.

Panting, he held his position, knees and palms pressed to the cold slab, head hanging between his locked elbows. Finally, he pushed back on his haunches and stared out at the endless expanse of water that stretched smooth and serene before him. There wasn't a wave—not even a ripple—to disturb the surface.

He didn't know where he was, didn't remember why he was here. Fighting the bile that clawed at the back of his throat and the dizziness that kept him on his knees rather than his feet, he stared at the horizon.

Shouldn't be like this. His wounds had healed. He ought to feel stronger.

His wounds. Wounded by what?

He remembered the tattoo. Black. All black. On his chest and down his belly, though it wasn't there now. And he remembered the blades. Cutting him. His skin tearing away—

Cold sweat slicked his skin.

Yeah. That was a memory he could do without.

Chanting. There'd been chanting. And a voice he ought to know. A voice he *did* know. Whose? The memory danced away, beyond his reach.

He kept his gaze locked on the horizon. Lifting his brows and widening his eyes, he tried to focus. Time passed, unmeasured, barely marked. And then there was something there. In the distance. A dark spot. It shifted and grew, sliding away from the line that demarcated sky and water, moving toward him.

Slowly, the spot took on shape and form. A longboat, both bow and stern high and curved. There were neither oars nor oarsmen, only a solitary figure balanced in the center, dark garbed and cowled, standing with a long, narrow pole in its hands.

A river.

A boat.

And, of course, a ferryman. There just had to be a ferryman.

Lokan pressed his palms hard against his thighs and struggled to his feet, swaying in place as the boat moved noiselessly toward him, finally gliding up to beach the bow on the sloping concrete. He could make out details now: The grain of the wood. The smell, like a basement that'd had a slow leak for years. The fact that the ferryman's head was turned the wrong way around on his body, so he watched the place he had come from rather than where he was going.

That had to be inconvenient.

His gaze dropped to the ferryman's hands where they curled around the pole. He could see the tiny bones, bare and skeletal and white, denuded of flesh and skin.

Lokan swallowed. The boat. The ferryman. The water reflecting the bleeding sky.

Okay, he knew where he was. Knew what he needed to do. Somehow, he'd landed in Hades's turf. Not great, but not as bad as it could be. Hades was no ally of

Sutekh or his sons, but Osiris's or Xaphan's realms would have been worse.

The fact that he knew all this was a relief. He knew the names of the forty-two gods. He knew the names of the deities of the Greeks and Romans. The Voodoo Baron Samedi. The Mayan Ah Puch. And all the others.

He knew those things and he knew his place among those who juggled and jockeyed for position in the Underworld's hierarchy.

Yes, he knew that now. He was Sutekh's son.

And looking at the boat before him and the river so wide he could see no land on the far side, he knew he was taking the long way home. He wasn't used to taking this route to the Underworld—soul reapers generally got to bypass the theatrics—but needs must.

The ferryman extended one skeletal hand, the draped sleeve of his robe falling back as he turned his palm up. Looking for payment. Lokan turned his head, only now noticing the endless line of shuffling mortals who moved toward the boat, each paying their pennies in turn.

Glancing down, he realized for the first time that he was naked. No clothes. No pockets. No coins to pay the fare.

That complicated things.

Well, he'd just have to trade on his father's name to pay for passage. Not that he liked that plan. But he didn't want to take the time to come up with a better one, given that he was feeling a whole boatload of urgency to get back inside Sutekh's borders.

Back to his brothers. The prospect brought a dark chill to his heart, and he couldn't explain that. Couldn't say why.

Stepping forward, he rasped, "I am Lokan Krayl,

youngest son of Sutekh, Lord of Chaos." Like this father needed any introduction. He was the boss of all bosses.

Despite the impressive introduction, the ferryman didn't so much as turn his head. Just held out his skeletal hand to the next mortal in line. Lokan saw now that the bones were held together by cobwebs. Tiny spiders, black and glistening—thousands upon thousands of them—crawled along the gossamer strands, past small, squared wrist bones to disappear in the long black sleeves of the ferryman's robe.

Cobwebs and spiders. He frowned. Shook his head. That wasn't right, was it?

Each in turn, the mortals dropped two coins in the ferryman's hand as they boarded, and he tucked them away, moving so quickly the action was little more than a blur.

Lokan took another step, directly in the path of the next mortal, a woman with smooth, fair skin, hair as black as onyx and denim-blue eyes. Seeing her here made him horribly afraid, not for himself but for someone else. For her? No, he didn't think so.

For an instant, he was certain that he knew her. And then he was certain he did not. He cleared his throat, tried again. "I need passage. Sutekh will pay." He hoped. One could never be sure his father would come through.

No one looked at him. Not the dead and yet-to-be-judged. Not the ferryman. No one. Annoyed, Lokan glanced over his shoulder at the woman—

—who shuffled through him as though he were made of air.

Through him.

And he knew that only because he saw it. He didn't feel a thing. Not a damned thing.

Annoyance shifted to wariness.

Something wasn't right.

He was a soul reaper. Son of Sutekh, spawned on a mortal woman. He was both alive and dead, mortal and not. He could traverse the realms at will: the Underworld, the world of man. There were few barriers to one such as he—that was the whole reason for his existence, and that of his brothers. They could go where the all-powerful gods and demigods of the Underworld could not.

His form should be as solid here as it was Topworld.

But it wasn't. It *wasn't*.

So what the fuck was going on?

Lokan closed his eyes and reached for his brothers, for the mental connection that bound them, the ability to touch the edges of each others consciousness. Not exactly telepathy; they couldn't speak in sentences and words. But they could sense if one of them was in distress.

He pushed the limits of his ability, but there was no answer. The connection was gone. And he had never felt loss such as he felt in that instant.

His heart cranked into superspeed. His mouth was as dry as dirt.

Stumbling forward, he reached for the boat, closing his fingers on the bow.

But he didn't.

There was nothing there. No boat. No river. No line of endless dead.

"Sutekh," he screamed, and again, "Sutekh!" The lapping of the water against the boat's hull answered his cry. And then that, too, disappeared, leaving him in choking darkness. No scents. No sounds. Nothing.

There was nothing.

Except the mind-numbing edge of his panic.

Toronto, Canada

PYOTR OFFERED A SHORT NOD to the guard positioned outside Djeserit's office door. The man took a single step to the right, effectively blocking Pyotr's path.

Anger sluiced through his veins, cold and sharp. He mastered it, giving nothing away. After all, the gorilla was merely doing his job. No sense in venting rage on an underling. He would save it and feed it and wait for the appropriate time to unleash it on Djeserit herself.

Pyotr stopped a polite distance away, and said, "I believe I am expected."

At that moment, there was an audible click as Djeserit released the lock on the door. Pyotr looked straight at the pin on the guard's tie and smiled for the camera. Idiot. Did she think he was unaware of her games? He knew about her spy cameras and the button under the edge of her desk that she used to release her door lock so she wouldn't actually have to stand and cross the room.

Djeserit was no fool. He never underestimated her. But predictability was her downfall.

Entering her office, he suppressed the urge to swipe his arm across the glass top of her desk, sending all her papers and treasures flying about. Instead, he lifted a pen that had fallen to the carpet and carried it to her, using that as an excuse to round the desk and loom over her.

With a smile, he set the pen down and said, "What have you done with our friend?"

Djeserit blinked, a slow lowering and raising of her

lids that made the first ember of unease flicker to life in Pyotr's gut. He'd thought this was her doing, that he was unable to reach the man he sought because Djeserit had somehow blocked him.

Her reaction told him that was fallacy.

She didn't know a damned thing.

"What friend would that be?" she asked.

"The friend who assisted us in skinning our last victim," Pyotr hissed.

Her head jerked up. Her nostrils flared. She didn't like to think of that. Likely, she preferred he not mention it at all. It was a dangerous thing they had done, a maniacal chance they had taken. But it had been necessary.

Then she mastered her emotions, hid her thoughts.

"You refer to Marin." Her expression shifted once more, a gleam of conceit lighting her dark eyes. She was the cat that swallowed the canary. Or so she believed. "Marin is dead. Your information is dated, my dear."

Pyotr said nothing for a moment, only rested his hand on the back of her outrageous, ergonomic chair and leaned close until mere inches separated them.

"I am not your dear," he said softly. Did she think him so inept as to lack key facts? Did she think he had not orchestrated every step of Marin's demise, his hand on the strings of the marionettes rather than on the knife? "And I am well aware that Frank Marin met an unfortunate fate."

No loss. He was actually quite pleased with the outcome. Given that the only one pounding on the door of the Temple of Setnakht was one lonely underling from the Daughters of Aset, he felt safe entertaining the possibility that Mr. Marin had revealed nothing of import before his death. And Ms. Tam had added nothing fur-

ther during her visit several days past; if she had, she would have been back by now, with reinforcements.

"To whom do you refer, then?" Djeserit stared at him owlishly.

Pyotr gritted his teeth. Was she baiting him? Testing him? She knew exactly who he would recruit for the task of skinning the lamb. "His brother."

Djeserit's dark eyes glittered, and his gut curdled. She *did* know something he did not. She had information that had failed to reach him. How?

"He is dead, as well," she murmured, her expression utterly flat.

Pyotr jerked back, leaving go his hold on the back of the chair so forcefully that it rocked and creaked. He clenched his fists against his thighs and then realized what his action betrayed and forced them to relax. Here was a complication he had not anticipated. Frank Marin's involvement had been fairly common knowledge. A calculated but necessary risk. So his death came as no real surprise. But no one had known of the brother. No one save himself and Djeserit.

"Did you have him terminated?" *Without my permission? Without my agreement?* Rage simmered, but he held it under tight rein. Where was his control, his calm?

He would not devolve to a gibbering, ranting ass. He was better than that.

Djeserit frowned. "I was planning to ask you the self-same question." There was no guile in her reply. Having known her for more than two decades, he believed he would spot a lie. She was telling the truth. She had not ordered Joe Marin's death. And neither had he.

"If neither of us—"

"His heart was taken." She cut him off.

Incredulity swelled. "I see."

She nodded, a slow, ponderous movement. "Torn from his breast. Which suggests that all our careful plans were for naught. He was killed for his darksoul in a completely unrelated and random act." Her face creased as she offered her repulsive smile. "Chance. Fate. Serendipity. It's almost…funny."

"Serendipity is defined as a gift for making useful discoveries quite by accident, so I make the assumption you refer to someone else's serendipitous act, rather than the congregation's?" He barely managed to keep the rancor from his tone.

Again, Djeserit blinked, her lids lowering then rising with exaggerated sluggishness, a habit that annoyed Pyotr to no end. "Serendipitous for the soul reaper who discovered Joe Marin."

Pyotr grunted his assent. A soul reaper just happened to find Joe Marin and kill him? Harvest his darksoul? Despite Djeserit's assertion that it was mere chance, a coincidence, Pyotr could not find it in himself to agree. Someone was playing puppet master. Someone had sent the soul reaper to Joe Marin. Who?

That was the question of the hour.

"We must find the child." Djeserit stared at him, eyes glittering, as though waiting for him to challenge her assertion.

"An excellent suggestion." He played the role of fool; it was not one that sat well on his shoulders, but it was a necessary concession. He had no desire for her to know that his own personal contacts were already looking. They had a lead. They would have her soon.

The child had been an important pawn. Then, task

complete, she had been rendered of no further use. Still, Pyotr was ever one to plan for all possibilities, and so he had had Frank Marin take her rather than killing her outright. The fool was meant to keep her safe for any future need.

But Marin had screwed up, stopping overnight in a place he was not supposed to stop and hence setting the whole plan awry. Pyotr had sent a contingent to retrieve the girl from Marin, but they had failed to complete their mission before Roxy stepped in. Which left Marin dead and the girl missing.

All very inconvenient, but fixable.

"Do you know where she is?" he asked.

Djeserit's lips thinned. Perhaps she saw through his ruse. Perhaps not.

"Do *you?*" She tapped the tip of her right index finger against the glass of her desk. It was enough to betray her unease. It was enough to tell Pyotr that she, too, had people looking.

"No." And that was truth. He didn't know. Not yet. But ask him in a matter of hours, and the truth would change. Circumstances would change. But one thing would remain constant. "We must stick by our plan. Detail by detail, we must not waver."

Djeserit nodded. "We will open a place for a new soul reaper in the ranks."

"Precisely," Pyotr lied. Let her think what she would. He had no intention of sharing his true plan. In time, she would know.

"We must continue to trust each other, Djeserit. There are only two mortals who know the truth of what passed that night, the truth of the soul reaper's death. Only two. You and I." Which gave them both foolproof

protection against betrayal each by the other. "I cannot sacrifice you without betraying my own involvement, and the same holds true of you. It is a perfect failsafe, yes?"

Had Djeserit possessed eyebrows, they would have risen. As it was, her forehead creased in a series of horizontal lines. Then she laughed, the sound tinkling and light, the only truly pretty thing about her. "Agreed."

He smiled to hear her say it.

The only thing that could ever guarantee complete protection for either one of them was not death of their co-conspirator, but complete annihilation. There must be no soul, no heart left to tell the tale.

How to accomplish Djeserit's annihilation was quite the conundrum.

CHAPTER TWELVE

YOU'RE GORGEOUS WHEN you're stabbing things, Roxy Tam.

Dagan thought she was gorgeous? Roxy hated the little surge of pleasure his words evoked. Almost as much as she hated the way her lips still tingled and her pulse still raced. The taste of him was on her tongue, and she wanted more.

"Fuck you," she muttered.

"Love to oblige. It's been a while. But this hardly seems the time or place." His gaze raked her, sending her thoughts spinning all kinds of places they had no business going. Then he leaned over and flicked off the light, cloaking them in darkness. The air stirred as he moved, shadow on shadow, his arm brushing hers. "Unless you're a fan of having an audience."

She pressed her lips together, willing herself to be silent.

"Define a while." Damn. She just had to go and ask. Why was she doing this? Baiting him? It was like stepping into a lion's cage, hugging an armload of raw steak. Even if she dropped the steak, she'd still be lion bait, covered in blood.

Again, that low laugh. Like sin.

"Longer than a month, less than a decade."

Well, that told her a fat lot of nothing. His words made images flash through her thoughts—skin to hot skin, his hips flush with hers, clothes on, then clothes off, bump and grind. Damn, why did she have the urge to end his dry spell?

Actually, she knew exactly why.

Because for the past eleven years he'd been the main feature in her x-rated girlie version of a wet dream. And for the past eleven seconds she'd had her tongue down his throat and it'd been far better than anything she'd fantasized about. What she really wanted to do was forget whatever was out there, whatever was coming for her, and focus on him, focus on now, rip his shirt open, flatten her palms against his chest, open her mouth on his skin, sink her teeth in his flesh as he pushed inside her.

She didn't have words for how that made her feel. Pissed off. At him. At herself. Embarrassed. Wary. So she changed the subject.

"What's out there?"

"Nothing good. And there's more than one."

Roxy opened her senses and reached for the unknown. Energy crackled through her like a half dozen cans of Red Bull hitting her system all at once, prickling and dancing and leaving the fine hairs on her arms standing upright. The something that was out there was moving in fast, and it was definitely more than just one something.

"Have you gone up against a supernatural before?" He paused. "Other than me?" Definitely amusement in his tone. Probably because she'd just been plastered against him about as up close as she could get. Or because she hadn't exactly gone up against him the first

time they met. More like sat there and let him happen to her.

"I've taken on a few Topworlders with a hint of supernatural." None of them any stronger than Frank Marin. And, like him, they hadn't proved much of a challenge. "Once, a lesser demon who works as an enforcer for Hades." Which had been a bit more than a challenge.

"How'd that turn out?"

"I won." Barely. There had been a heart-stopping moment or two where she hadn't been too sure that she'd be walking away from that one. It had been a good wake-up call as to the limitations of her supernatural enhancements. Yes, she was stronger than the average human, female or male, but that strength paled in the face of power such as that wielded by a soul reaper. So she'd trained harder, learned to think smarter and whittled away at her limitations. "We had a disagreement about three teenaged girls and what their future might hold. Asshole wanted to sell them to Asmodeus as psy-whores."

"Not a nice life, and certainly not a long one. I assume you had something different in mind?"

"I wanted them to head back to high school."

"Hmm. You sent them back to a normal life." He fell silent, the quiet lasting long enough that she thought he'd run out of things to say. Then, "What's out there is not like anything you've encountered. Do exactly as I say and you won't die here tonight."

"S'okay. I'm pretty adept at keeping myself safe." And that would include hiding behind him if it proved prudent, or running if that was her best choice.

She turned her face to the windows, searching for

any clue about what was coming. Didn't help. She could see only the dark outlines of her furniture and the night sky beyond the glass. There were no stars, no moon. It was too cloudy for that. But despite what she couldn't see, she knew that whatever was out there wasn't lesser anything. The vibe coming off them was incredible, and the vibe coming off Dagan Krayl didn't make the situation any easier to read.

"Just out of curiosity, why didn't we both run when we had the chance?"

"Because whatever brought these particular visitors to your door is probably something I'm interested in." His tone was dryer than a Bombay Sapphire martini.

Fair enough. Her thoughts were running parallel to his; that was pretty much the exact reason why she hadn't taken off in a burst of speed. Great, she was thinking like a soul reaper. She wasn't sure that ought to make her proud.

Seconds ticked past. "What, no smart-ass quip?"

"I'm all out," she muttered.

He made a sound that might have been a laugh before letting out a soft hiss. He pushed her back with the flat of his hand. Then he hooked a foot behind her leg and held her there, as though he expected her to leap to the fore.

She didn't argue, not by word or action. She wasn't so stupid as to jump into the fray before she assessed the risks.

"Fine by me. You stick your neck out, Krayl. I'll watch your style, judge theirs." She paused, considered and opted for the truth. "And, yeah, I'll run like hell if I think I'm outnumbered and outgunned."

Because that's what she'd been taught to do. Avoid

capture. Besides, she didn't exactly trust him to step up and keep her safe. Why would she? She'd made a habit of trusting no one but herself.

Silence. "Smart girl." A rough whisper laced with a smile. Another beat of silence, then he said, "Dae."

"Excuse me?"

"Don't call me Krayl. My name is Dagan. I prefer that you call me Dae."

Wasn't that just perfect? A soul reaper with a frat-boy nickname.

Roxy shook her head. "You can call me Ms. Tam."

And then she said nothing more because Dagan Krayl—Dae—tensed and shifted. They were out there now. Whatever *they* were. She took her cue from his posture and the hum of adrenaline coming off him, bringing her knives into defensive position.

"Don't bother," he said. "Steel will barely even slow them down."

"That's why my knives aren't steel. They're tungsten carbide sintered with cobalt. Hard enough to cut bone."

"And useless in this fight." His tone—part amused, part exasperated—got under her skin like grit in a scrape. "Hardness has no relevance—"

"That's debatable." Lord, he made it so easy.

The amusement disappeared, leaving only exaspera-tion. "You can't cut smoke and flame."

"Smoke and flame." Her gaze shot to the window. Dark shadows inside, darker night beyond. "Is that what's out there?"

"Might as well be." His body shifted against hers, tense muscle, alert and ready. "Shh. They're here. There are more than I expected."

"More what?"

He ignored her question, grabbed her wrist and hauled her toward the back door. "If you value your home, move. Confronting them inside won't leave you much more than ash and blackened stone to sift through."

She could smell it now, the sting of sulfur or maybe brimstone. Whatever it was, it was something that burned. "What are they?"

"Xaphan's concubines," he muttered, tearing open the door and shoving her through. She did a quick scan of the dark yard and saw nothing but the silhouettes of the trees, branches outstretched like skeletal fingers.

Ducking out, she eased into the shadows, careful, watchful. He did the same, so close his arm pressed against hers as he scanned the perimeter.

"Xaphan?" she whispered, hugging the house as she moved along the porch. That was the same name she'd heard at Tesso's Bar and Grill.

Dagan's reply was soft enough that she had to strain to make out the words. "Keeper of the furnaces and the braziers that light the lakes of fire."

Like that told her anything. Though the Daughters of Aset taught their foot soldiers little enough, Roxy had taken a couple of college courses on mythology and religion, and she had also done some research on her own. So she knew that pretty much every territory in the Underworld had lakes of fire. Which ones were Xaphan's?

Didn't matter right now. What mattered was knowing exactly what she was about to go up against. Going in blind wasn't the best option. "And his concubines are...?"

"You don't want to know." He gave her a little shove as they reached the corner of the house. "Go."

She went, darting around the corner and sprinting along the wooden boards, only to skid to a stop halfway across the wide porch.

Yeah, he was right. She *didn't* want to know, but it was too late for that. Her gut clenched.

Perched on the porch rail, toes curled so long black talons bit into the soft cedar, was a creature both lovely and grotesque. Her skin had the smooth, supple look of expensive leather, a deep burgundy red, the color of embers dancing against blackest night. She squatted on the rail, powerful thighs flexed, short black skirt hiked as high as it would go, stopping just short of baring her hoo-hah for the world to see. Black and sleek, her hair cascaded in a straight curtain over her shoulders. Her features were small and fine, and her smile bared pointed, white teeth, perfectly formed. Perfectly deadly.

From the darkness and shadow behind her emerged more of her kind, equally lovely, equally frightful. And they were all looking at Roxy.

Dandy.

"Over the rail," Dae snarled with a none-too-gentle shove at the small of her back.

Roxy didn't wait for him to repeat the directive.

Slapping her palm against wood, she vaulted the rail and came down like a gymnast, knees bent, feet planted for less than a heartbeat before she tore toward the woods, running flat out.

A quick glance told her he was right behind her. Why was *he* running? Why didn't he stay and fight? A soul reaper was one hell of a powerful being.

"I'm trying to lead them away and spare your damned house," he snarled, answering the question she hadn't asked.

"What are they?"

"Fire genies."

Creatures she wasn't familiar with. But now wasn't the time for an in-depth chat. Roxy bolted for the thick woods at the south end of the yard, her long legs eating the distance.

"Not so fast, Otherkin." The words came from too close. Something snagged her ankle and she went down, hard. The smell of burning leather stung her nostrils. Her shoulder slammed against the ground. Her chin bumped dirt and her teeth snapped together so hard that she expected to feel tiny chips of enamel on her tongue.

Twisting at the waist, she jerked her trapped limb and found it held in a solid grip. She was slipping and sliding as she rolled, and she struggled to right herself, ramming her free heel against the earth for leverage. She surged to a sitting position, and came face-to-face with the fire genie that was holding her ankle.

The smell of sulfur was stronger now, stinging her nose. A whitish-gray curl of smoke twined up through the cool night air between them.

From the corner of her eye, Roxy saw a tangle of limbs that appeared to be Dagan with at least three adversaries piled on his back.

She had the thought that she'd have to take down the genie that held her before she'd be of any help to him.

Then she took a hard look and realized that he didn't look like he was having any trouble fending them off. He didn't need her help.

And even if he did, she had one priority. Herself.

She couldn't let attraction or her history with him alter that fact. *Me first* was the key to her survival.

Xaphan's concubine tightened her grip and shook Roxy's leg like a dog at a bone. Her ankle felt hot, too hot, like she'd stepped way too close to a bonfire.

"Smells like barbeque," Roxy quipped, ramming her knee into the underside of the genie's chin. The cloth of her jeans burned away in a shower of crimson sparks, leaving a hole at the knee rimmed in blackened denim and her bared skin stinging and blistering. "Fuck. I loved these jeans."

The genie's head snapped back, but her grip on Roxy's boot tightened. Then her chin dropped, and she smiled, narrowed eyes glowing a deep orange, lips peeling back to bare those dreadful white teeth.

Reaching for her knife, the reaction honed to instinct without thought, Roxy tasted the bitter edge of panic as she came up empty. Her stomach dropped. She'd been holding both knives. Her sheath was bare. *Bare.* She'd lost her blades, dropped them when she fell.

"Looking for this?" The genie held her knife aloft, and to Roxy's horror the metal began to glow, then curl and finally drip, the heat of the genie's hand enough to turn it into tungsten carbide soup.

She looked around, desperate. As far as weapons went, her choices were limited.

Frantic, Roxy clawed at the ground, scratching up dirt and pebbles. Little treasures. She flung them at the fire genie's eyes.

Xaphan's concubine reared back with a startled cry, swiping her open palm across her face. Not waiting for an invitation, Roxy booted her in the chest, rolled and

planted both palms flat on the ground. She heaved herself into a crouch, then surged for the tree line.

And got nowhere.

With a cry, she fell hard, her foot still trapped in the genie's curled talons.

Damn, that creature could take a shitload of punishment.

Heat flared in her tethered ankle. Roxy bit back a cry. Her ankle was roasting, seared like chicken on a grill, the burn of the genie's grip seeping through her leather boot, accompanied by a disturbing hiss and sizzle. Pain beyond pain licked at her skin, plunging deep, clear to the bone. She kicked and jerked, but the genie held her.

Only willpower and gritted teeth kept her from screaming in agony.

Roxy shot a glance at Dagan. No help there. He was buried under a pile of concubines that clung to his back and shoulders, arms and legs tangled so Roxy couldn't even tell how many there were.

The pain in her ankle intensified, white-hot agony, and she did scream then, a short cry that she strangled almost as soon as it was born. Dagan's head jerked up and his gaze met hers. Lips peeled back in rage, he reared up. The fire genies tumbled to the ground, hissing and spitting like angry cats.

"Leave go, Naamah. If she is damaged, you answer to me." He directed his words to the one holding Roxy even as he kicked back, caught one of the others in the gut and sent her flying. A second creature clawed his leg, talons tearing through denim, leaving bloody runnels in their wake.

Naamah. He knew her name. "Nothing like a re-

union," Roxy muttered. "What, you two go to high school together?"

Neither one even glanced at her.

"You know my name."

"Your reputation," Dagan corrected, and Roxy revised her thinking. Guess this wasn't a reunion after all.

"You think I fear you, soul reaper?" Naamah's words were laced with scorn, but the heat in Roxy's ankle eased.

"I think you *should.*" Roxy felt the icy promise of those words.

But Naamah only laughed.

Interesting. If Xaphan's concubines were here for Dagan, they'd know he wasn't just any reaper but one of Sutekh's sons. Since they seemed to be oblivious of that fact, Roxy figured they were here for *her.* But she had no idea why.

With the fire genie's attention diverted, Roxy saw her chance. Hauling back, she punched her as hard as she could in the throat. The grip on her ankle loosened. Roxy pressed her advantage and summoned every ounce of her preternatural strength and speed. Catching a fistful of Naamah's long, black hair, she yanked as hard as she could, then slammed her cupped palm against an exposed ear. The resulting howl was more rage than pain. Still, it was satisfying.

Roxy's own yelp was exactly the opposite, as her palm bubbled and blistered at the contact.

Heart pounding, chest heaving, she cradled her freshly burned hand against her chest and scrambled away. She made it three feet before Naamah slammed her open palms against the ground. Flames arrowed across the dry grass, then burst into a ring of fire.

Roxy spun right, left, her escape cut off by a wall

of fire on all sides. She was trapped, the heat coming at her from every angle.

Through the fire, she saw Dagan surge toward her. One of the downed concubines threw her weight against the side of his knee. There was a sharp crack. Roxy winced. Classic football tackle; easiest way to shred the ligaments. That had to hurt. He didn't even flinch, just kept coming, the other fire genies surging behind him.

"Hold," Naamah ordered as her followers moved en masse. They held.

Simon says, "Stop."

It might have been funny under different circumstances.

Naamah turned to Dagan. "The Otherkin could have survived without a foot, but not without her skin." She offered a tight smile. "Shall I burn it away? Leave her a bloody, oozing mass?"

The ring of fire reached higher, closer, fingers of flame flicking sparks on Roxy's clothes. She slapped at the embers as they ignited. But she wasn't without recourse. She figured that if she rolled herself into a tight ball, she could somersault out of here with only moderate wear and tear. Taking a deep breath, she readied herself for the move—

"You damage her, I damage you." Something in Dagan's tone made Roxy freeze. Maybe it was the utter lack of bravado—he was making a statement of fact, not a threat. Whatever it was, she wasn't the only one who sat up and took notice. The ring of fire inched away.

True to form, Naamah laughed, but the sound was hollow. "And why do you think that your silly threats are of any consequence to me, underling?"

Dagan offered a tight, close-lipped smile. "I am Krayl."

Dead silence greeted that pronouncement, then Naamah peered at him, eyes narrowed, and asked suspiciously, "Which Krayl?"

"The eldest."

Burgundy skin paled to ashy gray, and the fire genie sucked in a sharp breath as she reared back. She made a quick gesture and the ring of fire receded further still—not completely, but enough that Roxy could take a breath without choking on heat and smoke.

"I beg pardon, son of Sutekh." Contrition warred with arrogance in her tone. To Roxy, it sounded like arrogance won.

"I do not grant pardon." Dagan shot a glance at the ring of fire. "Put it out."

The fire genie snarled, her eyes glowing an orange so bright and hot that Roxy could almost feel the temperature going up. But that was the extent of her reaction, flash without substance. Guess Sutekh's son outranked Xaphan's concubine.

Seeing their leader's reaction, the others surged forward, lips peeled back from pointed teeth, eyes glittering like fireflies, but a barked command—"Stay"—froze them in place.

Then Naamah rounded on Dagan, her entire frame vibrating with rage. "The *capo bastone* will be interested to know that one of Sutekh's sons has stepped over the line."

"'*Capo bastone*'? That's a joke, right?"

Roxy didn't get the reference, but Dagan seemed to find it amusing.

The fire genie stared at him, then finally shrugged

and rolled her eyes. "Xaphan's crazy for anything in mafia entertainment. *The Godfather. The Sopranos.* Had me buy him the complete series and a *'badda-bing'* T-shirt last time I was Topworld. Thirty-three discs. He insists we use the terminology. It's easy enough to pacify him."

That got Roxy's attention. If Xaphan's concubines could wander around Topworld, that told her two things. First off, they weren't as powerful as all that. The most powerful Underworlders had to stay put. They couldn't come to the mortal realm at all. They could only travel to each other's realms if specific invitations were issued and protocols followed.

Except for soul reapers, of course. They didn't seem to obey any laws but their own.

Second, it meant that the fire genies were able to alter their appearance to look more human. They couldn't exactly walk into Wal-Mart looking like demons from hell.

Dagan shook his head. "I don't care what Xaphan's interested in. On any level. Tell him anything you want about Sutekh's son stepping over imaginary lines. I'm not the one who's shoving my nose in someone else's concern." His tone hardened. "And tell him the girl is mine."

His assertion got Roxy's back up. She wasn't a girl, and she belonged to no one but herself. Still, she didn't think this was the time to argue. They weren't paying a shred of attention to her. So she ducked her head, wrapped her arms tight and somersaulted out of the burning circle. She came up gasping as her weight pressed on her burned ankle, singed leather rubbing blistered, oozing flesh. A slap here and there put out

the glowing embers that had caught her clothes. She inched back, babying her wound, trying to draw as little attention to herself as possible as the other fire genies watched their leader, obviously waiting for direction.

"The girl is yours?" Naamah sounded genuinely perplexed. Her gaze flicked to Roxy, who froze, squelching the surge of frustration at having been caught slinking off. Couldn't they have kept bickering until she had a solid head start? "Where is she, Otherkin? Where did you stash her?"

"Who?"

"The girl." Xaphan's concubine was clearly holding on to her temper by a thin thread.

"What girl?" Roxy asked, in unison with Dagan.

"What did that worthless piece of trash tell you?" Naamah demanded as she stepped forward.

Dagan shifted to block her path.

"Which worthless piece of trash would that be?" Roxy spread her hands, palms up. "I seem to know quite a few."

"Frank Marin."

What was it with everyone wanting info about Marin? Her eyes shifted to Dagan, but he was watching the other fire genies. They were huddled in a group, leaning forward. She had the thought that they were held back only by a thin, imaginary thread and that when it snapped they'd come at her like a pack of wild dogs.

"He didn't tell me much of anything—"

"And even if he did, you have nothing to share." Dagan interjected, sending her a hard look.

Roxy shrugged. "Yeah. What he said…"

Naamah looked back and forth between the two of them. "The girl is nothing to you," she said to Dagan. "Nothing. A mere human." She turned her gaze to Roxy. "Tell me where you left her."

Left her? Damn. Understanding dawned. They weren't here for Dagan. And they weren't here for her.

They really were here for "the girl." They were here for *Dana*.

She had no idea if Dagan knew what was going on. His expression was ruthlessly neutral and he kept any further questions to himself, probably saving them up like pennies in a jar.

But Roxy had pretty much forced the puzzle pieces together till they clicked. The genie knew about Marin, and she knew about Dana. In that instant, Roxy was damned glad she'd anticipated trouble—not that she'd known exactly what form that trouble would take—and asked Calliope to get the kid and her mom to a safe house. Which explained why the fire genies couldn't find her. Because Dana wasn't where they expected her to be, and Calliope was way too savvy to leave a trail of breadcrumbs.

But why was everyone so interested in that kid? And how had Frank Marin ended up with her in his closet?

The closet. The motel—

"You were there." At Roxy's accusation, Naamah offered a Cheshire Cat smile, pretty much confirming that the dark shape she'd seen outside Marin's motel room had been one of Xaphan's concubines. Probably this one. "You went in after I left…" *You saw me with the kid.*

"We missed each other by seconds."

"You two have met before?" Dagan sounded anything but patient.

"In a manner of speaking," Roxy answered at the same time Naamah said, "Shut your mouth, Otherkin."

"How'd you find me?" Roxy asked. Someone had sent these creatures to find her, in order to find Dana.

"It was easy enough to ask around, Otherkin. Your name, your face…they're well known among the Topworld grunts." Again with the creepy smile. "Big Ralph had a great deal to say. Amazing how much a man will talk when you got your mouth around his—"

Roxy shuddered and cut her off. "Thanks. I can do without the details."

The fact that her face was known wasn't news to her. It was one of her main duties to liaise with those "grunts"—humans with just a whisper of supernatural blood, and sometimes none at all—who did the Topworld dirty work for the more powerful Lords of the Underworld.

"You must have little value to your handlers," Naamah taunted. "Finding you was no challenge at all. There are few shields in place to hide your identity."

And that wasn't news to her, either. What was the point in being a liaison if no one could find you to liaise with?

If Xaphan's head bitch meant the information as a barb, she missed the mark. The Asetian Guard wasn't about to waste resources. Roxy wasn't a fish worth frying. Which was actually why she was so good at her job. She usually flew under the radar, asking questions, getting answers.

"Guess you're not too efficient, then," Roxy replied,

syrupy sweet. "Otherwise, why'd it take you so long to look me up for a visit? It's been...what? A week?"

The other fire genies hissed and snarled, but Roxy kept her gaze locked on Naamah, who was, in her opinion, her single greatest threat at the moment. She hoped Dagan was watching her back and would hold off the others if it came to it. Not that she trusted him, but he definitely wanted something from her, so he had a vested interest in keeping her alive. For now.

What the hell? The Setnakhts, the Asetian Guard and now Xaphan—a completely new and unfamiliar player to the game—were all interested in Dana. She was one in-demand little girl. A kid everyone wanted. And Roxy had left her unguarded, unaware, safe—or perhaps not so safe—in the arms of her sweet, flutter-brain of a mother who'd cried and cooed and offered Roxy cookies and milk.

Shit. What the hell had she been thinking?

But that was just it. She hadn't exactly been doing mental gymnastics. She'd been following orders. Rescuing the kid and taking her back to her mother had been secondary. Her main assignment had been to get information from Marin so the Asetian Guard could use it to make certain the dead reaper stayed dead.

Marin hadn't been particularly forthcoming, and it looked like she might have saved the kid only to leave her in worse danger. Not the most glowing success of her career.

But at least she'd had the foresight to ask Calliope to move Dana to a safe house. That'd keep the kid from getting snatched again. Calliope was good at her business. The best.

Roxy shifted her weight, hissed at the pain. She was

basted and cooked and a little charred, and no closer to figuring out what the hell was going on than she'd been before Xaphan's bedmates showed up to play.

"Guess Marin didn't give you enough info before you killed him. That why you came after me?"

"What are you talking about?" Xaphan's concubine threw up one hand in a dismissive gesture. "Marin was dead by the time I reached him. I couldn't exactly get information from his corpse."

A chill chased across Roxy's skin. "What are *you* talking about? I left him alive." And Xaphan's concubine had to have reached him within moments. How could he have been dead?

Her gaze slid to Dagan. His expression was unreadable, his posture alert.

She looked back and forth between her two supernatural inquisitors. An impossible scenario came to her.

She'd almost afforded Dagan the temporary position of ally. Maybe that was a mistake. Either Xaphan's concubine was lying about Marin being cold by the time she found him, or something else—something Roxy hadn't seen or sensed that night—had done the deed.

The casual impatience of Naamah's replies made Roxy inclined to believe her, which left her with only the *something else* option.

There was only one being she knew of that could slink anywhere undetected by another supernatural, one being that could possibly have slipped by both her and the fire genie unobserved: a soul reaper.

And if it *were* a reaper that had silenced Marin, was there even the remotest possibility that Dagan didn't know it?

That would be a "no."

So who was lying here, and who was telling the truth? The question actually made Roxy's lips twitch with dark humor.

They were all lying, including her.

CHAPTER THIRTEEN

She is a flame which follows after Osiris,
Burning up his enemies

—Egyptian Book of the Dead, Chapter 17

"ARE YOU CLAIMING YOU didn't kill him?" Roxy demanded.

Naamah flicked her wrist negligently. "It isn't a claim; it's a fact. I would have loved to kill Frank Marin, but I never had the chance." Her lower lip puffed out in a pout. "So I owe you for robbing me of a treat."

"Good luck getting payment on that debt," Dagan said, silky soft. *You get to her through me,* he didn't say, but Roxy heard it anyway. And judging by the belligerent expression on her lovely, terrifying face, so did Xaphan's pet. What was it with him and the macho thing? He'd left her to her fate for eleven years. Why did he suddenly care what happened to her?

Only answer she could come up with was that she had something he wanted. Something everyone wanted.

Nose to nose, Dagan and Xaphan's concubine did the death-stare thing. More power to 'em. The reaper wanted to stand in front of her with armor shining and white steed pawing the air?

Knock yourself out, buddy.

Roxy tested her weight on her injured limb. *Damn.* Her ankle felt like a well-turned pork roast. She had a hole in her new jeans and a massive blister on her knee where she'd contacted the genie's skin, never mind a burned and oozing hand. She felt like she'd been sent to cooking class in the pitch-dark, complete with sharp knives and a gas stove.

Slowly, she began to back away, thoughts spinning. She hated missing the obvious, and she was dead certain that she was doing exactly that. All these powerful Underworld factions wanted a piece of Dana. Question was: Why? She needed to figure out the answer. Fast. Not just because it was her job, but because she felt a personal connection.

She didn't like kids. Didn't like jobs that involved kids. Never went near a movie theater or a mall during rugrat high-traffic hours. But *this* kid was different.

This kid made her remember being five years old, being ripped from her mother, being shoved into a life that gave a panoramic view of the dark side and never quite being able to come back to the light.

"You overstep, reaper," Naamah hissed, her eerie orange eyes fixed on Dagan, her words jerking Roxy's thoughts back to the moment.

Damn, what was with these two and the pissing match?

"Overstep? I doubt that." Dagan eyed her condescendingly. *"Vae victis."*

"Now you babble. Is there a point to your words?"

"Vae victis," he repeated, closing his fingers around Naamah's wrist. "Woe to the conquered."

Dagan flicked a look at Roxy and jutted his chin

toward the forest. Guess he wanted her gone, and for once, she was in agreement. Playtime was over. She'd just leave these two to battle it out and see whose little yellow stream went the farthest.

"Conquered?" Xaphan's concubine laughed, a short, high sound that died as abruptly as it had begun. "I see no conqueror. I see a soul reaper backed only by his father's name."

She jerked her arm, but Dagan kept hold of her wrist.

Slowly, Naamah's head came up, her expression unquestionably satisfied, as though Dagan had done something she approved of. Like she'd been waiting for him to do exactly that. "Your action is one of aggression, son of Sutekh," she purred.

Roxy's instincts started to scream.

For a second there was complete silence, then a high-pitched whistling pierced the night, like a kettle on full boil, and it took Roxy a second to realize it was coming from the fire genie. The air shimmered and undulated, heat pouring off her in thick waves. Incredible heat. Roxy felt like her lungs were burning as she gasped and jogged backward with an ungainly lope, her ankle screaming in protest, her blood rushing loud in her ears.

The smell of roasting meat carried on the breeze.

"Now would be a good time to run," Dagan snarled, yanking back on his hand. But his grip didn't release. His fingers clung to Xaphan's concubine as though glued in place.

Melted in place.

To Roxy's horror, his hand burst into flame. The stink of seared flesh swirled through the air, stinging

her nose, and the other genies edged forward, humming with anticipation, obviously waiting for a single word of encouragement from their leader.

Roxy's gaze snapped to his face—his features were twisted in pain—then back down to his hand. Or rather, what had been his hand. The remains of Dagan's limb drifted to the ground in a sifting of ash, delicate as snow.

Staring at the blackened stump of his wrist, she swallowed against the bile that crawled up her throat, bitter and sharp. Horror congealed in her gut. Not just because he'd been hurt, but because he'd been hurt defending *her.*

Damn it to hell. Damn it to fucking hell. Another thing to add to her debt. If he hadn't pulled on his hero cape, that could be Roxy's foot burned away to nothing.

"Run," he ordered. He jerked his maimed forearm across his belly and his shoulders hunched forward as though to protect it as he kicked back at one of the fire genies that crept toward him, bolder now, her companions only a step behind.

Backing away, Roxy did a perimeter sweep, checking for a clear path. Maybe twenty feet away, the shadows shifted and moved. Shadows where none should be. Two forms appeared in the undulating darkness. She had a split-second impression of male bodies, moving fast.

Reinforcements or a new threat? She didn't stop to double-check. Instead, she did exactly what any smart person would do.

She turned, and she ran.

Heart pounding, ankle screaming, Roxy bolted for

the freestanding garage at the north corner of the church. She came in fast, skated across the gravel and went down, legs outstretched. She slid round the corner of the squat building like she was skidding into home base.

At the last second, before the side of the garage blocked her sightline, she shot a look over her shoulder. The concubines were all over Dagan. Or maybe he was all over them. Hard to tell.

She ought to leave him. He wasn't her ally or her friend. He was a soul reaper, whose goals were in diametric opposition to her own.

She ought to run like hell for the forest. This was her turf. She could navigate it with her eyes closed. Sometimes, she did exactly that, just to add a layer to her daily run. Xaphan's concubines would have a hard time following.

She ought to leave Dagan on his own.

Like he'd left her. For eleven years.

But something inside her wouldn't let her do it.

Something called idiocy.

She was seven kinds of fool for even thinking about protecting the soul reaper. It was anathema to her directive; Calliope would kill her. Possibly, quite literally. It was a betrayal of all she had become to help a son of Sutekh.

He'd helped *her*. All those years ago, he'd helped her, and now he was doing it again, protecting her, offering her a clear road to freedom. She didn't trust that, didn't trust *him*. But she couldn't just turn her back on him now and run like a dog with its tail between its legs.

Besides, she could tell herself he had information

that might help her. All she needed to do was pry it out of him. Like teeth. That bit of logic kept saving his ass from being a betrayal of the Asetian Guard.

She surged to her feet, tore open the door of the garage. It was dark as a cave, but she knew where everything was, knew exactly what she sought. Not her gleaming black Corvette. At the moment, she wanted a weapon, not an escape route. Besides, her keys were back in the church in the rose-colored glass bowl.

Her hands closed around the cool metal cylinder, and she yanked it from the wall. Securing her grip, she spun and sprinted back the way she'd come.

Clumps of dry grass were burning, lighting the night with a red glow, the flames highlighting the burgundy skin of the fire genies, dancing across their features. Two were on Dagan. One was on the ground. Blood smeared all three of them. Whose blood? It was impossible to know.

The air smelled like a cookout, fire and charred meat.

Only three of Xaphan's concubines…where were the others?

From this angle, the corner of the church obscured her view of the porch, but she could hear the sounds of a scuffle. The shadows she'd seen earlier…Dagan's reinforcements? Maybe. She didn't dare assume anything. There could be a third player in the melee.

Naamah leaped away from Dagan and turned her attention to Roxy. Dagan was a shade faster. He caught her by the hair and jerked her up short, his attention divided between the genie struggling in his hold and Roxy.

"I told you to run," he snarled.

She didn't bother to waste her breath with an answer.

The concubines caught hold of him wherever they could—skin, hair, clothing—and lit him up like a bonfire. Roxy leapt forward, but Dagan was faster. He took all three with him as he dropped and rolled, moving with preternatural speed.

One tore free and leaped to her feet. Her eyes widened as she focused on Roxy, then narrowed, and she padded forward with lethal grace. Roxy wasn't so refined. She was perfectly happy to play down and dirty, and that's exactly what she did as she pulled the pin on the fire extinguisher, aimed and squeezed.

White foam hit the fire genie full in the face. The creature froze. Roxy jogged back half a dozen steps, waiting to see the result of her handiwork. Xaphan's concubine swept her palms across her cheeks, coming away with handfuls of chemical flame retardant. She flicked it aside and stalked Roxy, a step forward for each step back. She looked anything but happy. In fact, she looked downright pissed.

Roxy kept up her retreat, the fire extinguisher clutched before her. This was not going as planned.

Fuck. Fuck! She'd been so sure. So she'd taken a risk, committed to the plan and it looked like her gamble hadn't paid off.

Panting, she switched her grip on the heavy canister, planning to use it as a club. Then the fire genie stopped dead in her tracks and made a sound between a gasp and a grunt. Her hands flew to her face, her palms clapping against her cheeks, her mouth a round O of horror. Roxy actually took a frantic look over her shoulder to see what terrifying apparition lurked behind her.

But there was nothing there. It was the foam, she realized as she turned back to her opponent. Looked like her plan had worked after all, albeit with a slightly delayed reaction; the foam was eating away at the fire genie's skin like acid.

Better late than never.

Figuring *if some is good, more is better,* she flipped the canister and hit the concubine with a second shot, this time on her legs.

Seconds ticked past. Roxy didn't dare look away, but she was peripherally aware of Dagan putting up a fight some twenty feet away, engaged with Naamah and, at this point, what appeared to be one other. Something about the way he was moving nagged at her. Something not quite right.

With a low cry, Xaphan's concubine bent and slapped at her ankle, like she was slapping at ants, doing a little two-step at the same time. It made for an interesting picture.

The fire genie smacked harder and danced to the side, a series of short, sharp cries escaping her lips.

From the corner of her eye, Roxy caught a flash of movement. She spun, crouched low, and raised the canister. A second concubine came off the porch, arms tight, knees tucked, like she was doing a cannonball off a dock. Roxy rocked back, fell to one knee, and shot.

Concubine and foam collided midair. The fire genie hit the ground, uncurled and took two or three loping steps. Roxy was on her feet, retreating, waiting for the foam to do its job.

Another few seconds and the fire genie stopped in her tracks and began scraping her palms along any exposed skin in broad sweeps.

"Two down," Roxy murmured, spinning back toward Dagan.

Naamah still clung to him, nails and teeth and feral snarls. One more. There should be one more...

Roxy started to spin. Too late. She went down hard, feeling like she'd been hit in the back by a freight train. Her skin sizzled. Talons dug through her jacket, tearing the full length of her sleeve and reaching deep into skin and muscle. Pain rocked her. She bucked, rolled, brought the fire extinguisher up in front of her and emptied the last of it in her attacker's face.

Xaphan's concubine screeched but held on, her talons like grappling hooks. Gritting her teeth, Roxy grabbed hold of the genie's wrist, pressed hard on the front, just the way Dagan had done to her earlier. She couldn't match his strength, so the move wasn't perfect. Still, it loosened the genie's hold enough that Roxy could claw at her fingers and pull each talon free, like she was plucking thorns. It hurt like hell.

She said a silent prayer of gratitude that the chemical foam had either distracted the creature or weakened her enough that she hadn't incinerated Roxy's arm. Or maybe that was a talent possessed only by their leader.

Turning the canister on its side, she used it like a ram to force the fire genie away from her. Then she surged back to her feet, panting, her gaze scanning for imminent threat.

Dagan rounded on her, Naamah nowhere in sight, his maimed wrist pressed against his belly, his eyes narrowed dangerously. "Nice work."

He didn't sound sincere. Or grateful.

"You're welcome," Roxy snapped, watching his

blood ooze into the speckling of white foam that clung to him in splotches, turning it pink. Guess her aim hadn't been specific enough.

For a split second, his attention shifted to a point behind her.

"You need to go. Now."

Roxy turned, and saw nothing. Just shadows and night and the empty front porch of her house.

"Get the fuck out of here," Dagan snarled.

She turned back, the fire extinguished held across her chest.

Damn. Where had they all come from? There were at least a dozen concubines now, advancing like a pack of hyenas, eyes glowing orange, lips peeled back.

They were looking at her. And they didn't look friendly.

Dagan's gaze met hers. The connection lasted no more than a frozen millisecond. Gray eyes. Pewter and mercury. The rage and power he held leashed were palpable, like a wave of heat steaming off concrete, bending the air.

She backed away. Her bag of tricks was empty. Right now, there was nothing more she could do here. Not for him. Not for herself.

The promise he'd made earlier hung between them. *Remember, if you run, I will find you.*

Good luck with that.

Decision made, Roxy aimed the extinguisher can at the advancing fire genies. They stopped midpace. Guess they didn't have a clue that the average can only had about ten seconds' worth of foam—and she'd already shot at least eleven.

They pinned her with malevolent gazes. It gave new

depth to the idea *if looks could kill.* Then one grew bold and crept forward.

As Roxy backed away, a glint of metal on the ground caught her eye. It was her second knife, the one that hadn't been melted. She dove, rolled, grabbed and surged to her feet.

She flicked the blade open and threw.

It landed dead center between one of the concubine's eyes as she leaped forward, blackened talons outstretched. Roxy hurled the empty fire extinguisher with all the force she could muster. It hit the creature square in the chest.

Dagan moved into the path of the advancing group, one man against a small army. He lunged and caught the hair of the fire genie closest to him as she made to slither past.

Roxy turned to the woods and ran. The pain in her ankle was so bad she wanted to howl. Later. No time for that now. She could hear the snarls of the fire genies, and the harsh rasp of labored breathing, but she didn't look back. She'd done all she could for him, more than a self-proclaimed enemy of the Daughters of Aset deserved. Her conscience ought to be clear.

So why did guilt bite at her like a rabid rat? It slapped her, but she slapped it right back. No sense wasting energy on futile emotion. He'd made his choice. She was making hers.

Still, she regretted the lost opportunity to find out what he knew. That had been her justification for not hightailing it in the first place.

Forcing everything else from her mind, she focused on running, the pounding of her heart, the rise and fall

of her chest. She could hear something behind her. *Don't look. Even a glance will slow you down.*

So she didn't look. She ran, dodging trees and fallen logs and ruts that could snap an ankle. She'd run these woods a thousand times, part of her regular training. Her pursuers hadn't.

Good luck to them keeping up.

Eventually, the sounds of pursuit faded. There were fewer of them now. Roxy had no idea how long they could keep coming, how fast they were. How many there were. She couldn't simply count on outrunning them; they might be able to outlast her, and she was running out of forest. Pretty soon she'd hit fields cut by flat road. Not great cover.

She needed to out-think them, throw them off her scent.

A small boulder lay in her path. She stopped dead, squatted low, hefted it and then threw it as hard as she could into the dense undergrowth. It rolled and bumped, and Roxy hoped the noise carried and drew them off course.

Leaping high, she caught a low branch and swung herself up like a gymnast at the rings, coiled, controlled, silent. She bent her knees and hooked the branch, then hung there briefly, upside down, facing back the way she'd come. Nothing moved. There was no one behind her. Not yet.

With an easy roll, she curled her body upright then scrambled higher, careful to make no noise. Finally, she stopped and crouched on a branch, muscles tense, senses humming. Closing her eyes, she let the subtle vibrations of unseen molecules tell her what was close. She could feel the unique pulsa-

tions, feel the energy signature that marked every supernatural.

The air shifted—not the stirring of the breeze, but something more sinister. Where? She didn't move, didn't blink, didn't dare breathe.

Heart pounding, she waited, mouse to cat. Run, and Xaphan's concubine would catch her when the trees stopped. Fight, and the creature would sift her to ash. Which left *hide* as the only logical choice. She hadn't fed recently—not since the few drops she'd taken from Frank Marin; she couldn't count that microscopic bit she'd taken from Dana—and she knew from experience that her own signature was negligible unless she fed. She could pass for human, a bonus in the world she lived in. It let her blend in, unnoticed.

The vibration cycled through the air, growing closer. Closer.

The fire genie stopped.

Roxy moved only her eyes, scanning the shadows, the trees and the night surrounding her like a cloak. The sky was overcast, clouds blocking moon and stars, the trees here in the forest further dampening what light eked through. Sight was little use to her. But she didn't need it. She *felt* the threat, in her gut, in her veins.

There, to her left. One of Xaphan's concubines.

Only one. The others must still be back with Dagan.

Guilt pricked her. That was an improvement. At least it wasn't gnawing her raw anymore. *Get over it.* Not a productive use of energy. There was nothing she could have done to help him. It had been all she could manage to save herself.

The fire genie tipped her head, sniffed the air, then turned in Roxy's general direction.

Fuck. She was going to have to fight. What had Dagan called them? Smoke and flame.

She swallowed, feeling sick as she thought of his hand burning away to ash. She wasn't in the mood for a cookout. Especially not if she were the meat.

The creature moved, a single step toward her—

Roxy tensed, ready to spring, to fight, to claw tooth and nail for her life.

Then she heard a shrill, teakettle whistle in the distance, coming from the direction of her house. Once. Twice. She thought there was a hint of desperation to the sound. Or maybe that was just wishful thinking.

Dead silence for a heartbeat, then the fire genie left, her footsteps less than stealthy, almost careless.

Roxy slumped against the rough bark at her back, infinitely grateful that the fire genie hadn't scented her energy signature. For a slow count of twenty she held her place, then she pulled her cell out of her pocket and dialed.

"I have a situation," she said when Calliope answered. "I need you to move the girl again. Different city. Better yet, a different state. It's best if as few people as possible know about it. I'll explain when I can."

Ending the call, she stared hard at the shadows, looking for even the slightest hint of movement or light.

Then she dropped to the ground and spun, ready to move.

She didn't even have a chance to breathe before something fast and lethal got her from behind.

CHAPTER FOURTEEN

The slaughterhouse of the god is what I abhor
And my heart shall not be taken from me

—Egyptian Book of the Dead, Chapter 28

DAGAN HAULED ROXY AGAINST HIM, his front to her back, his hand tight against her mouth, his maimed forearm pressed to her belly. Barbed shards of agony pierced him, running up his arm like an electric charge. A new limb bud had already started to form where his hand had been, and the process was promising to be less than pleasant.

For about a millisecond Roxy stayed still, stayed quiet. Then she elbowed him in the ribs, brought her heel down on his instep and smashed the back of her head against his cheek. She missed his nose only because he read her intent and shifted just in time.

"It's me," Dagan rasped against her ear, his arm tightening around her abdomen till he figured he'd forced every molecule of air out of her lungs. "Hold still."

She stopped struggling and gave a single sharp nod, but her body was rigid, her muscles humming with tension.

The situation was too tempting to resist. So he

didn't. He let himself enjoy the sensation of having her in his arms—however mutinous she might be—lowered his face and inhaled the scent of her hair, vanilla with a top note of smoke.

She made a strangled sound, and he figured he'd pushed as far as he could, for the moment.

Easing his hold, he let her get her balance on her own two feet. For a second, he debated whether to draw his hand from her lips slow or fast. There was always the risk she'd bite him.

But she surprised him as he uncovered her mouth, doing nothing more violent than whispering, "Follow me."

No questions. No polite chit-chat. Just an order she expected him to obey.

His amusement knew no bounds.

"Follow *you?*"

"I know this terrain better than you. Wanna trip over a log and break an ankle?"

She glanced at him over her shoulder. Then she froze, sucked in a sharp breath and jerked from his loosened grasp, going down in a defensive squat.

He knew what she saw behind him: two shadows, close at his back. Though how she managed to differentiate them from the crowded, dark shapes of the trees was a mystery to him. He could see Alastor and Gahiji just fine, but he had the eyes of a soul reaper. She didn't.

"Don't stab them." Because he couldn't guarantee that they wouldn't stab back. "They're with me."

She straightened, but her body language screamed distrust, and he noticed that she gave no assurance that she wouldn't do other bodily damage. She stared hard

into the darkness, but he doubted she could see more than indistinct shapes. His companions knew the art of camouflage. Soul reapers specialized in that. And killing.

Still, he couldn't help but be impressed that she was actually looking in the right direction.

"That answers the question about what was on my porch," Roxy murmured. "Reinforcements."

He hadn't been aware there was a question, but the answer seemed accurate. "You could call them that."

Best Dagan could figure, Alastor had sensed the horrific pain he'd experienced when the bitch had seared off his hand, and he had arrived in the midst of the battle, dragging Gahiji in his wake. Dagan suspected that Gahiji hadn't come by choice, but because the two had been together at the time, following Sutekh's rule about pairing his sons with a reaper to watch their backs.

As far as options went, Gahiji wasn't all that bad. He'd been a soul reaper longer than either of the brothers had been alive. He was as predictable as the path of the sun, unwavering in his loyalty to the old man. He never strayed, never broke the rules. He harvested hearts and darksouls. He was Sutekh's man.

Dagan had once asked his father how he had earned such loyalty.

"An iron fist in a velvet glove," Sutekh had replied. Which, as usual, was no reply at all.

"This once, expand the concept," Dagan had said, exasperated.

"I make him feel worthy because he *is* worthy. He is important to me, and he knows it. He has only one fear, and that is the fear of disappointing me. He cares

not about ending his existence, only that that end not come at *my* hand."

And Dagan had understood. Because that was the exact loyalty Sutekh had nurtured in his sons. Only it hadn't played out exactly as the old man had envisioned. He'd meant to spawn four sons with loyalty only to *him*.

What he got were four sons loyal to each other. And to him, despite their mixed feeling of love and loathing. Not exactly what he'd bargained for.

"Be at ease," Dagan murmured when Roxy failed to relax her stance even a little. "I told you, they're with me."

"Which is such a wonderful recommendation."

"Don't trust me?" he asked.

"Not in a million years."

Smart girl. He didn't trust her, either.

"You should have run when I told you to."

She stared at him, crossed her arms over her chest and raised her perfectly arched brows. Her full lips tightened. "I saved your ass."

"You spoiled my plans." He mirrored her movements, crossing his arms over his own chest. "I told you to run."

"And leave you outgunned and outnumbered?" Her brow furrowed as she studied the position of his arms, then she dropped her own to her sides. "Besides, I don't take orders from you."

"Outgunned and out—" he echoed. Her response drew him up short. He'd thought she had her own agenda. But she'd thought she was *helping* him? *Protecting* him?

From behind him came a sound suspiciously like a

snicker. Roxy shot a narrow-eyed look over his shoulder, appearing no more pleased than he felt.

"Perhaps empirically I was outnumbered, but I was definitely not outgunned. I played with them long enough to buy you time to get the fuck out of there," he explained, forcing himself to go against his inclination not to. He wasn't used to justifying his actions, except occasionally to the old man, but she needed to understand that her behavior had been ridiculous and unnecessary. And he needed to know she wouldn't repeat it. He couldn't have her in danger every time he turned around. He found that...unsettling. "Once you were out of the hot zone, I intended to question Naamah, find out what exactly they were after. You destroyed all hope of that."

"*I* destroyed it?" Her tone was low, despite her blatant incredulity. Her hands fisted. Her chin came up. She glared at him with her tiger eyes. "What, you think I'm a mind reader? A single sentence or two up front would have cleared things up nicely."

What did she imagine was the basis for her righteous indignation? He'd had his hand burned off for her. Why the hell was she looking at him like *he'd* done something wrong?

"Right, then," Alastor broke in. "You two done?"

"Not quite," Dagan growled at the same instant Roxy said, "Not hardly."

"Location's a bit dodgy. Perhaps we could adjourn to a—" Alastor glanced around "—less vulnerable premises before you continue?" He sounded amused. And curious. Both of which served to tweak Dagan's temper a little more.

"Fine," he amended, even as Roxy offered a terse, "Works for me."

He huffed a breath. She huffed a breath.

And he felt like an idiot. What was it about Roxy Tam that made him behave like a sixteen-year-old with a perpetual hard-on, a possessive streak and a chip on his shoulder the size of Mt. Everest? Better question: What was it about *himself* that made him act that way in regard to Roxy Tam?

He wasn't so sure he wanted to know the answer.

He uncrossed his arms, and her gaze dropped to his maimed limb. Even in the dark, she couldn't miss the carnage that had been done.

Reaching out, she laid her hand on his forearm, her expression one of compassion as she stared at the blackened stump of his hand. Then her gaze lifted to his.

"I'm sorry."

Her words nearly made him grab her and haul her close and press his mouth to hers to taste that compassion, that warmth. But even a small taste would lead to weakness. He had no doubt of that. And he already seemed to have a hole in his armor when it came to her.

"This'll heal." He shrugged. "Told you, I cut my heart out and put it on a platter in order to find you. Trust me, that was worse."

A short exhalation escaped her. "You say the strangest things."

"He does, doesn't he?" Alastor stepped closer and gave him a hard look. A *What the bloody hell is wrong with you—why the bloody hell are you telling her this?* look. Dagan didn't have an answer, and as Alastor and Gahiji crowded forward, Dagan had to fight the completely unreasonable instinct to turn and bare his teeth, to snarl a warning. He didn't like the way Gahiji in par-

ticular was looking at her. Like she was a rare butter-fly, and he was a collector.

In those circumstances, rare butterflies tended to end up pinned to a board with their wings spread.

He had the insane urge to gather Roxy against him, open a portal and find a nice dark hole to crawl into. Just the two of them.

Which made about as much sense as anything else that had happened tonight. He had no business feeling territorial and protective. She was a human who had chosen to ally herself with his enemies, the Daughters of Aset, despite his warning. A mortal woman he had met in passing eleven years ago, and left behind. For-gotten.

No.

That was a lie.

He had left her behind, but he had never forgotten her. No matter how hard he'd tried to bury any thought of her, she'd crept up on him at times in a sort of weird waking dream; at least, that's what he thought it was.

Even though soul reapers didn't dream.

There was wakefulness and there was the sheer blackness of sleep. Yet over the years she had come to him, usually naked and hungry, sometimes clothed and sated, laughing, sparkling, slipping into his thoughts uninvited.

He'd asked his brothers in a subtle, offhand way if they'd ever experienced the same. They hadn't. They'd had no clue what he was describing, so he'd let it drop. And she'd kept coming.

No one else. Only her.

"By the by, any idea what Xaphan's concubines were doing here?" Alastor asked.

"Looking for marshmallows," Roxy offered at the same time Dagan shot her a look and said, "Looking for information."

He wanted her quiet. The less attention Gahiji paid her, the better. She seemed to get the message because she didn't say anything more.

"I sent Mal to meet with them," he said. "They were asking questions about a mortal named Frank Marin."

He sensed Gahiji's attention sharpen. He'd been there when Sutekh bid Dagan to collect on the debt Joe Marin owed. No doubt Gahiji suspected the two were linked.

"And you think Mal sent them here?" Alastor asked.

"Unlikely. He didn't know where I was going. And there was no reason for him to direct them here. I sent him to get information, not give it."

Dagan noticed that Roxy had suddenly gone quiet. She didn't volunteer for public consumption the fact that she'd almost encountered the fire genies outside the Tee Pee Inn. And for some reason, he didn't offer that tidbit, either. He tried to tell himself it was because there was no relevance, but the truth was, he didn't want to share his insider's knowledge. Something about the entire situation was nagging at him like a stone in his boot, and he wanted to follow it up firsthand without anyone else muddying the water.

"I can handle things here, Alastor." It was a neat, tidy way of telling his brother to grab Gahiji and get lost. "I suggest we split up." He jerked his head in Roxy's direction. "But *she* stays with me."

"Why?" Gahiji asked, surprising Dagan that he spoke at all. Usually, he observed. He rarely asked questions.

"Are you asking why we should split up, or why she stays with me?"

"Both."

Roxy glanced toward Gahiji when he spoke, her head tipping to one side, a small frown creasing her brows.

"We split up because I'm not inclined to take on the two of you as reaper shadows," Dagan said, "no matter what the old man prefers. And she stays with me because I'm not done with her yet."

"Keep arguing, boys." Roxy shook her head and stepped away. He caught her hand.

She glanced down, then up. It was too dark for her to see much of anything, he knew. But he was under no such limitation. Her features were as clear to him as if she were standing under the full force of the sun.

"You wanna lose that one, too?"

He laughed then. He couldn't help it. She amused him. Enraged him. Confused him. Made him want to drag her up against him and push his tongue in her mouth, close his hand on her breast. Made him want to take her, and let her take him.

Abruptly, he dropped her hand and broke the connection.

It worked, at least to a degree. The lust that had hit him like a brick wall eased, and he could think. He could breathe.

Whatever the hell was between them, she felt it, too. Her pulse was racing. He could hear it.

"Quite finished, are we?" Alastor muttered. Dagan figured he'd be called on the carpet to answer a shit-load of questions at some point, but not now. Not in front of Gahiji.

It wouldn't do to let their father's mole know any unnecessary details. The soul reaper was already watching Roxy much too closely, like he was trying to figure out what made her tick.

"So what happened to Xaphan's concubines?" Roxy asked. "Where did they go?"

"They're carrying coals to Newcastle." Alastor laughed at his own joke, but Roxy only looked confused.

Dagan realized she had no idea what his brother was referring to, and he found his spirits strangely buoyed by that. Nice to know he wasn't the only one who didn't always get the joke. This one, he happened to know because Alastor had used it before, and the Internet was a wonderful thing.

"He means they're doing something pointless and superfluous," he offered. "I sent them running off toward a dead end."

Roxy made a sound of impatience. "Yes, I know what the expression means. I was just wondering what that pointless, superfluous thing might be."

So much for feeling like she was a kindred spirit.

"What do you know about Xaphan's concubines, human?" Gahiji asked, his tone soft.

Roxy turned and peered into the darkness, her expression betraying confusion, her head tipping to the side again, as though she were listening for something, trying to get a handle on it. "I don't know anything. Why don't you tell me what *you* know?"

"We owe you no information." Gahiji smiled coldly. The expression was one Dagan had seen before. His hackles rose. Something didn't feel right. Gahiji didn't lead. Ever. He worked alone, or he worked as subordi-

nate to one of the Krayl brothers. For him to take on lead role, even nominally, felt off. Wrong. Dangerous. "And I wonder at your curiosity."

"Hey," Roxy shrugged. "I'm an inquisitive kind of girl." She tapped her index finger against her lower lip. "Don't take this the wrong way, but, do I know you? Your voice sounds familiar."

"No." Gahiji turned away and studied the dark woods, as though ascertaining if the perimeter were safe.

It was safe enough. The fire genies were occupied elsewhere, chasing their tails.

"Too bad it's so dark. Maybe if I could get a look at you…" Roxy prompted.

Gahiji ignored her.

"Alastor, you and Gahiji see if you can meet up with Mal. I sent him after Xaphan's concubines earlier, but he seems to have taken the scenic route. See if you can find him, then find them. As I said, they were asking questions about Frank Marin, and about a girl—" his gaze slid to Roxy and he stared at her for a slow count of three, saying nothing, letting her know that he knew she'd been holding out on him "—a kid. Name of Dana. She's in Oklahoma City."

Roxy's expression didn't change, but he felt the tension crawling through her, nearly crackling off her skin. She hadn't shared that information with him, and if he was placing bets, he'd wager that she didn't like the fact that he pulled it like a rotten tooth out of one of Xaphan's pets.

"Dana…in Oklahoma City," Alastor echoed. "That's it? No last name? No address? No idea what they want with her?"

"None."

"Any idea what *we* want with her?"

"No." Not yet. But soon. Because his gut was telling him that Roxy might have the answers to his questions. And he meant to stick closer than glue on a stamp until she shared. "Which is why you're going after Xaphan's concubines, and I'm going after the kid. With Ms. Tam." He shot her another hard look.

She gave him a tight smile and turned away, as though their discussion was of absolutely no interest to her, but he noticed that she kept looking at Gahiji, clearly trying to get a good look at him despite the darkness. Not a likelihood.

But the thing that ground at him was the fact that Gahiji was watching her, too.

Suddenly, Gahiji let out a low hiss and struck like a snake, catching hold of Roxy's wrist and shoving the tatters of her coat sleeve up to her elbow.

"What the fuck?" she snarled, and she slammed the heel of her hand against the reaper's nose. He moved his head only enough to avoid the blow. Then he let her go and took a single step back, his head swiveling as he settled a dark glare on Dagan.

"She is of the Asetian Guard," Gahiji said, his voice low.

Roxy took a step to the side, taking her away from Gahiji, and even farther away from Dagan. He didn't like that. His instincts were clanging like a firehouse bell.

"Roxy," he murmured.

She glanced back over her shoulder, her expression guarded. Then she closed her hand over the opposite forearm, as though guarding her mark. She slid one foot toward him, but Gahiji took another step, placing himself directly between Dagan and Roxy.

The clanging bell turned into a full alarm fire.

"We're working toward a common goal," Dagan offered, subtly claiming her as an ally and under his protection.

The tension coming off Gahiji crackled in the air. Alastor moved closer to Dagan's side.

"A common goal," Gahiji echoed, his tone flat and cold. "What protection do you have from treachery? She knows your face, and now ours."

So much for subtle.

"Not yours. It's too dark." Dagan took a step. Gahiji took a step. "This isn't your call, Gahiji. She's mine."

Roxy backed up, clearly sensing the tension. Unfortunately, she backed away, rather than toward him. Not that she had much choice. Gahiji stood squarely between them now.

"You have erred, Dagan Krayl." There was accusation there. A hint of belligerence.

"Dagan!"

He heard Alastor's warning a split second after his own instincts shot into overdrive. Too fucking late. Gahiji moved, a blur of speed and deadly intent.

Dagan surged forward but felt like he stood still. He leaped, twisted, reached for Roxy even as she leaped toward him. Her movement brought her face-to-face with Gahiji.

And Dagan was too late. Too fucking late.

His burned hand had begun to regrow, but it was yet little more than a limb bud—numb, weak, useless. His usable hand was too far away.

Gahiji was closer. He had two working hands.

And one of them was now buried in Roxy's chest up to the wrist.

CHAPTER FIFTEEN

"No!" DAGAN'S CRY WAS WORTH NOTHING. It couldn't stop what had already happened.

Spine arched, limbs taut, Roxy froze. Then her head jerked back and a sound escaped her lips, like the air escaping from a deflating balloon.

Leaping forward, Dagan closed his one working hand around Gahiji's forearm, exerting every ounce of his control and power. He moved his damaged limb to Roxy's back, pressing hard with the flat of his forearm, holding her in place.

The three of them wove a tight circle, a macabre embrace.

"What the fuck are you doing?" Dagan roared, the words barely intelligible.

Roxy clawed at Gahiji's arm, scraping skin, drawing blood, then she just held on, digging deep. Her eyes were wide, her toffee-cream skin paler than chalk. Then she turned her head and her gaze met Dagan's and he read all the horror and fear she was feeling.

Lips pressed in a taut line, thick brows drawn low over his small, close-set eyes, Gahiji glared at Dagan.

"She is our enemy," he said, his tone reasonable, calm, detached. Everything Dagan wasn't. "Let me harvest her and go. Let me bring her darksoul to

Sutekh. He will find whatever answers she hides." He shot a look at Dagan's fingers where they curled around his wrist. "Why do you hamper my intent?"

The question was genuine, not meant as a challenge. He clearly had no idea what Dagan was about.

Welcome to the fucking club. Dagan had no idea what Dagan was about. He only knew Roxy Tam couldn't die here tonight. He would do anything, kill anything, swear fealty to any lord or god if she could just live.

He had saved her in the past. He would save her now.

Impossible. She's already dead. Her mind only doesn't know it yet.

Something broke inside him, a tidal wave pounding through a dam, casting aside everything in its path in the face of its surging fury. He was left shaking. With rage, yes, but something more. Something that left his skin cold and clammy and his tongue tasting like metal.

Keeping his grip tight around Gahiji's wrist, he held the reaper as still as he could.

"Help me hold her," he gritted at Alastor, then realized his brother was already in place, his hands on Roxy's waist, his chest against her back, a bolster to offer stability.

As though anything would help.

There would be questions later, but in this moment, Alastor stood by him, without question, without argument. His brother had his back.

If any of them moved even a matter of inches, Roxy's heart would be left in Gahiji's hand and she'd be dead. Gone. Sent to Osiris and the Field of Reeds. Or maybe sent to Hades. To Ah Puch. To Yama or

Gauna. There were so many damned gods and demi-gods ruling over territories he could never hope to enter. How would he find her in the vast Underworld?

Or maybe Roxy Tam would go somewhere else, to a heaven Dagan knew nothing about. He had no idea which god or goddess would open their arms to her. He didn't want to know. Didn't want to find out.

He wanted her right here, Topworld, alive and bitching.

But, viscous and dark, her blood was welling from the edges of the wound in synchrony with the beat of her pulse. Gahiji's hand was acting like a poorly fitted cork. If he pulled it free, the wound would bleed like a fountain, a geyser. She would bleed out in minutes, maybe seconds, and there wasn't a thing Dagan could do to stop it.

He raised his eyes and found Roxy's gaze focused on him. She was aware, he could see that. She knew exactly what had happened, exactly how dire her situation was. He didn't know what could possibly fix this.

He killed things. He didn't save them.

Gahiji turned his implacable gaze on Dagan. "Unhand me. Let me finish it. You only prolong her pain."

"Leave go her heart, Gahiji. It is not yours to take." *It's mine, you bastard. Her heart is mine, has been since I let her keep it eleven years in the past.*

"She saw me. Saw *us.*" Gahiji paused, as though letting the import of the assertion sink in. "She will carry tales. More than that, she has information that could be a threat, knowledge that might be of value to Sutekh. Let me take her soul. You cannot mean to let her live? A Daughter of Aset. You know the rules. She must die."

"Shut the bloody hell up," Alastor interjected. "I

don't know what is going on here, but I do know there are no sodding rules about Aset's Daughters. Are you trying to start an all-out war, Gahiji? Leave go, man. Dagan claimed her under his protection. You have no right to this kill."

Roxy held incredibly still. Dagan could hear each breath coming shallow and fast, rattling in her chest. Alastor shifted closer, held her tighter, made certain that he balanced Dagan's hold and Gahiji's thrust, and Dagan felt a swell of gratitude. He hadn't said a word, but his brother understood.

Funny, that, because *he* didn't understand. He only knew that if Roxy Tam closed her tiger-bright eyes and let her lungs deflate on a final exhale, a part of him would close his eyes with her and not rise again.

Beneath his grasp, he felt a minute loosening of Gahiji's hold.

"Let me take her heart and her soul. At least that way Sutekh can gain the answers you failed to obtain," the reaper said, shifting to accusation as a bargaining tactic. "She will die now, regardless. You fight the inevitable."

"She will not die." Dagan kept his hold on Gahiji's wrist, preventing him from either digging deeper or withdrawing. "And I'll get my own damned answers in my own damned way. Leave go."

But Gahiji only stared at him and held his place, and with each second they argued, Roxy's life slipped away. Dagan wanted to howl. To rant. To rip the other soul reaper limb from limb and paint himself with his blood. But more than any of that, he wanted to save her.

"What do we do?" Alastor asked, his tone calm and clipped and proper, his accent thicker than usual. His calm helped pull Dagan back from the edge.

"We fix her," Dagan said, frantically sifting through ideas and discarding each one. If they pulled out Gahiji's hand, Roxy would bleed out in seconds, but how long would she survive with his fist buried in her chest?

"Dae," she rasped, the word faint. She shifted her gaze from Gahiji to Dagan, and he saw hope and determination there, as though she thought she could survive. As though she expected him to save her. He felt the weight of her expectations, too heavy. He was sickened by the knowledge of his impending defeat.

For all his supernatural skill and power, he had no clue how to fix this. Even Sutekh couldn't return the dead to life.

But he could make soul reapers out of them...

The second the thought hit him, he discounted it as a possibility. To a one, soul reapers were male.

Besides, he couldn't see the old man welcoming a Daughter of Aset to the fold.

She was going to die, and he'd brought that death to her door. Had he not come after her, his brother would not have followed with Gahiji in his shadow.

"Blood," she whispered.

He glanced down. There was a river of blood. It snaked along Gahiji's forearm and dripped to the ground.

She tried again, but the words were lost. She had almost no breath. He could see her weakening, feel her weight sagging onto his arm where he held her.

His eyes met hers. She was telling him something, something he couldn't understand, but she thought he ought to. He could read that expectation in her eyes.

Her lashes fluttered.

Her head lolled to the side.

"Roxy!" Dagan choked on the swell of liquid-nitrogen pain, the cold burn of desperation as he thought of her gone to the Underworld, gone beyond his reach, for though he knew not what god would claim her, he knew it wasn't Sutekh.

Again, her lashes fluttered and she opened her eyes. "Pa…ra…siiiite."

It took him a second to figure it out. Parasite.

"Yeah, I guess I am." But he had no idea why she thought it was so important to tell him so with her damned dying breath.

His reply agitated her. Her bronze-green eyes flashed and she shook her head. He had it wrong. Whatever she was trying to tell him, he had it wrong and he was out of time.

Gahiji's lips tightened until his mouth was a hard, thin slash in his face. He was going to tear her heart out. Dagan could sense it.

"I invoke my place as Sutekh's son and bid you release her heart. You take her darksoul, Gahiji," he promised, "and I'll claim yours."

The other soul reaper froze. Dagan watched the shock flicker across his features like the flare of a match, there and then gone. He could feel Alastor's tension as he watched them both, but he didn't dare pull his attention from Gahiji. He'd already made a mistake that would likely cost Roxy Tam her life.

He wasn't about to nail her coffin shut by making another.

His words hung in the air. He'd never pulled rank like that, never invoked the old man's name, not once in three hundred years. But now he did. And he'd

gladly pay whatever price doing so cost him, because if the look Gahiji shot him was any indication, there was going to be hell to pay.

Eyes blazing, Gahiji made a sound of frustration. "You choose an Otherkin over your own?" His words dripped disdain.

"I choose to keep her alive for my own reasons," Dagan clipped. "You have no right to question what they are, and I deny you the privilege."

Gahiji stared at him, his face an expressionless mask. Then he loosed his hold on her heart and pulled his empty fist from her chest, leaving a gaping, ragged hole and a geyser of blood.

Roxy was left hanging, held up by Dagan's one-armed embrace and Alastor's grasp on her waist, and nothing more.

Deadweight.

"GET HIM THE FUCK OUT OF HERE, Alastor, before I take his soul and feed it to Sutekh in a soufflé."

The words jarred Roxy from a place where there was only darkness and pain. The voice was Dagan's, harsh and low, the sound tinny, distant, as though it were traveling along a twisted, narrow tunnel.

Something moved close beside her, and she felt like her chest was being crushed by a garbage compactor. She tried to move, to push it away, but her limbs were leaden, refusing to obey her will. With a jolt, awareness of her position snapped into place. She wasn't standing anymore; she was flat on her back. She could smell the forest floor—earth and damp leaves and rot. She thought she might be dying.

Roxy turned her head toward Dagan, trying to grab

hold of an anchor, feeling as though she were a tiny boat in a murky, roiling sea.

"She is a Daughter of Aset." *No shit. Give the reaper with the lightning fist a prize.* What had Dagan called him? Gahiji. She knew that name. It meant hunter. Seeker. She found that funny, in a not-so-funny way.

Then she wondered *why* she knew that name, and how. *Gahiji.* The answer drifted just beyond her reach, and she let it go, too cold, too tired. She couldn't seem to hold on to her thoughts.

"What the bloody hell were you thinking, Gahiji? She was offering up no threat." British accent, hard and clipped. It took her a second of swimming against the brutal tide before understanding hit her. It was the third soul reaper talking now.

"She is of the Asetian Guard. That is threat enough."

She tried to focus her thoughts, and all she could come up with was that she'd been right about the name. Gahiji. Hunter. Seeker.

Hunting *her.* No that wasn't right. He'd been hunting someone else. She wanted to shake the cobwebs from her head and pull a clear thought from the bunch. Instead, all she got was cotton floss.

"Take him with you, Alastor." Dagan again, speaking from close beside her. His voice was taut, angry. He sounded like the slightest push would send him over the edge.

"Take him where?"

"Anywhere but here. Go hunt down the Setnakhts. Find out about what made Frank Marin so special." Staccato bursts of words. Like bullets. "Then go make nice with Xaphan and his concubines. Smooth over tonight's debacle before it turns into a war."

Roxy tried to open her eyes, or maybe they were open and she just couldn't see. She knew Dagan's hands were on her chest, pressing, hurting. She wanted to push him away. But she was weak. She was cold and shaking. So she just lay there and let him do whatever he was doing. Somehow, she thought he was the least of her problems.

She could smell blood, metallic and sweet. But it didn't rouse the hunger, which could mean only one thing. It was *her* blood. Damn.

There was a faint rustling and more words, low voiced, angry. She couldn't hear them, just the tone. Or maybe she heard nothing at all. No sound. Maybe all was just a void, an empty place that was cold and silent and the voices were inside her head, crawling out of the open grave of her darkest nightmares.

Her mother's face was before her, streaked with tears. She saw a glimmer of silver in her mother's hand, then felt the cold weight of a heavy chain around her neck. She heard a man's voice. She didn't like that voice. It made her afraid. Then she saw only darkness.

She had no idea where she drifted or how long, but suddenly there were knives inside her. No, not knives. Saws, buzzing and whirring and shredding her skin and bone. Agony ripped her from the nothingness. She screamed and screamed, but no sound came out. There was no breath for sound, so her cries echoed only in her head, in her heart, terror and dread.

"Roxy." Her name was a command, the single word bringing her back from the edge of mindless panic. "I have to lift you and it's going to hurt."

Hurt. Was this what Rhianna had felt? Such pain? Or was it different when all your nerve endings were burned away?

Thoughts of Rhianna nearly undid her, layering a different kind of agony on the physical. Memories and wishes. She could feel the pillow in her hands.

"Roxy! You fucking stay with me."

She knew that voice, crème brûlée with a hint of crackle, only it was rougher than before. Harsher.

Then the meaning of the words hit her and the pain in her chest took on a different flavor as her circumstances came rushing at her like a cart on a hill. She was dying.

"My heart," she gasped.

"Still in your chest, but barely."

"Blood." Disgorging that single word took all her concentration. She willed him to understand.

"Yeah, you've lost a lot of blood—" No! He had it all wrong. Why didn't he understand? "—Your chest's ripped open. Your ribs are cracked. Your left lung's collapsed."

Ah, so that was why it was so hard to breathe. Or maybe it was because he was leaning over her, pressing on her chest. At least, it felt like he was. She tried to reach for him, to make him stop.

"Be still. I'm trying to control the bleeding. You aren't helping."

What did he think she ought to do? Sew herself up?

She gave up on trying to speak. Waste of energy. Every breath was a gasp, every beat of her pulse an agony.

Forcing her eyes open, she focused on Dagan. He was an obsidian shadow against blackest night. Paltry light filtered through the canopy of leaves, shimmering in his hair, making his eyes glitter. He looked fierce, angry. And something else that she couldn't quite name.

"Don't die. I'm not done with you."

Now, there was incentive.

Her tongue darted out. She tried to wet her lips, but there was no moisture.

This was not supposed to happen.

She wasn't supposed to be here on the forest floor, bleeding, dying.

In her dreams, her nightmares, Dagan took her heart. But it never ended like this. This was different. For some warped reason, it bothered her that someone other than him had gone rooting around in her chest. In her dreams, it was always Dagan.

Why the hell had the other reaper turned on her? Memory coalesced. Her mark. He'd seen her mark.

No, that wasn't right. He'd *looked for* her mark, like he'd expected to find it.

Well, he'd found it. He'd seen her as the enemy, and he'd acted.

A second of hard-edged clarity touched her thoughts. If Aset's Daughters were such an enemy, one to be killed on sight, why hadn't Dagan done the same?

He knew exactly what she was. Had known all along. Why had he let her live eleven years ago? And why was he now trying to stanch the flow of her blood and save her life?

Questions that begged for answers. She tried to lift her hand, to motion him closer, but managed only to twitch her fingers. It was enough. He saw it and leaned in, his pupils dilated, leaving his gray eyes dark and fathomless.

She could smell his skin. She could smell his wounds. And just like that, the instant of clarity faded and she was almost overwhelmed by the blood, the hunger, the need.

Blood. She needed to make him understand. Was it only a couple hours past that she had wondered what his blood would do to her? Had she really thought that she didn't ever want to find out? How one's perspective changed given the right incentive.

Willing him to watch her lips, she mouthed the words *Need blood.* Then she traced her tongue along her lower lip, praying he would understand.

For endless seconds she thought he didn't.

He was motionless, leaning so close that his hair fell forward to brush the skin of her cheek.

"Parasite," he said softly, more to himself than to her.

Still he did nothing. She knew it was only seconds, but they felt like hours. Like an eternity.

Maybe he didn't want her to survive after all.

She was his enemy. He had told her she would be. Years ago he had warned her. And now, his comrade had near to killed her. She needed no greater proof. As a member of the Asetian Guard, she'd been warned that the reapers were no friends of Aset or her Daughters. But the Daughters were not so bloodthirsty as their enemies. They only warned their soldiers to avoid the soul reapers; they never instructed them to kill.

After this encounter, she thought perhaps it was because the Daughters of Aset wouldn't stand a chance in hell of succeeding.

What the fuck had she been thinking when she went back tonight to save Dagan Krayl? She should have run. Should have kept on running.

Her vision was fading in and out. Black to gray and back again. Then she heard noise, loud, discordant and she forced her thoughts to reform from the splintered shards they'd become. She realized Dagan was right in

her face, yelling, calling her name, forcing her back from the place she had floated to.

"Don't you fucking die," he snarled, eyes blazing, features taut. "Look at me, right here." He made a V with his index and middle finger and pointed at his eyes. "Stay with me, Roxy."

She tried. She really tried. But she felt like she was watching an out-of-focus movie as her vision wove in and out. Her exhalation was ragged, more sob than breath. The urge to howl rose inside her, because she had no strength. Weak. So weak.

"Blood." She needed a raging river of it.

Please. The word had no voice, no volume. She was too weak to speak anymore, too weak to move. She could do little more than raise her hand ineffectively.

Then he *did* understand. She saw the minute widening of his eyes. Only that. It was enough to tell her he'd caught the gist.

Jerking back, he stared down at her, and she thought he meant to decline, to tell her she was touched in the head, to refuse her the only thing that would save her now. He had to know his blood could save her. He'd made her, done this to her, turned her into a parasite that fed from human hosts. Blood had to do the same for him, keep him alive when nothing else could, or maybe reapers were built differently.

She closed her eyes, so very tired.

A faint sound came to her, foreign, out of place. Like tearing cloth. And then she felt the warmth splash her lips.

Her lids flipped open. His wrist was directly above her, torn open, a wide flap of skin hanging loose, and beyond that, the fresh pink flesh of his reforming

hand. The blood dripped in a luscious torrent. She opened her mouth. It splashed on her chin, her lips, her tongue.

An inhuman sound escaped her, half ecstasy, half desperation. He seemed pleased by that, his lips curving in a grim smile. They were rimmed in blood. She realized he'd used his teeth to open a vein.

Panting, she tried to rise, to arch forward, to clutch his wrist and claim her prize. But her body failed her.

He moved, almost faster than she could see, straddling her chest, his knees on either side of her, his torn wrist pressed hard against her open mouth, his free hand cradling the back of her skull, holding her to him.

The flow surging with each beat of his pulse, his blood filled her mouth. She swallowed. Let her mouth fill again. Swallowed again.

It didn't taste like ambrosia. The blood was metallic and sharp, pungent, a little salty, a little sweet, rich with power and life and the lure of the forbidden. A reaper's blood. Dagan's blood. How many times had she tasted him in her dreams?

With a moan, she sank her teeth deep, searching for the fount as she tried to pull more.

More.

He made a harsh sound. She knew she hurt him. But he didn't draw away, and she didn't stop.

There was only need and his blood rushing through her, filling her, feeding her. Life. She wanted to *live*.

Agony suffused her, multiplying exponentially, and with it came a sharp and over-focused awareness of her heart, her pulse, the scents and sounds around her. She welcomed it all.

But a part of her knew that she was damaging him.

She eased back a little, letting the flow come to her rather than tearing at him like a starving beast.

She was alive, and planning to stay that way. But she didn't need to maim him to do it.

She fed from him and knew she would survive. Not an easy task. She wouldn't heal in a blaze of instantaneous glory. She would suffer and she would ache. But she *would* survive.

How long did she feed?

It felt like an eternity of bliss, but was more likely only seconds.

Still, he held his wrist to her mouth and let her drink and drink and she was filled with him, aching for him. Somewhere inside her, she recognized the shift, recognized that she wanted to surge over him and push him to the ground and, with her lips suctioning his vein, she wanted to take him inside her, feel his cock fill her, feel the thrust and grind of his hips against her own.

But the mind and the body were not synchronized. Despite the luscious bent of her thoughts, she was too weak to force her limbs to act.

Enough.

She must have taken enough. Perhaps too much. He'd been hurt earlier, his hand burned away. How much blood could he afford to lose? Or did such things matter to an immortal soul reaper?

With a gasp, she tore her mouth away and turned her head to the side.

"Better?" he asked, his voice thick.

Was she?

Raising her hand, she brought it toward her ruined chest. Strength failed her at the end, and her hand flopped down to lie against torn cloth and torn flesh,

warm and sticky with her blood. But there was no longer a massive gaping hole. Had there ever been? She thought so. She thought the other reaper had had his hand full inside her.

"My..." Was that her voice? That pathetic rasping whisper?

"Shh." He rested a finger against her lips, his head cocked, muscles suddenly taut and humming with tension. He still straddled her body, forming a shelter, a shield. "I need to get you somewhere safe."

Somewhere safe. *Calliope.* It was the closest thing to safe she could come up with.

Great plan. She could just imagine Calliope's expression if she showed up with a soul reaper in tow. Well, actually, he'd be towing her, or probably carrying her, leaving a trail of blood in their wake.

What were her options? Die here on the forest floor, or trust him with Calliope's location.

She swallowed. Her throat felt raw, like she'd screamed for hours then downed a mug of lemon juice.

Dying didn't really appeal. But neither did betrayal, and that's exactly what she'd be bringing if she brought a soul reaper to Calliope's door. Bad enough that she hadn't left him to his fate when the fire genies attacked. Worse, she'd fed on his blood.

But somehow bringing him to Calliope's home seemed a step beyond either. It was like bringing the wolf to the door. And opening it for him.

In the end, she didn't have to decide. Dagan shifted so he no longer straddled her chest but instead knelt at her side. His forearms slid under her shoulders and her hips.

Harpooned by her agony, she cried out as he tried to lift her.

The pressure eased as he let her rest fully on the ground once more. His expression hardened, but his touch was gentle as he reached up and stroked her hair back from her face. Then he leaned in until he was so close that his breath brushed her cheek. She could smell the faint citrus of his skin and the stronger scent of smoke from the fires Xaphan's concubines had started. And she could smell his blood where it yet smeared his lips.

She stared at his lips. His mouth was drawn in a taut line, hard and tense. She wanted to feel his mouth on hers, to taste him. She wanted to kiss him—not in case she died, but in case she lived.

His hand slid to the angle of her jaw, then her throat. She could feel her pulse beating against the pads of his fingers.

"Don't you fucking die," he breathed.

She didn't think she would. Thanks to him.

His gaze locked on hers. She didn't know how long they simply stared at each other.

He made a primitive sound, deep in his chest, and then he kissed her, his mouth hard on hers. She opened and took his tongue in her mouth, tasted his desperation and his fear for her, his dominion and power, and his blood. It stained his lips, and hers, and it was there in their kiss, electric and forbidden, salty and sweet.

His breath was hers. His blood was hers. The electricity of his power thrummed between them.

With a groan, he drew back. "I need to move you."

"I know."

"I don't want to hurt you."

"I know." But it *would* hurt. Not much anyone could do about that.

There was an odd look in his eyes, one she couldn't quite read. Not just because the night was dark, but because she had the feeling he was guarding his thoughts, forcing his features to betray nothing as he studied her face, her throat, her bloodstained chest. Then his gaze lifted to hers once more.

"I guess one more won't matter," he said.

"One more what?"

"Bruise."

His hand closed tight around her throat. His fingers pressed deep. And everything went black.

CHAPTER SIXTEEN

I will not let you take away this heart of mine
Which belongs to the living who move about

—Egyptian Book of the Dead, Chapter 29

A SOUND DREW HER FROM THE DARKNESS. Crinkling. Like plastic wrap being pulled off a candy. Roxy reached for that sound, tried to grab hold of it, an anchor. It disappeared, and she was left in the dark, surrounded by thick fog.

At some point the fog receded. She lay on her back, drenched in sweat, covered by something soft and warm. The air smelled a bit like smoke, a bit like citrus potpourri and a bit like lemon cleaner. Lemon. She'd always loved that smell.

Well, maybe not always, but for years. Years and years.

She liked lemon lollipops. The thought made her smile.

She faded, drifted, and let the fog and dreams take her.

"Drink."

There was something resting against her lips, something hard. A cup. It tapped against her teeth as she opened her mouth and drank. Blood. Warm, salty, metallic.

Blood from a cup.

She wanted blood from his wrist. His neck. His groin.

Did she say that out loud? He made an impatient sound that made her think she might have.

She swallowed the last of it and laughed, though she didn't know why. It came out brittle, and a little wild.

"Sleep." Tense. Terse. Not laughing like her.

Bossy. But for some reason, that made her feel comforted rather than angry.

She slept.

She tried to wake, clawed through the cobwebs that clung to her thoughts, but never quite tore all the way free. She could hear water pounding. The shower. Someone in her shower. She turned her head toward the bathroom and saw light leaking from beneath the door. Then it was gone, and all was dark.

Again, the pattern repeated. How long she vacillated between sleep and almost awake, she couldn't say. Throughout her lost hours—or was it lost days?—she knew Dagan was there. Watching over her. She heard him, felt his hand on her hair, or at her back, propping her up while she drank, or tucking the covers around her when she shivered.

He brought her water, ice tinkling in the glass.

"Slowly," he said as she guzzled, so thirsty she felt like the sand of the desert filled her. "You'll make yourself sick again."

Again?

"Blood," she demanded.

"Water," he said.

"Why do you get to choose?"

He laughed. "Because you're in no position to argue."

"Asshole. Why are you laughing while I'm dying?"

No answer, and then, just as she drifted away, he said, "Because you're *not* dying."

Later, she felt a cool, wet cloth on her skin, stroking her arm from shoulder to fingertips, stroking her leg from thigh to toes. It felt good, so good, and she arched and moaned and opened her eyes.

Awareness skittered through her, sensitizing every nerve ending in her body. It was one of those dreams where Dagan Krayl stood over her and she was naked. But this dream was different somehow. Then it hit her. He was clothed.

In all the dreams past, he'd always been naked, hard muscle and hot skin. Reaching out, she trailed her fingertips along his denim-clad thigh.

"Take them off," she said.

He made a sound low in his chest. She reached for him…reached…and then the dream disappeared and she slept.

The sound of a spoon tinkling against glass woke her. She turned her head. Dagan was sitting in the overstuffed chair in the corner. On the low table was her glass pitcher with the swirling blue handle, a glass full of cloudy water and her sugar bowl. He took a spoonful of sugar and dumped it in the water, stirred, studied the results, then added another spoon and another.

He looked up and caught her watching him. "Ran out of lollipops," he said, and she thought that was the most bizarre thing she'd ever heard.

Tipping back his head, he bared the strong column of his throat, and she watched the movements as he swallowed, downing the glass of sugar water, cloudy

white. Her teeth hurt just watching him. She wanted to ask him why he was doing that but, again, her thoughts faded to black.

The next time she roused, she climbed out of the dream as though she were hauling herself out of a sucking bog, the last tendrils clinging to her, refusing to let her go. A final surge and she opened her eyes and knew exactly where she was: in her bed, in her room, cream walls and rich, warm-honey wood floors, and her own pillows, fluffy and full.

The curtains were drawn, the air stale.

She wanted light. She wanted a breeze and the smell of the outdoors.

She wanted to know what the hell had happened and how long she'd been out of it.

"You're awake."

She turned her head and found him lounging in the doorway, one shoulder propped against the frame, arms crossed over his chest. His hair was loose, damp, falling around his shoulders.

Faded jeans rode low on his hips. He wasn't wearing a shirt. He was all sleek lines and ridges, biceps and pectorals and washboard abdomen. He was a work of art. The kind that begged to be touched.

"How—" She paused, cleared her throat. Her mouth felt like she'd been eating sawdust.

Dagan pushed off the door frame and crossed to the small table in the corner by the window. He lifted the pitcher, the one with the swirly blue handle—so that part hadn't been a dream.

"No sugar," she rasped as he poured water into a glass. "I don't have your sweet tooth."

"You remember that?" He shot her a glance.

She didn't bother to answer, just stared at the glass. She was parched bone-dry, so thirsty she didn't want just a single cup—she wanted the whole pitcher.

The glass he brought her was less than half full.

Clutching the sheet against her breasts, she pushed to a sitting position. She waited for the inevitable wave of dizziness and was grateful that it never came. Tipping her head back, she looked at him where he loomed over her like a great gold-and-bronze beast. Bare torso. Rippling muscle.

She was surprised she was lucid enough to notice.

Actually, no. No, she wasn't. A build like that was impossible to miss. She'd have to be dead not to notice.

"Slow," he said as she took the glass from him, "or you'll just end up puking it out again."

Again? Which meant she'd already puked some out? And he'd done…what? Cleaned her up? Changed her linens? A charming possibility.

"How long?" she asked after she'd downed the water and handed the glass back to him.

"Three days."

She blinked. Three days. Memories flashed like a slide show. Pain. Blood. Him carrying her to her bed, talking to her, calming her. Carrying her to the bathroom, holding her while she—

No, please, no. That was too mortifying.

Surreptitiously, she ran her hand along her thigh and encountered only skin. Her heart thudded in her chest. Sliding her palm up to her hip, her waist, she found more skin.

"You stripped me!"

His smile was mocking. "Would you have preferred that I leave you in your blood-soaked, ragged clothes?"

"Yes!" He'd seen her naked. Completely, utterly naked. And at her worst. *Dandy.*

He laughed, a dark, low sound. "Well, you weren't conscious to express your preference, so I followed my own. Leaving you in blood-spattered, mud-caked clothing seemed the greater of evils."

Heart hammering, she stared at him, broad chest and taut belly, faded denim hugging muscled thighs.

"What happened to your shirt?"

Again, that mocking smile. "You bled on it."

Fair enough.

She knew there were things she ought to be focusing on. Instead, her gaze slid to his mouth, and she focused on the one thing she oughtn't.

He'd kissed her.

That's what filled her thoughts. She had bigger, more immediate problems. She'd almost died. She had no business thinking about his mouth on hers, no business thinking that eleven years of naughty dreams should have made his kiss mundane. But she couldn't seem to stop obsessing about that single point.

He'd kissed her.

Twice.

The first kiss, the one before the fire genies had come, had been hot and wet and deep. Exactly the way she'd thought it would be. It had sent a flash flood of lust drumming through her.

But the second kiss was the one that cut her open and laid her bare. Because that's what he'd done out there on the forest floor when he'd pressed his mouth to hers and let her feel his emotions.

He'd cut himself open, laid *himself* bare.

His every thought had been in the touch of his lips

and the thrust of his tongue and the taste of his blood shared between them. Desperation. Rage. Futility. She had tasted his emotions, blending with her own.

That kiss had been something more than she'd ever dreamed about, and the thought of finding out what that something more might be scared the shit out of her.

She realized she was still staring at his mouth. And he was staring at hers.

"What?" he murmured. "Nearly dying cranks your handle?"

She opened her mouth to offer a sassy comeback, but what came out wasn't anything she wanted to say.

"You left me." The words surged and tore free from somewhere deep inside, a place she had always refused to acknowledge. She immediately wished she could call them back. They made no sense. Her feelings about him made no sense.

He raked his fingers back through his hair and then glanced down at the glass in his hand, as though wondering where it had come from. He set it on the night table.

Don't answer, she thought. *Let it go.* Safer that way. Safer to cling to the possibility that maybe she'd misread, maybe he didn't feel a damned thing for her and saving her was all about getting information.

Then he did answer, and blew that theory all to hell.

"I wanted you to have a nice, safe, normal life, Roxy. A mortal life." His tone was low, and he didn't look at her, just kept his eyes on the empty glass, tapping the tip of his index finger against the rim. "You wouldn't have if I was in it."

"So you left me to figure it all out alone?" He hadn't even told her what he'd done to her, hadn't warned her

how horrible it would be to ache and crave and lust for blood.

He glanced up, stared at the far wall, his jaw taut, his lips drawn in a hard line.

"I left you to have a life. I told you to stay away from the Daughters of Aset. I warned you." Finally, he did look at her, his eyes bright and hard, his words so low she had to strain to hear them. "You weren't supposed to go looking for them, draw their attention, get snared in their web. You were supposed to marry a fucking accountant and live in a house with a picket fence."

"An accountant—"

"You were supposed to have babies and a dog—" his words grew louder, more forceful "—and drive them around in a fucking minivan. You were supposed to go to fucking yoga on fucking Wednesday nights."

"Yoga?" Bewildered, both by his words and the barely suppressed violence behind them, she stared at him. "Did you really believe that was going to happen?"

He raked his fingers through his hair. "Yeah. I really did."

And she sort of understood that. Hadn't she wanted exactly that for the girls she'd saved from the lesser demon who worked as an enforcer for Hades? She'd wanted them to head back to their normal, high school lives.

She stared at Dagan, suddenly seeing the tension in his features, the dark shadows beneath his eyes.

She ought to leave it alone. She knew that. Instead, she swallowed and asked, "How did that make you feel?"

"What?"

"The idea of—" she lifted one hand and waved it, palm up "—me living the life you describe? Marrying an accountant and ferrying my kids around in a minivan."

A hard bark of laughter escaped him. "It made me feel like I wanted to rip the heart and darksoul out of the worthless human who got to lie beside you at night. Except he wouldn't have a darksoul. He'd be all shiny and bright."

The way he was looking at her made her shudder. Possessive. Dominant.

"But you left me." Like everyone else.

"Because there's no place for you in my world." His tone was savage.

"I don't even know you," she whispered, completely at a loss to understand the feelings churning inside her. A match to his, if his words and actions were any indication.

"But you do. And I know you." He leaned down and fisted both hands on the mattress, her mother's pendant still hanging around his neck, swaying forward, then back. His pupils were dilated; there was only a thin rim of gray around the endless dark depths. "Dream much?"

She sucked in a sharp breath. He offered a feral, knowing smile, white teeth, zero warmth.

"I know you hate chocolate."

"Fine, but do you know *why*?"

"Tell me," he whispered, but she pressed her lips together and said nothing, too confused to even know what to say.

"You like sweet wine," he continued. He frowned and narrowed his eyes. "You have a subscription to

Forbes. You like your privacy, hence the house in the middle of nowhere. You never eat steak." He paused then and met her gaze. "You kept my jacket in the back of your closet. For eleven years." Seconds ticked past. "And you took it out every so often and wrapped it against your naked skin."

She looked away from the intensity of his stare, feeling out of her depth.

Some of these things he could have gleaned from going through her drawers while she was out of it, but not all of them. Not the part about wrapping herself in his battered leather coat and wondering what it would really feel like to be wrapped in *him*, his arms, his legs, his scent.

Reaching out, he curled his fingers under her jaw, and gently turned her head until she had no choice but to look at him.

"You wanna know how I know this shit? I snooped through your dreams, just like you snooped through mine."

She took a long, slow breath, fighting for calm, searching for some reasonable explanation, not willing to believe what she thought he was telling her. That all those nights she'd touched him, stroked him, tasted him and let him taste her, she hadn't been flying solo. He'd been right there with her.

No.

That was wrong. Just *wrong*.

"Do soul reapers do that? Dreamwalk—" she lifted her hand, dropped it "—or whatever you want to call it?"

"No." He snorted. "Reapers don't dream."

"But you just said—"

"Yeah. I know what I said."

Clutching the sheet against her breasts, she studied his face, not even knowing what she was looking for. She felt at a distinct disadvantage. She was naked. He loomed over her, practically naked, with only those low-slung jeans between him and the altogether.

As though he understood the bizarre thoughts flashing through her mind, he pushed his fists against the mattress and straightened, then took a step back, giving her space to breathe.

Or maybe, giving himself space.

Reaching up, Roxy pushed her hair back off her face. It felt lank, and if she wasn't mistaken, she smelled like a dead goat.

Her hand was shaking as she moved it to her chest, sliding it beneath the sheet to feel between her breasts for the healing wound she knew would mark the place Gahiji had torn her open. It was there, smooth and raised. With a gasp, she peeked beneath the sheet and found a scar that looked months old.

Misreading her actions, Dagan soothed, "It's healing. The mark will fade in time."

"Fade? It already looks three months old rather than three days!" Though she tended to heal quickly, this was crazy weird even for her.

She stared at him, and it hit her that he had two perfectly formed hands.

Catching his wrist, she dragged his hand closer, inspecting it—first palm up, then palm down. He let her, offering no resistance. His palm was creased with the usual lines, fingers long and tapered, fine gold hairs on the back of his hand.

Not a mark. Not a scar.

He'd regrown a full hand in three days or less.

He must have figured the path of her thoughts, because he said, "I always heal, Roxy."

"Always?"

"Yeah."

From his tone, she could tell that he meant that as reassurance, but it wasn't. Because it made her think of exactly why he'd come to find her the night the fire genies attacked, and it made her wonder what the fuck was going on.

"If you can heal like that, heal *anything,* how the fuck did the Setnakhts kill one of you?"

The air hummed with tension as her question hung between them.

"The Setnakhts?" He pulled his hand from hers and arched one straight brow. "You know that for certain?"

"You knew they might be somehow involved," she hedged.

"*Might be* is very different than definitely. You sound very sure."

She thought about it, tried to figure all the angles. Answering that question would be yet another betrayal of her allegiance to the Asetian Guard. Because going back to help him when he'd faced the fire genies hadn't exactly been in her mandate.

Which was worse, saving her enemy's hide, or giving him information about the Setnakhts?

He'd saved her hide first. Did that make it okay?

Damn, she definitely didn't do her best thinking when she'd barely survived getting her heart ripped out.

"Why do you want to know? You looking to avenge your brother's murder, kill the killer?" Of course he

was, but she'd rather be asking the questions than answering them, and that was the first thing that popped to mind.

Dagan offered a predator's smile, bared teeth, no humor.

"I share, you share?"

"Something like that."

"I want to find his body and bring him back."

Yeah, she'd figured. But hearing him say it made the situation very sticky. "So you can find not just the one who wielded the knife but the one who set the plan in motion."

"Great minds think alike," he murmured, the words heavy with sarcasm.

There you go. Proof positive that what he wanted and what she'd been assigned to achieve didn't mesh so good. "So, let's say you succeed, let's say you bring him back and he fingers the ones behind the plan. What then?"

"Then—" he shrugged "—I kill them all. A quick strike."

"Even if it pisses off their allies? Even if you throw the Underworld into chaos? Even if your vengeance ultimately costs hundreds of thousand of human lives? They'll all come after you. Then your crew will go after them. And so on and so on. You're going to start a fucking Armageddon. Is one soul reaper's life worth that?"

He moved so fast, she didn't have a hope in hell of ducking. His fingers closed around her wrists, not hard enough to hurt, just firm enough to hold her still. He was bigger. And he hadn't been near death for the past three days. But she wasn't afraid of him.

"I know what's inside your skin, Dagan Krayl," she whispered, her eyes never leaving his.

"There's a soul reaper inside my skin, Roxy Tam." His fingers tightened.

"A soul reaper who's spent an inordinate amount of effort keeping me alive." She traced the tip of her tongue over her lower lip. "Don't pretend you'd hurt me now."

They clashed in silent challenge, then he jerked his hands away and stepped back. He shoved his hands in his pockets, which only served to push his jeans down so far she could follow the treasure trail right down to the very top of the triangle of hair at its base.

"I could kill you if I wished."

"Without a doubt," she conceded to assuage his stupid male pride. Because actions spoke far louder than words, and he'd just spent three days doing everything he could to keep her alive.

He was torn. She could see that. His anger at her words meant he cared at least a little about the humans who might die if he followed his plan. But did he care enough? Or was his brother's life worth everything to him?

He was quiet for a moment, then he said, "What if you could find your mother's killer? Wreak bloody, brutal revenge? Would you turn down that opportunity—" he slanted her a dark look "—even if it unleashed a fucking Armageddon?"

Her mother's killer. There it was. Cold and ugly and bare. Her mother had been murdered. Somehow he knew that for certain.

She knew her pain was etched on her face, bare and raw. She knew it, and she couldn't find the strength to try and hide it.

And if she did have the opportunity he described, wouldn't she take it, no matter the price? Wouldn't she?

"We're not so far apart, Roxy."

No, she supposed they weren't.

"I killed him," he said then, his expression one of satisfaction. "The one who murdered your mother. I tore open his chest. I pulled out his heart. And I sent his darksoul to Sutekh." He bared his teeth in a parody of a smile. "How did you describe it? Ah, yes…I broke the cycle. No chance for rebirth. He is simply—" he snapped his fingers "—gone."

Rage and nausea and hate boiled in her gut. "I wanted to be the one—"

"Precisely."

Their gazes locked and she acknowledged game point. She knew exactly how he felt about his brother's killer.

Why did she have to feel that affinity with him? It made everything…complicated.

"I need to know what you know," he said softly.

She owed him her life. Twice over. She owed him a debt for killing her mother's killer. But a decade ago, alone, confused, hungering for blood and terrified of what she'd become, she'd accepted Aset's Daughters as her family. How to honor both debts?

She mentally tested—and discarded—tidbits of information she could share without betraying the Asetian Guard or her own morals. Finally, she settled on information he already knew, with just enough fresh meat to satisfy. Frank Marin was dead, his soul gone to wherever it was meant to go. If that was Sutekh's realm, then Sutekh had probably already pried whatever answers he could from Marin's darksoul. But if it

was someone else's realm, she didn't want to betray any more than necessary.

"Frank Marin was there, the night they brought your brother in," she said. "He told me he didn't see the actual killing. But he saw them bring your brother to the Temple of Setnakht—"

"Where? They have several worldwide."

She hesitated. How much information was too much? But he was staring down at her, arms crossed now over his broad chest, expression cold and flat, and she figured she'd give this much and no more. Because in the end, despite the things he'd done for her, their goals were still diametrically opposed. "Toronto."

The only response she got was a grunt.

End of conversation.

Neither of them said another word about it.

She figured the time for a quick exit was as ripe as her smell. "I need a shower," she muttered.

With the sheet clutched to her breasts, she swung her legs over the side of the bed, then just sat there, staring at the floor, getting her bearings and waiting to see if her head started to swim.

When nothing dire happened, she raised her head and found herself staring at the mirror above the dresser. It reflected an image from the mirrored door of her closet behind her: her shoulders and back naked. The cream-colored sheet, a vivid contrast to her dark skin, was pooled low at her hips. Her hair hung in tumbled disarray.

But the image revealed more than the curve of her spine and the flare of her hips. It reflected Dagan, close behind her, shirtless, arms crossed, his head turned toward her, his expression stark and hungry.

Dangerous territory.

Her breath caught and she felt electricity spark on her skin.

Then he looked up and caught her watching him, and their gazes locked and held. Did she breathe? Did her heart beat?

Finally, he looked away.

She rose, clutching a fistful of sheet to strategically cover her ass. He stayed perfectly still.

"No need to rush to my assistance." She was a bit breathless.

"I know."

She gave a snort of strained laughter.

"What's so funny?"

"You." When he shot her an offended look, she hastened to smooth his ruffled feathers. "I can't decide if I ought to be thrilled that you think I'm back to being able to handle things on my own, or offended that you're done playing the gentleman."

She watched in the mirror as his gaze dropped once more to the naked expanse of her back, dipping to the barely covered swell of her buttocks, lingering there.

"*Playing* the gentleman," he mused. Then his gaze snapped up and met hers in the mirror once more. "You need help getting to the shower?"

"You hoping I'll say yes?" She turned her head to look at him over her shoulder.

One side of his mouth curved. "I'm just hoping you'll shower—"

"Thanks." Nice. That had put her in her place. She imagined she smelled like a sewer.

Reaching back, she hauled the sheet higher, then shuffled forward, feeling like all kinds of a fool.

She was halfway to the bathroom door before he said, "You didn't let me finish."

Again, she glanced at him over her shoulder, acutely aware that he'd seen her naked, that he'd stuck around through the worst of times. Bad-ass soul reaper playing Florence Nightingale. He'd tended to her most primitive, basic needs, fed her his blood and saved her life. Again.

He hadn't left her this time.

She wanted to touch him.

She wanted him in the shower with her, soapy, wet hands gliding on her soapy, wet skin.

"So finish." Her mouth was dry, her pulse racing.

He rounded the bed and prowled closer. She did a half turn, keeping him in her sights, and backed up a step just a millisecond too late. He lunged, caught the edge of the sheet and gave it a tug. Struggling to hold it in place, she fisted one hand at the front, one at the back, holding fast to clumps of material.

"I'm just hoping you'll shower—" he gave the sheet another tug. She tightened her hold and scooted away, toward the open bathroom door "—and let me watch."

Her head jerked up. She met the glittering gray of his gaze. Not cold now. As far from cold as anything could be.

"Not gonna happen."

"No?" He arched one straight brow. "You might change your mind."

She tried to edge sideways, but he had a solid grip on the sheet, limiting her choices. Either she stayed exactly where she was and kept her cover, or she dropped it and bolted.

He was too close, too tempting, and she was wearing

a film of three-day sweat. That was pretty much the only thing that kept her from dropping the sheet and grabbing him.

The pounding of her pulse marked the seconds.

She held his gaze, aching, wanting, knowing on every level that letting him get close to her was a mistake. *Don't touch him. Don't ache for him. For the love of Aset, don't have sex with him.*

But that was the thing about common sense. It was only worth something if she chose to heed it.

And right now, the way he was looking at her, like he was starving and she was a nice, rare steak, made her want to bury her common sense six feet under.

She took a single step toward him. His expression shifted, hardened, like that of a predator catching a scent.

Dropping the sheet, she bolted.

CHAPTER SEVENTEEN

As for all the evil which is on me,
It is what I have done among the lords of eternity
Ever since I came down from my mother's womb

— Egyptian Book of the Dead, Chapter 17

DAGAN BENT AND RETRIEVED the discarded sheet from the floor, rolled it into a messy ball and just stood for a second, holding it, seeing Roxy in his mind's eye, naked skin and tumbled hair. The length of her legs, strong and brown and so fucking long they made his mouth go dry just thinking about them.

He wanted her legs wrapped around his waist. Hell, he wanted them up over his shoulders and her underneath him, moaning and clawing at his skin.

Tossing the sheet on the bed, he glared at the closed bathroom door. He could hear the water running in the sink and the soft scrape of her brushing her teeth. Then the sink turned off and the shower turned on.

He fought the urge to test the lock. To kick the door down and climb in with her, skin to wet skin, her back against the glass tile shower stall, her legs around his waist, the hiss of her breath in his ear as he pushed himself inside her.

His body definitely liked that image.

Sliding his hand inside his jeans, he shifted himself to a more comfortable angle, and felt a little ridiculous for getting a hard-on from just thinking about her.

"Fuck." She had him tied up in knots, wanting her safe, wanting her alive. And just plain wanting her.

Not her fault. He knew that. He was the one with all sorts of bizarre things going through his head. Things like possessing her, protecting her, fucking her till she came fast and hard, screaming his name.

The way he felt about Roxy Tam made no sense at all. Never had. He was getting the feeling it never would.

Blowing out a breath, he crossed to the window and drew the curtain aside with the tips of his fingers, narrowing his eyes against the glare of the sun. He did a quick scan of the empty drive and rolling front lawn. A habit more than a precaution. He'd sense any supernaturals by means other than sight long before his eyes could perceive them. But he was antsy. Too many days cooped up in this house, this room. Too many days thinking he might lose her.

Which was crazy thinking, because he sure as sugar hadn't had her in the first place.

That had been his choice. His fault.

He'd walked away.

From the second he'd laid eyes on her he'd known he wanted to stay, known he'd have to go. She'd had sass and spice. Guts. Tiger-bright eyes and a face that he'd never forgotten.

She'd had the most gorgeous breasts he'd ever laid eyes on.

And she'd been nineteen. And a half. And mortal. What the fuck else was he supposed to do but walk away?

It was exactly what he ought to do right now, for a whole different set of reasons. Caring about a mortal—caring about *anyone*—made him vulnerable. He'd nearly lost it when Lokan was killed. He didn't want to feel that way ever again, and if he let himself feel for Roxy, he *would* know that pain once more. Because she would die. She would leave him, and he would be alone. Again.

He hit the side of his fist against the wall. He had some crazy shit going through his head.

Letting the curtain fall back in place, he sprawled in the overstuffed chair in the corner, took out his cell and dialed Alastor's number.

"Wanker. I've rung you a dozen times," Alastor clipped. "Nice if you'd return a call in a timely manner."

"I was busy. I'm not busy now. You alone?"

"Yes."

"What happened with Gahiji and the old man?"

"Bugger went straight to Sutekh. Listed his complaints against your handling of the situation."

"Hmm." Dagan poured himself a glass of water and started ladling in spoons of sugar. He'd run out of lollipops days ago, and since Roxy hadn't had anything in the house that was sweet—not candy, not chocolate, not even ice cream—and since he wasn't about to leave her alone and unguarded while he went shopping, he'd made do with what he could find. Refined sugar. Not ideal, but going without was even less ideal. Especially since he'd been slitting his wrist open at regular intervals to bleed into a cup. "And?"

"And Sutekh listened to what Gahiji had to say."

"Hmm." He chugged half the glass. Grimaced.

Chugged the rest. A translucent, goopy sludge of half-dissolved sugar sat at the bottom. With a sigh, he grabbed the spoon and scooped it out, then licked the spoon clean. Nice. Sugar rush. "And?"

Alastor laughed. "Any of Dad's troops show up to keep you company?"

"No."

"Then you can figure the rest yourself."

"You talked the old man down." Dagan set the spoon on the table. "I owe you one. How did you manage it?"

"I merely pointed out the obvious. That Sutekh is the one who called a peaceful gathering of the heads of the Underworld to be held three days hence. Slaughtering one of Aset's Daughters practically on the eve of that meeting might lead to the entire Asetian Guard showing up looking for blood. Hardly a way to support his assertion that he's looking for a lasting peace."

"Not good politics."

"Precisely."

"And Sutekh prides himself on being a good politician. Nicely played."

"Thank you."

"And Gahiji?"

"He's dancing a very careful waltz at the moment, slow and controlled. He knows Dad's not pleased, and he knows I'm watching him." Alastor was quiet for a second, then he asked, "What the bloody hell was he thinking? It was as if he had a personal grudge against your Roxy Tam."

"Yeah." Dagan paused. Gahiji *had* acted like it was personal, though he'd offered generalizations as justification. But the whole thing had felt off. Wrong.

Something dark and dangerous uncoiled inside him. Suspicion.

He had a flash of recollection, like a flare going off, of Lokan mentioning Gahiji's name before he'd headed off to get himself killed. Nothing unusual there. Gahiji often conveyed the old man's orders. Why was that particular time suddenly jumping out at Dagan like a plaid tie against a paisley shirt?

He shook his head. He was clutching at any and every straw. What was he thinking? That the old man was harboring a traitor? Gahiji had been his father's right hand since at least a millennium before Dagan was born.

"Speaking of...how *is* Ms. Tam?" Alastor asked.

Dagan glanced at the bathroom door. "She's alive, and I intend to make certain she stays that way."

"You realize you sound positively rabid?"

"No." *Yes.* Rabid. Possessive. Territorial. Out of his fucking mind.

Taking a deep breath, Dagan consciously willed himself to tone down the snarl. His emotions were gut deep and murky. He couldn't explain them because he didn't understand them. Had never understood them. Not since the first time he'd laid eyes on her.

Ah, but he did finally have clarity on one point. He'd left her eleven years ago so she could have normal, human life. He'd convinced himself it was the correct line of action.

Now he knew for certain that altruism didn't pay. He'd made the sacrifice for nothing, because obviously her life was neither human nor normal.

Lesson learned.

He wouldn't make the same mistake again.

He realized Alastor was talking, and he forced himself to focus on his brother's words. "…and find out if Gahiji has had any direct contact with the Toronto branch of the Setnakhts."

"I'll take care of it." He paused, thinking of the way Alastor had stepped up three nights past, no questions asked, standing with him against Gahiji to save Roxy's life, then covering for him with Sutekh. "I owe you, Alastor."

Silence. Then Alastor said softly, "No, you don't."

And that simple assertion said it all. His brother was there for him, no matter what. The moment stretched, and Dagan had the urge to ask his advice, to find out if a woman had ever gotten to Alastor like Roxy'd gotten to him. The question clamored to crawl free, his natural reticence holding it back. Finally, he asked, "Hey Alastor, you ever read *The Godfather*?"

A huffing exhalation, then, "I saw the movie."

"Not the same."

"Why do you ask?"

How to explain? He tried to think of a way to come at the question from an angle that actually made sense, but he came up with nothing. He shook his head. What was he thinking? Alastor knew as much about women as he did.

"Let me know what you find out about Gahiji," Dagan said, dropping the subject, knowing that his brother was probably wondering if he had gone *bloody daft*.

Next up, Dagan dialed Mal, listened to the ring, then the message. *"You got Mal. Talk. If I like what you have to say, you'll hear back from me."*

Dagan didn't talk; he just disconnected the call.

He'd barely shoved his phone in his pocket when it rang.

"Yeah."

"A little surly today?"

Ignoring Mal's question, Dagan asked, "Does the old man have a reaper shadowing you?"

"He did. Samuel left about an hour ago."

"So you're alone?"

"For a short while."

Of course. Mal liked to entertain, as long as his guests were female.

"Find out anything from Xaphan's concubines?"

"They want that kid. Dana."

Dagan drummed his fingers on the table in a slow roll. "We knew that three days ago. You got anything new?"

"She's not where she should be. I checked the house in Oklahoma City. Two dresser drawers were left open in the kid's room. Looked like someone had grabbed handfuls of clothes in a hurry. A single suitcase was missing from the matched set in the master bedroom closet."

"Signs of forced entry or struggle?"

"No."

"Blood?"

"No."

"Anything else?"

"Looked like Dana's mother took the time to lock the door behind her."

"Or whoever took them locked it. Was there any supernatural vibe left behind?"

"Nothing."

"So a human took them." Dagan paused. "Or they took themselves. You got anything else?"

"Frank Marin's travel itinerary." Four little words, uttered with barely suppressed glee.

Dagan pinched the bridge of his nose and sighed. "Okay, I'll bite. Tell me about Marin's itinerary."

"He flew from Oklahoma City to Toronto. Stayed a night and a day. Then flew Toronto to Houston, rented a car and drove to Amarillo."

"Fascinating. You wanna tell me what he ate for breakfast, too? He a bacon guy, or sausage?"

Mal laughed. "How about I tell you that the kid was with him the entire time?"

Dagan sat straighter in the chair. "That *is* fascinating."

"Gets better. I got a witness, a young Setnakht recruit, Marie Matheson. She remembers seeing Lokan walking into the temple just as a little blond girl was walking out. She says he stopped and ruffled the kid's hair. Marie claims the kid looked all friendly and pleased to see him, that she hugged him."

"What the fuck?"

"That was my exact reaction. Wanna bet that kid was the mysterious, missing Dana?"

"I don't make losing bets. You got anything else?"

"Your guy, Joe Marin, he flew in to Toronto the same day as his brother and Dana."

"Alastor has a Toronto parking stub I lifted off Joe Marin—"

"I'll check with him. I'm betting the dates match."

"So we have the Marin brothers, the Setnakhts, this missing kid, Dana and Lokan, all in Toronto…"

"A fucking party," Mal agreed.

"Two days and a night…not long, but long enough. My gut's telling me they're all connected to Lokan's murder."

"Looks like."

"And the kid? What's her role?" What purpose could she have served?

"The sixty-four-thousand-dollar question. Maybe she had no role. Maybe she was incidental."

"Your witness says Lokan knew Dana, so I'm doubting she was incidental. Roxy was sent by the Asetian Guard to find her. Marin was holed up with her in some rat-shit motel. Xaphan's genies came here looking for her. Everyone seems to want a piece of that kid." Dagan picked up the spoon and tapped it lightly on the edge of the empty glass. "She wasn't incidental. She's a game piece. I just need to figure out the board."

"Maybe she's a witness. The last living witness to Lokan's death."

Dagan considered that, added the possibility to his mental list. "Maybe."

"You don't sound convinced."

"Because I'm not."

Mal laughed. "Neither am I, brother. Neither am I."

Dagan's gaze slid to the closed bathroom door. How much did Roxy know? How much was she keeping to herself? He had every intention of finding out, by fair means or foul. "Get anything else from Xaphan's concubines?"

"A great deal." Mal laughed again, obviously relishing the memory. "They were chock-full of energy. And information. Lovely creatures. Inclined to be helpful. But I believe I was entertaining a different group than those you met with."

"'Met with.' That's a polite way to put it." Dagan set the spoon down with exaggerated care. "I'm thinking Xaphan had a crew in Toronto at the same time that the

Marin boys were in town. Otherwise, it's too coinciden-
tal that the fire genies showed up at Frank Marin's motel
in Amarillo, looking for the kid at the same time as
Roxy."

"Yeah." Mal was quiet for a few seconds. "You do
realize your Roxy's in this shit at least hip-deep. Maybe
neck-deep. She was the first one to reach Frank Marin.
The only one we know of to talk to this amazing, dis-
appearing child. All of which points to the likelihood
that Aset's involved."

"A supernatural's involved. Of that I have no doubt.
Whether it's Aset remains to be proven." Again, the coil
of suspicion slithered through him. "I'm thinking it
might be closer to home."

There was a beat of silence as Mal digested that for
a second. "How close?"

"In our fucking front yard."

Mal gave a low whistle. "You care to elaborate?"

"Just as soon as I have something to elaborate on."

"Your Roxy, she say anything about Marin?"

"He admitted he was there when the Setnakhts
brought Lokan in."

Mal's voice was flat as he said, "The Setnakhts
worship Sutekh. And they're mortal. How the fuck
could they kill Lokan? And why? I really hate it when
the puzzle pieces don't fit."

Dagan dropped his gaze to his hand—the one
Xaphan's concubine had burned away—and clenched
his fist a couple of times. Good as new.

*If you can heal like that, heal anything, how the
fuck did the Setnakhts kill one of you?*

Mal's question echoed Roxy's, and Dagan didn't
have an answer for either of them.

Because he could come up with very few possibilities except a traitor in Sutekh's ranks, working with the Setnakhts. Who themselves were supposed to be worshippers of Sutekh. So why would they go after one of the old man's sons?

Could they not have known who Lokan was? Could that be the answer? But then why wouldn't Lokan simply have revealed his identity? Or annihilated them all? Either option would have saved him.

And as for a traitor...those closest to Sutekh were his sons, and Gahiji.

Gahiji? The fucker was eternally loyal to the old man. Why would he kill Sutekh's spawn?

But without a supernatural's help, how could a cult of mortals have taken Lokan down?

Which circled right back to the possibility of a traitor.

The worm had uncoiled in his thoughts, and he couldn't shake it now. It was no secret Gahiji had never quite approved of Lokan. Not that he'd overtly displayed it by word or action. It was just something the brothers sensed.

"You ever find out why Gahiji went for Roxy like that?" Mal asked.

"Other than the fact that she's a Daughter of Aset?" Dagan's tone was dry.

"Today's enemies are tomorrow's allies, Dae. Hey, I just crawled out from under one of Xaphan's genies. If I'd been with you three nights ago, she would have smoked me, right?"

He couldn't argue the fact. "True."

"So why did Gahiji attack Roxy? Makes no sense, even if she is one of Aset's."

Dagan played the scene in his mind. "He went for *her*. Not just an Asetian, but her, Roxy Tam. Like he had a more personal reason."

"Then all we gotta do is find that reason."

Dagan's thoughts had already started to wander that path. Everyone who'd shown up at Roxy's three nights ago had been interested in Marin, the Setnakhts and Dana.

All of whom seemed to be connected to Lokan's death.

What if somehow Gahiji's attempt to harvest Roxy's heart was linked to Lokan's death? A stretch, but Gahiji's behavior had been out of character. He was usually even as a sheet of glass. Taking the harvest when both Alastor and Dagan outranked him wasn't something he would normally do.

So why try for Roxy's heart?

He glanced at the bathroom door, drummed his fingers on the table, thought about his own peculiar preoccupation with Roxy Tam and said, "Hey, Mal—"

He almost stopped there, almost didn't ask, then he pushed himself to get it out there, figuring Mal, the consummate ladies' man, might actually be able to explain this shit. But he couldn't ask outright, so instead he used the same analogy he'd tried on Alastor. "Did you ever read *The Godfather?*"

There was a protracted silence, as though Mal were wondering what the hell he was talking about. Dagan almost laughed. *He* was wondering what the hell he was talking about.

Then Mal said, "Yeah. Years ago."

"You know that part where Michael Corleone sees the girl, Apollonia, for the first time?"

Again, Mal was quiet, probably thinking back to the exact scene. "Yeah. When he gets hit by the 'thunderbolt,' right?"

"Right." He paused. "You, uh, you ever been hit like that?"

"Like a thunderbolt? By a female? What a question, Dae. I get hit like that every day. Sometimes twice a day. Every time I see a sweet ass, a great rack, a set of lips so plump I want to bite them. What the hell is wrong with you?"

"No," Dagan said softly. "Not like that. Like in the book." In the book, the guy had wanted the girl to be *his;* he'd wanted to protect her. Possess her. She had been his fucking world.

Mal was quiet. "The book? Didn't she die?"

A dark smile twisted Dagan's lips. Okay. So maybe he hadn't chosen such a good analogy.

"Yeah, she died." He felt completely ridiculous. A sweet ass. A great rack. Roxy had both. Maybe that was what had him tied up in knots. He punched the side of his fist against his thigh. "Yeah. Forget it. See if you can find out anything else about that kid, and let me know."

Ending the call, he sat there staring at the floor. What the fuck was wrong with him? Roxy Tam had wormed so far under his skin she'd taken up permanent residence. And he'd let her.

He'd done things for her that had pushed the boundaries of both his nature and his experience. He'd stood against one of his own kind, his father's man. He'd stayed by her side, nursed her as she recovered. What the fuck did he know about nursing anyone?

Only what he'd seen from a distance as he watched

the ever-changing landscape of human lives. He'd sure as sugar never taken care of anyone before.

But he hadn't been able to *not* take care of her, hadn't been able to just sit back and watch her life—or death—play out as it would. He'd felt the burning urgency to *do* something. So he'd done whatever he could think of, and some things he never would have thought of.

Like feeding her his blood.

That was new. Whether she wanted to get all chatty and personal or not, he and Roxy were due for a little talk about that. He could still see her expression as she'd lain on the forest floor, bleeding, dying, begging him to feed her his blood. Her eyes had told him she thought he ought to know exactly what she needed.

So, yeah, the girl had some talking to do.

He could hear the water pounding on the walls of the shower. He heard her humming, softly at first, then a little louder.

That sound made him picture her, in the shower, water sluicing over her smooth, brown skin, her hands slick with soap, rubbing her calves, her thighs, her belly. Her breasts. His own hands slick with soap...

He thought about taking her breasts in his hands, pinching her sweet brown nipples, rolling them between his fingers. He thought about cupping the smooth, round swell of her ass, getting inside her, his tongue in her mouth, his fingers pushing up into her, and finally—

He surged to his feet. But he didn't move. Instead, he stood there, arguing with himself.

She'd been at the brink of death for three days.

But she isn't at the brink of death now. She's been

feeding on my blood for three days. She looked damned hale and hearty sprinting to the bathroom, naked.

There could be no future for them.

Who the fuck wants a future? She in there, now, squeaky clean and ready.

He crossed the room, paused in front of the bathroom door and stared down at the handle. He meant to keep arguing with himself, but he couldn't think of a single reason not to kick the damned door in.

Then he closed his hand on the knob and turned it, and he had his reason.

She'd left the door unlocked.

CHAPTER EIGHTEEN

ROXY BRACED HER PALM against the mosaic glass tile of the shower stall. She hung her head and let the water pound her back, releasing the knots, easing the aches.

She'd shampooed twice, conditioned once, washed every part of her body, then washed them again. But she couldn't seem to make herself turn off the tap and wrap herself in the towel she'd laid out. The water just felt so damned good that she wanted to extend the pleasure, make it last.

And in a way, she wanted to hold fast to her moment of solitude. She wasn't eager to face Dagan, not with the bizarre intimacy between them now. Intimacy implied trust.

She wasn't so good at that.

She'd been on the brink of death, her chest ripped open. He could have left her to die. He hadn't. Did that mean she could trust him? She honestly didn't know.

She glanced toward the bathroom vanity. Steam condensed on the glass shower door, blocking her view, but she knew what was there: a second glass beside hers, a second toothbrush in that glass. She supposed he'd raided the stash she kept in the medicine cabinet.

Her toothbrush had been flying solo for more years

than she cared to count. Safer that way. Now he'd gone and messed things up.

He'd nursed her, cared for her, bled for her.

She ran her tongue along the edge of her teeth. She knew his taste, uniquely his, familiar now. Too familiar. Like she'd tasted something similar before. The thought made a short laugh escape her. She'd tasted *him* before, eleven years ago; that's why it was familiar.

Only that wasn't it.

She felt like she was missing something. Something important—

A cool wash of air touched her skin, and she froze, the fine hairs at her nape prickling and rising. *Dagan.* A shudder rocked her from crown to toes.

There was a faint suction sound as the glass shower door pulled open. Her breath hitched. Raising her head, she slicked her wet hair back off her face, but she didn't turn, didn't move, just stared straight ahead at the glass mosaic tiles.

"I didn't invite you to join me," she said, a little breathless. *Damn.* She cursed herself for that.

"You left the bathroom door unlocked." His voice was a low rasp. Just the sound of it stroked her senses. "I took it as an invitation."

Another faint shush of sound told her he'd pulled the glass door open a little wider. She closed her eyes for second, knowing he was looking at her, the curve of her spine, the swell of her ass, the length of her legs. She opened her eyes and shivered.

Finally, she turned her head, looking back at him over her shoulder. He was all golden skin, smooth over hard muscle, planes and angles. Dark gold hair curled on his chest and tapered to a thin line down the center

of his belly. He was sex on two legs…two long, muscled legs, wrapped in faded denim.

She swallowed, forced her thoughts back to the point she meant to make. "I live alone," she said. "There *is* no lock on the bathroom door."

Hooking his thumb in the waistband of his jeans, he cocked one hip to the side. She held her breath as the cloth slid dangerously low. A bit more…just a—

"My mistake." He didn't sound particularly apologetic. "You want me to leave?"

Did she? Her gaze searched for his, only he wasn't looking at her eyes.

"And if I say yes?"

His eyes narrowed; his lips thinned, but his tone stayed neutral. "Then I'll leave."

Heart pounding, she weighed her options and choked back a hard laugh. Options? She was already wet for him. And all he'd done was look at her ass.

She didn't move, didn't breathe. She wanted this. Wanted him. But she wasn't so foolish as to think there wouldn't be repercussions.

There was always a price.

What did he expect from her? What did he want?

He wanted sex. Only sex. She had to believe that.

Animal release. They'd come together, and they'd move apart, like it had never been. Because there could be no chance for anything else between them.

"No," she whispered. Then, louder, "No, I don't want you to leave."

Roxy straightened and turned, moving one arm to shield her breasts, while the other hand dipped lower.

"Don't do that," Dagan rasped. "I want to look at you."

The way he said it made her want him to look at her.

His eyes were mercury bright against the dark fringe of his lashes, and the look he settled on her was hotter than an arc welder, searing her, making every nerve in her body jump to electric alert.

Hard-edged lust boiled her blood, electrified her skin.

She'd made her choice, and she intended to enjoy it. So she dropped her hands back to rest against the glass tile of the shower stall, palms flat, back arched. Her nipples puckered; her pulse raced.

"So look."

His gaze slid from her face to her neck, lingered on her breasts, then moved lower, nice and slow and smooth, molten silver leaving a track of heat in its wake.

She did her own perusal, taking in the shadows and angles of his face, the corded muscle of his arms, the swell of his pectorals, the flat, hard planes of his belly.

Lust, raw and ragged, tore through her. *Just lust.* She wasn't about to give it more significance than that. When they were done with each other, bodies sated, dark needs quenched, he'd still be a soul reaper, son of Sutekh, and she'd still be Otherkin, a Daughter of Aset.

But in this moment, they were just two creatures, two beings, sleek and hungry and oh-so-ready.

Reaching up, she dragged the heavy mass of her wet hair back, baring her shoulders, her breasts. Then she slid her hands along the wet tiles, stretched her arms up and out to either side, and pressed her palms flat to the opposite walls of the shower. Let him look, let him want and ache, as she had wanted and ached for eleven fucking years.

His lips drew taut in a knowing, masculine smile. It told her clear as day that he knew her every thought, her every need.

His cock strained against the faded denim of his jeans, hard and thick, the heavy bulge impossible to miss. She wanted to see it, wanted to touch it. She wanted to feel the slick glide of it in her fist, in her mouth. Inside her, fast and deep.

Desire kicked her in the gut. She wanted to scrape her nails and her teeth over his skin. Lick him. Bite him. Touch every part of him like she had done a thousand times in her dreams.

His fingers slid toward his button fly. But he only paused there, waiting.

"Is there an accountant?" he rasped.

"A wha—" She froze, thoughts spinning like radial tires on black ice, and then she got what he was asking her. Was she involved with anyone, with some mortal guy who could offer her the picket fence? "No. No accountant."

Not that she hadn't tried. But over the years, no one had measured up to the lover who haunted her midnights, and eventually she'd stopped trying. "There's no one."

Holding her gaze, he offered a feral smile, a reward for her answer. His long, tapered fingers worked the top button of his fly, sliding metal through cloth, his movements spare and precise.

She wet her lips, waiting. She wanted those fingers on her skin, on her breasts, between her legs. She wanted that cock in her mouth, in her fist, inside her, hard and deep.

He took his time working the second button and the

third, and the whole time, he kept his eyes on hers, watching every nuance of her reaction.

The water pounded down on her, running in rivulets over her shoulders, her breasts, teasing her nipples.

Fisting her hands against the urge to reach out and grab him, she let them drop to her sides, digging her nails into her palms.

Anticipation was a luscious treat. She held herself still, her heart slamming against her ribs.

He undid another button, the tease heightening her arousal.

Her breath came in short little gasps. And he hadn't even touched her yet. Just looked at her, eyes narrowed and glittering, lips parted, teeth bared.

She wanted to feel those teeth on her skin, on the corded tendons of her throat, on the sensitive skin at the insides of her thighs.

A tiny moan escaped her as the last button flicked free. The faded denim slid lower, baring the arcs of his hipbones and the lowest ridges of his abdomen. They slid lower still, all the way down his hips, his muscled thighs, his calves. The thick length of his cock jutted forward and up, a vein tracing the length, full with his arousal.

Her mouth was dry. Her pulse raced.

She leaned back against the shower wall, damned grateful for the support, because without it she would have sunk to her knees.

Now there was a lovely plan. She *wanted* to sink to her knees, to take him in her mouth, to suck him the way she did in her dreams. Now, she reached for him, wanting to fist his cock, to stroke its hot silky length, but he caught her wrist and stopped her.

"My rules," he said, stepping all the way into the shower, the water beading on his smooth skin as he dragged the shower door closed behind him.

"Yes." His rules. The thought made her shiver.

He trailed his free hand along her shoulder, her collarbone, to the healing scar between her breasts. His lips thinned, but he said nothing, only stroked the tip of his finger so gently over the ridge of tissue before gliding his touch to the edge of her breast.

Anticipation ratcheted through her.

Panting, she arched her back, offering, demanding.

With a dark laugh, he let the tips of his fingers drift lower, circling first one nipple, then the other. A rush of electric heat knifed through her, and she surged into his touch with a low hiss, wanting more, wanting his mouth, his tongue, his teeth.

Fisting his hand in her wet hair, fingers tangling in the long ringlets, he angled his mouth on hers. He kissed her, wet and deep, his tongue teasing her, inviting her to play.

Oh, she wanted to play. She thrust her tongue in his mouth, tasting him, her teeth grazing his lips.

He tasted so good. She clutched at the slope of his shoulders, corded muscle and male strength, as he let his weight fall against her, pinning her between hot man and cool tile, the water beating down on them both.

Coiled tight and heavy with anticipation, like the air before a tropical storm, she rubbed against him, her legs scissoring. Open. Closed. He thrust his knee between them, his thigh against her mons. She did a slow grind, the pressure making her gasp.

He kissed her like she was ambrosia, like he

couldn't get enough. Deep. Wet. Lips and tongue and teeth. Sucking on her lower lip. Biting her.

She had no breath. She had no awareness of anything but him, the slide of his body on hers, the taste of him, the scent of his skin.

He palmed her breast, took the nipple between his fingers, teased her, pinched her. She cried out as a jolt of sexual anticipation arrowed to her groin. The sound she made was primitive, raw.

"Offer them to me, Roxy," he ordered against her lips. "Offer me your breasts."

The words made her hot, wet. She cupped her palms under her breasts and lifted them, offered them.

His head dipped. His hand slid between her legs and he pushed his fingers inside her as he closed his teeth on her nipple. She jolted, moaned, the pleasure so intense she thought she was going to unravel right then.

"Not yet," he whispered, his tongue stroking her nipple, gentle now. Then he closed his lips on her and sucked, a hard, sharp pull that made her fist her hands in his hair and moan and squirm.

She arched her hips against the thrust and retreat of his fingers.

Reaching for him, she closed her hand around his cock. So hard. Silky skin. She stroked and rocked and made sounds that could only be read as invitation.

He tugged her head back, and stared into her eyes, his mouth a hard line.

She'd done this. Pushed him to the edge of control.

"I want your cock. Inside me. Filling me." She scraped her nails over the sensitive head. "My rules now."

"You think?" Two little words that told her he had no intention of letting her lead.

Somehow, that added to the thrill, layered arousal on arousal.

Curving one hand around her lower back, he brought their bodies tight. With a dark smile, lust and promise, he reached between them to guide the head of his cock over her mons, over her clitoris, between her swollen, slick folds. He rubbed back and forth, making her gasp at the contact.

She pumped her hips. Not enough. He controlled the rhythm, the depth, just the head of his cock sliding inside her. And she wanted it all. Greedy girl, she wanted it all.

She felt stretched, but not full.

"Please," she breathed, and he gave a low laugh of pure masculine pleasure.

Closing his hands on her buttocks, he lifted her, his mouth on hers, hungry, demanding. She wrapped her legs around his hips, and one arm around his shoulders. Her free hand tangled in the long, wet strands at his nape.

He pressed her back against the tile and thrust inside her, full and deep. A smooth, slick glide. A moan tore from her lips. He was inside her, deep inside her, filling her almost to the point of pain, so big, so hard.

She wanted to move, wanted to thrust, but he dug his fingers into her flesh, holding her still, holding her exactly where he wanted her.

With a cry, she shoved her fingers through his hair and met the thrust of his tongue, sucking on him, drawing on him. She pulled him into the kiss, making it harder, wilder. So good. So damned good. She tasted him, raking her teeth along his lower lip, biting him until she tasted blood.

His lips slanted on hers, vying to set the pace, small nips of her lips and the sweep of his tongue.

He was all the way inside her now, and she rocked and writhed, but he wasn't in any hurry. He moved his hips slowly, shallow thrusts that made her whimper and moan and struggle for more.

The angle he held her at was perfection, letting him rub against her sensitive flesh.

"You're so hot. So damned tight." He dropped his face to the curve of her neck. She felt his teeth on the cord of muscle, and she gasped at the sensations he roused in her.

Thighs trembling, she locked her legs tighter around his hips.

One hand under her bottom, he closed the other on her breast, kneading it, squeezing the nipple as he upped the pace, pumping into her in long, deep strokes.

He played her body like an instrument, making her sing, almost to the crescendo. Almost. Her body was his to command, his to rule. She was near mindless with the hunger that spiraled and pulled her deeper.

He knew just how to move, how to bring her to the razor's edge.

Poised there, she raked her nails down his back, clawed at his ass. He moved faster now, grinding and deep, quickening the pace, tipping her body to an angle so exquisite that she jerked and sank her teeth into his chest, biting, sucking.

He gripped her ass tighter, slid his fingers down between her buttocks. With a scream, she tore over the edge, falling, falling. Flying. Shattering into a million shards.

She came hard, fast, clenched muscles and raw sensation. Like nothing she'd ever known.

Breathing raggedly, she clung to him, her face buried in his throat, her heart racing, the pleasure going on and on as he kept riding her.

Head back, he plunged into her, muscles clenched, body shaking. She could feel him coming, feel the throb of his orgasm, the coiled tension of his release.

To her shock, she climbed fast and hard and came again in crashing, wild waves.

"Fu-u-u-ck." She gasped.

She was trembling and he was trembling and they both hung there, together.

She thought he held her there for a long time as she found her way back. A very long time.

"Damn," she whispered. "Damn."

Shifting his grip, he held her with one hand under her bottom and reached out to adjust the taps. Only in that second did she realize the water had gone winter cold.

He played with the tap, turning down the cold, turning up the hot. Only when he was satisfied did he let her slide down his body, skin to wet skin.

Taking up the soap, he washed her, washed himself.

"I already scrubbed everything—" she laughed "—twice."

He nodded, his expression solemn, but he kept working soapy hands between her thighs, then up over her hips, her ass, kneading, touching.

"It's about needing to have my hands on you," he murmured, "not about getting you clean. I sat out there and listened to you humming and thought about my hands on you, just like this."

Their gazes met, held.

"What else were you thinking about?" she whispered.

"Then or now?"

She swallowed. "Now."

He gave her a look so sexy it reached inside her and touched the fading embers of desire, fanning them, stoking them. "My mouth on your clit."

LATER, THEY LAY ON THE BED together, her back to his front. Dagan had one arm thrown across Roxy's shoulders and one leg draped over her thighs. He had her pinned in place, and he liked that. He thought the only position he liked better was her beneath him, held down by his weight. It was a primitive, primordial instinct that made him enjoy the idea of possessing her, dominating her. She was *his*.

As if he could ever fully dominate a creature such as she.

The thought made him smile.

More likely she'd stand toe to toe with him, nose to nose. And she'd hold her own.

In a moment of stunning realization, he thought that maybe that was the appeal. That's what it had been all along. He could think of her any way he wanted, think of dominating her, possessing her. But in the end she wouldn't break, wouldn't even bend.

He stroked his hand along the curve of her hip, then slid his fingers between her thighs.

She shifted and slapped his wrist. Then slapped him again when he didn't withdraw quickly enough for her liking.

With a grin, he went back to stroking her hip.

He'd licked her until she screamed. He'd caught her wrists and pinned them above her head as he drove into her.

And he'd liked that. A lot.

But after they'd both reached a shuddering, panting release, after she'd clung to him, pliant and soft, as she caught her breath, she'd slapped at his shoulder and muttered, "Get off."

So he'd settled for holding her pinned at the limbs.

Now, she made a little humming sound and wiggled her ass against him.

"At some point," she murmured, "we need to talk about—"

"About?"

She waggled her fingers. "Things."

"Things," he echoed. "Okay. Pick a thing."

She was quiet for a moment, then said, "The shadows under your eyes. You look like you haven't slept in days."

"I haven't. I stayed awake to make sure you were safe."

"For three days?" She sounded shocked.

"Yeah."

She tried to squirm around in his hold so she could look at him. "But you were feeding me your blood. And you were injured yourself. You—"

"Pick another thing," he said, holding her tighter, uncomfortable with the topic.

He thought she would argue. He could feel the tension in her limbs. But in the end she relented and picked another thing. "You're Sutekh's son. What the hell was that like growing up?"

Not the *thing* he'd been anticipating, and not a topic he really wanted to touch on. But something told him that shutting her down right now was a move he didn't want to make.

"What was that like?" he repeated. *Hell.* Solitude. His father's rages. Expectations Dagan could never meet. And finally, liberation, so very long in coming. Then understanding of the bitter truth that freedom is not always sweet.

But he said none of that. Instead, he said, "I grew up alone."

The second the words escaped, he thought he must have lost his mind to allow them to burst free. Why did he tell her that? He never talked about it. Not with anyone. Of course, his brothers knew his childhood had been far from pleasant. Dagan was the son Sutekh had decided to raise in the Underworld while his brothers were fostered out Topworld. Luck of the draw—except luck wasn't a particularly apt descriptor.

He rarely talked about that with his brothers, and they rarely told him of their own experiences. Thinking about it now, he realized he'd avoided asking because he hadn't wanted to have to answer if they returned the inquiry. Besides, they all knew exactly what it meant to be Sutekh's son. In the end, regardless of how their earliest years were spent, they'd all ended up in the same place.

Roxy was quiet for a time, and then she said, "So did I. Grew up alone. At least, in part."

When she didn't offer anything more, Dagan prodded, "Tell me."

Still she said nothing, only lay there, curled in his embrace, breathing slowly.

"You said your mother left when you were five."

"You remember that?" She gave an incredulous laugh. "It's weird." She paused. "I didn't remember anything about the night she left for so long, except the

face of the cop who sat with me in a room at the police station and the fact that he fed me chocolate wafers." She shook her head. "I fucking hate chocolate. And steak. Guess we associate certain memories with certain smells or tastes."

"I like steak. Rare."

"Of course you do." She took a slow, deep breath, then let it out. "You sure you want to hear this?" She turned her head to look back at him over her shoulder, and snuggled her ass invitingly against his cock.

Tempting. But he actually *did* want to hear this. He wanted to know everything about her.

"You said you didn't remember for so long…but now you do?"

"Flashes. A lot of them came to me while I was out of it for the past few days. Guess a near-death experience brings your life into sharp focus." Her fingers stroked his skin from wrist to elbow, and back again, then she dipped her head and let her tongue wander along the swell of muscle at the side of his forearm.

"What else do you remember?"

"My mother's face. She was crying. I remember she had a mark on her forearm, an ankh. It's how I knew where to put mine." She gave a soft exhalation. "I remember the way she smelled. I remember what she said to me right before she left…something about a seeker, a hunter. That if she left me, he wouldn't be able to find me."

"A hunter," he echoed, a feeling of unease stirring in his gut.

Roxy rolled and sat up, dragging the sheet with her, shifting so she was cross-legged, facing him. He didn't want to let her go. He wanted to keep her inside the

circle of his arms, keep his hands on her, keep touching her.

He closed his hand around her ankle, needing to maintain the physical connection. To keep her close. Like he had to make up for the years he'd allowed himself to keep her far away.

"It's funny. I feel like the second Gahiji's hand went into my chest, it was like a switch got flipped to the 'on' position and all sorts of memories came on like a bunch of light bulbs." She stared down at him. "I dunno. Maybe I'm creating memories.

"Gahiji," she mused. Frowning, she shook her head, her fingers idly tracing his where they curled around her ankle. "It's a unique name. When I was lying there, bleeding, I kept thinking I'd heard it before. That *he* was the hunter. The seeker."

"You've heard Gahiji's name before?" Tension sifted through him. She could have. It was possible. What if Gahiji *had* been the hunter after her mother?

If he had, then how had Roxy's mom ended up in Joe Marin's collection?

Roxy swallowed, her eyes shimmering as she met his gaze. "She's dead, isn't she? My mom?"

He didn't have to kill her hope; he could lie. He almost did. Then he thought of the depth of that betrayal, and he said, "Yes. She's dead."

"I knew that." She blew out a breath and seemed to deflate before his eyes. He felt her pain. This loss was one he understood. Then she squared her shoulders and let out a sharp exhale. "I knew she would have come back if she could have." Rage and hate glittered in her eyes, and her words came harsh and fast. "*Was* Gahiji the one who killed her?"

"No." Gahiji hadn't done the deed, but had he hunted Roxy's mother? Had he brought her to her murderer?

Why?

Alastor's questions came back to him: *...wouldn't he have had to practice on something weaker than a soul reaper first? Shouldn't there be something other than human bones and body parts in the mix? Maybe a lesser Underlord or a succubus?*

Or a Daughter of Aset.

Click. The game board shifted, the players moved. Gahiji's game piece changed sides.

Dagan couldn't be sure. Not yet. But he wasn't surprised. A part of him had been suspecting this since the night Gahiji had tried to take Roxy down. The attack had been too strange, too personal. This was just one more bit of evidence to be weighed.

"It wasn't Gahiji that killed your mother. But I killed the one who did."

"Not good enough." Her eyes narrowed, her lips drew back from her teeth. "I wanted it to be *me.*"

"I know." He did. It was the exact way he felt about Lokan's killers. "But it was me, and that's the best I can offer. What happened after your mother left?"

"Foster care," she bit out.

They were words that had little meaning in his existence. But he noticed there was an almost defensive note in her voice.

She mistook his silence and plunged on, "It's not always what you hear it is."

He knew nothing of foster care, had heard nothing. It was not part of his reality, but he didn't say that, just nodded and listened.

"Yeah, in the beginning I made the rounds of a few dumps. Wasn't good, but wasn't terrible. No one beat me. No one did…other things to me. There were just apathetic adults, and way too many kids in way too small a place. The apartments in Rogers Park aren't exactly spacious. Not enough clothes or food. Blah. Blah. Blah." She shrugged, made a soft sound of dismissal. "I was a cliché…. Never alone, and completely, utterly alone—you know?"

Her gaze locked on his, tiger bright, and he felt like she was looking for something specific, something inside him. What? What did she see when she looked at him? He felt oddly exposed, and to his surprise, he allowed himself to be even more exposed as he murmured, "I was alone. Utterly alone. No crowd. Just me."

"What about your mother?"

"I never knew her." Sutekh had taken him when he was an infant and left Dagan's mother freshly pregnant with a second child, Alastor.

Had she mourned him? Or had she known by then what Sutekh was, what her son was? They were questions he hadn't allowed himself to think about in centuries. What was the point? He could never find the answers. The mortal who had given him life had died nearly three hundred years in the past, shortly after giving birth to his brother.

But lying here, looking into Roxy's bronze-green eyes, listening to her share her memories, he wanted to offer her something, share something. It was an odd experience, this wanting to tell her about himself.

"My father visited from time to time," he said at length, pleased that he'd found some personal tidbit to share.

She nodded, solemn, intense, and he was glad he'd given in to the urge to exchange memories.

Still, she said nothing. The silence dragged. Too long. He had the uncomfortable, horrible realization that she expected him to say more.

At last, she asked, "What about your brothers?"

He stroked the skin of her ankle, up her calf. Smooth skin. Like satin. Dipping his head, he traced his tongue along the bone at the side of her ankle. He contemplated the length of her leg, considered tracing his tongue from calf to thigh to—

"No," she said.

He dragged his gaze to hers.

She made a huffing exhale and prodded, "Your brothers?"

"We weren't…raised together," he said. "I never met them until I was an adult."

She frowned, clearly perplexed. "How many brothers do you have?"

"Thr—" Pain knifed him and he stopped, gathered his thoughts. "Two. Lokan is dead."

Of course, she knew that already.

"I'm sorry," she whispered. "I am." Her lips parted as though she would say more, but he rested his fingers against her mouth, stilling the words. She might be sorry, but she was still of the Asetian Guard. Would she choose duty over him, or him over duty, if it came down to a choice? Would she look away as he continued his hunt for Lokan's remains, or would she try to stop him, as he'd come to suspect she had been ordered?

Would he allow her the choice?

He didn't want to know. Not right now, with the

taste of her still on his lips, and the feel of her imprinted on his skin.

Time enough to face questions of duty later.

Right now, he just wanted to saturate himself with her. The smell of her skin. The sound of her voice. The secrets he could coax from her lips. Not the secrets of Aset. Only *her* secrets. Roxy's.

"So you were alone in a crowd," he prompted. "And then?"

"I moved around to a few places. When I was eleven, I got with good people. They didn't have much, but they had good hearts. They both worked long hours, though, and sent money back to relatives in Haiti. I was alone a lot. A neighbor was supposed to keep me when they weren't around. She never paid much attention. The year I turned twelve, my foster parents took in another kid. Then I wasn't alone anymore." She pressed her lips together and drew a shuddering breath. "For a while."

"But the night I found you, you were alone again."

He felt her tense beneath his touch, the muscles of her calf twitching, like she meant to bolt. She shifted on the mattress, tried to pull away, to withdraw. Not gonna happen.

Pushing to a sitting position, he stared at her, face-to-face. He stretched his legs out on either side of her, his knees slightly bent so he created a sort of open-ended circle with her in the middle.

"Alone." She jutted her chin forward and nodded slowly. She took a breath, opened her mouth. Closed it. And again. Until she summoned whatever strength she needed and finally continued. "You know what it feels like to burn. The pain. The heat. Indescribable, right?"

A question, but he knew she wasn't looking for an answer.

Her gaze dropped to his hand. "My foster family burned. We lived in Valleyview Village, a low-rise apartment complex. Still the projects, but better projects than Rogers Park. I came back from a track meet one night. The whole block was lit up like a sunrise. Most people got out. Some didn't. My foster parents were home at the same time for the first time in months. They died together when the roof collapsed."

Her face was expressionless, her tone flat.

"My foster sister, Rhianna, got out, but there was a price. She was burned. I saw her. I thought water was pouring down her arm. But it was her skin melting off." She pressed her lips together and nodded. "I won't tell what it was like, what she suffered. The burn baths were the worst. At least, that's what I thought until they started cutting off bits. Toes, then a whole foot. The fingers on her right hand. I went to classes at night, then worked graveyard at a gas bar, so I could be with her during the day. I think I never got more than four hours sleep a night for five, maybe six months."

She dropped her head, closed her hands on his wrists, and he looked down, shocked to see that his fists were clenched. His heart was pounding, his stomach tight. He felt pain and horror for a human girl he hadn't even known.

Because it caused Roxy pain.

He *felt* her pain. Wanted to take her pain.

Her gaze held his, burning bright. "She begged me to kill her. To stop the misery. Every day, I'd go see her. Every day, she'd beg me to put the pillow over her face and just let her go to sleep. Every damned day.

"I kept thinking it would get better, and for a bit it did. But, see, the thing about burn victims…even after months and months, they're not out of the woods. There's still the risk of infection. She got one. She died. End of story."

But it wasn't.

"Tell me the rest."

She shook her head, dipped her chin and let her long hair fall forward to hide her expression.

Dagan cupped her face, his palms on her cheeks. He made her look at him. Made her face him. Her pain was terrible. Soul deep. He could see it.

"Tell me the rest," he ordered softly.

"I stood there beside her bed," she whispered. "I picked up the pillow. She was looking at me. Her eyes were beautiful. Her face was beautiful. She was burned almost everywhere except her face. She didn't move. Just smiled at me. Like she was glad to finally go."

"You ended her pain," Dagan said.

Tears welled in her tiger-bright eyes, spilled over onto her cheeks, pooled at the corner of her mouth.

"The person I am now would have. The person I was then… I couldn't do it. I didn't love her enough or I wasn't brave enough or I told myself she could still make it, still win…or maybe I was just too selfish, wanting a few more hours, more days until I was alone again. Whatever the reason, I put the pillow down. She begged me, 'Don't,' but I did. Then I sat by her bed, and I let her live. For four more torturous, horrific days, where every breath was an agony, every second an eternity, four days where I *knew* she was going to die in the end…those four days of hell are on me because I let her live."

She ran the tip of her tongue over her lips, catching her own tears.

That wasn't all, though. He held his silence because he sensed there was one last bit to the story.

"Finally, I worked up the guts. I came one morning and she was sleeping, and I did it. I put the pillow over her face and I held it there. She didn't even move. Not the whole time I held it there. I threw that pillow across the room. I was crying so hard I couldn't breathe. I thought I was going to be sick. Then the nurse came in and she put her hand on my shoulder and she told me that Rhianna passed about ten minutes before I ever got there. She didn't know what I'd done. *I* didn't know what I'd done."

She stared at him, breathing hard.

"Nothing. I didn't save her. Didn't ease her suffering, either. And in the end, I was alone again."

And suddenly, Dagan understood everything.

That night, when he'd told her to run from anyone with the mark of Aset, when he'd told her that if they found her, they'd keep her, his words hadn't dissuaded her. They'd fucking sent her running out in search of them.

So she wouldn't be alone.

CHAPTER NINETEEN

They have made war, they have raised up tumult,
They have done wrong, they have created rebel-
lion
They have done slaughter

— The Egyptian Book of the Dead, Chapter 175

The Underworld, The Territory of Sutekh

MAL STOOD IN SUTEKH'S GREETING chamber. He'd been about to head out the door for a run, when he'd felt dark wisps of power prodding at the edges of his thoughts. It had been almost two centuries since he'd learned to completely block his father's intrusions, but Sutekh never got tired of trying. Mal had considered ignoring the summons, but in the end, he set his iPod on the shelf, opened a portal and headed for Sutekh's realm.

The room was empty when he arrived. Typical. Send him an urgent summons, then make him wait.

He sauntered past the rows of painted columns toward the open doors that led to the secluded garden. He could smell the lotus blossoms, hear the trickle of water from the pool. He got only as far as the chairs at the far end of the room before he sensed his father's presence behind him.

Turning, he grinned. "Top of the morning, Sutekh. Nice hat."

Today his father had chosen to don the guise of traditional Egyptian royalty. Over a long linen tunic he wore a transparent robe that grazed his ankles. He was youthful in appearance, barely past the flush of childhood. His olive skin was smooth and utterly hairless, and he wore an elaborate gold headdress, inlaid with glittering stones.

Shiny.

Mal itched to get his hands on those stones. He knew a Topworld fence who could work wonders...

Of course, stealing from his father was out of the question, but it would be such damned fine fun.

"You will go to Osiris as a hostage," Sutekh said, obsidian eyes flat and dead.

"Sounds like a blast."

Sutekh made a dismissive gesture. "You will listen to everything my enemy reveals. You will watch. You will commit every shred of information to memory and bring it to me upon your return."

"That's quite a list. Maybe I should write it down." Mal considered asking if Sutekh wanted photos. But Sutekh didn't have much of a sense of humor, so instead Mal asked, "My return? You're convinced Osiris will keep me alive?"

There weren't many things that could kill a soul reaper. Sutekh himself. Certain lakes of fire. And Osiris's sidekick, Ammut the Devourer. Lovely creature. Head of a crocodile, body of a leopard, ass of a hippopotamus. She was the eater of the unworthy dead. Pretty much like Sutekh. Only she played for the opposite team.

Oh, and Sutekh packed a bigger punch.

And of course there was the new possibility, the unknown thing that had butchered Lokan. With *unknown* being the not-so-comforting point.

"He will keep you alive." Sutekh glided across the space and settled himself on his gold-inlaid, carved throne. "He knows my vengeance will know no bounds if he does not."

Nice. Mal would be dead, but he'd be avenged in a big way.

Like you avenged Lokan? Mal bit off the question before it could tear free. He'd be smart to walk softly. Sutekh wasn't known for tolerating criticism.

"Can't promise information will be all I bring on my return." Mal grinned. "Osiris has some lovely baubles that hold definite appeal."

Ah, the telltale tic. A tiny vibration beneath Sutekh's right eye, almost imperceptible unless one knew what to look for. And Mal knew. From long, long years of experience, he knew. *My work here is done.*

Mal cheerfully helped himself to a square of baklava from the platter on the sideboard. Sutekh always kept a ready supply of sweets for his sons brought in from Topworld because if they ingested the food of the dead, they'd be trapped in the Underworld forever. They each had their poison. Dagan's was lollipops. Alastor preferred English toffee. Lokan had been crazy for Swedish berries. But Sutekh never stocked their preferences, just his own.

Fortunately, Mal didn't have a preference. Sugar was sugar. He ate it because he had to.

Sutekh glared at him, saying nothing. Mal popped the baklava in his mouth. The time had long since passed that his father's glare had much impact on him.

Of course, he would do exactly as Sutekh asked.

Not because it was an order, but because he had his own agenda.

His father's Machiavellian plots were ongoing and ever present. Mal had lost interest in them a couple of hundred years back. Pretty much when he'd started hatching Machiavellian plots of his own, but on a far less grand scale. For him, it wasn't about politics and power. It was about fun.

Live long enough, and any day that provided entertainment was a day worth waking up for.

Actually, the only one who'd followed the twists and turns of Sutekh's mind and machinations had been Lokan. He'd found the politics of the Underworld fascinating.

Mal had been happy to leave his brother to it. They all had. And Lokan had seemed happy to be left to it.

So what the fuck had happened? How had Lokan ended up dead, with Sutekh the All Powerful unable to finger the perpetrator?

That question underpinned Mal's main reason for heading to Osiris as a hostage. If anyone was a prime suspect, it was Osiris, or possibly his sister/wife, Aset. Either way, a visit to Osiris's territory might provide clues.

His previous opportunity to glean information had been lost when Dagan took his place at the scale in the Hall of Two Truths. He didn't intend to let a second chance slip by unused.

"What are you expecting I'll learn?" Mal asked, just to see if Sutekh would reveal even a hint of his thoughts. Not fucking likely, but always worth a try. Nothing ventured, nothing gained. "Osiris won't even be there."

Osiris would be with Sutekh and the others, meeting on neutral ground on the far side of the river Styx. "Guess I can always play poker with Anubis, but, you know, a two-player game isn't much fun."

He shot a glance through the open doors to the private gardens. He could see Gahiji standing there staring into the pond, hands clasped at the small of his back.

Of course. His father's shadow was never far away.

"Send Gahiji," Mal said, testing, poking. He didn't expect his father to entertain the idea, and he didn't actually want him to. But he saw Gahiji's shoulders stiffen ever so slightly, and he was glad he'd made the suggestion. The other soul reaper's response suggested that Gahiji didn't want to go. Interesting.

Did he have a particular reason for wanting to accompany Sutekh to the meeting of the Underworld gods and demigods? Perhaps a reason that had something to do with the way he tried to eliminate Roxy Tam, who just happened to be a Daughter of Aset?

Questions upon questions.

Sutekh glanced into the garden. "I need Gahiji at my right hand."

Mal tamped down the rage that swelled. He kept his tone mild, but his words were blade sharp. "Lokan was your right hand."

What was unsaid hung in the air between them. *Maybe Gahiji got tired of playing second.*

Sutekh stared at him, obsidian eyes flat and soulless. "You will go."

"Yeah." But not because Sutekh decreed it so. Mal would go to Osiris's realm because it suited *him* and his current purpose: to find and punish Lokan's killers. Unlike Dagan and Alastor, Mal wasn't convinced they

could bring their dead brother back, even if they did manage to find his remains. Was there a time limit on such dark magic?

Yeah, there was. Even if they did find Lokan's body parts, they still had to find his Ka and bring it back. Problem was, the Ka was sustained by food and drink. Go without, and it withered, maybe even died. They were racing against time to find him before his Ka partook of the food of the dead. That would seal the deal. Eat the banquet, pay the price: no way back.

And what would it cost to reanimate him? How many innocent souls? Was there a price beyond that which any of them would be willing to pay?

More questions without answers, and he didn't like banking on theoreticals. Alastor was the one tasked with finding the details on the reanimation. He had the most truck with demons, and they were going to need demon magic to work this.

The one definite was the possibility for vengeance. Mal dealt in that, intended to have it. Served cold and raw and bloody.

He was convinced that Osiris knew something about Lokan's death, and he meant to ferret out what he could while he was there. It actually suited his purposes that Osiris would be away at the meeting. Osiris was too savvy to give anything away for free. But he had daughters. Wives. Concubines. Slaves. And Mal had confidence in his own charms.

"So I go to Osiris. And he's sending you…Aset?"

Sutekh shot him a look. "Aset has her own territory. She is a power in her own right. She goes to the meeting."

Mal shrugged. "Just confirming my facts. So who's he sending?"

"Ammut."

A surprise. He'd have thought Osiris would keep her close to hand with Mal coming for a visit. "She's coming here?"

"No. You know how this works."

He did. If it were a small meeting, those involved sent hostages to each of the players.

If it were a massive gathering, the rules changed. Sutekh's reply had just told Mal exactly how big this meeting would be.

There was a protocol to such things. With so many gods and demigods scheduled to attend, a simple exchange of hostages between any two wouldn't do a whole hell of a lot toward keeping the peace. They'd just slaughter each other and be done with it.

Instead, each ruler sent a hostage to another ruler, who in turn sent a hostage to a third ruler and so on down the line. That way, if one was slaughtered, it automatically dragged an ally into the war.

Of course, bloodthirsty creatures that Underworlders were, the god whose hostage had been killed would kill the one in his possession even though they were unrelated to the one who'd done the killing in the first place, and so on, until everybody had a dead hostage. And the 6,000-year-old ceasefire would be over.

Mal found a certain dark irony in the whole setup.

"So who's sending *you* a hostage?" he asked, mildly curious.

"Hades. He sends Persephone."

Mal gave a low whistle. Hades was putting big-time

trust in Sutekh, thereby making a clear statement to every other god and demigod as to whose side he was on.

Since Sutekh had arranged this meeting of the top dogs, they were likely coming into it expecting he meant to initiate a massacre in payment for his butchered son. But they couldn't outright decline to attend, just in case he meant to meet for exactly the reasons he gave: to open a bid for peace.

It was a tricky dance. One that might end up in slit throats and dismembered bodies.

Of course, Mal would be relatively safe, given the limited number of ways to kill a soul reaper.

"You really bidding for peace?" Mal asked.

"At this precise moment, yes."

Mal laughed, his deepest suspicions confirmed. At this moment, Sutekh would lobby for peace. But somehow, he was initiating some convoluted, far-reaching plot to discover and punish those who had killed Lokan. And then he'd kill them all.

Sutekh was nothing if not patient. He'd wait years, even centuries, to see his plots reach fruition.

"A dish best served cold?" Mal asked.

One side of Sutekh's mouth curved up in the barest hint of a smile. "As an arctic wind."

Toronto, Canada

ROXY SAT FACING DAGAN ON THE BED. She'd bared her heart, her soul. Let him dig out truths she'd kept hidden even from herself.

She had no idea why she'd trusted him with her secrets.

Or perhaps she did.

A shudder chased up her spine. Fear. She didn't want to understand her actions, didn't want to acknowledge any underlying emotion.

But apparently, he had no such qualms.

"You are mine, Roxy Tam. Mine to hold. Mine to keep. Mine to protect." His gray eyes glittered with a feral light, wild, untamed. A little frightening. "You are mine."

Her heart twisted, then slammed against her ribs, too hard, too fast. She jerked away from him and skittered on all fours to the farthest corner of the bed. There, she held herself poised, ready to run. Maybe ready to fight. She wasn't sure, wouldn't be sure unless he tried to touch her.

He seemed to understand that, because he stayed exactly where he was, watching her with eyes that were mercury bright. He made no move toward her. But he wanted to. She could read it in the way he balled his hands into fists and the tense lines that bracketed his mouth.

"I belong to no one but myself." She kept the words toneless, cool. But inside, she was a bubbling cauldron.

What exactly was he saying? What claim was he making on her?

She felt breathless, her heart too tight, her pulse racing uncomfortably fast. "You can't just grab me by the hair, club me over the head and drag me into your cave—"

"Why not?"

"Why—"

She stared at his mouth, his lips quirking up at the corners, and she realized he was *laughing* at her. On the inside. Trying very hard not to laugh on the outside.

"Oh!" She lunged and punched him, her fist connecting with his shoulder. He didn't flinch, didn't even roll with it, just sat there and took it.

Rubbing her fist, she glared at him.

"You're gorgeous when you're hitting things, Roxy Tam," he murmured, and moved so fast she didn't even have time to blink.

He took her down, flat on her back, pinning her with his weight.

"So that whole 'you are mine' speech was just teasing? Right?" She didn't know what she wanted him to say. She only knew she held her breath, waiting.

He said nothing, just stared down at her, gray eyes glittering with that same intense light. It unnerved her. Attracted her. Drew her in and frightened her all at once.

Gently, so gently, he kissed her, his mouth warm and open, his tongue teasing, luring, until she wrapped her arms around his neck and kissed him back.

Tearing her mouth from his, she gasped for air, fought for lucidity. She should let it go, should just enjoy the moment and the sex and not look for anything else. Life had taught her not to look for anything else. But a part of her wanted to know, *needed* to know. "You didn't answer me."

"Because I never lie."

"What? Never lie? What does that have to do with anything?"

"You want me to tell you I was teasing. You want me to tell you that I don't feel like chaining you to my side and never letting you go. You want me to tell you that I don't regret eleven years of dreaming about you and never touching you. And I can't say any of that without lying."

And then he surged over her, sleek, predatory, his hands touching, seeking, making her moan, making her wonder how she could want him again so soon. Making her wonder how she could ever stop wanting him.

With easy strength, he grabbed her hips and rolled her until she lay facedown, prone beneath him, his weight pinning her, his cock, hard and hot, pressing against her ass.

He pushed her thighs apart, his legs coming between hers. Then he gave a grunt of dissatisfaction and pushed her legs wider still. She gasped as he reached underneath her and stroked her clitoris until it was swollen, sensitive, aching for his touch.

"I want to take you like this. Pinned underneath me."

She understood. He was a primitive being, for all his longevity and experience. He ate. He slept. He killed.

Now that he'd found her and decided to claim her, in his mind, he *possessed.* She was his.

And for her, he would do anything. Nurse her. Bleed for her.

She wasn't certain why the realization didn't send her screaming for the hills. Maybe because she herself wasn't so far from primitive.

But if it came down to choices, with what she was and what he was—a Daughter of Aset, a son of Sutekh—what would he do then? Would he even have a choice? Would she?

His teeth grazed her shoulder, the back of her neck. "I want to make you come. I want to make you scream."

"So make me scream," she said, and spread her thighs wider still.

LOKAN OPENED HIS EYES and stared at the darkness. Utter and absolute. No moon. No stars.

He blinked, the sensation gritty and uncomfortable. And still he could not see.

He touched his face.

Or did he?

He felt nothing. Not his fingertips. Not his cheeks.

Then he remembered the river, the boat. He rolled to his side, the movement making his stomach heave and his chest ache. The experience seemed wrong somehow.

Was he dead?

It was a foreign concept. Impossible. Could he die? Was he mortal?

He shook his head, trying to remember.

His name was Lokan. He was…what? Who?

He tried for other names, other thoughts, and only one came to him.

It was a memory. The sound of laughter. It was beautiful. Musical.

Suddenly the darkness receded and he was bathed in light, bright hot sun and the smell of summer. The laughter came from all around him, varying tones and timbres. And then a high-pitched shriek of sheer joy, followed by more laughter.

He felt the sun on his face, the breeze in his hair, heard a whoosh of sound.

"Push me, Daddy. Push me higher."

He felt metal beneath his fingertips, and he looked down to see chains, looked up to see a metal pole held aloft by other metal poles set at angles.

The chain fed down, down—

Don't look.

But he did. And there she was. Blond hair. Eyes like washed denim, like his own. Wide smile with a little girl's pretty white teeth.

She looked at him.

She looked *like* him.

His chest hurt to look at her. Unbearable pain.

"Push me higher, Daddy. Higher."

He did. He pushed. He could feel the tension in his muscles, the flex and release.

Slowly, he lifted his head and glanced to his left. There was a woman standing there. He felt affection of a sort, but nothing more. She was the child's mother.

His wife?

No. She was someone he had known but not loved. She was the child's and he was the child's, but he and the woman did not belong to each other.

But the child was *his* and he…loved her. Yes. The pain, the agony that burned in his heart. It was love. And it was fear. No, more than that, it was sheer terror.

They would hurt her. Cut her. Because she was his.

Him, or her. One of them would die. But he couldn't die, could he?

Him, or her.

He had to find a way.

He thought of his brothers. He had brothers. He knew it. He reached for them now and found only darkness. Endless, cold nothing. What were their names? He didn't know. He'd lost their names in the endless nothing.

He reached for the swing, for the child, but she was gone. Nothing there. Just the ghostly trail of her laughter.

The light receded and it was dark once more. Not

as dark as before. Light enough that he could see robed and cowled figures.

There was danger here. For her.

And something else. Betrayal.

A voice behind him. Someone he couldn't see. But he knew that voice. It was familiar. It was—

"Daddy! You came for me!" A soft, warm little body flinging herself against his legs. Tiny arms wrapping around his thighs, holding as tightly as her little muscles would allow.

She was here, and he wanted her to be anywhere but here.

"I don't want her to watch. She's to know nothing," he said.

"Of course."

Frustration surged. He should know that voice. He *did* know that voice. It was—

Hands were prying her from him, and she cried out, her face a mask of fear and uncertainty. He reached down. Ruffled her hair. Soft. Precious. Every hair on her mortal head, precious.

He would die for her.

He was *going* to die for her.

"You will make certain she is safe, that she's returned to her mother?" He spoke to the one directly behind him. He didn't turn to look over his shoulder, because he hadn't then, so he couldn't now. He understood in that second that he was living a memory.

"I will make certain."

He believed the promise. His betrayer made this promise, and he knew he would keep it. But he needed insurance.

"I need one phone call," he said. "In private."

"Yes."

The child was crying, great, fat tears that rolled down her cheeks and dripped off her chin.

"Daddy loves you," he said. "*I* love you."

Love. Could his kind feel love? He hadn't thought they could. Of course, he had never thought his kind could sire children, but he'd been proven wrong. She was there, looking at him with her washed-denim eyes, crying, her very existence proving his assumption wrong.

They took her away. His heart shattered into a million scattered slivers, cold and bright and broken.

Someone put a phone in his hand. He summoned every drop of supernatural ability he had and molded it into a shield, for his thoughts and his words, just in case they listened. He was powerful. He could hide this from them. But he could not use his power to save himself, because that would doom his child.

He called the child's mother, the woman he didn't love. She thought he was part of something called the Mafia. The thought made him laugh out loud, though he didn't know why.

In terse sentences and strangled words, he told her to trust no one. He told her not to contact his brothers, not to call any of the "safe" numbers he had given her in the past. Not to trust anyone he had trusted.

Betrayal wore the most unexpected face.

Then he gave her a name and contact information for his enemies, the Daughters of Aset, the Asetian Guard.

Only his enemies could keep his daughter safe. Only they *would* keep his daughter safe.

CHAPTER TWENTY

ROXY STRETCHED, FEELING LIKE a cat who'd been lying on a sunny step for hours, so relaxed she could barely move. "You hungry?"

"For you or for food?" Dagan didn't open his eyes. He just lay beside her, legs splayed, arms wide, unabashedly naked. Clearly, modesty wasn't a soul reaper trait.

"You already had me."

"True." He turned his head, opened his eyes. The look he gave her told her he was already growing hungry for her again. But he looked tired, too. Exhausted.

"Hungry for food," she prompted.

"You got anything sweet?"

"I think there's an old box of Frosted Flakes in the back of the pantry."

He grinned—white teeth, gold skin, a dimple peeking in his left cheek. It was incongruous, that dimple, in his hard, angular face. It was sexy. She wanted to lean in and press her lips to it. So she did.

"Sex, or cereal?" he asked, rolling, reaching for her, drawing her close. She felt the stirring of his cock against her thigh.

"Are you always like this?"

"Actually, no." He dipped his head to nuzzle her neck. "Your skin's delicious."

"If you compare it to chocolate, I'll kill you."

He licked along her neck to her shoulder, drawing a shiver. "It's like toffee. Like the sauce on a caramel sundae. Like coffee ice cream. Like—"

"Is there a reason you're comparing my skin to every sweet under the sun?"

"Sugar addict," he murmured, then he traced his tongue over her collarbone and down toward her breast.

She sighed, arched and he asked again, "Sex or cereal?"

Her stomach chose that moment to rumble. "Cereal—"

"Hmm." It was impossible to miss the affront in that sound. He drew back, frowning down at her.

"—then sex." She laughed at the expression on his face. "Hey, if you don't fuel the vehicle, it can't perform."

"Where do you want to eat?"

"That's a loaded question, isn't it?"

He laughed, the sound rich and full and beautiful.

"The kitchen," she decided. "It's more likely we'll actually end up eating something."

"Fine." The mattress dipped as he rolled and pushed to his feet. Then he padded from the bedroom, completely nude, without a backward glance. She watched him go, admiring the high, round curve of his ass and the long, lean muscles that roped the backs of his thighs and calves.

She bounced from the bed, feeling like she could run a marathon. Which made no sense because she'd almost died, had eaten nothing but his blood for three days and then had had marathon sex for…how many hours?

Her sense of time was completely screwed.

Of course, subsisting on his blood had probably given her the boost of energy. It was like nothing she'd ever experienced before. Like can after can of Red Bull poured down her throat.

She opened a drawer and grabbed a pair of underwear and a long T-shirt. Some habits were hard to break. She'd spent too many years in foster homes where there were too many kids, too little space and definitely zero privacy, so walking around completely naked wasn't something she was exactly comfortable with, even in her own home. She'd been alone in the crowd. God, she couldn't believe she'd said those things to him, told him private realities she'd shared with no one else.

She'd told him about Rhianna.

That she'd done so was both intimidating and freeing.

Running a hand along her hair, she glanced in the mirror. Her lips were red, puffy from Dagan's kisses. Her eyes were bright, her ringlets standing out in every direction. She looked like a woman who'd been well and truly fucked. Because she had been. And shortly, she would be again.

The thought made her smile.

She found him in the kitchen, eating stale Frosted Flakes by the fistful from the box.

"You're a Neanderthal."

"Yeah." He grinned, unashamed.

She scrounged through the fridge and found eggs, bacon, milk that hadn't yet hit its due date. There was some bread in a bag on the counter, sort of stale but not growing anything. Yet. He took the milk from her, tipped his head back and drank it from the carton.

"Oh, for God's sake."

He looked at her, brows raised, gray eyes wide. "What?"

"What."

"What?"

Shaking her head, she pulled out a pan. Then—surprise, surprise—he pulled out a chair at the kitchen table, held it for her and waited till she sat. Then he cooked her breakfast for dinner. Fluffy scrambled eggs, bacon, toast that dripped butter.

She practically licked the plate.

They made love again, finding an innovative use for the dregs of a bottle of maple syrup Dagan discovered at the back of the fridge. He said he needed sugar—something about his jacked-up metabolism—and that licking it off her naked skin was the only way he wanted it.

Who was she to argue with a physiologic necessity?

She hopped in the shower when they were done, and when she came out, Dagan was asleep. She was surprised, and not. He'd stayed awake, standing guard over her the entire time she was recovering. She'd seen how tired he was. And she took the fact that he'd let himself rest as a sort of statement of his confidence in her ability to take care of herself now that she was healed.

So maybe he was only partly Neanderthal. Looked like he meant to let her wield her own club.

Standing over him, she studied his features, his frame. He didn't look boyish or sweet in slumber. His features were as angular and chiseled as when he was awake. The only thing missing was the hardness around his mouth. So it appeared that in sleep, he relaxed at least a little.

Roxy got dressed, making as little noise as she could. Yeah, she was tired. But she was exhilarated, too. And she needed to speak with Calliope. She's rather do it in person for a whole lot of reasons, some of which had to do with the Asetian Guard and with Dana, but most of which had something to do with the guy sprawled on her cream-colored sheets, sleeping the sleep of the dead.

Definitely not a snorer.

She wasn't used to explaining her whereabouts to anyone, but she left a note propped on the table by the bed, just in case he woke up while she was gone. It felt wrong somehow to just leave him here alone without any explanation. *Back soon. Leave me a number to reach you if you need to go before I get back.*

Staring at the message, she wondered if that was too casual. Then she shrugged. Too bad if it was. She couldn't be—didn't want to be—other than who she was. And she wasn't about to expect him to sit here waiting for her, either.

They'd existed in separate lives for a very long time. They'd existed in the same life for three—or was it four now?—whole days.

They'd both need to do some adjusting.

She left him sleeping, grabbed her keys from the glass bowl in the entry hall and headed for the garage. Once inside the car, she opened the glove box and took out a disposable cell. She dialed the number from memory. She hadn't written it down, hadn't wanted to risk leaving any evidence, any trail.

Calliope's people had moved Dana and her mom twice now. But Roxy wanted them moved again. This time, without anyone but her knowing about it. Because she had the inside track here, information that no one

else seemed to have. Actually, she wouldn't have it either except for following her gut the night she'd saved Dana.

Roxy had tasted her blood. The kid had been out for the count. Roxy'd seen a scratch on her arm, tiny droplets welling in a neat line. A swipe of her finger. A swipe of her tongue. And she had a surefire way to track the kid if she got nabbed again.

She didn't know why she'd even considered that a possibility. But she had. And she wasn't one to pass up a perfect opportunity.

There'd been something odd about the kid's blood. A strange energy. But Roxy had chalked that up to never having tasted a child's blood before. Now, she wasn't convinced.

The kid's blood had had a familiar taste to it.

And if what she suspected was true, then she was on her way to figuring out at least part of the riddle of the dead soul reaper. If she were right, then she knew what role Dana had played. And she knew how they'd managed to kill Lokan Krayl.

A sleepy, feminine voice answered the phone on the seventh ring. "Do we need to go right now?" Dana's mom whispered, not even bothering with a greeting. There was only one person who would call this phone. Roxy'd given it to her, and Roxy was the only one who knew the number. "Dana has nightmares. I've just gotten her to sleep."

If someone else found them, Dana's nightmares would spill over into the bright light of day.

"I told you that if I called, you'd need to do exactly as I say, when I say it. I'm calling. That means you need to go."

There was beat of silence, then Dana's mother whispered, "I know. I'm sorry."

"If you can't do this, you need to say so now."

"For my daughter, I can do anything."

The words were fervent. They brought out gooseflesh on Roxy's skin. She had a flare of memory, her own mother saying something very similar, years and years in the past.

"You have your funds all set, the way I told you?" Roxy asked.

"Yes."

"You go straight to a motel. Somewhere clean but not expensive. Tomorrow, you go to the safety deposit box I set up for you. There's ID there, cash and instructions. Follow them to the letter."

"I will." Her voice was still soft, but now it was laced with steel. Roxy actually believed this might work, that between them, they'd manage to keep Dana safe.

"And you know not to call anyone. *Anyone.* Not even the number you dialed originally to get in touch with my superiors when Dana was taken."

She could hear Dana's mom breathing fast and shallow.

"Yes." The woman gave a harsh laugh. "You know, I never thought I'd be grateful that Dana and I have no other family. But right now, I am. I'm grateful I'm not leaving anyone for them to find. To hurt. And that I'm not leaving anyone behind to miss us when we disappear into thin air."

Her words reached deep inside Roxy and twisted her gut tight. "Yeah, that's a good thing. But at least you'll be together. You have each other." That was her gift to Dana. The chance to grow up with her

mom by her side. Or maybe it was the chance to grow up at all.

The same gift her mom had given her.

"You're certain—" the voice on the other end dropped so low Roxy could barely hear her "—the Mafia won't find us."

"Yes." That, Roxy could definitely swear to. If the woman wanted to believe Dana's dad had been Mafia royalty, more power to her. She was probably safer believing that than knowing the truth. "You do exactly what I told you, exactly what the instructions say, and no one will find you."

But I will if I have to because I can track your daughter's blood.

"Thank you. I'll do everything just the way you said. Thank you. I mean that. Thank you for everything."

Something tightened in Roxy's chest. The woman's gratitude made her uncomfortable. She was thanking her for tearing her life apart, for forcing her to leave everything known and familiar. How fucked was that?

"Destroy the phone as soon as you hang up," Roxy said, and disconnected the call.

She pulled the SIM card out of her own disposable phone, opened the car door and set both the card and the phone side by side on the ground. She smashed each one under her boot heel. Then she carefully collected the broken bits, intending to throw them out the window a little at a time as she drove.

Not that she was in favor of littering, but this situation demanded an exception.

As she pulled the Vette out of the garage, she had a momentary thought, a sort of belated curiosity about

why Dagan had decided to take care of her here, at her place. She remembered him saying something about needing to get her somewhere safe. Her home had already been breached by fire genies. How had he by any stretch of the imagination thought that that was safe?

Maybe he'd had some inside info that the fire genies wouldn't be back.

She shrugged, hit the gas and chewed up the highway. Caution was a hard habit to break, so she took the long route, doubling back on herself, even ducking onto a sideroad and cutting the engine as she watched for anything coming up behind her. No vehicles. No fire genies. Not even a whisper of supernatural vibe. Still, caution won out over haste. Only when she was absolutely certain that she hadn't been followed did she head for Blackstock doing double the speed limit, flat out.

It was her lucky night. No cops.

That would have been all she needed, a fucking ticket.

The gray ribbon of road unfurled under the cloud-smeared night sky. There were no lights on this stretch of highway, and the houses were set way back from the road. She knew this route almost as well as the route to her own front door. Even so, she almost missed the turnoff to Calliope's, hidden as it was by trees and overgrown wild grass.

Truth was, her concentration wasn't all it could be. Her thoughts were back with Dagan. What was she supposed to be thinking here? That the soul reaper had lost his soul to her. Not hardly. That he'd…what? Fallen head over heels in lo—

In *lust*. Lust was tangible, skin to skin, mouth to mouth, peg A in slot B. *That* she could deal with.

The other *L* word? Not so much.

Roxy cut sharply to the right, following instinct rather than visual cues, and the shadows broke, revealing a driveway that was little more than short grass grooved by parallel dirt lines. She slowed to a crawl, followed the S-curve of the drive, then slowed even more as she broke through the thick clumps of evergreens that hid Calliope's modest two-story period farmhouse from the road.

Calliope had chosen the place with care. The trees were perfect cover in any season, but past them was an oasis carved out of the woods, set on a couple of acres northeast of Toronto. The lawn out front was freshly cut, the garden well tended. The porch was butter yellow, the wood siding painted a pale shade of gray. Picture postcard perfect.

A lie of omission. It didn't reveal what lay beneath.

Years ago, wide-eyed and overwhelmed by new and strange knowledge, Roxy had looked around and observed, "No one would ever imagine the place belongs to—" She'd pressed her lips together, unsure if she ought to give voice to her thoughts.

"Go on," Calliope had urged.

"A member of the Asetian Guard."

"Which is exactly the point," Calliope had replied, her lips curving in a beautiful, serene smile. More than once over the years, Calliope's smile had grated on Roxy's nerves like a cat yowling at 3:00 a.m., mostly because Roxy and *serene* didn't inhabit the same dictionary. And partly because Roxy wanted just a sliver of that tranquility for herself.

"Where should I live, Roxy?" Calliope had continued. "In a fortress? No man-made wall can hold back my enemies. Or yours, now."

Hadn't that proven to be the truth. All those years ago, Dagan had warned her about the Daughters of Aset. Would have been nice if he'd thrown in a mention of fire genies.

And soul reapers and demons and gods and demi-gods.

Killing the engine, Roxy sat in the car for a second longer. The kitchen light was burning despite the hour. Looked like Calliope was expecting her. No surprise there. That was one of Calliope's talents—prescience. Roxy might sense a supernatural's energy vibe, but unless she'd encountered the individual before, she wouldn't necessarily know *who* was coming for a visit, just that *someone* was. And she'd know if they were friend or foe.

But Calliope knew a hell of a lot more than that. Generally, she knew exactly who was about to arrive at her door.

Roxy took the front stairs two at a time, crossed the wide porch and raised her hand to knock. Before her knuckles could hit wood, the door swung open.

"That's creepy." She dropped her hand.

"I'd think you'd be used to it by now." Calliope pulled the door fully open and stepped back in invitation. "You disappeared for three days without checking in," she said, her gaze intent.

"I've disappeared for longer than that before."

"True. But right now there are—" Calliope paused, as though weighing her choice of words "—circumstances that made your disappearance a cause for concern."

"But you won't tell me what those circumstances are."

"No."

"See, that's exactly the problem. You tell me nothing. I have no tools to work with. I go in blind and unprepared."

"It's safer that way."

"For who? Not for me—"

"Actually, yes. For you. You can't be held accountable for things you don't know. I'm protecting you."

Roxy threw her hands up in frustration. "I need to protect *myself*. And if I don't know what's going on, how am I supposed to do that?"

Her expression betraying none of her thoughts, Calliope pulled the door open a little wider.

"There are huge chunks of information I don't have leave to reveal," she said. "But I can tell you this. There's a meeting of the gods of the Underworld three days hence. It's a strategic and logistic nightmare involving the exchange of hostages as blood guarantors. I am to be one of those hostages. Which means you'll be on your own as long as I'm gone." She stepped back and swept her hand before her. "Come inside."

Headway. Calliope had actually revealed something important. Roxy walked past her into the house, then offered tit for tat, information flowing both ways. "I was out of touch because I had a less-than-friendly visit from an entire platoon of fucking fire genies." She waited a beat, not really expecting Calliope to express surprise but offering her the chance just in case she wanted to break tradition.

"You do attract the oddest friends."

"Do tell."

Calliope reached past her and closed the door. She didn't lock it. What was the point? Calliope was in no

danger from the average human. And a lock wouldn't offer any protection from even a low-level supernatural.

And locking a wooden door against something like, say, a fire genie was probably more than a little redundant.

Calliope turned, looked at her, and went still. Her eyes narrowed then widened a fraction of an inch. Without asking for leave, she reached out and caught the neckline of Roxy's T-shirt, dragging it down to bare the top of her chest. Roxy followed Calliope's gaze to the raised ridge of her healing scar.

All color washed from Calliope's face. She looked sick, shaken. Which left Roxy feeling sick and shaken because Calliope never lost it. Ever.

"You—" Calliope's voice cracked, and she pressed her lips together and took a slow breath in through her nose. Roxy could actually see the way she centered her thoughts, see the subtle changes in her posture, her carriage. "You had a run in with something more than Xaphan's concubines. What happened?"

"My chest got caught on a soul reaper's fist." The second the words were out, Roxy knew she'd made a mistake. She'd gone for flip, light, a little shared joke to dispel the tension. But Calliope wasn't laughing.

"I'm okay," Roxy said, but she could see that Calliope wasn't okay.

Then her mentor got herself together, or at least she appeared to. It was like a mask slid in place, a perfectly etched version of Calliope that was all surface, no depth. *Shit. Shit!*

Without another word, Calliope turned and headed for the kitchen.

Following behind, Roxy froze, turned, double-

checked that the door was closed. Something didn't feel right. The fine hairs at her nape prickled and rose. Something out there. Or in here.

"What is it?" Calliope asked as Roxy leaned one hip against the tiled counter.

"You picking up anything out of the ordinary?"

Calliope took her time answering. "No."

"Then it's nothing," Roxy said. If Calliope wasn't sensing anything, then there was nothing to sense. She was better at this than Roxy, more attuned to even the slightest change in molecular vibrations.

Turning to the counter, Roxy lifted the lid of the ceramic cookie jar and peered inside. Empty. Damn. Usually it was at least half full of homemade cinnamon cookies.

She was starving. With a mental shrug, she headed for the fridge, yanked it open and sagged in disappointment.

"Tomorrow is shopping day," Calliope commented as she filled the kettle and set it on the stove. Her voice was tight, and Roxy knew the whole scar-on-her-chest issue wasn't resolved yet. Might as well feed herself while Calliope decided exactly what she wanted to say.

Bypassing the leftover steak, she reached behind a carton of plain yogurt for a plastic container. She popped the lid. Looked like cold rice, chickpeas, and...dried cranberries? Weird. She leaned in and sniffed. Balsamic vinegar. Feta. With a shrug, she got a fork from the drawer and dug in, leaning one hip against the counter.

Again, she felt that odd sensation, not quite a feeling of being watched, but something similar. A warning.

Setting the fork down, she straightened off the counter.

"Calliope," she said. "You getting anything?"

Her mentor was instantly alert, features taut. Her brows drew together in a frown.

"I sense nothing, but it doesn't mean that nothing is there. What do you feel?"

"Cold. Not like a temperature, like an emotion. Inside me. I—"

She broke off. Calliope was no longer there. She'd moved with abnormal speed, almost faster than Roxy'd been able to see. Damn. Roxy hadn't known Calliope could move like that.

Then she sensed him. *Dagan.* Somehow, he was here.

Her gut clenched.

"Fuck."

She was already sprinting flat out for the entry hall. Chest heaving, heart pounding, she went skidding around the corner, then stopped dead. She shook her head, held her hand up, palm forward, as if that feeble gesture could ward off catastrophe.

Poised in the center of the room were Calliope and Dagan, locked in a lethal, frozen tableau. He was wearing only his faded jeans, his feet and torso bare, his hair wild and tangled to his shoulders, as though he'd leapt from her bed and paused only long enough to pull on the single garment.

Calliope curled her fingers against Dagan's throat. Her green eyes were bright with hate and rage, her lips peeled back in a feral snarl, her fingers white knuckled with the amount of pressure she was applying. Her chest heaved in a harsh, fast rhythm, her breath loud

in the quiet. In her hand was a bone-handled blade, pressing into the skin above Dagan's heart. A trickle of blood oozed along the swell of muscle, working its way toward his belly.

In ten years, Roxy'd never seen her mentor lose her cool. She'd rarely seen her show much emotion. But this wasn't just emotion. This was all-out, Grade A hate.

And Dagan was returning the aggression measure for measure. His fingers dug into Calliope's throat and his other hand was drawn back, fingers clawed, like he was about to punch through ribs and muscle and take her heart.

His gray eyes were colder than frost. He didn't move. Didn't breathe. Didn't look her way as he said, "I told you, if you run, I will find you."

Roxy took a careful step forward. She kept her gaze locked on Calliope, though she wasn't certain her normally even-tempered mentor was the sure bet.

"I didn't run. I drove." Okay. Lame. But she wasn't coming up with a whole hell of a lot here. "I left you a note."

He flicked a glance at her. "A note?" The way he asked made it clear that he hadn't read it, hadn't seen it. And it probably wouldn't have mattered if he had.

"Dae, don't hurt her."

Her words made Calliope flinch.

Bad choice. She changed tactics.

"Calliope, stand down," Roxy said, heart hammering so hard she thought she might be sick. He could kill her. One serpentine flick of his hand and he could rip out Calliope's heart. Surely Calliope knew that; she had to know she didn't stand a chance.

Or did she? Roxy had never seen Calliope move as fast as she had just now. So maybe there was more to her than Roxy had ever imagined.

"He tried to kill you, yet you would defend him?" The words were hard and cold.

"No! He isn't the one who hurt me. He saved my life." She shook her head. "Calliope, you can't kill him. You know that. And he won't hurt you if you stand down."

She hoped.

She was betting Calliope's life that she was right, that Dagan wouldn't simply thrust his hand deep inside her chest and rip out her beating heart then harvest her darksoul just the way she'd seen him do it in the past. Just the way Gahiji had tried to do to her.

He was what he was. A killer. A soul reaper.

A few hours in her bed didn't change his nature.

The knowledge rocked her.

What had she imagined? That he was tamed by her love.

No. She couldn't love him. Couldn't love anyone. If you loved, you lost. If you loved, you hurt. If you loved, you got your heart torn out when they left.

"Calliope," she tried again, her voice shaking. "You can't kill him."

Neither combatant moved a muscle, though she knew they'd both heard her.

Then, voice humming with tension, with hate, Calliope asked, "I can't kill him because he cannot be killed or because you do not *wish* him to be killed?"

The moment of truth. The moment of lies.

What was she supposed to offer in response to Calliope's question?

Roxy sensed a sharpening of Dagan's attention, as though somehow her answer would decide something important, something that had nothing to do with who was going to end up bleeding all over the hallway floor.

The answer choked her. She saw Calliope tense ever so slightly and she realized she had no time to think. No time to decide.

She was going to have to sacrifice something here tonight. She couldn't have both Dagan and the Daughters of Aset. She saw that with brutal clarity.

"Both," she snarled. "I don't want him hurt, and even if I did, you couldn't."

"Why?" Calliope asked, her tone sharper than Roxy'd ever heard.

Again, Roxy felt that surge of panic. Why what? Why didn't she want him hurt? She didn't want to say. She just wanted it to be what it was, without words marking it, defining it.

Slowly, Dagan turned his head toward her. She felt like everything else in the room disappeared. The floor, the walls, even Calliope. Gone. And there was just Dagan, seeing clear to her soul.

She wanted to beg him to let Calliope go, to do this for her, to walk away. A part of her was terrified to ask. What if he felt so little for her that he said no?

She was risking everything here, and she could be left with nothing.

His gaze flicked to Calliope, and Roxy's heart slammed against her ribs.

He dropped the hand he'd been about to tear her heart out with. Roxy felt the first spark of relief. Then he lowered the hand from around her throat.

Calliope stared at him, cold, disdainful. She still held him in a choke hold, her knife still pressed into his chest.

He didn't look particularly concerned.

"I could kill you," she whispered, every word dripping venom.

"No. But you could hurt me." His mouth curved in a dark smile, as though he promised to hurt her in return.

On a sharp inhalation, Calliope took her hand from his throat, let her knife slide away, though she didn't pull the tip from his skin until she'd marked a line from chest to hip. Blood welled, red and bright, and Roxy had to consciously hold herself back from leaping forward and tearing the knife from Calliope's hand.

She didn't want him hurt. Not even a scratch.

Yet, four days ago, she'd been doing worse than what Calliope was doing now, digging her blade into his thigh deep enough to hit bone. She flinched at the memory.

He'd been patient with her, even then.

Calliope shot a glance at Roxy. Her eyes were like emeralds lit from behind, the fire of fury, the fire of hate. "You brought a soul reaper here, to my home?"

It struck Roxy then, clear as a lake on the laziest day of summer. For Calliope, this was personal. It wasn't just about being a member of the Asetian Guard. She had a personal grudge against soul reapers.

Both Dagan and Calliope jerked back, almost in tandem. Calliope stepped to her right, legs bent, body coiled.

Dagan mirrored her movement, prowling like a

beast about to spring on its kill, matching each step Calliope took. They circled, and circled again.

Seconds oozed past, and Roxy fought the sick feeling that burned high in her gut. This moment was only a reprieve. She was going to have to betray someone tonight. Dagan? Calliope? Maybe even herself.

Roxy leaped between them, one hand going flat on Dagan's chest, the other catching Calliope's forearm.

"Enough," she snarled. Then she turned her face to Dagan and barked, "I need five minutes of privacy. Now."

Beneath her touch, she felt Calliope tense. Guess that barking orders at a soul reaper just wasn't done.

Dagan narrowed his eyes. She thought he would argue. Maybe even move past her to get at Calliope. He was faster than she could ever hope to be.

"Please," she gritted.

His nostrils flared, then he gave a sharp nod and stepped away. He turned and stalked from the house, slamming the front door behind him.

CHAPTER TWENTY-ONE

I am strong as Thoth...
In order to seek out my foe,
He has been given to me
And he shall not be taken from me.

—Egyptian Book of the Dead, Chapter 11

THROUGH THE NARROW STRIP of glass beside the door, Roxy could see Dagan pacing the lawn.

She shook her head and turned to Calliope, assessing her mood.

Calliope's lips curved in a mocking smile. "I want to go after him and stab him a thousand times. But first, I want to hear your explanation."

With a nod, Roxy let go of her forearm.

They stood, separated by an arm's length. Separated by a great, yawning chasm. How to cross it?

"Talk," Calliope ordered.

So Roxy did. She started with the least provocative information, telling Calliope in concise terms about Xaphan's concubines, their questions about Frank Marin and their interest in Dana.

Leaning to the side, she tried to catch sight of Dagan on the lawn, but he'd paced beyond her field of vision.

"That's why you wanted Dana moved a second

time," Calliope observed. "You were concerned the fire genies were going to find her."

"Yeah." Roxy felt a pang about keeping quiet that she had moved the kid a third time, and about the certainty she had that Dana was by no means an incidental pawn. She was a key piece on the chessboard. In some ways, she was the queen.

But if Roxy's suspicions proved true, then Dana's life could well depend on no one knowing where she was. So she didn't tell Calliope that she'd made the kid disappear. That information would surface in its own time, and she'd pay the piper then.

Calliope's brow furrowed. "And you never thought I might need to know more? What if Xaphan's concubines had reached her first? You should have contacted me immediately."

"She couldn't. She was dying." Dagan's voice interrupted them, and from the way Calliope jerked to attention, Roxy was fairly certain that she hadn't sensed his return any better than Roxy had.

She remembered Calliope's past description of soul reapers: *…you would never have known he was there. Not unless he wanted you to. They can practically move between molecules, disturbing nothing. Not air. Not sound. Not light. They are there, but not there.*

So very true.

"Must you sneak around?" Roxy snapped.

"Sneak around?" Dagan looked completely flummoxed. "You said five minutes. It was five minutes."

She sighed. He really had no clue how eerie it was to have him simply appear at will. "People like to have a bit of warning when someone arrives."

He shrugged. "I'm here. There's your warning."

Great.

Calliope was regarding them as though they were a foreign species. "What do you mean, she was dying?" she asked Dagan, her distaste at speaking directly to him apparent in every word.

For some reason, Roxy didn't want him to answer. Everything that had happened for the past few days— being nursed by Dagan, protected by him, drinking his blood, making love with him—it all felt too personal, too private to offer up for public consumption.

Besides, there really was no way to tell a part of the story without revealing most of it. She'd spent ten years hiding her parasitic nature—and the fact that she had to feed from a human host—from Calliope and the Asetian Guard. She hated for the jig to be up now.

Dagan's gaze met hers, flat, implacable.

"I was injured," Roxy hedged. "He helped me heal. Clearly I wasn't dying. Do I look like I was dying?"

"You tried to take her heart," Calliope accused, her gaze sliding to Dagan, her hand flexing on her knife.

"A soul reaper did. But it wasn't me."

Calliope's breath hissed from between her teeth, a sound so unlikely to be coming from Calliope Kane that it made Roxy freeze.

"Calliope—"

"I saw the scar, far too smooth and even to be only a few days old. You are a mere infant among the Daughters. You do not yet have the power to heal like that." Her eyes narrowed. "How did he help you heal? Please the goddess Aset, tell me you didn't drink his blood."

Roxy stared at her, uncomprehending. "What?"

"Whose blood healed you?" But her gaze was already shifting to Dagan, as though she knew.

Roxy felt like the world was tilting upside down, everything she knew turning inside out, leaving skin on the inside and raw, bloody flesh out. The things Calliope was revealing. She was an infant among the Daughters? Was Calliope implying that her supernatural power would grow? But more than that...the blood. Calliope knew about the blood.

"What—" Roxy's breathing was way too fast. She tried to slow it, tried to stay calm. "What do you know about the blood?"

"Excellent question," Dagan murmured. "I'd be very interested in the answer. Quite the shock. One minute Roxy's bleeding all over me, the next I'm bleeding down her throat. Fascinating turn of events. Especially when the hole in her chest started to knit like it was kicked into fast-forward."

"What?" Roxy whirled to him. What was he saying? That he *hadn't* known she drank blood? Hadn't known what she was?

"But you made me," she cried. "You turned me into a blood-drinking fiend. A vampire. Why are you asking *her* about this?"

She heard Calliope's sharp intake of breath, felt the tension in the room thick as a pea-soup fog. Turning, she met her mentor's gaze. The expression on Calliope's face made her stomach churn. Something wasn't right. In fact, something was terribly, terribly wrong.

"Not my doing," Dagan said, his hands spread before him, palms up. "And you're not a vampire. There are no such things as vampires. They're a myth perpetrated by a panic-stricken public in response to natural changes of decomposition."

"What?" Roxy felt like a contestant on some bizarre

game show. She wanted to go look for the cameras, because nothing else made any sense. Panting, she turned to Calliope. "Talk. Now."

Calliope looked stricken, her cheeks drained of color, her eyes wide. She shot a glance at Dagan, as though willing him to leave, but he only crossed his arms over his chest and stared her down.

"I thought you knew," Calliope said, turning back to Roxy. "You came to us already blooded, with the mark carved in your skin. Why would I think you didn't know?"

"Know what?" Roxy snarled. "What are you talking about? Already blooded? What does that mean?"

"The Daughters of Aset are pranic feeders. I thought you knew. We sip from the life force of others. It is Aset's gift to us, what defines us as her Daughters, passed to our daughters in maternal blood, if we have them." She paused. "Not all of us do. It would upset the natural balance, given our longevity."

Natural balance. Longevity. Roxy's head was reeling, her emotions so raw and ugly that she had to fist her hands by her sides to keep from hitting something. Everything she'd thought had been wrong. This was too much to take in all at once. So she picked one question, one thing to focus on.

"Sip the life force of others," Roxy echoed. "How? By drinking their blood?"

Calliope shot another look at Dagan, her expression pained. Clearly, she didn't want to talk about this in front of him. But in this moment, with horror and anger and confusion swirling in a brutal mix inside her, Roxy didn't give a flying fuck who heard what. She'd been living a lie for eleven years.

"What do you think you're going to say that he doesn't already know?" Roxy demanded. "He's been feeding me his blood out of a fucking cup for three days!"

"Except when I fed you from my vein," Dagan murmured helpfully, and Roxy had a vivid flash of memory, her mouth sealed to him, her teeth sinking into his flesh, the feel of his life force filling her.

"Shut up," she gritted.

"She would have healed faster if you stuck with the vein," Calliope said. "Blood taken directly from a living donor is the most beneficial source of natural prana."

Dagan dipped his head in acknowledgment. "I'll remember that for next time."

Rage and confusion and a sense of betrayal churned inside Roxy. She fisted her hands at her sides, wanting so badly to hit something, to lash out. "You've known me for ten years, ten goddamn years, and you never thought to mention any of this?"

Head tipped to one side, Calliope studied her, then she said softly, "Roxy, sit, please."

"Sit?" Her world was falling apart, everything she knew—or thought she knew—turned upside down and backward, and Calliope wanted her to sit.

Dagan moved until he was directly behind her. His arms came around her, his chest against her back. He was solid and warm. Safe. She could feel his heat through her T-shirt, feel his strength.

And it was only in that second that she understood why Calliope had told her to sit. Because she was shaking, her whole body trembling, her fury and confusion manifesting in a physical breakdown.

Which made sense. She'd been at death's door for three days. Then she'd fucked Dagan until both of them were replete and drained. Physically, she was on her last leg.

"Go on," Dagan said.

Calliope stared at his arms where they wrapped Roxy from behind. For a second, her facade cracked, just a little. Enough to glimpse confusion behind the mask.

"When you came to us, you had the dark mark already etched in your skin. It was perfectly executed. Beautiful."

Roxy swallowed, nodded. "I'd been looking for the Daughters of Aset for a little more than a year. I'd discovered the dark mark, recognized it as the symbol from my pendant, and I—" She broke off, gathered her thoughts. "My mother had the same mark."

She could summon a clear recollection of her mother's forearm, the skin smooth and coffee-brown, with a raised pattern. Roxy remembered tracing her childish fingers over the mark. She could almost feel it beneath her fingertips even now.

"Okay, so I had the mark when I came to you. But didn't it occur to you to sit me down and make certain I knew the basics? To make sure I understood what I was? Just a nice friendly chat over a microwaved mug of blood?"

Dagan made a choked sound, and she felt his chest move against her back. He was laughing. *Laughing.* She wasn't sure if she wanted to kiss him or hit him.

She jerked from his embrace and stood on her own, facing them both down.

"And you," she said to Dagan. "Did it occur to you

to explain that you hadn't turned me into a blood-sucking fiend? That it was—" She jerked around and glared at Calliope. "What? An accident of my birth?"

Calliope looked affronted. "Not an accident. A gift. You say it as though it is some dreadful curse that's been perpetrated on you."

"Isn't it? I suck blood to survive! I did it in secret, hiding what I was, taking tiny bits, going as long as I could between feedings! The pain was horrific, like hunger pangs multiplied by a thousand. The first year, before I found you, I thought I was dying. Every day, I thought I was dying." She spun back to Dagan. "I thought you did this to me! I cursed you, hated you—" *longed for you, loved you.* She didn't say that. Didn't even want to dare think it. She took a shaky breath— "I blamed you for all of it."

Calliope was staring at her now, green eyes bright with horror and dismay.

"Am I to understand that *he* was your First Blood? A soul reaper?" Her tone was flat.

Roxy nodded. Dagan moved up beside her again, protective, possessive, close enough that his arm rested against hers. "Does it matter?"

"We do not feed from supernaturals. It can breed an…unwanted connection."

Guess that explained the waking dreams.

"He saved my life. From a rapist and his partner. Dagan came and harvested their hearts. Their souls."

"She watched you harvest darksouls?" Calliope looked at Dagan. Her tone was colder than liquid nitrogen, laced with disbelief. "She saw what you are and you let her live? You gave her First Blood. Was it a plot, a ploy—"

"No. I knew nothing of what you are. I had no idea you were pranic feeders. No clue you drink blood." His smile was mocking. "The Daughters of Aset don't exactly advertise what they are. Fuck…Roxy lived as one of you for ten years and didn't know what you are. Maybe I *was* her first, but it was an accident. She bit me."

Calliope blinked and shot a glance at Roxy. Surprised. Assessing. "And still you let her live. I don't believe your words. No soul reaper would let her live."

"Because you know so much about us?" Dagan arched a brow. "Believe what you want. I wasn't sent that night to harvest her."

"And if you had been?" Calliope's eyes narrowed. "If you had been sent there for her, would you have harvested her soul?"

Roxy's heart slammed against her ribs. There was an intensity to Calliope's words, a hidden meaning. She was asking something more from Dagan, more than just the answer to the specific question.

Dagan hooked his thumbs in the waistband of his jeans, his expression implacable, his eyes flat gray. Cold now. He didn't like being put on the spot. Didn't want to answer. And then he did.

"No."

One word.

Whatever Calliope had been looking for, he'd given it to her. Her shoulders relaxed ever so slightly, her expression softened.

She moved close and stared into Roxy's eyes.

"I didn't do a very good job," she said, and her mouth turned in a sad smile. "I hadn't been a mentor before. You were my first pupil. So prickly, so private.

I didn't push for personal information because you seemed to prefer distance, and because I didn't want to make you withdraw even more. I see now that that was a mistake. I've lost you and I'll have to answer for that."

"You haven't lost me." Roxy shook her head. "Answer to whom?"

Calliope cut Dagan a look. Roxy had the feeling she was choosing the right words, the ones she thought were best. Best for what?

"You're the bottom rung of the Asetian Guard," Calliope said at last. "You're privy to no secrets."

"Apparently, I wasn't even privy to the secret of what the hell I am," Roxy muttered, unable to squelch the hint of resentment.

Calliope's lips twisted in a wry smile. "My error, Roxy. You have my apology and my regret, but the truth is, given what has now come to light, it seems that even from the first day I found you, you were never meant to be one of us."

"What? Why?"

"I didn't know you'd taken First Blood from a soul reaper. If I had—" she shook her head "—well, it doesn't matter. You'd already been blooded and marked. Already fed from his pranic force. I can't imagine what that was like." There was both awe and a faint tinge of disgust in her tone.

"So what are you saying?" Roxy felt a surge of panic. "I'm no longer a Daughter of Aset? Because I fed from a soul reaper's life force?"

Genuine terror congealed in her gut. Calliope was cutting her loose. After ten years of security, ten years of having a family with the Daughters of Aset, she was

going to be left with nothing. She thought of her mom. She thought of her foster parents. She thought of Rhianna, her sister in everything but blood. Every single one of them had cut her loose. They'd fucking *died* and left her alone.

And now Calliope, her sister in the Daughters of Aset, her mentor, her friend, was going to leave her bobbing, a small solitary boat in a roiling sea.

Her breath came in hard gasps, the pain in her heart a twisting agony. She breathed, breathed, tried to focus her thoughts and it hit her then, like a bolt of electricity.

In the end, wasn't everyone alone?

Hadn't she always stood on her own two feet?

It wasn't as though the Asetian Guard had given her security or answers. It had been about doing the job. Nothing less, nothing more.

She could find another damned job.

A moment later, she felt it, Dagan's hand in her own, his fingers long and elegant, interlacing with hers.

Not so alone, then.

To her surprise, Calliope stepped forward, and there was a suspect sheen of moisture in her eyes.

"Oh, Roxy," she whispered. "Is that what you think of me? After all these years? You think I would cast you aside like you have no meaning, no value? Of course you are a Daughter of Aset, my sister, my pupil. My friend. You were always a Daughter, from the second you were born. But you cannot be of the Asetian Guard anymore. Knowing what I know now, I must say, you never should have been in the first place."

She shot a glance at Dagan, who stood silent and glowering at Roxy's side.

"You have fed on the life force of a soul reaper. You are unique among our kind." She shook her head. "But it is ever the way of mortal and immortal to hate what they fear." She shot a dark look at Dagan, and Roxy knew that whatever acceptance and love Calliope was showing her, it didn't extend to him. She was suffering his presence, that was all. "Perhaps it would be best if this information were not made public at this very moment."

This very moment. Roxy remembered what Calliope had said when she first arrived, about the upcoming meeting of Underworld lords and the exchange of hostages. She had a feeling that this was an oblique reference to that information.

"So this is supposed to be our little secret? And our superiors in the Guard? What happens when they find out?"

She could see the conflict warring inside Calliope, see the banked rage every time she glanced at Dagan. She'd been right earlier. She was convinced of it. Calliope hated soul reapers with a personal fire.

"You have tendered your resignation from the Asetian Guard. I have accepted it," Calliope said. "You are no longer a member. You had no access to sensitive information, so your mustering out presents no logistical threat. If—or rather, when—they find out, they might argue that I ought to have shared your personal information. I shall argue in return that I had no obligation to do so. I have no intention of telling the Asetian Guard about you and—" she slanted a knife sharp glance at Dagan "—him. Not right now."

So it wasn't a pardon. It was a reprieve. Not what she might have hoped, but definitely better than nothing.

Calliope's expression underwent a subtle shift, her lips parted and Roxy knew she was going to say something more, something important, but she never got the chance to hear what it was.

Senses suddenly on high alert, Roxy swayed, feeling like she was being battered by some sort of electrical storm. Her skin tingled to the point of pain, like a thousand needles were jabbing her at once.

Calliope stiffened and jerked back, clearly bombarded by the same sensations.

Roxy froze, then turned. The air shimmered. Changed. She spun, searching out the threat, knowing it was there but unable to see it. Then a choking smoke filled the space in front of her—a dark, undulating cloud.

Dagan moved between her and the cloud, his lips peeled back in a wolf snarl, his body settling in a ready crouch.

The air twisted and bent, the dark blot before her defying logic and physics. Then it pulled in on itself before thrusting forward into the room.

Three soul reapers appeared—two Roxy had never seen before, and one she knew far too intimately. She knew the thin, cruel lips and small dark eyes, the massive skull and hawkish nose. She'd been face-to-face with him, inches away, while he got all up close and brutal with her heart.

Cold terror chilled her. It was Gahiji.

Hunter.

Seeker.

She knew whom he hunted. Her. He hunted her.

To her shock, his words proved her wrong.

"The child," Gahiji barked, his gaze fixing unerringly on Calliope. He prowled toward her. "Do you

think you can hide her? I found your first safe house, and your second. But she is gone, now. You moved her in a hurry. The mother left behind their clothes, the child's toys. Everything."

Dagan stepped forward, and Gahiji turned to him, his expression flat. "You interfered in your father's business already this week. Will you do so again, son of Sutekh?"

Beside her, Calliope gasped. "Not merely a soul reaper, but Sutekh's son."

No one bothered to confirm or deny her observation.

"Will you betray your own father, your remaining brothers, in this matter?" Gahiji demanded.

Roxy saw Dagan flinch, and it didn't take a stretch of logic to know Gahiji was pushing exactly the right buttons.

From his pocket, Gahiji withdrew something small and soft. Dana's Flopsy.

A wild flood of relief washed through her. Dana's mother had done exactly as she'd said. *Everything* left behind. Not a toy, not a book, not a photograph taken with them when they fled. Not even Dana's precious toy. Roxy felt a pang for the child's loss, but better to lose a stuffed toy than her mother. Or her life.

Leaving everything behind was the only way to be sure, 100 percent sure, that they would disappear without a trace.

And she'd made the call just in time, from the looks of things. Dana's mom had gotten her out of there before Gahiji found them.

To her left, Calliope shifted onto the balls of her feet, tense, ready. Roxy had a good idea what was going through her head. No doubt she thought Dagan had

brought the other soul reapers here. No doubt she thought it was just Calliope and Roxy, two Daughters of Aset, standing against four soul reapers.

Maybe she was right.

Roxy cut a glance at Dagan. She remembered the way he'd looked at her and said, *"You are mine."*

She thought that she knew where Dagan would stand in this fight.

She'd have confirmation soon enough.

"Where is she?" Gahiji asked again, taking another step toward Calliope.

Dagan shifted so quickly, Roxy felt the brush of the air rather than actually saw him move. She blinked and he was standing between them, at right angles to both her and Gahiji.

Rivaling the soul reapers in speed, Calliope darted forward, a blur of action. She had her knife in hand and she settled in a defensive crouch.

Roxy wasn't far behind. She had her own blades out and at the ready. They weren't her favorites—those had been destroyed the night Xaphan's concubine's attacked—but they would do.

"I seek the child," Gahiji repeated. "I offer you your pathetic lives in exchange for that information. She is nothing to you. A mere mortal."

Mortal. The way he said that made Roxy certain he *knew*.

Dana might be mortal, but she'd been fathered by a soul reaper.

Roxy hadn't been sure until she'd fed from Dagan after her injury. There was a signature there. It had confused her at first. But something had nagged at her, a similarity between Dana's and Dagan's blood.

They shared a genetic match, not as father and daughter, but as uncle and niece.

Roxy would bet her church that Dagan's dead brother, Lokan, was the child's father. And her gut was telling her that he'd died to protect the child.

She had no doubt that Dagan didn't know about Dana.

And now she had no doubt that Gahiji *did*.

"YOU ARE BREACHING POLITICAL boundaries coming here like this," Dagan snarled. "Are you trying to start a war on the eve of Sutekh's bid for peace? What could be so important about a mortal child that would make you risk my father's wrath?"

He could feel the hate and suspicion pouring from Calliope Kane as he spoke. No doubt she thought he had brought the others here, led them to her. Perhaps he had. Perhaps they had followed him when he had come after Roxy.

But he didn't think so.

He thought Gahiji had come to Calliope's, looking for information about Dana, that he was as surprised to see Dagan here as Dagan was to see him.

The two other soul reapers circled forward. They gave Dagan a deferential berth, but they seemed bound and determined to obey Gahiji. They were new. Very new. He didn't even know their names.

In that second, it was like blinders dropped from his eyes.

Gahiji wasn't here at the old man's behest. He wasn't even here with the old man's knowledge. Gahiji didn't give a shit about the upcoming meeting of the leaders and gods of the Underworld.

Because just as Dagan had begun to suspect, Gahiji wasn't playing on Sutekh's side of the board anymore.

The Marin brothers. The kid, Dana. The question of how the Setnakhts had managed to kill a soul reaper.

The Setnakhts hadn't; a soul reaper had.

Everything clicked.

"You're here to cover your own ass," Dagan said, soft voiced in his rage. "You're here to find that kid because she saw you. She knows your face. You fucking killed Lokan, you bastard. You fucking killed my brother."

He surged forward. The other two soul reapers fell on Roxy and Calliope.

Instinct warred with hate. *Protect Roxy. Annihilate Gahiji.*

Could she hold off the other soul reapers while he killed Gahiji?

Dagan couldn't be sure.

The decision twisted him in knots.

Gahiji moved. Dagan surged after him. From the corner of his eye, he saw one of the other soul reapers go for Calliope. She was fast, hitting low and hard. She could handle things for the moment.

The soul reaper on Roxy went for the kill strike. Dagan saw his arm cock back, his fingers claw. With a cry, Roxy brought her knife up and forward, cutting him from gut to breastbone. It didn't stop him.

Dagan thought his own heart would rip out of his chest as everything seemed to move at a snail's pace, the reaper's arm coming forward, Roxy arcing back away from the strike as she pulled her knife free.

The soul reaper's blood spattered in a wide arc.

Instinct won. *Protect Roxy. Keep her safe.*

At the last second, he contorted away from Gahiji. He couldn't risk her life.

Clawing his fingers, Dagan pulled back, then struck, whipcord fast, his hand tearing through skin and muscle, shattering bone. He closed his fist on the heart, tore it free with such force and speed that it flew from his grasp to spin through the air until it landed with a splotch against the far wall.

It hung there for a millisecond, then slid down the wall, leaving a trail of blood behind.

With a feral snarl, Dagan tore the darksoul free and tethered it with a band of fire. He would take it to Sutekh. Until it was ingested, there was always the possibility it could be returned to the traitor's body and the traitor could heal.

The thought of that made him realize that Gahiji had to have had help to take down Lokan. Powerful help. A god strong enough to banish Lokan's soul to somewhere it could never return from.

He stored the thought away to ponder later. To find Lokan's Ka, he needed to find Gahiji's ally.

Calliope struck, then dipped. Roxy was already diving into the fray, knives ready as she went to Calliope's aid.

Again, everything seemed to slow down, passing before his eyes like frames of stop motion.

Gahiji glancing over his shoulder at the dead soul reaper and the band of fire in Dagan's hand.

Calliope stabbing the second soul reaper in the arm even as he went for the kill, his hand speeding toward her chest.

Roxy screaming Dagan's name as she realized she was too late.

Gahiji spinning away and surging for the portal.

Dagan froze, torn in two. Everything he was, everything he had always been, wanted to go after Gahiji, to stop him, to catch him. He needed to avenge Lokan's death. He needed to find his brother's remains. He needed to bring him back. And Gahiji was the key.

But Roxy was screaming his name, the syllables drawn out in the milliseconds before the other soul reaper would connect with Calliope's heart.

He didn't give a shit about Calliope Kane. Live or die, she made no difference to him.

But she mattered to Roxy.

And Roxy mattered to him.

More than mattered. He didn't know what name to put on the burning, tearing pain that made his heart twist and made him feel both sick and wonderful at the same time. He figured it must be what mortals called love.

Lucky him.

Gahiji dove for the portal.

Last chance. Last fucking chance.

"Fuck," Dagan snarled, pouring his rage and disappointment in the one word as he spun, lunged and rammed his hand through the other soul reaper's back, straight to his heart.

He didn't need to turn to know Gahiji was gone. He'd lost his chance.

No, not lost it. He'd made his *choice*.

Raising his head, he found Roxy staring at him. Her face was less than an inch from his own, her knife buried to the hilt in the soul reaper's chest. She was looking at him like he was a god, like he'd hung the fucking moon.

And Dagan did the only thing he could do. With the dead reaper pinned between them, he leaned in and he kissed her, hard, fast, and as he pulled away, her lips clung to his. That told him everything he needed to know.

It told him he'd made the right sacrifice.

She stared up at him, tiger eyes bright and fierce.

"You let him get away. He probably helped kill your brother, but you gave up your chance at him to save Calliope."

"I'll have another chance at him," he said. *But there would have been no second chance for Calliope.* "I made my choice. I chose you."

Calliope made an odd, choked noise, but he didn't look at her, didn't look anywhere but straight into Roxy's eyes, into her heart, her soul. And he let her see into his.

"I love you, Roxy Tam."

She opened her mouth, closed it, opened it again, and whispered, "I fucking love you, Dagan Krayl."

He thought that as far as moments went, this one was damned near perfect.

Then he pulled the heart free and let the reaper's body slide to the ground. Glancing down, he realized he had no pouch and the heart was still twitching in his hand.

He needed to harvest the darksoul.

Grabbing Roxy's wrist, he turned her hand palm up and dropped the heart into it.

"Here," he said. "Hold this for me, would you?"

EPILOGUE

As for all the evil which is on me,
It is what I have done among the lords of eternity
Ever since I came down from my mother's womb.

—Egyptian Book of the Dead, Chapter 17

GAHIJI HUNKERED DOWN IN THE CORNER, shivering with cold in a cave few knew about and even fewer dared to seek. Those who ventured here rarely returned, for this cave was steeped in death.

But Gahiji did not fear death. He had been brought through that journey long ago.

"Gahiji." His name echoed through the space, seeming to come at him from all sides at once.

"You have failed."

"I have." There was no point in denial. It was plain that he had failed, that the child was not in his keeping, that the witness to his perfidy and the perfidy of his current companion had escaped their net.

"You have been branded a traitor. They seek you. They hunger for your darksoul."

Gahiji bared his teeth in a parody of a smile. "They do."

"Did you betray me? Did you betray my identity?"

Gahiji wanted to answer the question with a

question, but he dared not anger this territorial, mercurial lord.

"I did not."

"And the child did not, or we would know it by now."

Gahiji took a breath and dared much. "As I stated before, I do not believe she saw me, or you. She is no threat, no danger."

His companion was silent for so long that Gahiji wondered if perhaps he were alone.

And then the voice came to him, so close that it fanned the back of his neck, like ice and fire on his skin.

"You left it too late to terminate her. Even if you could find her, killing her would serve no purpose now."

Gahiji said nothing, only waited for the explanation.

"Dagan called a meeting. He wanted his brothers there, and his father. His father's closest allies. It was enlightening. It seems that the eldest Krayl figured out the puzzle. He knows Dana Carr is his niece."

Gahiji sucked in a sharp breath. He hadn't expected that.

"That information is an unpleasant surprise, isn't it? I know *I* was surprised."

Gahiji swallowed, feeling truly nervous for the first time since he'd helped facilitate Lokan Krayl's demise. He'd thought everything was neatly sewn together. Now, he knew that threads were unraveling.

"So now those at that private, well-guarded meeting know that the Setnakhts had supernatural help to kill Lokan. They know Lokan let himself be killed to save his daughter. What they do not know is where Lokan's body is or where his soul was sent."

Panting now, Gahiji stared straight ahead. He could feel death at his nape, smell its rotting scent.

"There's one other thing they do not know," the voice whispered, close at his ear now. "They do not know the identity of the supernatural you betrayed them to. Let's keep it that way, shall we?"

Gahiji was dead before he even registered the threat.

* * * * *

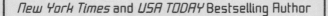

REQUEST YOUR
FREE BOOKS!

2 FREE NOVELS
FROM THE SUSPENSE COLLECTION
PLUS 2 FREE GIFTS!

YES! Please send me 2 FREE novels from the Suspense Collection and my 2 FREE gifts (gifts are worth about $10). After receiving them, if I don't wish to receive any more books, I can return the shipping statement marked "cancel." If I don't cancel, I will receive 3 brand-new novels every month and be billed just $5.74 per book in the U.S. or $6.24 per book in Canada. That's a saving of at least 28% off the cover price. It's quite a bargain! Shipping and handling is just 50¢ per book.* I understand that accepting the 2 free books and gifts places me under no obligation to buy anything. I can always return a shipment and cancel at any time. Even if I never buy another book, the two free books and gifts are mine to keep forever.

192/392 MDN E7PD

Name	(PLEASE PRINT)

Address	Apt. #

City	State/Prov.	Zip/Postal Code

Signature (if under 18, a parent or guardian must sign)

Mail to **The Reader Service:**
IN U.S.A.: P.O. Box 1867, Buffalo, NY 14240-1867
IN CANADA: P.O. Box 609, Fort Erie, Ontario L2A 5X3

Not valid for current subscribers to the Suspense Collection
or the Romance/Suspense Collection.

Want to try two free books from another line?
Call 1-800-873-8635 or visit www.morefreebooks.com.

* Terms and prices subject to change without notice. Prices do not include applicable taxes. N.Y. residents add applicable sales tax. Canadian residents will be charged applicable provincial taxes and GST. Offer not valid in Quebec. This offer is limited to one order per household. All orders subject to approval. Credit or debit balances in a customer's account(s) may be offset by any other outstanding balance owed by or to the customer. Please allow 4 to 6 weeks for delivery. Offer available while quantities last.

Your Privacy: Harlequin Books is committed to protecting your privacy. Our Privacy Policy is available online at www.eHarlequin.com or upon request from the Reader Service. From time to time we make our lists of customers available to reputable third parties who may have a product or service of interest to you. If you would prefer we not share your name and address, please check here. ☐

Help us get it right—We strive for accurate, respectful and relevant communications. To clarify or modify your communication preferences, visit us at www.ReaderService.com/consumerschoice.